"Fans of books like A Beautiful Mind or The Quiet Room will appreciate this account of people living with schizophrenia and the loved ones that are affected by their mental Illness. Additionally, this would resonate with readers who liked Jeannette Walls' The Glass Castle about her eccentric and emotionally unstable family."

—Pacific Book Review, by Ella Vincent

"*Killifer* and Martin are direct, detailed, and painstakingly honest—requirements for any interesting autobiography (...) there are no easy answers for dealing with mentally imbalanced loved ones. Still, this sometimes painful retelling of the family's struggles is a gift to society because it sheds light on a subject not often discussed."

—The US Review of Books, by Toby Berry

"It is not an easy book to read—or, no doubt, to write. But it is a well-crafted story that will be deeply touching to many readers as you follow two girls going from childhood to adulthood trying to navigate the difficult and complex situations that Jane puts them in (...) As Louise stated, 'You can't fix the situation and you can't feel guilty. You just have to go with it and do your best.'"

—The Pagosa Springs (Colorado) SUN, by Carole Howard

OVERTAKEN

INSANITY

TWO SISTERS LIVES ARE BURDENED
BY ELDER SISTER'S MENTAL ILLNESS

LOUISE KILLIFER
&LOIS MARTIN

ISBN: 979-8-89031-649-3 (sc)
ISBN: 979-8-89031-650-9 (hc)
ISBN: 979-8-89031-651-6 (e)

THE EWINGS
PUBLISHING

One Galleria Blvd., Suite 1900, Metairie, LA 70001
(504) 702-6708

To everyone whose lives have been affected by a
mentally ill family member, friend or acquaintance.

CONTENTS

ACKNOWLEDGEMENTS

To all our friends and family, thank you for supporting us through this overwhelming endeavor, as we portrayed our lives throughout challenging situations, never knowing what would manifest next.

A big thank you goes to our high school friend, Pat Sloss, who spent many hours from her busy life to edit and offer valuable suggestions.

Most importantly we thank our husbands, Don and Bill for their suggestions, cooperation and encouragement.

INTRODUCTION

The mentally ill are among us everywhere, whether we acknowledge them or are even aware of their prevalence. According to the National Institute of Mental Health, research shows mental disorders are common throughout the United States and affects tens of millions of people each year. This same reference goes on to state *the main burden of illness is concentrated among a much smaller proportion (about 6 percent) who suffer from a seriously debilitating mental illness.* Our story is about the more serious debilitating form of mental illness, which our oldest sister, Jane, displayed.

The following story describes circumstances involving a highly intelligent, extremely mentally ill sibling. From my earliest memories, Jane presented an upheaval in both my younger sister, Lois, and my childhoods. I received the brunt of Jane's physical abuse, which was hardly noticed by our parents who were lost in their day-to-day routines.

Being the oldest, Jane assumed a role of dominance. She looked down on Lois and me as mere nuisances of little importance. Normal interactions with her were rare. Jane immersed herself in books when not stirring up trouble.

Jane craved our mother's attention and gravitated toward her instead of having friends. Lois and I were accustomed to Jane siphoning away our mother's time and attention. It was difficult for our mother to accept Jane's mental illness. She desperately looked for explanations and solutions. She had strong convictions, believing a cure lay in a healthy diet of fruits and vegetables.

Lois and I hid from our feelings of embarrassment and shame, which were too difficult to acknowledge. We were good at pretending things were normal; and in a way, they were normal for us, at least. We were used to Jane's peculiar behavior ever since we could remember.

As adults, Lois and I moved away, which allowed us to continue coping by putting Jane's issues in the background. We were uncomfortable in her presence. Our solace was found in avoidance.

Jane's initial incarceration as a teenager was the beginning of a lifetime of bouncing in and out of mental health facilities. With each episode of being committed, once stabilized, Jane was released. After being home a short time, she stopped taking her medications. It was a matter of time before she got in trouble again. The vicious cycle kept repeating.

During the time, our mother suffered several heart attacks; and after her death, Jane went out of her way to complicate matters. Dealing with Jane was at times, like dealing with a child having a temper tantrum. We strove to get through the worst times as best we could despite Jane's demented beliefs and opposition to traditional common sense actions.

We invite you to join us in our journey through life, through growing up, happy times, sad times and crazy times.

Perhaps you can relate to similar circumstances that have come your way not only through mental health issues but also in your own crisis with a family member who is addicted to drugs or alcohol, which has brought cruel discord to your life.

—Louise Killifer

REFLECTIONS

Louise's Reflections

It is difficult to openly admit my inner most feelings that express negative thoughts towards my mentally ill sister. As far back as I can remember, I never liked Jane. It brings tears to my eyes as I recall discovering my baby book and reading my first words were "don't" and "stop it." Why would a baby's first words be verbs commanding to be left alone? It was evident Jane was mean from the beginning. She was continually trying to hit me, kick me, scratch me or interfere with anything I was doing. There was no peace when she was around.

Even though we grew up in what was for all practical purposes, a normally functioning family, my younger sister, Lois, and I knew other families were not like ours. Jane's weird personality and actions were as obvious to us as knowing the sky was blue, but our parents were blind to it.

Jane's cruelty and our overly strict parents, who spanked us for the mildest infraction, stole the joy from my younger years. I can still remember when the school photographer for my fifth-grade picture kept telling me to smile. I thought I was smiling, but I was not. I had nothing to smile about.

I found my big happy smile when I was twelve. It was not a smile of vengeance. It was an innocent smile of relief. That was the year Jane broke down mentally and was taken to a hospital and was gone the majority of the school year. There is no way to describe the peacefulness our home enjoyed in her absence. Life was simpler, and I was happy, turning into a silly seventh-grader who had found joy and freedom from Jane's menacing presence.

Upon her return, Jane did not dominate the years that followed. Lois and I had developed confidence and, for the most part, were rarely home. When we were not in school, we were enjoying the company of our friends or going to our jobs, making it easy to avoid and ignore Jane, for which we felt no guilt.

As Lois and I built our own lives, the unpleasant memories of growing up with Jane were locked away and seldom thought of; however, I was not aware that it was evident on my face.

During the years I worked at the college, I was fortunate to become acquainted with George, my supervisor's husband, who was an extraordinarily intelligent psychiatrist. He would sit in a chair next to my desk while reading a magazine as he waited for his wife, Barbara. After his death, Barbara shared an observation he had made. He told her he could tell from a look in my eyes that I was a tender flower that did not receive water at a crucial time. It was amazing he could tell I lacked healthy nurturing.

After our mother's death, Jane and I spoke frequently over the telephone. She talked incessantly, babbling while I tried to decipher what point she was trying to make, if any. Attempting to reason with Jane was futile and exhausting. Her fabricated stories left me astounded. Insults and derogatory statements routinely flowed freely from her wild thoughts. As her sister-in-law said, "Jane has used up my *lithium crystals*." I related exactly to what she was expressing. As kids, Lois nor I talked about Jane's mental illness, not even to each other or to any of our friends. The first time I ever brought up the subject was as an adult in my forties. I mentioned Jane to one of my friends, whom I had worked with a number of years. I was amazed to learn her first husband had extreme mental health issues and had been committed to a mental institution, where he remained until his death. No one would have ever guessed what she had been through, nor would anyone have any idea of the secret I had been harboring as well. At that point, I did not feel so stigmatized to talk about Jane and have finally reached a point in my life where I can comfortably talk about my sister's mental illness. Even though it is a guarded topic, as we open up our vulnerability, we realize we are not alone.

Lois' Reflections

I naturally looked up to my oldest sister, expecting her to be my role model. At some point, I noticed Jane acted weird.

Jane had no childhood friends. Our mother blamed Jane's failure to assimilate with her peers on them for ostracizing her from their clique, believing it was not Jane's fault. In place of having friends, Jane latched onto our mother and monopolized her, creating their special camaraderie, literally robbing me and my sister, Louise, of our mother's attention. Louise and I were left emotionally abandoned.

Our overbearing parents did not tolerate disobedience, turning Louise and me into exceptionally well-behaved, submissive children with low self-esteem. I left home at the age of seventeen, two weeks after graduating from high school, to escape my parents and Jane's strange presence. I felt liberated and glad to be "free."

After one failed teenage marriage, I married a military pilot, at the age of twenty-five. I moved frequently, usually, long distances from my family home. My attention centered on my husband and personal goals with little thought of Jane and whatever trouble she was getting into. I felt sorry for her. I could not imagine the personal turmoil she was going through. At the same time, I wanted to stay away from her, and I did.

Jane dispensed havoc on all our lives. There were times she appeared relatively normal but peculiar. I learned through much frustration not to make the mistake of assuming I was communicating with a normal person who is capable of logical reasoning.

With further contemplation, I have come to the conclusion that Jane and our mother never came to grips in recognizing there was a major problem and acknowledging they could not cure Jane's mental illness using their methods.

I escaped the full impact of the multitude of Jane's mental health disorders, until our mother had a heart attack. Jane consistently complicated the situation. Once we got through this critical time, I declared I would never ever speak to Jane again. Eventually, I learned to accept her on a clinical level, realizing her mental illness drove her aggressive and hurtful behavior.

Overall, the mental health system protocols were unable to provide the care Jane required. The system could only keep her stable for the periods of time she was in their custody and shortly thereafter. She defied court orders to remain on psychotic medications, which resulted in relapses into her insane behavioral pattern.

Her continual episodes of being committed or arrested by the police were difficult for Louise and me to accept. Each incident brought us emotions of embarrassment, disgust and hopelessness that it would ever end.

Looking back as an older adult, I acknowledge growing up with Jane was a bizarre experience, which along with lack of parental encouragement and support, thwarted my development to feel like an adult in my own right until later in my life.

Bringing this point to attention, emphasizes the importance of recognizing the need that our mother completely missed regarding paying attention not only to Jane's mental health, but to her own and Louise's and mine, as well.

Those dealing with mentally ill individuals need to be aware of their tendency to give too much of themselves, as this puts a strain on themselves and takes away from paying attention to others for whom they are responsible.

CHAPTER ONE

Days Gone By

Jane was annoyed with me from the moment I was born. Jane was no longer the focal point of our parents' attention.

In the late 1940's Jane Graham lived with our parents, Milton and Marie, and me, in the small mountain community of Gunnison, Colorado. Jane christened the primitive stone house in which we lived, the *Cricket House*. There was no plumbing for a bathroom. Our mother, a small woman of five foot two and dark brown hair and vibrant blue eyes, cooked on and old coal cook stove. Occasionally, Jane talked about the time she dropped me on my head in the coal bucket when I was a tiny baby. Jane said that explained why I was the way I was.

Jane wanted to be held even when our mother was occupied nursing me. She tried to climb to our mother's lap, not heeding the warning to get down because there was not enough room for two. Jane slipped and went tumbling onto the hard wooden floor, resulting in a broken arm.

Jane 26 months, Louise 7 months

When I was five months old, Mama went deer hunting with Daddy. Daddy was not tall, only about five foot 8 with sandy red hair and blue eyes. He was an accomplished hunter, and the game helped feed our family. Mama got excessively tired, causing her to lose her milk, resulting in me being fed from one glass baby bottle. I was frequently left unattended in the crib with the bottle that Jane consumed. It was not until Jane broke the bottle that our mother realized the reason I cried so much was because I was hungry.

In a conversation with Mama before she died, she talked about losing her milk and Jane breaking the only bottle.

"So, did you go out and buy another bottle?" I asked.

"No," she replied.

"Well, how did you feed me?"

"From a cup," she answered.

From a cup! That was way too young to take a bottle away from a baby.

Louise 2, Jane 3 ½

Daddy built a swing and attached it to a branch on one of the huge Cotton Wood trees in the large yard of the Cricket House. He took a picture of us swinging together. Jane made reference to that picture while talking to me after our mother's death.

"It hurt me when Daddy put you on me so I pinched you and you cried. Do you remember that?"

"I remember when Daddy took that picture. I have a copy of it in my picture album. But I don't remember crying," I answered. Getting hurt by Jane was a routine occurrence.

"Mama got mad at me and told me never to pinch you again and I didn't, did I?"

Jane started talking about when she was little. "When I played outside, the older neighborhood kids came over and played with me. They had a wagon that they pushed me up and down the street in. I learned how to pinch from them. Mama didn't like me to play with them because she didn't know where I was. After that Daddy rigged up a rope and they tied me to the clothesline so that I could run back and

2

forth and stay in the yard. Can you imagine that? I liked playing with older kids. I never did play well with younger kids."

One August day, Daddy took Jane and me to stay with the Cowans when Mama was in the hospital giving birth to Lois. We followed the tall teenage sons around the ranch as they did their chores. We particularly liked watching the cows chew their cud as they were being milked every evening in the barn.

Log house under construction. July 4, 1950

Soon after Lois was born, our family moved into the partially finished two-story log house that Daddy built. Before contracting the mail route, he worked for the U.S. Forrest Service. The house was built from large lodge pole pine trees that were cut down to clear camp ground areas.

Lois' crib was temporarily placed in the bathroom in the space of the future shower. A doorway with a curtain separated our parent's bedroom from the bathroom. Another door on the adjacent wall of the bathroom opened into a short hall that led past the other downstairs bedroom and opened into the "front room" as Mama called it.

A door off the kitchen and garage led to the upstairs that would not be finished until ten years later.

I observed mornings beginning with Mama donning her darkpurplish chenille housecoat, and nursing Lois as she sat on the edge of the bed.

Visitors came by to see Lois. One asked if I was jealous; Mama answered, yes. Afterward I asked her what *jealous* meant. Upon learning the definition, I resented her response. I liked having a baby sister even though she cried a lot. I liked hugging and kissing her and touching Lois' soft baby skin.

At the beginning of the following summer Mama took Jane and me to Bible school. I loved to hear the Bible stories and was fascinated by the cutout characters as they were displayed on a felt board illustrating the story of Joseph and his coat of many colors.

One morning after Bible school was over and the children were leaving, Mama appeared with a pair of panties, asking if I was wet. I was three and knew I was dry, but after a hasty check, Mama decided she needed to change my panties. Right there in the open, Mama took off my panties and put on a fresh pair. That was embarrassing but later it worked to my advantage.

One Sunday morning after another usual night of sleeping on the edge of the double bed I shared with Jane, I awakened to observe Jane still sleeping sprawled out. For no particular reason I decided to sit on top of her. The idea of peeing on Jane entered my mind. After a moment of contemplation, I gave into temptation and let the flood waters flow, whole heartily expecting to get spanked. It took Jane a little while to realize she had been presented a present.

Jane 4 ½, Louise 3, Lois 9 months

All of a sudden Jane yelled, "MAMA, LOUISE PEED ON ME!" In an instant our mother appeared.

"What did you do that for?" she asked.

Immediately, Mama began stripping the bed while, I climbed off my drenched sister. To my glee and satisfaction I did not get spanked. Mama surely must have thought I had a control problem. But oh no, it was done on purpose. How sweet it was!

Jane started kindergarten that fall. Of course, I wanted to go too, but I was only three. Jane was actually too young, also. Jane would not be five until November, but she was allowed to enroll early. Mama had spent a lot of time preparing Jane. She even knew how to tie her shoes.

Daddy left with Jane every morning returning at noon. Lois was too young to play with me. I played alone with my dolls or went outside and waited for the train to go by. I waved at the train and the engineer blew his whistle a couple of times and waved back.

Sometimes I picked wildflowers and brought them in to Mama; and sometimes I caught bugs, especially grasshoppers, and crushed them into the holes in the concrete. The following year I taught that trick to Lois. There was always a plentiful supply.

Mama rarely insisted we wash our hands. At times, my hands were covered with grasshopper juice for an extended period. Mama gave us a bath every Saturday night in the large kitchen sink. Dial soap was used for both our bodies and hair. Mama made great devil horns, which we could see in our reflections in the big kitchen window above the sink.

Train going by house

When we out grew the kitchen sink, all three of us were herded into the shower at the same time. We were not particularly well scrubbed as it was not always possible to get much of a turn under the shower before our mother announced it was time to get out. We could not run too much water because of the septic system.

One Sunday morning when our parents were sleeping in, I noticed it was unusually quiet. I gathered up my clothes and dressed myself. I hunted down my favorite pair of shoes, taking notice of the absence of Lois' usual crying. The shoes were an ugly brown pair of very comfortable high topped baby shoes. I crunched my feet in them, even though they were too snug.

"Jane, will you tie my shoes?" I asked.

"No!" Jane said emphatically.

I begged Jane to tie my shoes to no avail.

"Tie your own shoes," Jane retorted.

I removed my old favorite shoes and instead put on a pair of hand-me-down buckle shoes, never to don my favorite brown shoes again.

Jane displayed more disfavor to me than she did to baby Lois. Jane and I were always bickering, and we both got spanked a lot for fighting. I got the worst end of the encounters, and was always sporting scabs from Jane's clawing attacks.

Visits from grandparents were rare as Mama's parents lived in Oregon and came every few years. Grandma looked like one would expect a grandmother to look. She was chubby with totally white hair pinned back. She would respond to grandpa's high pitched voice, with a soft sweet, "Yes." Grandpa's voice was derived from a farming accident where his vocal cords were injured. During the visits, they never carried on conversations with us kids. We never really knew them. For Christmas, grandma sent fabric for Mama to make us dresses; however, most of the fabric was not designed for children.

Daddy's mother died when he was still in his teens. He had a stepmother, Deborah, who had no affection for her stepchildren or step grandchildren. Mama told us about the time Deborah took after her with a butcher knife. Mama got away unscathed. Daddy's father lived in

Mama, Grandma holding Lois, Jane and Louise below

the same town. He was the father of nine children; the oldest of which was old enough to be Daddy's father. He died in his nineties when Lois was three.

All of us kids were blue eyed, towheaded toddlers. As we got older, Lois was the only one who retained her blond hair.

Jane and I attended church regularly and participated in church activities. One summer evening we prepared to go to a gathering to roast weenies and marshmallows. Jane and I piled in the back seat of the Sunday school teacher's car with several other children.

As we traveled down the dirt street to pick up another child, the Sunday school teacher asked if we wanted to go faster. Everyone shouted, "YES," except Jane who said "NO, it burns up more gas." I had no idea going fast would burn more gas and wondered how Jane knew that, but what was wrong with having fun?

Jane clashed with her first grade teacher, Mrs. Barns. Mrs. Barns resembled the *Wicked Witch of the East* and was very stern and strict. It was not known exactly what the problem was, but I could not say I was disappointed later when Mama made sure neither Lois nor I got in Mrs. Barns' class.

Finally, it was my turn to go to kindergarten, where I got to play with other children. I was surprised that my friend, Carlotta, and others could even read *Goldie Locks and the Three Bears*. When talking to Mama about my classmates being able to read, Mama replied, "Jane was bored with kindergarten, so I didn't bother to teach you." I was nothing like Jane, and with Mama's assumption that I would be bored also, I felt cheated from learning and receiving rare one-on-one attention.

At that time, it was required for all kindergarteners to be vaccinated from small pox. We were told that for the vaccination to be effective we must let the pox, that forms, fall off on its own. I was mortified when one morning Jane thought it was time to come off and chased me around our bedroom with a huge open safety pin, until she cornered me and flicked the pox off. I thought I would surely die from small pox now.

Jane had become mortal enemies with Linda Morin, who rode the same school bus. Linda was two years older and a lot bigger and heavier than Jane. They got into knock-down, drag-out fights and truly hated each other. I met Linda on the first day of school when starting the first grade. Linda approached Jane and me as we waited for the bus after school outside of the old yellow brick school building.

"This is my little sister," Jane volunteered.

Linda nodded to me. Before long, Jane and Linda were engaged in a quarrel about how much they did not like each other.

"Your sister doesn't even like you, do you?" stated Linda.

Being the naïve little sister, who had no allegiance to my abusive big sister, I answered honestly, "No."

Linda reveled in my answer. "See, even your sister doesn't like you."

Just then, the bus pulled up. When we got home, Jane told our mother about the incident.

"Why would you say such a thing?" Mama questioned, receiving no answer.

I thought about that many times. If given a second chance, would I have answered differently? Unless I was lying to myself the answer would be "No."

Jane did very well in school. She did not socialize with her classmates but related more to her teachers and made excellent grades. Daddy bragged to everyone how smart Jane was and gave her a dollar for each A and more for straight A's.

I was another story. I had so much difficulty reading that my teacher told Mama I was retarded. Later when my second-grade class was given eye exams, it was discovered I could not see. I had the dubious honor of being the first one in what seemed like the entire elementary school to have glasses. I would never be a fast reader, and reading certainly was not my favorite activity as it was my straight A sister. Lois was not a straight A student either. That was Jane's claim to fame, which was not challenged by either Lois or me. We preferred not to study all of the time.

Mama made her own clothes and most of us kids' clothes. She made each of us three new dresses every year to start school. By Mama's standards from growing up in *The Depression*, that was plenty. She always said what you put in your stomach was more important than what you put on your back.

Every year before school started and during the Christmas break, Mama cut our hair and gave us a home permanent. Lois and I hated looking like *Little Orphan Annie* and finally got freed from that look when we were older and told Mama we could take care of our own hair.

There was no television reception when we were little. Daddy spent his evenings reading, while Mama cleared the dinner dishes and us kids played among ourselves in the one bedroom we all shared. One evening when Daddy was reading, my sisters and I were playing in our bedroom. As usual, Jane instigated squabbling. We got a little too noisy for Daddy's liking. He hollered at us and commanded we sit still on the couch and not let out a peep or we would get paddled with the infamous board.

The board was over a foot in length with one end whittled down for a handle, flaring out and then narrowing down to a rounded point. When Mama said to do something *or else*, it was assumed getting paddled with the board was the *or else*. Beatings with the board were brutal, leaving us with lingering stinging pain on our posteriors and uncontrollably sobbing.

As I sat quietly on the couch, glancing at Daddy and then Lois and then Jane, I contemplated to myself. What will we be like when we are grown ladies? Will we be pretty and have nice things? Will Jane ever stop being so weird?

Jane broke her arm a second time when she was in the fourth grade. I was pushing Jane in a swing when she decided she was going too high and jumped out. According to Jane, both times she broke her arm were my fault, along with her buck teeth, which she blamed on me because she bumped her mouth on the ground when she bailed out of the swing. I ignored Jane's version and never said anything in my defense. It was obvious Jane's accidents were due to her own poor

Jane 9, with broken arm, Lois 5, sitting pretty, Louise 7 with doll and biting fingernails, dog Sparky

judgment. Jane's accusations were false, and they added to my dislike for my insufferable sister.

When Lois was five, our mother enrolled us in a beginning swimming class. The closest swimming pool that was open to the public was twenty-seven miles away at a summer resort. Our mother was always deathly afraid of the water and wanted us to have the opportunity to learn how to swim. After having the lessons, Daddy took us on swimming jaunts throughout many summers. On one occasion in particular that I vividly recall; during the return ride home, rain began coming down in torrents. Jane broke out in song, singing at the top of her lungs, and continually repeating, "It's raining, it's pouring. The old man is snoring. Bumped his head and he went to bed and he couldn't get up in the morning." She could be most annoying.

Birthdays were celebrated after dinner with homemade cake and ice cream. Daddy got out his harmonica and played "Happy Birthday" to the honoree, while the others sang. After the candles were blown out and the cake and ice cream were served, Daddy entertained by playing old favorites, such as *Red River Valley* and *Home on the Range*. It was a fun family celebration. We never had birthday parties with presents and friends. When we asked if we could get presents like our friends, we were told our present was, "getting us here."

We never went *trick-or-treating*. There was never an actual reason given. It seemed most of the time when we asked if we could go somewhere or do something, if the answer was not "No," it was, "We'll see," "Maybe," or "I doubt it." One time I asked Mama why she did not ever say "Yes." She said she did not want to promise something and have to break it if something came up. If there was such a concern something would come up, why couldn't she say "Yes, as long as nothing comes up." In my opinion, she did not want to be bothered. I made up my mind that when I had

Lois 6, Louise 8, Jane 10, sitting on over turned canoe

children, they would go trick-or-treating and have birthday parties with gifts and friends like other children.

Mama was obsessed with everything being equal, so much so that everything we received for Christmas was identical – identical dolls, identical sweaters, etc. When Jane declared she did not want any more dolls, all of us stopped getting dolls, even though Lois was only seven. Jane had never been a doll person. Her idea of playing with dolls was to twist off their arms, poke out their eyes, and squeeze their soft plastic faces into a permanent distortion.

One Christmas Mama decided to ask each of us what we wanted. Lois was eight then and did not remember what she asked for. I wanted a little loom to weave pot holders on, like my friend Peggy had. And Jane wanted a chemistry set. Jane had decided she was going to be a scientist. She even made ammonia with her chemistry set.

Several years after Daddy and Mama moved our family into the log home, we got new neighbors. The Morgans had a similar log home built down the road. The Morgans were older than our parents. He was tall and thin with graying hair and was dominated by his wild blue-eyed wife. They had two older children in high school and a younger son, who was in the grade ahead of Lois. The Morgans were hateful neighbors. *Old Lady Morgan*, as Mama called her, made many trips back and forth into town each day. She watched for Mama to be outside hanging up clothes or working in the yard, and then drove by glaring or yelling at her.

Old Lady Morgan continually looked out her upstairs window watching every move Mama made. Daddy built a twelve foot high fence between the properties to provide privacy. When Daddy's dog, Sparky, died he bought a pure bred German Shepherd dog, named Patrick Henry. Old Lady Morgan called Pat, behind the fence and beat him, until his ears would not stand up.

Mama called the sheriff when the neighbor's antagonizing got out of hand. The sheriff was of no help. He came by to talk to our parents saying, "Can't you people get along?"

One summer afternoon as she drove by, Old Lady Morgan yelled, "We're going to have a show down tonight!" Daddy loaded his 22 pistol. They would be ready in case the Morgans were not bluffing.

Daddy took us girls to the drive-in movie as planned. The evening progressed normally until we arrived home. Walt Morgan and his lunatic wife were lying in wait for our return and appeared ready to cause trouble. Walt Morgan would have had second thoughts engaging Daddy, if he had known of his military service as a marine during World War II. Even though Daddy was not a big man, he was very strong and was no one to reckon with. Mama instructed us kids to go inside and stay away from the windows, as she grabbed the pistol and headed out the door.

Paying no attention to our mother's instructions, Jane proceeded straight to the large front room picture window, followed by Lois and me. Nothing could be seen but the pitch blackness of the night.

There was yelling and then a gun shot. The confrontation was over.

Mama and Daddy came inside the house reminiscing over what had just occurred, as the Morgan's old truck could be heard starting up and sped off.

Walt Morgan had come at Daddy with his fist, swinging and missing. Daddy's blow connected with Walt. He was knocked against the metal handle that protruded from the rear of the 1945 Ford Jeep. Walt was not in the best of shape when he stood up preparing to lunge at Daddy again. Mama shot the gun over his head.

"That's a warning," she announced. "Leave now or the next one won't miss."

The incident brought a culmination to the feud. Our parents went to court with the Morgans. Both parties were put under a peace bond, not to come within a set amount of feet of each other.

Being the oldest, Jane naturally got to try things first. She joined the Camp Fire Girls, which was a disaster. She did not get along with any of the other girls. Most of them were from prominent families with money as opposed to our family, who was always scraping the bottom of the barrel. Because of Jane's experience with the clique, I was not allowed to join, even though I was invited by my friend Nancy.

The narrow gauge railroad train stopped running and the tracks were pulled up, which gave us freer rein to play where the train used to run. During a game of hide-and-go-seek, I discovered the most perfect hiding place ever. It was across from where the railroad track had run parallel to Chinery Hill and behind a willow, where there happened to be a small hidden cave in the hillside. It was a perfect vantage point, where one could see the house and entire yard but not be detected. After a game with Lois, where she came close but passed by, I showed her the discovery. We hid there after talking Jane into a game. It was a mystery to Jane where we were. Our secret spot was never revealed to anyone.

The highway department condemned our home when I was nine. The house was located in the path of the future service road that was going to be constructed next to the new highway. Chinery hill was to be cut back by explosives to make room for the new highway. When our parents could not find a place they liked in town, it was decided to move the house to a different location. Daddy instated a house mover from Montrose, a town sixty-six miles away, and purchased two acres of land closer to town farther up on the Gunnison River. There was one major obstacle in that the house was too large to pass through the existing bridge and could not be moved until the new bridge was constructed. The house was moved to where it was deemed to be out of the path of rocks hurling through the air from the blasting. It sat on stilts for one year, awaiting the completion of the bridge. Our family continued living there; however, the indoor bathroom facilities were replaced by an outhouse Daddy built.

The log house's journey to a new location

During the year, while waiting for the bridge to be completed, Daddy prepared the foundation and cleared the new site. When the bridge was finished the house made the journey across the river to its new location.

Daddy planted grass and a few trees and put in a hedge of honeysuckle along the irrigation ditch that emptied into the river from the front side of the property. Nearby, another irrigation ditch made its way through a swampy area. It was a special place full of new areas to explore. The irrigation ditches were full of wonders – minnows, snakes, frogs, spiders and leeches. Lois and I waded several times near the honeysuckle, but the other ditch was the best as it had an island and in the winter it froze over to make an excellent place to go ice skating.

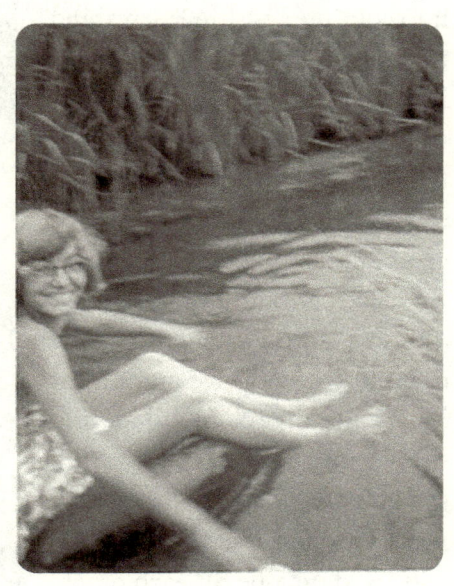

Lois age 13, tubing the ditch

Since we did not live in the city limits or close to other children, we spent the summers at home, playing among ourselves. Jane immersed herself in the *Encyclopedia Britannica* or books that were checked out weekly from the public library. On Saturdays, Daddy dropped us off at the theater to see the afternoon matinee.

We were never given an allowance. On Sunday afternoons, Daddy would take us on rides in the jeep. When a pop bottle was sighted alongside the road, he stopped for one of us to run and get it. When we had a tidy collection, we turned in the bottles for their deposits and shared the money.

I was ten when my new friend Peggy moved to Gunnison from California. She had pretty auburn hair and a crooked front tooth. Peggy loved to joke around. I was thrilled to be invited to Peggy's house to play one Saturday afternoon. I was even more thrilled to be asked if I could spend the night. After that, I spent lots of nights with Peggy until she moved back to California.

I continued to be Jane's punching bag until during one attack, I bent one of her fingers backward, which brought her to her knees in pain. From then on, she did not try to hit me anymore.

After Jane's experience with the Camp Fire Girls, she was not into joining anything. I wanted to join 4-H when invited by my friend, Vera. Finally, Mama let us join when she was convinced there were sewing and cooking categories, and having a cow or an animal was not a requirement. By then, I was in junior high.

Louise age 12, ice skating, wearing her red car coat

Lois and I knew we were dreaming when we asked for horses, like my friend, Vonda and her sisters had; however, we did get bicycles. Daddy located old, used bicycles that he painted and fixed up, one for each of us. They were bare-bones bikes with no gears. Lois and I spent many summer days packing lunches and riding our bikes to explore Hartman Rocks and other areas near our house. Jane was rarely interested in going with us.

Daddy talked a lot about taking a trip to Disneyland. The trip never materialized as from year to year, he was always busier than the previous year taking tourists on fishing trips down the Gunnison River in a rubber life raft.

Jane age 13, Louise age 11, Lois age 9 at Hartman Rocks

Jane was in the eighth grade when our family took our first trip to visit relatives.

It was our first trip outside the state of Colorado, and we were thrilled to go. It was December. We donned our matching red car coats with wooden buttons that Mama had purchased through the Army Surplus catalog. We visited relatives in Oklahoma, Arkansas, and Texas.

When Lois was nine she met a new friend, Ruthie. Ruthie was cute, with a face covered in freckles and a crooked smile. Ruthie's father was part of a huge crew that constructed the Blue Mesa Reservoir. Ruthie's family lived in a trailer park, which was a quick jaunt away on the bicycle. They became inseparable.

Later Ruthie's family moved to a park twenty-four miles away, which was closer to her father's work. Lois and Ruthie went on adventures with Ruthie's brother on the Dillon Pinnacles, where they found arrowheads. Occasionally, in the isolated areas, they came across boulders that were three to four feet in diameter. They loosened some and sent them bouncing down the mountain like a rubber ball, watching the exhilarating scene until each boulder came to a resting place on the flats at the foot of the mountain. Lois remained friends with Ruthie into adulthood, although Ruthie's family moved away in their sophomore year of high school.

When Lois was ten, each of us bought a young rabbit from our cousin, Katheryn, who was a year younger than Jane. She was the daughter of Daddy's sister, Mildred, whose family had a large ranch on a section of land and operated a coal mine. Mildred was strong and short and stocky. She shared the same blue eyes and sandy red hair as our dad. Lois chose a little white bunny with pink eyes, black ears, and a black wiggly nose. He was named Vanilla. I chose a little black bunny with a patch of white below her chin. Jane wanted me to name her Licorice, but she looked like a Sally to me. Jane had a pretty light brownish-orange rabbit, which she named after the flavor he resembled, Butterscotch. Lois and I played a lot with our bunnies. Jane did not pay much attention to Butterscotch. He got away and was never seen again. Lois and I took turns taking care of the rabbits. When Sally and/or

Vanilla got out of their cages, Lois and I always caught them. In fact, we got so good we trapped a wild rabbit in a pipe and then let him go.

Sally had a litter of eight babies. Daddy built more cages to accommodate the additional bunnies. Vanilla had gotten out of his cage but stayed around the yard and was allowed to run loose. One day Vanilla was not to be seen. Around that time, Lois observed Mama had a lot of scratches on her arms. Absentmindedly, she mentioned she was surprised it was so hard to drown a rabbit and then caught herself. Lois did not make the connection until sometime later, it occurred to her why Vanilla had vanished.

One afternoon after school, I went out to feed the rabbits to find them all gone, along with their cages. In the house, I ran. "Where are the bunnies?" I asked.

"Your dad gave them to a family on his mail route. You weren't feeding them every morning, so we got rid of them." Mama said coldly. Lois and I felt betrayed. Our parents should have first discussed with us about giving the rabbits away.

Sex was a big mystery. Perhaps our mother thought by not talking about it, we would remain pure as the driven snow. I asked innocently numerous times, "How do you get pregnant?"

Mama's response for the longest time was always, "You climb a telephone pole." Of course, I knew that was another one of Mama's silly answers that lacked credibility. Our mother always kept us protected from any conversation or situation that would disclose the facts of life. I was twelve by the time our mother rounded us up for the "birds and bees" talk.

When we got older we earned money working around the house. I ironed Daddy's clothes and both Lois and I mowed and watered the huge grass areas. One summer I applied varnish to the outside of the log house. Lois and I also baby sat routinely. Jane was not interested in doing those types of things. Apparently she had enough money from her grades.

Mama and Jane started speaking Pig Latin to each other. They changed words around in a manner, adding "ay"s to words in their jovial conversations. I could generally get the just of what they were saying, but never did get the hang of speaking it. Lois and I did not appreciate the fanfare.

Jane and Mama researched a type of mushroom that was growing in the lawn. They harvested the mushrooms and fried them in butter and ate them. No one else was interested in partaking. Jane also did some kind of science experiment letting mosquitoes bite her. What she was trying to prove was anybody's guess.

One day after school a misfortunate garter snake crossed Jane's path. She picked it up by the tail and whirled it around her head and then released it toward the river.

By the time Jane was fourteen, Daddy completed the upstairs of the house, providing each of us a bedroom of our own. There were no handrails on the staircase, but that was not an obstacle as Lois and I ran up the stairs usually two steps at a time.

One evening in the fall, shortly after Jane started her freshman year of high school, things began to significantly change for the worse. We were in bed, each in our own room upstairs. Jane would not settle down and go to sleep.

"Ouch! Ouch! Ouch!" she cried out periodically. Finally, she grabbed her pillow and blanket and went downstairs to sleep on the couch. Daddy told her to go back upstairs and go to bed, but she refused.

Jane age 14, with snake

The same thing happened the following night. Jane said spiders were biting her. In succeeding nights, she yelled out, "Bats in the belfry! Bats in the belfry!" She continued to have the perception of spiders biting her and insisted on sleeping on the couch. She also claimed there were people living in the unfinished part of the upstairs that was accessed through her room. Her behavior could not be ignored. Our mother conferred with the family doctor, and an appointment was made for our parents to meet with a psychiatrist at a hospital in Denver.

My sisters and I were left at home while our parents went to make arrangements for Jane to be admitted. That afternoon, Jane began pulling the living room drapes closed.

"Stop closing the drapes, and open them," I commanded. "It is daytime. We don't close the drapes during the day." I had grown to be stronger than Jane, and was prepared to go to battle if need be.

To my surprise, Jane was insisting a wolf was looking in at her. Jane removed the lamp shade from the floor lamp, put it on her head, and began dancing around. "If that wolf is going to look in here, I'm going to give him something to look at!" Jane exclaimed.

"There is no wolf out there. Take that lamp shade off your head and put it back!" I exclaimed.

I was not informed of what behavior to expect or how to deal with Jane. I did not know Jane's hallucinations were real to her.

Our parents returned late that evening. Mama read Jane's diagnosis from a list of sophisticated psychiatric terms that were not familiar. Arrangements were complete for Jane to be admitted.

Dr. Phillips was Jane's psychiatrist. He requested to meet with Lois and me. Our parents brought us to speak with him in Denver. The doctor wore a long lab coat. He was tall, and thin, and very nice. After the interviews, he conferred with our parents, telling them Lois was the most likely to have mental problems later in life. Several years later, Dr. Phillips was killed by one of his patients.

Jane played mind games with her doctors. She thought it was funny to trifle with her psychiatrists, leading them on with made-up stories, and then laughed about how she had fooled them. She thought she was so smart, but surely the doctors saw through her nonsense.

There were lots of speculation as to what caused Jane to be mentally ill. One story was her mental illness resulted from spinal meningitis, which she caught from mosquitoes. Another excuse related to having a bad reaction from punch spiked with LSD at a church function. Mama even thought maybe she got *sick* from the mushrooms they had been eating from the yard.

Whatever the actual reason for Jane's full-blown psychosis, no one could say. The onset of some mental illness begins at puberty, and that is when Jane's schizophrenia became apparent.

With the essence of Jane's influence gone, for the first time there was serenity and peacefulness in our home. The consistent tension from Jane's presence had vanished. There was tranquility.

Jane was released in May after missing the majority of her freshman year and began the next school year again as a freshman. Things were different now. I was a teenager, and Lois was not far behind. We had gone on with our lives normally and spent a lot of time with friends and activities.

Lois loved swimming and completed the more advanced classes. By the time she was thirteen, Western State College had built a beautiful indoor swimming pool, where she swam frequently and joined a summer swim team. Lois got up early in the mornings to ride her bicycle two miles to arrive by seven o'clock for swimming practice. Our parents never attended any of Lois' swim meets.

Daddy's afternoon coffee-drinking friend was the manager of a clothing store. As a favor, Jane was hired to be a store clerk. She was not comfortable around people and switched to working in the stockroom. She did not like the stockroom either. That did not last long.

I wanted to get contact lenses. Daddy agreed with the stipulation I had to pay half the cost. I got a summer job cleaning cabins at Longs Motel down the road. I began working every day walking to the motel, throughout the summer until two weeks before beginning my junior year.

There were no optometrists in our town. Our family's optometrist was Dr. Swigert, who had an office in downtown Denver. I would need to see him periodically throughout a two-week period. Since neither parent could go, Jane accompanied me on the Continental Trailways bus. Our mother considered Jane cured, since she was currently functioning well. An outgoing older girl sat in a seat near us. She was a singer, and before long, our section of the bus was singing joyfully. That set the tone for the entire trip. Jane was amazingly amicable, and we had a good time together. We stayed in a residential hotel that was down the street from the optometrist's office. For entertainment, we went on a sightseeing trip across Denver by way of city buses and crossed the street daily to ride the escalator at the Denver Dry Department store.

The following spring, I had the opportunity to clerk at the clothing store that was not copasetic to Jane. I continued to work there summers and after school my junior and senior years. I sparingly purchased clothes using my discount and saved the majority of my earnings for college.

When Lois turned sixteen, she wanted contacts lenses. Dr. Swigert invited Lois to stay at his home with his family during the two-week period that she would be staying in Denver. She rode the bus and went by herself.

Jane continued to excel academically in high school; however, she had little interaction with others her age. According to one of her classmates, it was like Jane was invisible. She hardly talked to anyone.

Jane had one friend, Jean, who had attended a country school until she entered high school. Jean was the oldest of ten children. She had brown hair and wore glasses. One of her brown eyes tended to cross. She did not dress like the other girls. Jean did not fit in very well with most of the *city* girls in her class. Jane befriended her, and they remained friends throughout high school.

Jane loved to show up her classmates. Barry, a friend of mine, stopped me during class changes to tell me he was repulsed by Jane's smug, gloating know-it-all air when she answered a question no one else had a clue about.

Jane definitely did not fit in. During a conversation I had with our mother about being different, she said, "We are different from other people." She made it sound like a good thing, but to Lois and me it was more like being outcasts.

Jane took a class in shorthand in which she did very well. Later as an adult, she sent letters to me written in shorthand. I had taken one semester of it in college, but hardly used it, except to decipher her letters. I believe she used it to show she was superior, which was an unspoken feeling I got from both Jane and our mother.

Jane joined the Candy Stripers her junior and senior years of high school. She performed volunteer work at the hospital doing nonmedical tasks, such as delivering patients' meals. She received satisfaction from helping people.

Jane was not particularly interested in boys, however, in her senior year, she did have a date to go to the drive-in movie. When her date tried to kiss her, she yanked off his glasses and licked the lenses. She walked home, which was not far from the house.

Lois and I both had numerous boyfriends in high school. Mama would not allow us to date anyone who was not in high school. She said college boys had *ideas*.

Many times Lois and I asked if we could go skiing. Mama always said, "No, you'll break your neck and it's too short to tie." We knew the true reason for not being allowed to go was that it cost money to rent equipment and buy lift tickets. Our parents guarded their money too closely for such frivolous activities. Lois was fortunate her junior year to have a boyfriend, Wally, who lived in Crested Butte. He was a tall blond fellow with a slender build. Wally worked in the ski rental shop, and his mother worked in the ticket office. He decked Lois out in skis, boots and poles. His mother provided complimentary ski lift passes and he taught her to ski.

I had spent so much time working at the clothing store, babysitting and keeping up my grades, there was not much time to spend with friends; however, I did go on a legal senior ditch day with my boyfriend, Don, and some other classmates. Don had dark brown hair and brown eyes. He was big and hefty, being the tackle for the high school football team.

Even though I got my driver's license when I was sixteen, I never drove a vehicle to school. I either rode the school bus or relied on a boyfriend to give me rides.

Lois enjoyed high school and had a lot of friends. She was allowed to drive "the bomb,"

Lois with the bomb in background and German Shepard puppy (Notice W Mountain in the background) which was a 1948 Willys Jeep Station Wagon. She knew how to have a good time and had great fun taking her friends around.

The home high school football games were always on Friday afternoons. Before the games, Lois drove the bomb packed with her friends up and down Main Street, yelling cheers as was tradition with the high school kids. If our parents would have found out, she would have gotten in trouble.

Louise age 17, cutting a cake she baked for senior ditch day

Like me, Lois worked her last two years of high school in addition to babysitting. During the school year, Lois had a clerical job in the office of the Superintendent of Schools. She also had weekend jobs.

Prior to beginning her senior year, with some of her savings, Lois went on her first excursion to shop for school clothes with her friend, Gail. She had dark hair and brown eyes and a great sense of humor, with a little mischief mixed in. Gail drove her car. They spent the night at a motel in Montrose, where they drank a beer and smoked cigarettes.

Lois and I had dreams of living fulfilling lives under our own terms. We were full of hope and high expectations.

CHAPTER TWO

Lives of Our Own

Upon graduating from high school, Jane received a full scholarship to Northern Colorado University in Greeley. That fall, our mother took her to college. In departing, her farewell words to Jane were "Don't call home asking for money." Mama's parting words were very upsetting. Jane was in no way prepared to be dropped off where she had no friends or even knew a soul. She felt abandoned with no one to fall back on. Two weeks later, Mama received a call from a college official, informing her Jane had not attended classes and to come get her. Mama returned to Greeley to bring Jane home. Jane had a relapse and went back in the hospital.

My boyfriend, Don, had moved to Gunnison his freshman year of high school when his father retired from the army. Don was born in Texas but lived in Germany as a toddler and all over the United States from then on. He asked me to the prom our junior year of high school, and we started seeing each other regularly.

We enrolled in the same required general classes our freshman year at Western State College (currently named Western State Colorado University), and became engaged in November shortly after Don's father was killed in an automobile accident. We decided to get married before starting our sophomore year in college. Lois was in her senior year of high school and Jane was living at home.

A simple wedding was held at the log house, followed by a reception. While Mabel, Don's mother, an average size woman with short chestnut hair and hazel eyes, shed a few tears, Mama showed no sign of sentimentality or sadness. Someone mentioned something to her about missing me, to which she replied she would have more time to pursue her own interests. Overhearing this coldhearted response sent pangs through my heart. I had always longed for a more heart-warming, loving mother.

After honeymooning in Denver, Don and I returned home and lived with Don's mother in a mobile home that was jointly owned by Don and his mother. Several months into the fall semester, I discovered I was expecting. I was excited about the baby.

Daddy had put in three mobile home spaces in the open area in front of the log house. He proposed putting in another space behind the log house, where we could live rent-free if we paid for having the space added. The deal was made, and we planned to move the twelve by sixty foot mobile home soon after the baby was born.

During a visit with my parents, Don joined Daddy in the garage, while I chatted with Mama in the living room. She informed me Mabel, Don's mom, was not allowed to live there. She did not give a reason but was very adamant about not allowing Mabel to live on their property. I was caught off guard and totally speechless. I had always been intimidated by Mama. There was no arguing with the authority figure, whose demands were adhered to with the sanctity of the almighty. I was terribly upset and mortified of the thought of having to say anything to Mabel.

Upon arriving home, I went into the bedroom and broke down in tears. Don's mother owned half of the mobile home. There was no way I could tell my mother-in-law she had to move out. We had already invested in the construction of the mobile home space. By the grace of God, the following day, Mabel announced she had made plans to take a government job in Alaska and leave soon after the baby was born.

Don was working his night job cleaning the college student union when I went into labor. After a long night and through the following morning of back labor, I was rolled into the delivery room. Rather than going in the delivery room, Don chose to bide the time in the waiting room.

I had a precious little son, whom was named after Don. Don got a quick glance of his new baby son through the nursery window and left to attend class, rest and go to his evening job.

The second morning after little Don was born, the nurse brought him in for his early morning feeding, saying something about him being fussy. Minutes later, the nurse took him back to the nursery. That was the last I ever saw him.

Being a new mother and ignorant of hospital protocol, I was wondering why it had been so long since they had brought in little Don. Questioning authority was not something I had ever been allowed to do. That evening, Don visited me. We were waiting for the nurse to bring our baby when Dr. Thomas entered. He announced our little baby had died. He did not know why.

Graveside services were held. Besides being devastated, I was a mess. I was recovering from the birth. My breasts were engorged with milk, which had come in the day little Don died. I had cried so much it hurt to breathe. My life was upside down. I felt empty but knew I could not wallow in grief. Don was in class when I visited Dr. Thomas to learn the results of the autopsy. He reported the hospital staff was very surprised when our baby started having breathing problems. There was blood in the baby's stomach, which he could not explain, and there was amniotic fluid in his lungs that he explained resulted from the baby taking a breath too soon. I could not understand how little Don could live two days with enough fluid in his lungs to cause his death that was not detected. I had visions of him not being dead at all. Perhaps one day little Don would come to find me.

I learned of an office job opening with the City Recreation Department, for which I applied. I started the day little Don would have been four weeks old. Since we needed the income, I continued to work and did not enroll in fall classes. I missed taking classes and being with people my age.

After graduating from high school, Lois wasted no time going out on her own. She was ready to get out from under the watchful, judgmental, and overbearing eyes of our parents. Within two weeks after graduation, at age seventeen, she was enrolled at a business college in Denver. Daddy said Lois would be back in two weeks, but she was never to return, except to visit briefly.

The business college Lois attended was for women only. Lois completed the one-year course, in eight months and got a good paying job with a trucking company in Denver.

One of her roommate's relatives owned a television store that was looking for an attractive model to appear in their newspaper ads. After inquiring about the job, Lois was hired as Pistol Packing Maggie to promote Magnavox televisions.

Lois posing for Magnavox ad

It was difficult to meet decent young men. A year, after graduating, Lois was introduced to Lawrence on a blind date setup by her roommate. Lawrence, age twenty, was stationed at Fort Carson Army Base at Colorado Springs with the rank of private. He was muscular and over six feet tall, with a short, groomed military haircut. After a short romance, consisting of fun-filled weekends, Lois married him at the age of nineteen and moved to Colorado Springs. Marrying him was the biggest mistake of her life. She did not realize he partied during the week, as well as the weekends. Due to behavioral issues, the army gave Lawrence a general discharge. He hawked Lois' personal belongings, such as her silver coin collection, to get money to purchase alcohol.

Lois supported them on a meager secretary's salary, while living in an apartment complex. Lawrence claimed to be looking for employment, but instead, was having an affair with a young woman who managed the apartment complex. Lois became aware of the affair one morning when she woke up early, alone. Looking out the window, she saw him leaving the manager's apartment.

Lawrence was both physically and mentally abusive, threatening to kill Lois if she left him. Even though Lois was very attractive and smart, she lacked the self-esteem and courage to leave.

Lawrence began bringing marijuana into their home, smoking it every night. Several other popular drugs followed, such as LSD. This did not set well with Lois. She could not persuade him to give up the alcohol and drugs.

Lois worked a few blocks from a large church with beautiful, inspiring, stained-glass windows. She began visiting the church on her lunch hours, in awe admiring the spectacular windows and crying. She prayed in desperation, "Please, Lord, PLEASE HELP ME!!"

Lawrence started dealing the illegal drugs he was so fond of. That did it! Lois knew if he got arrested, she would get arrested as well, and wanted nothing to do with it. After two years of hell, Lois left and hid from Lawrence.

By the grace of God, Lois worked for a government contractor in a building that had a security guard at the entrance. She spent several days with a friend from work and did not drive her 1968 Dodge Charger to work. Lois found a small apartment of her own, and then used her car for transportation to work; however, Lawrence stole it. Through friends and the police, she got it back. After filing a restraining order, she had no more trouble from him, but still looked over her shoulder. Lawrence did not appear for the divorce hearing. She was now on her own, a little older and a lot wiser. She thanked God for giving her the courage to leave and start healing.

Don and I were friends with Bob and Linda Garfield. Don knew Linda, a confident young lady of our same age, who worked at the Trailways bus station across the street from the Conoco gas station where he pumped gas. Bob, also our age, and I were in the same accounting classes. Bob was tall and slender with short curly hair. He was the night clerk and bookkeeper for Dos Rios Restaurant and Motel. One evening when we were having dinner together, Bob told a story about this crazy woman coming to the lounge a few nights previously, causing trouble.

Bob began relating the event as it was told to him. "Several evenings ago, a wild woman came in the lounge and approached the owner. She took his drink and poured it over his head. Then she approached the band. She grabbed the maracas and smashed them together, breaking them into thousands of pieces with beads scattering everywhere. She was shouting, calling everyone sinners and reprimanding them for drinking and smoking." As he was telling the story, he was laughing. It sounded very amusing. Bob did not realize he was talking about Jane, and I did not tell him.

The night the incident took place, my parents received a call from someone who recognized Jane. Unbeknownst to them, Jane had slipped out, riding her bike to the restaurant, which was a mile down the highway. Jane was totally out of control when Daddy and Mama physically carried her out of the bar. Once they were home, Daddy began unloading the bike from the back of the Willys Station Wagon. Mama tried to keep Jane restrained as she climbed out from the back seat of the two-door vehicle. Jane fought, yelling and kicking and flailing her arms around. She bit Mama on the hand, which later developed into a serious infection.

That was the start of Jane making a nuisance of herself around the community. She went to the house of one of her favorite teachers. Jane must have scared her because she would not answer the door. Many years later when I learned of the teacher's death, I informed Jane. To my surprise, Jane responded, "Good. When I went to her for help, she turned me away."

Jane kept slipping away on her bike. On one occasion, she rode out to Parlin, a small ranching community twelve miles east of town. People were complaining about a strange person riding a bike through their yards. The sheriff arrested her for trespassing, and she was locked up. While in jail, she ripped up the sheets and stuffed them down the toilet, causing a big mess. She thought it was very amusing.

Jane bought a junker Morris Minor car for a couple hundred dollars and registered it under Mama's and her name. To keep Jane from driving and getting in more trouble, Mama removed the distributor cap. Mama found a buyer and returned Jane's money to her. Jane was locked in the upstairs to keep her confined to the house. She tried to escape by climbing onto the roof and jumping off from the garage. She did not get away though. Another time, Jane decided to tie sheets together and lower herself down from what had been my bedroom. Her foot got caught in a sheet. She was hanging upside down out the window that faced the river. Someone in the house across the river saw Jane dangling from the window and called Mama.

"I know," Mama told them nonchalantly, "I'm going to get her down in a minute." Jane was admitted to the state hospital, in Pueblo.

While in Alaska, Don's mother found a new husband, William Bennett. He had seven children, of which the three youngest, all boys, were living with them. Mabel and her new family stopped by to visit us on their move from Alaska to Texas, where William owned a home. During their visit, I miscarried at sixteen weeks. The miscarriage was traumatic but did not leave the void that I was still feeling from the loss of little Don.

Don graduated from college with a double major in mathematics and accounting. He continued taking graduate courses. Meanwhile, I conceived, and Caroline was born in 1971. She was beautiful beyond compare as her face turned red, and she was crying healthfully– "Weh, weh, weh." Don was jubilant, as he left the hospital, singing at the top of his lungs while driving to one of his part-time jobs.

I was pleasantly surprised when Daddy appeared to see Caroline and me at the hospital. "Third time's a charm," he said.

I quit my job and stayed home to take care of Caroline. It was a very happy time for me as I followed Caroline's development. All was well, even when I discovered I was pregnant again. Caroline was only seven months old, but I felt ecstatic. Another little baby was a gift from heaven. Since we had no insurance, I got my old job back, which was opening up. Jane had stabilized and was doing well taking business correspondence courses. Jane babysat Caroline. Caroline gave her purpose, and she truly loved Caroline. Caroline was easy to take care of, walking at nine months old, she was a very adorable little blond doll. Jane played with her and put her hair in pig tails. The arrangement worked well with no concern of Caroline not receiving appropriate care. Mama was close by if Jane needed help.

We had hoped to stay in Gunnison. Don was still pumping gas and had another part-time job while we were waiting for a teaching position to open. With our second baby on the way, Don could not continue to pump gas indefinitely.

Job applications were sent out, and I started packing. He accepted the offer from Farmington, New Mexico, which came on the day Christopher was born. Chris was eight weeks old and Caroline was eighteen months when we arrived in Farmington with all our worldly possessions.

Our budget was too tight to survive on a first-year teacher's salary. The lady next door agreed to babysit, while I went to work afternoons at the high school as a bookkeeper for the school's activity accounts. Later, I became secretary to an administrator and worked full time during the school year. During that time I suffered three miscarriage; however, I successfully conceived again, and Curtis was born in 1976. He was a wonderful blessing. I had been through enough emotional turmoil from losing so many babies and was happy to now have my family complete.

My parents moved to Delta in 1975. Their new place consisted of two acres with a four-bedroom house. The property included a large garage, an outbuilding, a chicken house, a root cellar, and a barn. Mama was happy to have a place where she could keep chickens. Daddy had been talking about retiring to a warmer place to get away from the excruciatingly hard winters that aggravated his arthritis, which resulted from a war injury he acquired while fighting on Midway Island as a marine during World War II. Shortly after moving, Daddy had knee replacement surgery. Jane followed and got her own place to live, supporting herself with a job in a secretarial pool for a canning company.

Lois was still living in Colorado Springs when she met Hans a couple of years after divorcing Lawrence. Hans was a handsome man; short in stature, but made up for it by his honest character and soft brown eyes. Being in the military, his blond hair was cut short. She first noticed him at a Bible study class in the fall of 1975. He said he was from L.A. (Lower Alabama). Lois loved his southern accent. He was a second lieutenant in the air force and was an instructor pilot at the Air Force Academy. Hans was from Montgomery, Alabama, and a graduate of the University of Alabama. On their first date, they took a drive to picnic in the mountains and observe a protected buffalo herd. They enjoyed each other's company so much that after returning to their homes, they changed clothes and went out to a restaurant that evening. From then on they saw each other every day until they got married the following April.

One of Hans' brothers, one sister, and a friend came to the wedding. Our parents and Jane attended also. Daddy walked Lois down the aisle with the assistance of his cane. I was unable to attend as I had recently given birth to Curtis. Lois and Hans went to Lahaina in Maui, Hawaii, for their honeymoon. When they returned, the military packed Hans' house and Lois' apartment into a moving van. They were on their way to Lubbock, Texas.

Soon after arriving, Hans was sent to a base in Florida for three months of special training. Lois accompanied him, while their new home was being built. Hans was the oldest boy of seven children of divorced parents. Hans' mother operated a small market which had been held up by thieves. The thieves did not get money but Hans' mother was hit with the butt of a rifle that left a big knot and bruise on her head. Lois met the rest of Hans' siblings when going to Montgomery to take care of his younger brothers and sisters and maintain the house, while his mother was in the hospital.

Upon returning to Lubbock, they settled in their new home. Hans taught pilots to fly T-37s at the base. Lois got a civil service secretarial job on the base. Her office supported flight simulators which were controlled by computer programs. Although Lois did office work, she had the opportunity to climb in a simulator from time to time and "fly" the plane, usually crashing. Lois became interested in becoming a computer programmer and enrolled in classes at Texas Tech.

Jane moved to Colorado Springs in 1977, where she worked in a secretarial pool at a hospital. She decided to pursue a career in nursing and enrolled at Pikes Peak Community College. Jane was very opinionated regarding the care of patients. She did not approve of the routine use of prescription drugs. She did not complete nursing school; however, she did complete the certified nurse aide requirements and then worked as a nurse's aide at St. Frances Hospital.

Mama had an unquenchable thirst for knowledge. With her daughters gone, she began researching many topics, such as family linage, UFO's, numerology, and the lost continent of Atlantis. She talked about the San Andreas Fault and believed California was going to fall off into the ocean any day. She did research on Admiral Byrd's exploration to the North Pole where he discovered the earth is hollow, a fact that is not generally known per Mama. She believed in reincarnation and cited two lives she had lived previously. In one life, she was a man on Atlantis and was herding cattle onto a boat when she drowned. In another life, she told of being a girl around the age of seventeen, living in New England in the 1700s. She died from a spider bite. Mama claimed to be clairvoyant on limited occasions, such as envisioning Don's father appearing before her with blood dripping from his fingers the evening he died. She also told of experiences she had knowing when her grandparents had died before she was notified.

Daddy, Mama, and Jane became absorbed in a church with which we were not familiar. They had become fanatical about the church.

Mama talked about it constantly. They said prayers called decrees from a book, chanting quickly and loudly in unison to the ascended masters.

The church taught meditation and practiced astral projection or out-of-body experience, which according to Mama explained why she and Daddy could hear Jane making noise upstairs when she was in body, confined to a hospital during one of her breakdowns. Mama and Daddy went to many church conferences. Mama talked about church leaders, auras, karma, chakras and the predictions of Edgar Cayce, St. Germaine and Nostradamus. They

Don, Caroline, Chris, and Louise with Curtis in front

purchased countless church tapes and books and hung a picture of a temple with an all-seeing eye on the wall in their living room. The religion incorporated teachings from Buddhism and other world religions. It was a conglomeration of everything. Hans called it the Baseball Religion because it covered all the bases of the major religions. Mama said it was the answer to what she had been seeking. They gradually drifted away from the church when the headquarters moved to another state.

Don thought Mama was a bit dingy. Lois and I were used to our mother and accepted her with an open mind, not judging her one way or another.

Don and I bought our first house in 1977, and I began working at San Juan College. I enrolled in an evening class and was up every night until midnight studying. I received an A in the course; but it was evident I could not continue to be a good mother, work a demanding job, and have any sanity left with that kind of a schedule.

Going back to school would not be in the cards.

Our children were fascinated with dinosaurs. Don decided to take our family to Vernal, Utah to see dinosaur exhibits and invited Daddy to join us while Mama was in California, taking a writing course. We had a carefree, enjoyable visit going through the exhibits of relics and the museum. Don purchased a number of unique small realistic plastic dinosaurs for our children, while Daddy purchased a brontosaurus that cost $7. I was amazed. I had never seen that side of him. On the drive back, Daddy mentioned something to the effect of not wanting to live forever. That comment went over my head. I did not know then Daddy was hinting of not being around much longer, and this would be the last time I would see him alive.

Hans' next assignment was at RAF Woodbridge near Ipswich, England. Before leaving, Lois took a side trip to Delta to spend a few days with our parents before venturing abroad. A month later, Lois and Hans were living in temporary quarters when Hans went on a week-long assignment to Germany. Soon after Hans' departure, Lois received an early morning call from Mama informing her of daddy's death. Hans returned to England immediately. After fifty-two hours of travel, Lois and Hans arrived in Delta.

Mama, we three daughters, and our families viewed Daddy's body, which was laid out on a granite slab. We could hardly speak. He looked calm like he was sleeping. A small group of people were present at the memorial service, including Daddy's only surviving brother, William, known as Curly, for his full head of curly red hair. Mama did not show any signs of grief. She had not come to the realization of Daddy being gone. It was like one big reunion. This was the first time we had been together since Lois left home over ten years previously.

A blood clot had lodged in Daddy's heart. The blood clot originated from his knee joint replacement, which caused blood clots to continually form. He knew it was a matter of time but did not tell anyone. Daddy died way too young at age sixty-two, cheating his grandchildren out of anticipated fishing outings

Funeral gathering Jane, Lois, Marie (Mama) Louise, Don Front – Caroline, Chris, Curtis

and stories about when he was in the war.

When visiting with Mama about losing Daddy, Mama told me that several evenings prior to his death, they were sitting quietly in the living room, reading, when they heard the sound of a loud horn, which lasted several seconds. "They are coming to get me," Daddy said calmly. Daddy had been painting the barn from a faded-out brown to a sparkling green. On the afternoon of the day he died, he stroked in bold green lettering on a replacement section of plywood "Milton May 1980." Later that summer, it was painted over when Don and I returned to finish painting the barn.

When Lois and Hans got back to England, they moved into a small house in Felixstowe on the coast of the English Channel. Anxiously, Lois watched as job openings were posted on base, but she was not eligible since the positions were reserved for British nationals. Not to be dissuaded, she found a job on the British economy as a data entry operator for a company that leased shipping containers and tracked them all over the world on ships and trains. The office was so close to her house Lois generally walked to work until the office moved ten miles away to Ipswich. She began taking the train, stowing her ten-speed bicycle in the bicycle car, and riding her bike the rest of the way to work in four-inch heels and a dress, just like the British women.

Lois worked in a large room alone with a dreadful English woman, who took pleasure in tormenting her. Emma was tall, and stocky, and homely, with dull blue eyes and short curly hair. She spoke with a smooth British accent, mocking and bulling Lois continuously. Even though this woman's ridicule made Lois' life miserable, Lois was not comfortable initiating a confrontation. Lois was conditioned to be submissive after growing up on the receiving end of our overbearing mother. She was fearful she would lose her job if she brought attention to the conflict. After two years of abuse, Lois finally lost it. In no uncertain terms, she told this egotistical bully where to go and exactly how to get there. Emma instantly ceased harassing her from that moment on. At age thirty-four, she finally allowed herself to set boundaries. Lois learned one very important lesson—some people will not respect you until you stand up to them.

Back in Farmington, Don and Ken, a teaching colleague, decided to start a small janitorial service. The main client of the janitorial service was a large drug store. Every other Sunday, Don and Ken stripped the floors and put down a fresh coat of wax. Besides keeping the books, I went in an hour to wipe down the stainless steel counter bases.

At that time, besides teaching, Don was driving school bus and working all night on Saturday, cleaning floors for another large store. Don was also working toward his master's degree, while I typed his critiques and projects.

CHAPTER THREE

Years Roll By

In 1982 Mama married Albert Archer. She met him at the Salvation Army store, where they both worked. He was sixteen years her senior, closer to her father's age than he was to hers. Albert was a retired railroad worker and kept milk cows. Albert had eight grown children. When Mama called to inform me she had decided to get married and asked what I thought, I replied, "We want you to be happy, and if that is what you want, then go ahead."

I was expecting to be invited to the wedding, but upon making reference to coming, Mama replied, "I got married the first time without you, and I can do it again without you." Her response was absurd, but consistent with her personality. Marie's marriage to Albert was a simple affair with family who lived nearby.

Soon after Mama married Albert, they came for a visit to Farmington. Albert was nothing like Daddy in any way. He was an old man of short stature with a growth on his nose. The remains of his jack-o'-lantern teeth were crooked and yellowing. His conversation focused around his cows or church.

Our family group went to a cafeteria for lunch. We all sat around a large round table with Mama and Albert. Albert announced he was going to say grace. Everyone held hands as Albert started to pray. He spoke in a low, monotone mumble. The cafeteria was very noisy with dishes clanging and conversations among the patrons, all speaking loudly to be heard above the noise. Several times, I looked up to see if Albert was still praying. Finally, after the longest meal prayer I had ever experienced, the hand holding ended signifying the prayer was over.

The first time our family went to visit Mama after her marriage to Albert, I was horrified to see what Albert had done to Daddy's meticulous yard. Fruit trees had been planted in the front lawn with furrows dug to provide water to the trees from the nearby irrigation ditch. Further exploration behind the house revealed a rickety fence that had been jimmy rigged with bailing twine and wire to hold it together. There were milk cows grazing in the previously unused field.

⚬❧⚬

Back in Farmington, the street where we lived opened up, turning it into a major thoroughfare. After living there five years, it was time to move to a suitable place where our children could safely ride their bicycles. The house was put on the market and sold within several months. A new house was

Louise and Lois in Munich

being built, which would take three more weeks to complete by the time we had to vacate our old house. Lois invited us to join her and Hans on their vacation to Germany. This was the perfect time to go. All our household belongings were stored in a moving van. While our good friends watched our children, we vacationed with Lois and Hans.

Lois and Hans planned to spend their vacation camping all over Europe, taking their English BMW with the steering wheel on the right-hand side of the car. We brought dome tents and spent most nights in campgrounds, mingling with the Europeans. A memorable stop was a concentration camp outside of Munich. It was a sobering experience to visit the camp, where millions of Jews perished during World War II.

While in Berchtesgaden, it was eerie to walk the streets where Hitler had walked. Many castles and palaces were visited, each revealing elegant and spectacular displays of their own.

Suddenly, Hans was called back to his unit temporarily in Germany, leaving the rest of us to find our way back home. An express train out of Koln took us back to our parked car. Lois was not used to driving the autobahn, where speed limits generally did not exist. Road construction made it confusing. We decided to follow the signs to Umleitung and get our bearings from there. We never actually made it to Umleitung, but finally found our way back to the ferry. Later, we learned *Umleitung* meant "detour" in German.

After three years in England, Hans was reassigned to Colorado Springs and Lois and Hans bought a new house. Jane was still living in Colorado Springs. She met Wes at the public library. Within five days, they decided to get married. Lois helped by making a bouquet of lace, pink ribbons and flowers. Jane and Wes got married at the Justice of the Peace with Lois being their witness. They lived in a mobile home park on the outskirts of town. Wes had worked twelve years for an electrical company when he lost his job and then became a truck driver. Jane continued to work as a nursing assistant. She did not communicate with me about events happening in her life. It was assumed all was going well.

Lois and Hans decided to visit Mama and Albert one Christmas and called about coming. After spending one night, Mama told Lois undiplomatically she had to leave because they were going to one of Albert's children's home for dinner. On Christmas Day, Lois and Hans left to go back home. Their Christmas dinner consisted of tacos, which they bought at a restaurant on the summit of Monarch pass.

Lois shared her experience with me. "Mama kicked us out on Christmas Day to spend time with Albert's family. I don't understand why we were not welcomed to the family Christmas dinner. Why couldn't she have asked if we could come to dinner with them?"

It appeared to me Albert's family, who visited frequently, had priority. "Our mother has been hijacked," I expressed in a joking manner. But it was true. That experience created ill feelings. Hans said if he ever visited again, they would stay in a motel.

Hans was not fond of the idea of going to see Mama. The next time Lois visited, she drove to Delta alone. Mama had let her hair grow longer than Lois had ever seen it before. She was annoyed that it was in her face. After asking Lois to cut it, she looked much better with her white hair in a becoming, neat, layered style.

Sunday morning, Lois joined Mama, going to church together, before leaving the following day. As they entered the church, they saw a congregation of nearly forty people waiting in the auditorium for the service to begin. They seated themselves in a pew half way down from the front on the right side. Mama pointed out the pastor's wife, who was seated at the piano. She was a small woman with long salt and pepper hair and an expressionless, submissive face.

The short, dark haired, wiry pastor entered the stage in a confident, stern demeanor. Mama had mentioned the pastor did not approve of women cutting their hair, which was evident when during the sermon he looked straight at Lois, adamantly proclaiming that some people in the congregation had been persuaded by evil influences from out of town to break God's law. It was obvious this old fashioned preacher's remarks were directed toward Lois. She was mortified.

After the service, Mama gave the pastor a dozen of freshly laid eggs, in lieu of a monetary contribution. He rudely grabbed the eggs, tucked them under his arm, and walked off. Being a strong Christian, Lois could not wait to escape from the church.

Lois' bad vibes influenced her to question Mama about her church. "Do you really feel this church is meeting your expectations?"

"I don't agree with it all, but at least it isn't one of those highfalutin churches," she replied.

"When you pass on, is this the pastor you want to do your service?" A few months later Mama started attending a different church.

After two years in Colorado Springs, Hans was transferred to Germany. Lois got a civil service job in Bitburg, where she worked for the Operations Commander, who was the Colonel that commanded all the fighter squadrons. When the meetings were interrupted from the unbearably loud F-15s taking off, he would always say, "Ahhh, the sound of freedom!"

Our time was dedicated to our children. In the summer, we went tent camping and fishing at Haviland Lake, north of Durango. Sometimes we went on day hikes around Haviland Lake, Purgatory Flats, Engineer Peak, Potato Mountain or one of multiple other trails. In the winter, we took our children cross-country skiing; taking Curtis

Going fishing Curtis, Chris and Caroline

for the first time when he was three. That did not work out too well. Don and I ended up taking turns carrying him. During the school year, our children were kept busy participating in sports and various activities. Don generally assisted coaching whatever sport in which the boys were participating. Caroline was a Brownie and Girl Scout, and exceled at selling Girl Scout cookies, and also earned lots of badges.

Our family visited Jane in Colorado Springs, spending one night with her in her mobile home. Wes was gone driving truck. Jane got up at 5:30 A.M. to go to her job. Jane was functioning reasonably well. Wes had run up their charge card buying Western shirts and other clothing for himself, which made Jane angry.

Lois and Hans were back in the states in 1988 and were assigned to Tyndall Air Force Base outside of Panama City, Florida, on the Gulf of Mexico. Lois had been working on a degree in computers over the last twelve years and had finally graduated in 1989.

Hans retired and they moved back to Colorado Springs, returning to their Colorado home, which had been leased. Lois found a job, this time as a computer programmer with a company that contracted software development for NORAD. Hans was trying his hand at selling real estate while waiting to get a position as a commercial airline pilot.

Jane seemed to be functioning within normal limits. Her social awkwardness and inappropriate behavior was on display when she visited Lois at her home. During the visits, Lois noticed her staring at Hans. Jane routinely lashed out with ridiculing insults and telling Lois what she should do.

Lois mentioned Jane's behavior to a co-worker, who had previously worked at a hospital with mentally ill patients. She explained Lois was trying to relate to Jane as if she was sane and not to expect Jane's behavior to make sense all of the time.

Lois changed jobs to take a position with a Fortune 500 company, and Hans was hired by Delta Airlines. It was becoming increasingly inconvenient for Hans to make his flight connections, resulting in a move to Atlanta. Lois was able to transfer to another position within her company.

Jane wanted to move closer to Mama, but Wes did not. After five years of marriage, Jane divorced Wes. Years later, she regretted her hasty decision to dissolve their marriage. After divorcing Wes, Jane moved to Delta.

Jane got in the habit of calling us on our birthdays at seven A.M. to tell us "Happy birthday." I received a birthday call from Jane early one morning. Breaking away from the usual chat, Jane spoke. "I was going to break you and Don up, but I decided not to." I blew off Jane's absurdity. Jane was green with envy of my family. In another early morning birthday call, Jane did not get away with her belittling tactics. "You don't live in the real world," Jane remarked.

"What do you mean?" I asked. "You think raising children, going to work every day, and maintaining a household, is not the real world?"

"You have never been out there on your own," responded Jane.

"So you think getting in trouble, being thrown in jail, and being hauled off to the state hospital is living in the real world?"

"I didn't mean that," Jane stammered.

I received a letter from Jane, saying, "You hurt my feelings." Jane never cared if she was hurting anyone's feelings; that seemed to be her goal.

❦

Our children had grown up. Before we knew it, Caroline had graduated from high school and was off to college. The following year, Chris graduated and was off to college, also. Curtis was the only one left at home, not that we ever saw him, but could tell he was around from the trail of dirty clothes.

Chris married Phyllis, his high school sweetheart, in May after completing his first year of college. Chris was majoring in the field of computers. He had grown into a handsome young man; not quite six feet tall, with green eyes and blond hair that had gentle waves, when he let it grow. Phyllis had dark short hair and brown eyes, and was a talented pianist.

Caroline met Joe at the university and they married the following May. Don and I had barely recuperated from Chris' wedding, when it was time to plan for Caroline's. Mama did not attend any of her grandchildren's graduations or Chris and Phyllis' wedding. She had no plans for attending Caroline's wedding either until Lois *twisted* her arm. "What do they need me there for?" Mama asked.

The day of Caroline's wedding had been spent decorating the church and reception area and seeing to the details from music to flowers. Lois was the matron of honor. Her long blond hair was styled in a sophisticated up do.

I was getting worried when Mama and Albert had not arrived long after the expected time. Mama had been driving around for hours before stopping at a filling station to call for assistance. She had misread the map I drew and kept backtracking, going in circles. When she arrived, she obviously needed to have her hair washed. Caroline's wedding was a formal church affair, and her grandmother needed to look presentable. I volunteered to wash and curl her hair. She was not making the effort for her granddaughter's wedding that I expected. At least she was there.

The following year Curtis graduated from high school and chose to attend San Juan College. Curtis had his father's coloring with brown hair and brown mischievous eyes. He was the same height as Chris and like Chris was a good-looking guy with a great sense of humor. When our kids got together, we were kept in stitches. Curtis rented a house with two of his friends and worked at Radio Shack. It was a bitter sweet change to have all of our children out of the house.

We visited Mama and Albert once or twice a year. Jane rented her own apartment but never failed to be there upon our arrival. During one visit, Don went with Albert to check on irrigation ditches. Mama suggested Jane and I go for a walk.

As we began our walk along the well-established graveled county road, Jane started talking. "When I can't sleep at night, I like to take walks and sing. People sleep with their windows open and complain I'm waking them up. They call the police, and I get arrested. I'm not hurting anybody. If I had a lot of money and a lot of property, I could walk on my property and do what I wanted. They would just say I was eccentric."

Before I could respond to Jane's complaints of being treated unfairly, she changed topics. "I have a new boyfriend. His name is Jeff. He wants to get into my pants. He signed over an apartment to me. We want to get married, but Mama doesn't want me to. She said he is too old for me."

"Let's go back now," I choked out.

Jane continued talking as we turned around and strolled back toward the old farmhouse. "Believe it or not, but Mama is crazier than I am. You should be around her more, and you could see for yourself."

That thought had never occurred to me as I protested that idea. I had never considered Mama as having mental health issues, even though years later, that thought surfaced. For now, I interpreted Mama's behavior as *difficult to get along with*. I had always felt frustrated regarding her unconventional behavior. In hopes of achieving insight in dealing with Mama, I had attended a workshop on dealing with difficult people. According to the presenter, one has to adjust their own attitudes and accept there is nothing they can do to change someone else. I must have been delusional to think there was a solution. There was a choice between peace and conflict. I was consoled with my submissive choice of peace.

⚮

Jane did not marry Jeff. It was surmised Mama's objections resulted in their breakup: however, Jane maintained her residence in the apartment Jeff had signed over to her.

Our weekend visits to Mama entailed arriving Saturday afternoon, spending the night, and leaving Sunday morning. Since Mama left food out on the table with flies generally buzzing around the kitchen, Don was leery of eating there, which started a tradition of Don treating for pizza or other fast food. Jane monopolized the conversation, chatting about their church or people and places that were foreign to me, intentionally leaving me out of the conversations.

Mama had only met Chris' wife, Phyllis, briefly at Caroline's wedding and had never seen their baby son, Avery. For Mama to see her first great-grandchild, Chris' family joined us on one of our visits.

As had become customary, Don treated our group to dinner. Upon entering the Kentucky Fried Chicken, Albert staked out a table in the center of the seating area. While waiting for our group to place their orders, Albert handed out miniature booklets of Bible verses and engraved pencils to any children whose attention he could get. Mama and I were seated by Albert when Jane approached wearing a straw hat and sat down, offering to sing a song she wrote. Where Jane ever got the idea she could write songs, or sing, was a mystery to me. She made up words and tunes as she went along. As Jane sang, I looked around to find Don hiding out with the kids at a distant table. I felt very conspicuous after being deserted by Don. I put on the biggest smile I could muster and said to myself, "It's okay, no one knows you here."

Lois and I were surprised when in September 1994, we received announcements in the mail of Jane's marriage to Ben Jenson. Jane met Ben at a rehabilitation center while recuperating from her most recent relapse. Jane had made the announcements, which displayed individual pictures of each of them from the shoulders up. Ben had a balding head and a neatly groomed bushy white beard.

"Jane married Santa Claus," stated Lois.

"Yes, his beard sure makes him look like Santa Claus," I agreed, with a chuckle.

Neither Lois nor I had ever heard of Ben before. Jane did not waste any time dragging him to the altar. Ben and Jane took up residence in the apartment Jeff had signed over to Jane.

Don and I met Ben on one of our visits to see Mama and Albert. Ben's beard had grown unruly. He wore a hat that hid his balding head; his general appearance resembled an unmade bed. Ben had little to say until he got to know you. He had a great sense of humor and liked to tell jokes. Ben was a Vietnam veteran with an unexplained disability. From Jane's apartment, she took us for a walk to meet Ben's sister, Carrie, and her husband, Herman, who lived with their family in a house a short distance away.

It was too difficult for Mama and Albert to get away from the farm to come see us, so Don and I embarked on a visit bringing Chris and his family to Delta for a second time. This time there was also a little granddaughter named Kayla, who was two years younger than Avery. It was a delightful experience for Avery and Kayla. They had never been around farm animals and were fascinated by the three large wooly sheep that greeted them at the fence baaing.

The events of our visits had become routine. Being true to form, Jane would already be at the house when we arrived; she and Ben would always join us for dinner, and she would always make up an excuse to come back to Mama's house afterwards. By the time Jane left, it was late and time to go to bed. This practice eliminated any time I would have to chat with Mama out of Jane's presence before we had to leave the next morning.

After another evening out during one of our visits, Jane returned to the house saying she had left a book there. Albert had already retired to the bedroom. Moments after entering the house, Jane broke into a repertoire of obscenities. "Mother F… this and Mother F… that." Perhaps the attention I was getting from Mama had ticked her off. The air turned blue with a gamut of profanities. Whatever point Jane was trying to make was lost to the cosmic void.

I was stunned to hear such expletives erupting from Jane. Generally, whenever Jane heard even the mildest swearing, she would gasp and remark, "You said a bad word."

Mama stared in silence, while Jane raged on in her profanity frenzy. "Let's go home," Ben repeated several times, but Jane was not willing to give up center stage easily. When Jane and Ben finally left, everyone went quietly to bed, drained of their energy.

❧

Albert died in August 1999 at the age of ninety-two. His family had planned a Labor Day reunion before his death. Albert's body was preserved several weeks in order to combine his funeral with the reunion to accommodate distant relatives. Lois and Hans were planning to visit prior to Albert's death. Their plans were kept after first spending a few days with us. I rode with them to visit Mama, while Don stayed home with his teaching obligation. The funeral took place the week before we arrived. Albert's family had returned to their homes.

Previously, I had asked Mama for a set of dishes she had been keeping for me. Mama was digging through a closet, looking for the dishes, when I appeared to help. "I don't need help," she told me. "Go join your sisters outside." I stepped outside, taking note of the beautiful, cool September day as I joined my sisters by the goat pen.

Earlier that day, Mama told us she had changed her will. The topic was fresh on Jane's mind. She glared at Lois and me through glasses that shielded her distrusting eyes. Out of nowhere, Jane blasted away, "You are only interested in Mama's money. You are trying to cheat me out of my share!"

Lois and I were dumbfounded. We had no say in our mother's will. Jane was getting a good deal. The will made provisions for her to occupy the farm as long as she wanted. If she did not want to stay there or whenever she moved from the farm, the property was to be sold, and the proceeds were to be divided among us three. That was not fair by Jane's thinking; since Lois and I already had homes, the farm should be given to her outright. She was complaining that if she and Ben decided to move to Grand Junction or somewhere, the house would not be there for them if they wanted to come back. We assured her she would not be cheated. Jane finally calmed down after the backyard screaming match was over.

Lois and I brought to Mama's attention our concern for what we would do with all her stuff when she was gone. "You three girls should be able to go through it in a weekend," she responded.

Lois and I looked at each other with *huh* expressions. Who was she trying to kid? We both knew that was impossible, even if Jane was not instigating problems, which was another impossibility. Our mother had no concept of how involved it would be to clear out the overwhelming abundance of things that had accumulated.

During this trip, Lois confided Hans was having a medical issue, but the cause of his discomfort had not been determined. When he returned home, Hans was scheduled to go for a scan of his gallbladder. Mama's research of her medical books indicated pancreatic issues. After a conversation with Mama, Lois requested to have the test include checking Hans' pancreas. The test was changed after Lois' insistence. The diagnosis revealed advanced stage IV pancreatic cancer. Hans was not expected to live past six months. The news was devastating.

Don and I flew out to Peachtree City, Georgia, to visit Lois and Hans in July of 2000. Hans continued talking about all the things they were going to do when he got well. He was very frustrated but refused to give up as his body kept withering away.

As Hans continued to get closer to death, he was admitted to the hospital. A friend paid him a quick visit, but left and came back the following day "I came by yesterday to see you but you were sleeping," she told him.

"I was not sleeping," he replied. "I was watching you from behind that chair."

Hans was released from the hospital under hospice care. Being heavily sedated under morphine, Hans had strange hallucinations. "You have to get those cows out of the back yard," he told Lois in his semi-comatose state. Hans died at home two days after being released in the presence of Lois, his mother, and a sister. It had only been a month since our visit when Don and I returned with all three of our adult children to attend Hans' funeral.

Hans' death was very traumatic for Lois; she could not envision a happy future without him. She spent her days in a fog going through the motions of living and working. It was very lonely with no family or friends around other than work colleagues. After several months, she realized Hans had died; not her, and she needed to get through her grief.

Lois' company had been wanting her to move to their headquarters in Memphis. With Hans gone, Lois made the decision to move. After selling her home that she shared with Hans in Georgia, a new home was being built in Tennessee. The event of 9-11 had just occurred weeks prior to the scheduled closing. Planes were grounded and finalization of the mortgage was delayed. Fortunately, the builders let Lois occupy her new home before the actual closing. Her niece, Caroline, took off time from her job and helped Lois with the huge job of setting up her new house.

⁂

Our mother's siblings routinely communicated through emails and wanted her to join in. Lois decided to give her a computer that had belonged to Hans. It was sent to me for Don to set up. Curtis provided a printer, which he bought at cost through the Radio Shack store he managed. Lois and I went in together on a Christmas present to get our mother a chair with casters to use at the computer.

Don and I squeaked in a quick Saturday trip to Delta. Don assembled the chair, and the computer was set up. Remarkably, Jane was not there. Mama said Jane was not feeling well and suggested I call her.

I greeted Jane over the phone. She was cranky and rude. "You know I have Parkinson's disease?"

"No," I responded in surprise.

"Didn't Mama tell you?"

"No," I replied. "I'm so sorry."

Jane started, screaming, "No you are not sorry! You don't care about me. All you care about is yourself and your family! You don't care anything about me!" She slammed down the receiver.

I was in shock and extremely upset. "Jane said she has Parkinson's disease."

"It isn't for sure. I didn't think to tell you about it," Mama responded. As it turned out Jane did not have Parkinson's.

With a snow storm looming over Red Mountain Pass, Don and I left hastily. As we drove down the highway, I felt badly from Jane's verbal attack. Of course, I cared about Jane; but she certainly was not the focal point in my life, which Jane thought she should be.

Hans had been gone three years. During that time Lois started dating but was disillusioned with the dating scene. She was still grieving and began attending a grief counseling group at a church. During her third visit, Lois met Bill, a Tennessee cattle rancher with three grown children. Bill was a widower, who had recently lost his wife to cancer, after a lengthy battle. Bill was captivated with Lois; a while later they became engaged.

After their engagement, Lois and Bill traveled to meet our family, first stopping in Delta. They knew they would not be arriving until late afternoon and made arrangements to meet at a pizza shop for dinner. Lois and Bill arrived early. Choosing a table for six, Bill sat at the end of one side. Mama arrived soon after, sitting across from Bill. Jane and Ben were the last ones to enter and took the remaining seats across from Bill. Lois introduced Bill to everyone before the group ordered. Mama chatted with Bill in casual conversation with a few comments from Ben as they awaited the arrival of their pizzas.

Jane finally spoke as she addressed Bill from her cattycorner position. "You know why they didn't let me sit next to you? It's because I'm the crazy one." After Jane's proclamation, she nodded her head back and forth and smiled.

Throughout dinner, Jane refrained from speaking but constantly glared at Bill, peeking under the brim of her straw hat that she customarily wore. Lois had forewarned him of what to expect, but anything she could have described could not have portrayed the uncomfortable feeling of strangeness that accompanied Jane's presence.

After dinner Lois and Bill returned to their motel and left the next morning to visit us in Farmington for a few days. Then it was time to introduce Bill to her home town of Gunnison. They hired a fishing guide who was following in Daddy's footsteps. Daddy had been a trailblazer when it came to entertaining tourists, as he was the first one to offer guided fishing tours or "float" trips down the Gunnison River, beginning back in the 1950's. The fishing trip brought back sweet memories for Lois. Bill was impressed by the beauty of the area and the great fishing the Rockies had to offer.

Later that summer, Jane decided to paint Mama's barn white. The job was barely started with a few strokes of white paint over the previous green when the chore was abandoned. Mama asked us to finish the job. We agreed to complete the task and had Curtis join us. We arrived one Friday evening, ready to work, and began painting early the next morning.

Milton (Daddy) with his rubber life raft

All three of us worked briskly until lunchtime arrived on the hot August Saturday. Don began rinsing the paint from the brushes with a garden hose as not to return from lunch to find ruined brushes with dried paint. Jane appeared out of nowhere, lumbering up to the barn with Ben following behind. Jane announced they had been in a parade. She was dressed like a clown, wearing a plaid blouse and striped slacks topped off with her straw hat. We were invited to go rafting with them. Jane was not happy when her invitation was turned down. The barn had to be finished that afternoon.

"Give me the hose," Jane demanded. "I'm thirsty. I need a drink of water."

"The water in the hose is hot from sitting in the sun. Go into the house where you can get a cool drink." Don said as he continued rinsing the paint brushes, while Jane jabbered. The calm conversation changed in the blink of an eye. "Give me the hose!" Jane rudely insisted. Don repeated. "The water is not good to drink. Go to the house for cool water."

"Are you going to give me the hose or not?" Jane shouted. Don handed her the hose. It had a metal nozzle, which controlled the flow of water by holding down a lever. Jane grabbed the hose from Don's hand. Without removing the nozzle, she placed it up to her lips and pressed the lever. The water shot out with great pressure. It was rather hilarious as the water came spewing from her mouth, but no one laughed. Jane threw the hose to the ground with force, hitting my foot.

"Ouch!" I squealed in pain. Jane did not care she had hurt my foot. She marched off in a huff and drove off with Ben, not stopping for a drink of water at the house.

The following Monday, Jane began a writing class in which she had enrolled at a college in Grand Junction. Jane had a disagreement with her instructor, quickly getting on his troublemakers list. When the class was over, Jane lay down on a bench to rest while waiting for Ben to pick her up. She had been there a lengthy time when the college security asked her to leave. Jane had a breakdown and withdrew from her class. She blamed her breakdown on becoming dehydrated because Don would not give her water.

All of our children were coming for Christmas of 2001. Don thought it would be nice to have my mother join us. She had never seen Caroline and Joe's two children. Clara was three and Mathew was approaching his first birthday. Don and I arranged to pick her up and afterwards bring her back home. It was a great family Christmas. Mama was glad she had spent the time with her grandchildren and great-grandchildren.

Keeping up the farm was difficult for Mama. She decided to sell and find a place in town. She contacted a real estate agent and was trying to get organized. "How is the packing going?" I asked.

"Pretty good," She replied. "I'm making headway on sorting the mail."

I was mystified. Mama had been preparing for months, and all she was doing was sorting through old mail. "Why did you let so much accumulate?" I asked.

She replied, "A lot of it was Albert's. He didn't want to toss anything without looking at it. He said they wouldn't send it to him if it wasn't important. He was too tired to read it, so he kept it in a box."

"It is old. Why don't you just toss it rather than waste time going through it?" I suggested.

"It is a good thing I've been looking through it. I found some pictures of Albert's kids that would have gotten thrown out," Mama said to justify her project.

After a while, Mama's real estate agent contacted her with the prospects of purchasing a condo, which was exactly what she had been looking for.

Mama was in a quandary wanting to buy the condo but needed help in organizing the move. Lois relieved the situation and bought the condo with funds she received from Hans' life insurance. Without Lois' assistance, she would never have been able to sell the farm and move out while also coordinating the purchase of the condo.

I mentioned to my high school friend Vonda, with whom I had rode her sister's horse as teenagers, and who lived in Delta, of Mama's plans to move. Vonda volunteered the services of herself and her husband, Charles, to help. On the appointed day to move Mama's things to the condo, Don appeared with a rental truck. Our group got to work shortly after 7:00 A.M. Mama was unorganized and indecisive, by no means ready. Vonda and I made a box run, while Don and Charles started moving large pieces of furniture to the truck. Upon returning with an assortment of boxes, Vonda began boxing a multitude of books from a wall of bookshelves, while I boxed miscellaneous items that were lined up on the floor against the living room wall.

One of the bedrooms had been used for a food reserve, where Mama kept two freezers and a stockpile of canned goods. Don and Charles wrestled the freezers through the narrow door and out to the truck. Ben appeared and joined me in packing canned goods. Jane did not come to avoid exerting herself too much. I noticed several cans had begun to expand; one of blueberries had burst with dried blueberry juice on the side. "These need to be tossed," I expressed.

"You think so?" Mama questioned.

"You could die from botulism if you eat these!" I exclaimed.

"Well, okay, go ahead and toss those," Mama said reluctantly.

A lot was accomplished that day. Vonda and I made the beds at the condo, where Mama spent the night along with Don and me. The closets in the farmhouse were still full of clothes and items Mama had been hoarding for years. The bedroom that was used for storage had not been touched. It was still packed with all kinds of things, and the door would not open all the way.

Before her move to the condo, Mama had a series of garage sales; however, they hardly made a dent in her *stuff*. After moving to the condo, an auction company was contacted to sell items from the garage, out building, barn and miscellaneous things from the house. Don and I returned to help with the auction.

During the auction, I stayed in the house assisting Mama, and took on cleaning the refrigerator. Mama had neglected to clean a spill from years ago that had dried and was embedded on the lower section. I scrubbed the refrigerator over an hour before it was ready to be taken out to be auctioned. While the auction was taking place outside, Mama remained inside. The whole thing was too much. She was going in circles from one room to the next, confused as to what she should do next. After the auction, there was still a profusion of things lingering in the house.

The farm remained on the market for a year. Lois and Bill visited while Mama was still in transition to help clear more of her things. Lois returned another time by herself and took several trips to a recycling center and the county dump. The farm finally sold.

Our youngest son, Curtis, had remained a bachelor until he met Claudia in 2003. Claudia had moved recently from the East Coast when she got a reporter position with the *Daily Times*. She met Curtis at a soccer game after watching him play on an adult team. Claudia had been on her own, when she decided to follow her passion for writing and moved to New Mexico, alone with her cat. She was a natural light blond with blue eyes and very tall; almost six feet, towering over me.

Curtis wanted both of his grandmothers at his wedding in June 2004. Don and I retrieved Mama. Don's mother, Mabel, had flown in the week before. Her chestnut color-treated hair was cut short in a tightly curled permanent. The outdoor evening wedding was held at a special wedding venue on the river. It was an exceptionally fun evening with dancing and loud music, which resulted in a visit from the sheriff for being too noisy.

Marie (Mama) at the wedding

Unfortunately, Lois was unable to attend. She was still recuperating from surgery she had several weeks before. A small cancerous tumor had been found and she opted to get it removed as soon as possible. During her recovery, Lois stayed at Bill's home. He helped take care of her; and our daughter, Caroline, flew out to assist her during the most difficult part of her healing period.

Bill was biding his time, waiting for Lois to decide when she was ready to marry him. Bill was very supportive of Lois. His family was very fond of her as well.

I had retired from the college and, after a two-year stint with a credit union, was now working for the City of Farmington.

Jane and Ben had their ups and downs. Jane found herself in conflict with anyone who rubbed her the wrong way. Lois and I evaded dealing with her as much as possible and had little knowledge of Jane's day-to-day activities. Jane had been able to stay out of jail and out of the state mental hospital for a number of years, even though her mental health issues were rampant.

CHAPTER FOUR

The Phone Call that Changed Everything

The ringing phone broke the serenity of the peaceful Sunday evening in early November 2004. "Louise, it's your sister Lois," called out Don, as he went back to watching television in the living room. I was in my sewing room, finishing the inside edges on a fleece throw I was making as a Christmas gift for Don's brother, Adam.

I picked up the extension. "Hi, Lois. How are you?" Lois responded on a serious note, "I'm fine. I just received a call from Ben." That seemed strange. Why would Ben be calling?

Lois continued, "Mama may have had a heart attack. They took her to the hospital. They don't think it is very bad. Apparently she got sick while at church."

A barrage of questions sprung from my mouth. "How is Mama? What happened? Why weren't we notified sooner?"

"Ben didn't say much. He was very vague, but he didn't sound concerned. Jane will call us when she gets a chance."

Did our mother have a heart attack or not? Maybe there was nothing serious to worry about. After the brief conversation, I went back to sewing. As I paused to stroke back a lock of light-brown hair, tears began to roll down my cheeks. After no word from Jane and numerous attempts to call her, Lois located the telephone number of the hospital and passed it on to me. On Monday morning from work, I called the hospital and spoke briefly to Mama's ICU day nurse, Randy.

"Your mother had a tough night. She was woken up periodically for vital signs. She suffered a massive heart attack and will be in ICU several days. She is stable and is resting comfortably," Randy reported. "Call back at 11:45 when she will be awakened for lunch. Meanwhile, you can talk to your sister to find out more. She was with her all night."

I was in stunned disbelief as I attempted to call Jane, only to be greeted by the answering machine. I was upset and furious. Jane should have notified us of the severity of Mama's condition immediately.

Simultaneously, Jane called my home. On purpose, I had never shared my work number with her. "Mama is in the hospital. I am taking care of everything," Jane told Don confidently.

"How is she? What happened?" Don questioned.

"I'm too tired to talk, I'll call back later," Jane responded.

Don asked again, "How is she?"

"I'll call back later after I get some sleep," Jane repeated in her familiar demeaning tone, and then hung up. She was now fifty-eight, with graying hair but was still as mean and infuriating as when she was growing up.

Just as I was preparing to call Don, he phoned. "Jane just called, but she didn't tell me anything new."

"I just talked to Randy, the ICU day nurse. He said Mama had a massive heart attack and is sleeping. I will try to get in touch with her before lunch," I reported, still in disbelief.

As lunchtime approached, I phoned the hospital again. Mama was awake but sounded tired. "This was a big surprise. I had no idea anything like this would happen," she declared.

Mama was very talkative and rambled on about what the hospital was feeding her and all the medications she was on, including one for diabetes, which she did not know she had.

"I need to go home. Jane gave me some books the library was discarding, and I need to move them out of the way." Mama talked as if her heart attack was just a slight bump in the road.

I was happy Mama sounded so optimistic. "You need your rest. I'll call you tomorrow."

That afternoon, Jane called the house and spoke with Don again. "I have arranged for Louise to call Mama at 3 o'clock. You know she had a heart attack?"

"Yes, I know. I will call Louise," Don told her. Don phoned once more relaying Jane's message.

"I just talked to Mama. There is no reason to disturb her this afternoon. She needs lots of quiet and rest," I expressed.

I was perturbed with Jane. There was no need for her to set my agenda. At first I was not going to call; but as the afternoon progressed, I reconsidered. Mama may have been waiting for the call orchestrated by Jane. Before leaving for home, another call was placed.

Randy picked up the phone. "Hello, Randy." I said as I identified myself and informed him I was calling to check on my mother. "Did my sister make arrangements for me to call at 3?"

"No," replied Randy. I knew that question sounded strange. Randy gave a brief run down on how Mama's day had gone.

Before speaking to my mother, I felt I had to say something about Jane's mental status. "Before you transfer me, I need to talk to you." Having not planned what to say, I blurted out, "Jane is a fruitcake. If she starts acting strange or you need to talk to someone else about our mother's condition, our younger sister, Lois, or I should be called."

Randy opened up. "We are having problems with your sister. Dr. Nelson was having a hard time talking to your mother with her there." Randy went on describing Jane's actions. "She was telling us what we should do and bullied the night nurse, who is a small Filipina lady. She tried the same on me too, but I don't intimidate. I'm over six feet tall and can hold my own."

Randy made note of my phone number before transferring the call. After a short conversation with Mama, I drove home to be greeted by Don who had just arrived home himself. "There is a message on the answering machine to call a Dr. Nelson," he mentioned.

"He is Mama's cardiologist. I told Mama's day nurse we should be called regarding her care. He said Jane is—"

Just then the phone rang. Not bothering to complete my thought, I picked up the receiver.

"This is Doctor Nelson. Your mother is under my care." Choosing his words carefully, trying not to offend, he continued speaking. "I'm having problems communicating. Your sister wants your mother released, to go home, which would not be good. She needs to be transferred to Grand Junction. We do not have the right type of equipment here in our small hospital. St. Mary's Hospital has an excellent CCU. I recommend she be transported as soon as possible. Your sister is standing in the way. We have lost valuable time. Every time I try to explain a procedure to your mother, your sister interferes and has become a big hindrance."

Dr. Nelson was upset. He proceeded speaking quickly in an excited voice. "She was trying to give orders for your mother's care, questioning the medications I prescribed, along with my judgments. She called me a quack."

Dr. Nelson proceeded to give his credentials. "I taught at UNM Medical School in Albuquerque, for a number of years. If my mother had been in this situation, she would have been taken to Grand Junction the first night and would have already had a procedure." Dr. Nelson went on talking briskly and started repeating himself. Jane's behavior had turned this doctor into a babbling, nervous wreck.

Jane's goal had been to be a nurse. Jane talked with authority, and therefore, our mother thought she knew what was best.

Perfectly understanding the circumstances, I interrupted, "You don't need to explain any further. I can relate exactly to what you are saying." Words could not describe the wrath of Jane when she was in a rage. She was very aggressive and could be extremely unreasonable.

"My sister Lois has our mother's medical and legal power of attorney," I volunteered. "You should talk to her about making decisions regarding our mother's health care." I gave him Lois' phone number.

Dr. Nelson called Lois immediately. For the most part, the conversation was a repeat of his discussion with me. By then, he had become more relaxed in expressing his feelings. "I don't have to put up with the *bullshit!*" he exclaimed in frustration. He went on to give Lois test results and explained our mother's dire condition further.

It was obvious she needed specialized care, which the cardiac care unit in Grand Junction could provide. Lois reassured him she would talk to our mother right away about being transported.

Jane's behavior was not surprising. Lois and I were concerned our mother was allowing Jane to control the situation. It did not make sense to have lifesaving care withheld. Nevertheless, the decisions being made were not up to Jane. She had always thought being the oldest afforded her special privileges, which unequivocally included being the "boss."

Lois phoned our mother right away. "Mama, this is kid number 3. How are you feeling?"

"Weak," she replied. "I don't know what to do. Jane wants to take me home." She was not the forceful, strong-willed, decision-making machine Lois had known her to be.

Lois was no stranger to tough medical decisions. It had only been four years earlier since Hans had been stricken with pancreatic cancer. "Well, Mama," Lois proceeded, "the first thing we need to do is make sure you are well enough to be at home. I think we'd better get you to Grand Junction."

Much to Lois' surprise, Mama readily agreed. To reinforce the decision to transfer to the better equipped hospital, I called Mama. "There is no doubt in my mind, you should follow Dr. Nelson's advice," I stated.

"Jane is against the transfer," Mama expressed.

"Your condition is serious, and you need to be where you can receive the best available care. Since Jane is complicating your transfer, it is best for you to be moved without her knowing." I suggested with trepidation. I could envision Jane appearing in an irate state, causing a horrible scene and trying to sabotage the transfer.

On Tuesday morning when Jane appeared at the ICU unit, she was enraged to find our mother was not there. Lois and I felt badly about the deception but knew it was necessary to keep Jane from interfering.

Lois was feeling peace of mind in the satisfaction of knowing our mother had been moved where state-of-the-art equipment was at the doctor's disposal. The calm was squelched when Jane called yelling.

"They'll kill her! You are stupid, stupid, STUPID! You don't know anything about medical things!"

Jane called Lois back that evening, "I have the phone number for the Grand Junction Hospital, but I don't have time to give it to you. I'm late for choir practice." She hung up. Lois already had the number, she was not at Jane's mercy for locating information.

Dr. Conway, Mama's new cardiologist, talked to her about the possibility of having bypass surgery. Her brother, Jack, had a bypass several years previously. She had seen graphic pictures of his operation. "It looked like when you gut a deer," she told Lois. The thought of having to go through such invasive surgery scared her.

Dr. Conway kept in close contact with Lois. "Bypass surgery is continuing to be researched. It depends on if there are any healthy areas to which the bypass can be attached." Lois took notes as he explained details of our mother's condition.

Bill's eldest son, Michael, was a physician. Lois wasted no time contacting him. She repeated everything Dr. Conway conveyed. "Your mother seems otherwise healthy for a woman her age," Michael stated. "It depends if further research shows a bypass to be beneficial."

Mama agreed to have the surgery. Later that day Dr. Conway contacted Lois revealing his findings. "Unfortunately your mother is not a candidate for bypass surgery. The front part of her heart is not functioning, and there is nowhere to take the bypass. Your mother has less than a year to live."

In a telephone conversation I had with Jane, she was gloating, "See, I was right. I knew Mama should not have bypass surgery."

The expectation of our mother's recovery was gone, and now there would be other difficult issues. Because Lois and I did not call Mama just to say "Hi," months passed without hearing from one another. Even though we did not take the subject lightly, we had previously joked about Jane keeping our mother's death a secret when she eventually died, maybe not notifying us until after she was buried. If that thought was shared with anyone else, it would have sounded absurd, but Jane was capable of such behavior. It was feasible for Jane to keep our mother's death a secret for a short time anyway, at least long enough for her to help herself to Mama's possessions. Jane believed that because she was the oldest, she was entitled to everything. At least now nothing close to that scenario would take place. Our biggest concern was how Jane would function without our mother's stabilizing presence.

Lois spoke to our mother's attorney, James King, over the phone. "You can invoke your power of attorney now to take care of your mother's affairs. Making arrangements now for her final expenses will make things easier later on," he told her.

After dinner Lois checked her emails and came upon a horrible message from Jane, accusing her of all sorts of terrible things, such as wanting our mother to die and wanting her money, possibly projecting her own demented thoughts. The situation was difficult enough, and now it was compounded with Jane's ridiculous accusations.

That evening, I received a call from Dr. Conway, saying my mother was very ill; and if I wanted to see her, now was the time to come.

I was being bombarded with bad news. Just before Mama's heart attack, I had been diagnosed with atrial fibrillation and had been bouncing from doctor to doctor with my own ordeal. I had been admitted to the local hospital the previous week for constant monitoring to determine a safe medication dosage. The day before Dr. Conway's call, I had traveled to Albuquerque for a consultation with an electro cardiologist. He recommended I remain on heart medications and be monitored by my cardiologist.

Dr. Conway gave the impression Mama could die anytime. There was a fresh heavy snowfall on the mountain passes, which influenced our decision to wait until the weekend before making the trip.

Don and I left early Saturday morning, making our way steadily over icy Red Mountain Pass into Montrose and then on to Delta and finally Grand Junction, arriving at St. Mary's Hospital at 3:30 that afternoon.

Patients' rooms in the CCU occupied the circumference around the nurse's station. We could see Mama in a room to the left. She saw us in return, and waved. A monitor displayed a constant heartbeat reading, along with her blood pressure and pulse. An IV was taped to her hand. "It is good to see you, but you didn't need to come," she expressed.

Her remark caught me off guard. Did she realize the severity of her condition? She appreciated the soft blanket I brought and was pleased to receive the framed picture Claudia's mother had taken of her last summer at the wedding. She hardly resembled the healthy person, who just four months previously attended Curtis' and Claudia's wedding.

Mama related what had happened to her in detail. "After church services, I went to the car to bring in a cake I had baked for the potluck. I barely made it through the door. Someone rescued the cake as a tall strong man picked me up and carried me to a chair, like one would carry a small child. Another church member who lives across the street ran home and brought back an aspirin. She saved my life. I told them not to call an ambulance and to take me home, but it was too late. Someone had already called 911, and an ambulance was on its way."

She had been feeling excruciating pains throughout the services but did not say anything. Her general philosophy was *ignore it and it will go away.* She was an eighty-one-year-old independent widow, not taking any prescription medications, and did not even have a primary care doctor.

Mama desperately wanted to see her pastor. "Louise, will you contact Pastor Bedford for me and let him know where I am? I would really like to see him."

A smiling nurse entered Mama's room announcing, "Visiting hours are over. They ended at 4:00." It was already 4:30.

"Oh," I said in embarrassment. I had not realized we had overstayed our visitors' privileges.

"You just got here, so we let you stay a few minutes longer. You will be allowed back in at six."

We checked into a nearby motel and then walked over to a dinner, returning to see Mama precisely at 6 that evening. We visited briefly, but Mama was getting tired. We left to let her rest. On the way out, we met a professional looking man in a suit walking hastily down the corridor seeking the CCU. It was Pastor Bedford. We pointed the way and chatted for a moment. "Do you know how Jane is handling this?" I asked.

"She is doing okay. Come to think about it," Pastor Bedford, replied. "One thing seemed kind of strange to me. I called to let her know her mother had fallen ill and was on the way to the hospital in an ambulance. She said they had just sat down to have their lunch and would go to the hospital when they were finished eating. It seemed rather out of the ordinary that she took her time getting there."

On Sunday morning, we returned to Mama's hospital room. "Dr. Conway will be coming by soon to make his rounds, if you would like to wait and meet him, it shouldn't be too long," she said.

A short time later, a mature, robust man in a white lab coat entered. "Hello, I'm Dr. Conway," he said introducing himself, while shaking our hands. He went directly to Mama's status. "The blockage was extensive, much worse than originally thought. She had angioplasty, and three stents have been inserted. However, only one of the stents is functional. The myocardial infarction caused a lot of permanent damage to her heart. At this time bypass, surgery is too risky and probably wouldn't help."

Mama sat calmly in a bedside chair, appearing to be relieved she would not be facing surgery.

"You have less than a year to live. The medications will provide quality of life, not quantity. It is all in God's hands."

Matter-of-factly, Mama replied, "I am not afraid of dying. Whenever He wants me, I'm ready to go."

The room was silent after Dr. Conway's exit. Don and I were uneasy, while Mama did not show signs of concern. Time was flying, and we needed to get on the road to make the long drive back. We said our goodbyes. "I will notify Uncle Jack, Aunt Lorie, and Aunt Rebecca," I stated.

"No, don't bother them," she replied.

She was the oldest of her brother and two surviving sisters, who lived on the West Coast. They kept in touch by email and would be wondering why they had not heard from her lately.

As children, we learned to always obey without question. Contacting Mama's siblings was the right thing to do. After making that defying decision, Jack beat me to the punch. He had received an email from Jane.

"As you know, Mama had a massive heart attack." There was silence.

He continued speaking in a solemn tone, slowly answering, "We got this email from Jane saying Marie was in the hospital but is doing okay." I filled him in on the details as best I could.

"How are all of you *girls* doing?" Jack asked.

"Jane is not cooperating," I replied with frustration from fresh memories of the problems Jane was causing and the hateful things she was saying to Lois.

Jack took it lightly, "It's just sibling rivalry."

"Jane is interfering with life-and-death decisions," I expressed. Apparently, our mother's siblings had never been told the extent of Jane's problems.

Mama had stabilized and was ready to be released, provided someone could help her at home. Jane called me, complaining of the inconvenience it would cause her to bring Mama home. "Going to pick up Mama will interfere with my work hours! She will just have to stay there until I can get away!" Jane exclaimed.

Back in Tennessee Lois was spending an evening out with Bill. As they were entering a restaurant, her cell phone went off. It was Jane.

"I'm going to quit my job." Jane announced.

Catching Lois off guard, her immediate response was, "Don't quit your job." She knew Jane's financial resources were limited.

"You can't tell me what to do!" Jane screeched as she indignantly ended the conversation.

Jane only worked several hours a week, though Lois had assumed she worked considerably more. Her major source of income was received from Social Security disability benefits due to her mental illness.

CHAPTER FIVE

Lois Arrives

Believing our mother's time was near, Lois made arrangements to visit her prior to her discharge, from St. Mary's hospital. Lois spent every possible moment with our mother. When she was up to it, Lois assisted her with short walks down the hall and back. Mama instructed Lois to contact Samuel Harrison with Equitable Insurance where she had a long-term care policy.

Lois' trip was heaven-sent; she would be there to drive Mama back to Delta, eliminating the burden on Jane. Mama was delighted to be home. It was time to take care of some loose ends she had postponed for ages. "Lois, will you do me a few favors? There is some old grain fertilizer in the back seat of my car. Will you clean it up where it has spilled and throw it out?"

Lois meticulously scooped up the spilled contents of the broken fertilizer bag from the floorboard of the back seat and tossed it in the dumpster for the condo complex.

There was another request. "The top box in that stack next to the dresser contains arsenic. It was left over from when your father did taxidermy work. It needs to be discarded."

Lois saw to the proper disposal of the arsenic but was curious as to why it had not been discarded ages ago. "Why didn't you have Jane help you dispose of the arsenic before now?" Lois asked.

"Jane might breathe it in and get sick," She replied.

That answer hit Lois over the head like a ton of bricks. Why was she concerned about Jane getting sick but not worried she could get sick? In truth she probably did not trust what Jane might do with the toxin.

Lois had endured as much heartache as she could handle from the loss of Hans and had been in grief counseling from time to time. Because of the lack of childhood memories, her counselor thought she displayed characteristics of a person who had been abused and abandoned. Lois was confused from this observation. She considered her family to be stable with caring parents.

Lois' counselor thought perhaps this characteristic resulted from the many times Hans had been gone for extended periods throughout his career. Lois never felt abandoned by Hans and did not resent his absences. Even though they had no children, she was very busy keeping up with the obligations that went along with being the wife of an officer as well as her full-time job and working toward a college degree.

Something went off in Lois' head. The counselor's observation had nothing at all to do with Hans. Maybe she had been abandoned as a child, in a sense. Jane had demanded a lot of attention and got it. Maybe Lois did not consciously recognize she lacked attention. The focus was on Jane's needs, especially after her mental illness had been acknowledged. She began to think about her childhood. We were not encouraged to express ourselves. In fact, the opposite was true. Our parents' philosophy was *children are to be seen and not heard.*

Lois snapped out of her daze. This was her opportunity to learn important things. "The original to my new will is hidden in a brown manila envelope in that cardboard box at the foot of my bed." Mama pointed to a box that was peeking out from under a towel and some sheets. She had been postponing updating her will, which had become obsolete when the farm was sold. Previously, I had been appointed her executor and had told her, I preferred Lois be assigned.

The discovery of my heart condition must have motivated her to no longer delay the task, which could not have been timelier.

"Look over the will and the power of attorney documents," she directed. She shared information regarding where money had been stashed and other financial matters.

"May I make copies of your keys so we can get in your condo if we need to?" Lois asked foreseeing future necessity.

"Yes, that is a good idea," she agreed.

Lois was relieved. With Mama's permission, she promptly had several sets of keys made.

That evening, after going to bed, Mama started having difficulty breathing and was extremely clammy. "We need to call Dr. Nelson," Lois insisted.

"No. Don't bother him. I'll be okay," Mama stated.

In spite of her wishes, Lois called to speak to a nurse, who directed her to give Mama a nitroglycerin tablet from a supply she had received from the hospital. "Take this tablet. It should help," stated Lois as she handed Mama the nitroglycerin. She put the tablet under her tongue, but her irregular breathing did not subside.

"We need to call the doctor," Lois stated again.

"Give me another nitroglycerin tablet and let me rest. I don't want you to call the doctor."

There was no improvement, and Lois was getting anxious. She persisted in trying to persuade Mama to consult her doctor. "You can call the nurse," she reluctantly agreed.

It took an eternity for the nurse to return Lois' page. After describing Mama's symptoms, the nurse replied, "An ambulance is needed. Call 911 without delay. Your mother is having another heart attack."

A sea of boxes blocked the sliding glass door of her bedroom that faced the street. Lois removed the boxes to open the quickest path through which the medics could enter. After unlocking the bars that protected the sliding glass door, the entry was accessible. The medics arrived, swiftly transferring Mama to a gurney, and rushed her to the hospital. As the ambulance disappeared, Lois stood in the cold, dark night, scrapping the heavy layer of frost from the windshield of the rental car. It was midnight as Lois made her way to the hospital.

If Lois had not been there, our mother would have never called for help and may have died that night. It was fortunate her first heart attack occurred while at church; otherwise she would not have called for help then either.

Foreseeing the inevitable, the following morning, Lois set her emotions aside and began to make difficult arrangements to deal with our mother's affairs and prepare for the time when she would be gone. With the power of attorney document in hand, Lois proceeded to the bank. Lois had her name added to the account to permit her to pay Mama's bills. Unbeknownst to Mama, Lois opened a safe deposit box to insure safekeeping and accessibility of the new will and to prevent Jane from taking it or playing hide-and-go-seek with it. Mama believed banks could access safe deposit boxes and did not believe in having one. Lois ventured to the post office to arrange for the mail to be forwarded to her home. Lois then went by the funeral home, where she talked to Mr. Logan, the director, and acquired information and appropriate forms.

Anticipating lack of cooperation from Jane, Lois took one garage door opener for herself and left the other opener on the dining room table for me to take on my next visit. Jane already had her own keys and possession of an opener. A box of checks arrived in the mail the previous day. Lois took our mother's checkbook and most of the checks, leaving a book at the condo.

Lois reluctantly returned to her obligations while Mama remained in the Delta County Hospital. Before leaving she paid Mama a farewell visit. She hugged Mama goodbye, telling her she needed to catch her flight home, and informed her she had arranged for her mail to be sent to her home. "I will take care of your affairs until you are feeling better," she explained.

Mama expected to go home from the hospital soon, however, was disappointed when her release date kept being moved back. She would be spending Thanksgiving in the hospital. The evening before Thanksgiving, Dr. Nelson spoke with Lois over the phone. "Your mother has less than two months to live. The angioplasty did no good and congestive heart failure is resulting. Her EKG looks awful. I would not be surprised if she died within one month." He recommended in home care; however, he would not release her at this time, because she could not take care of herself. It was time to send her to a long-term care facility. He suggested Horizons Health Care Center.

Our three adult children, along with spouses and grandchildren, filled our home for Thanksgiving. "I want to see grandma before it's too late," stated Caroline. Early Friday morning, Caroline and Joe gathered Clara and Mathew, along with Kayla, to visit her grandmother.

Because of road conditions, it took longer to arrive in Delta than anticipated. Mama was delighted to see everyone; she especially enjoyed seeing her great-grandchildren. The group spent the night in a motel room. After bidding Mama a quick goodbye the following morning, they were on their way back to Farmington and would leave out early the next day to return home.

CHAPTER SIX

Horizons Health Care Center

I notified Mama we were planning to visit her the coming weekend. "Chris and his children and Curtis and Claudia are coming as well. Do you mind if we bring sleeping bags for the kids and stay at the condo?"

"All right, and while you are here, you can cut my hair. Jane has made arrangements to transfer me to a nursing home in Montrose. I will not be here when you come. Dr. Nelson doesn't practice in Montrose. I will have a new doctor. I prefer to keep Dr. Nelson. I really like him, but Jane thinks he is inexperienced and doesn't know what he is doing." Mama continued talking about how she did not know anyone at the Montrose home and stated she would rather not be moved there.

"Is there another place you would prefer to be?" I asked.

"Yes. I know of a nice rehabilitation center in Eckert. There is a couple that goes to my church; her ninety-three-year-old mother lives there. I could keep my own doctor. Nobody asked me what I want!"

"Is it too late to change facilities?" I asked as I heard someone talking in the background.

"The discharge nurse is here," Mama responded.

The nurse came on the phone, "Your mother says she doesn't want to go to the home in Montrose. I would like to place her where she wishes."

"Is it possible to send her to Horizons in Eckert?" I asked.

"She was scheduled to be moved this afternoon. There may not be an open room at Horizons. I will call around to see what options are available."

"The arrangements should be coordinated though my sister, Lois," I commented.

Complying with our mother's wishes, Lois finalized the arrangements for the transfer to Horizons after learning it held a five-star rating. It was confirmed to be a good choice by Gail, her old high school friend, whose husband was a caseworker for the area.

Jane was livid. She called Lois at work yelling, "You aren't competent to make those decisions! The home in Montrose is better! I stayed there for a while when I was convalescing, and I know firsthand it is a good place! I know the doctors there and they are very good. Mama should go to the home in Montrose!" Jane's attempt to intimidate Lois failed. She was overruled once more.

After our mother was transferred to Horizons, I phoned to confirm our plans for coming. Mama loved being there and sounded very happy. "This is a new wing. In fact, I'm the first person to occupy this room. It has a beautiful view of the mountains, and I like my roommate."

The garage door opener needed to enter Mama's condo, was in Jane's keeping. Jane was called to let her know we were coming and would be stopping by to borrow the opener that evening.

Upon arriving at Jane's ramble shack small apartment that evening, everyone got out of the vehicles and gathered in the alley around the door that Jane used. Don tapped on the door. Jane appeared with curlers in her hair and was wearing a bathrobe. "You woke me up."

Don spoke. "We need to get the garage door opener for the condo."

"Just a minute," Jane said as she vanished inside, leaving everyone standing in the cold alley. A few minutes later she appeared with the opener.

"We will return it early in the morning," I said unimpressed with Jane's hospitality.

Upon entering the condo, our family group was greeted by a familiar pungent, musty smell. I had hoped the odor would go away when our mother moved from the farm. The kitchen counter was covered with dishes and utensils. There were remnants of dried dill around the sink, counter and floor, left over from one of Jane's visits. The dining room table was fairly neat. Lois had cleared most of the table and tossed a considerable amount of junk mail on her last visit. The garage door opener Lois left was not in sight. It was rather obvious Jane had taken it.

The condo resembled a warehouse with boxes taking a fair amount of space throughout. Mama had been there nearly two years and was still trying to sort and organize the remainder of her belongings.

Chris and his children rolled their sleeping bags out onto the living room floor, while Curtis and Claudia occupied the once spacious guest room, which was overcome with stacks of boxes.

Don and I stayed in the master bedroom. Five large dressers hugged the walls. All of them were untidy with items scattered in disarray across the dresser tops. The boxes that had blocked the sliding glass entrance prior to the medic's visit were back against the door. A low row of boxes piled with indistinguishable items lined the foot of the bed. Behind the boxes stood a large closet with sliding mirrored doors that took up the entire north wall. How could Mama ever find anything?

Sunday morning revealed a new layer of freshly fallen snow. Everyone jumped out of bed and scrambled to get ready. After a quick fast-food breakfast at McDonalds, a stop at Jane's was in order.

Again, Jane met everyone at the door, leaving us standing outside. With the opener in hand, I spoke. "We brought back the door opener. Lois said there was an extra one on the dining room table. Do you know where it is?"

Jane hesitated, wanting to say no, but it would have been obvious she was lying. "Yes, I have it."

"Then do you mind if we keep this one, so we don't have to bother you the next time we come?" I asked.

"No!" she snapped. "Mama doesn't want you to have it. She wants me to know when people are there." I did not want to have a confrontation in front of my children and grandchildren. Jane was handed the opener, and we left to seek Horizons Health Care Center.

Our upbeat group headed for Eckert on the snow-packed rural highway. Out in the middle of nowhere, we came upon a group of isolated buildings. It was the Horizons Care Center complex. Everyone piled out of the vehicles and scampered for Mama's room. Our group inundated her at once. She was elated to see everyone.

I was shaken to see how frail Mama looked sitting in a wheelchair, receiving oxygen through plastic tubing. A portable oxygen unit was attached to the rear of her wheelchair. A wall divided the room down the center, allowing both occupants their own window view. Mama's half of the room was crowded with our entourage.

A passing nurse suggested we go to the dining area to spread out. Mama was too weak to wheel herself down the long corridor. Chris took charge, pushing her steadily to the distant room. Mama was presented with a conglomeration of items, including new slippers and a sweat suit. It was like an early Christmas. Pictures were taken as we visited. Eleven-year-old Avery eagerly told his great-grandmother his latest corny jokes.

The guys stayed in the dining room and brought out their laptop to play games, while the gals retreated back to Mama's room to give her a beauty treatment. I washed and cut her hair while, Claudia gave her a manicure.

Throughout the visit, we chatted continuously. Mama was in good spirits and displayed her sense of humor. Her brother Jack, and sisters, Lorie and Rebecca, had been taking turns calling. Along with them, Albert's children and church members, she had plenty of company.

A nurse stopped briefly. "Your mother has improved greatly from when she first arrived. She should be well enough to go home soon."

The idea of Mama going home soon did not seem realistic. She could not even stand by herself, except with the help of a walker, and she needed assistance getting up. She would have to improve a great deal before I would feel at ease with that happening.

It was almost time for lunch and time for us to leave. Mama was happier than words could describe. She thoroughly enjoyed the invasion. "You can do this again," she said.

I lingered to say goodbye again. I told her of the conversation with Jane patrolling her condo. As I suspected, Mama had not assigned Jane authority over the garage door openers.

I did not feel comfortable leaving her there; but it was time to join the rest of my family who were outside engaged in a snowball fight.

CHAPTER SEVEN

Staying the Course

Jane emailed Lois about my family visit.

> *Don and Louise were here. Mama said she does not want them having a garage door opener because it is needed here and she does not want to buy another one. I told Don we want to have them check before coming in. Both may or may not be true. So you are not the only one getting the brunt of my terribleness.*
>
> *It has not been easy. I have loads of house work to do. When this all happened I had four or five bowls of fruit I was making into jam. I prepared 7 or 8 jars but the rest had to be dumped.*
>
> *I'm very glad Mama is ok. We wouldn't know how to act without her around to referee everything, would we? I'm the boss. No you're not. So who is to blame? No one. Then why fight? It's the luck of the Irish, that's it. Hit um slug um.*
>
> *I am doing my best for Mama. What were you going to do? Have her die on the operating table just because some zealous people wanted practice with the knife?*

We can work together and not walk over each other. You think you need to have some kind of power position in the whole mess, maybe you can understand that even if you are making the final decisions if those decisions are bad, we all will have to suffer the consequences.

I didn't know if we could even budge her out of the hospital room, getting weaker and weaker. You can tell donkeys some things but you can't tell them much and since we belong to the best donkey family around I guess we should all put up or shut up.

L ois was making health decisions as responsibly as anyone could and discussing them with our mother every step of the way. Jane's behavior was wearing thin on Lois.

Lois noticed Mama's checkbook revealed $10 contributions to many nonprofit organizations, about five or so a month. These organizations covered things from "Save the Whales" to political contributions for out-of-state politicians. It was curious she gave to so many causes but did not send Christmas or birthday gifts or even cards to her own grandchildren or great-grandchildren.

The first week in December had passed. Mama was stronger and was hoping to be home before Christmas. Ellen, the administrator at Horizons, suggested she be moved to assisted-living. Mama was planning to go home and was not considering other options.

Four days before Christmas, our mother had improved enough to be moved to a room with a kitchenette. She was required to demonstrate she could cook for herself before being released.

"They are trying to teach me to cook pancakes. I never eat pancakes and now I can't keep them down anyway," she told me.

January 2005 was here. Dr. Nelson planned to do an echocardiogram sometime in the coming week to give him a better idea of Mama's present prognosis. "She won't be released from the nursing home until I give the green light," he informed Lois. "Ten days ago, she looked great. Four days ago, she had declined a little. There is roughly a thirty percent chance of her dying in the New Year." Our mother's life was on a countdown, even though her doctors were not consistent with their guesses.

I called Mama. "We will be coming to see you this weekend. I would also like to meet Dr. Nelson."

"You can use the condo," she offered. "Horizons is planning to discharge me January 18."

"The discharge nurse is pushing to have Mama go into assisted living quarters," Lois informed. "Ellen, the discharge administrator is surprised Mama wants to go home. Can you and Don move Mama's belongings to assisted living?"

The thought of being alone with no one to take care of her was irrelevant as far as Mama was concerned. She would never go willingly into assisted living in a million years. In my mind I envisioned Mama holding on to a bed post for dear life, refusing to budge, as her fingers were forcibly pried loose and being carried out screaming—a scene that was portrayed to me by Barbara, a previous supervisor, who was describing what had to be done when her frail Swedish grandmother was no longer capable of living alone.

"We don't have a choice," stated Lois. "Mama cannot manage by herself."

Ellen was called regarding the assisted living facilities and apartments. From the description, I knew the limited space would be too confining. The idea of moving Mama into a tiny place against her wishes would be a horrendous undertaking. What about the condo and its contents that would not fit in the assisted living quarters? The thought of it all made my head spin.

Mama had an episode of breathing difficulty and was transported by ambulance to the Delta Hospital, during the night.

Don and I left to see Mama early Friday morning. Lois had sent me an extra garage door opener that she had purchased. It was not programmed yet. We needed to deal with Jane again.

We arrived at Jane's apartment early afternoon. "Can I come along with you to the hospital?"

"Sure," I agreed.

"I need to get my coat." Again not inviting us in, she disappeared back into her apartment. She reappeared wearing a long old light blue ragtag coat that went down to her ankles. On her head was a plaid scarf that had been folded in a triangle and tied under her chin like we used to wear when we were kids in the fifties.

Jane gave directions to the hospital and took the lead to our mother's room on the second floor. I began to chat with Mama, while Jane stood quietly, leaning against the wall, censoring the conversation. Mama was coughing a lot, which was very frustrating to her. "If I could just get this cleared out of my chest, I would be fine. They brought me here because they thought I was having another heart attack, but I knew I wasn't. Now that I am here, they are going to see what they can do about this cough."

Mama continued to speak. "I need to get home. I can't keep going back and forth from the hospital to Horizons. Dr. Nelson was here a short time ago. He would like to talk to you kids while you are here. You can go over to his office later this afternoon. It is within walking distance from here."

"It is getting late. I have lots of things to do, and I don't want to talk to Dr. Nelson," Jane said sheepishly. "Don, will you take me home? I'll call you in the morning," she said giving me a glance. They left while I remained with Mama.

"Jane has been making things especially difficult for everyone," I mentioned. "Randy, the ICU nurse told us she was giving orders to the nurses. She was very obnoxious the night of your heart attack."

"I didn't know Jane was giving them a hard time," she replied, shirking off any signs of being perturbed by Jane's inappropriate behavior.

"Lois and Jane are in a power struggle. Jane is acting mean, just like when we were kids," I revealed.

The opportunity came up to express my frustrations of growing up with Jane. I talked about how Jane hogged the double bed we shared as kids. "She would kick me to move over so she could sprawl out, allowing only a narrow strip on the edge of the mattress for me to lie on."

"I started kindergarten with scabs all over my hands from Jane's clawing with her long, sharp fingernails." This was evidenced by faint jagged scares that could still be seen on the backs of my hands. Reminiscing, I talked about fighting with Jane when we were children. "Jane was always starting fights and when I tried to defend myself, I got spanked."

"Why didn't you tell me?" Mama asked genuinely.

I told on Jane all the time, but Mama never listened. Jane's excessive fighting and tormenting of Lois and me had been viewed as normal sibling spats. *How could you really not know!* I thought. *Weren't my scratch marks and scab-covered hands a clue?* Instead, all I could say as I remembered being intimidated by my domineering mother was "I was just a little kid."

Don finally returned. A nurse came in to check on Mama and asked us to leave for a while. We walked down the hall and found the ICU, where we met Randy. We introduced ourselves and apologized for Jane's behavior. He was very gracious. "People get upset and act strangely in times of crisis," he said.

It was approaching 5 P.M. and time to meet Dr. Nelson. We left Mama to rest and walked over to a nearby complex of offices. As the last patient left and his staff bid him good evening, Dr. Nelson joined Don and me in the waiting room. I could see where Jane thought Dr. Nelson was inexperienced, as he had a young appearance. A closer look revealed him to be in his forties and short in stature. His lack of size gave Jane a sense of superiority and reason to try to dominate him. "Your mother is a delightful lady," Dr. Nelson began, turning to a serious discussion. "Yesterday we did an electrocardiogram. It was a disaster. Her heart is functioning below the lowest level the machine can register."

He estimated her heart function to be around twenty percent. As he went on describing one bad thing after another, I asked, "If it is so bad, how could she still be alive?"

"That is the typical question of a first-year med student. Her heart has become much enlarged. It is a natural way for the body to compensate to pump enough blood."

Dr. Nelson then said, "I would not be surprised if she died tomorrow. She could last another six months. I spoke with Dr. Conway recently. He was surprised she is still alive."

"Can anything be done to stop her coughing?" I asked. "She said there is something in her chest she is trying to cough up."

"There is nothing to cough up. That is the sensation she has from the fluid collecting around her heart. Her heart is too weak to keep the lungs clear. It is developing into congestive heart failure. She has been given diuretics to help get rid of excess fluid, and that should relieve her coughing."

"If we are lucky, she will go just like that in an instant. If she lingers, she will die from the congestive heart failure. That is hardest, to watch them suffer," he said.

Oh my gosh, I thought. Mama kept saying she was getting better. The discussion then turned to getting Mama home. She definitely did not want to go in assisted living. "Is she a candidate for hospice?" Don asked.

"Marie has been a candidate for some time, and that is a possibility. I am the head of the local hospice board and can arrange for assistance. Hospice nurses will monitor her vital signs and provide most of the medications. They come in two or three times a week to help bathe, care for hair, and check things in general. Your sister would have to agree to spend the nights and check on her periodically throughout the day."

I was confident Mama would agree to in-state hospice care. It would be an enormous relief not to face moving her to assisted living.

With Jane being a topic in the conversation, more of the events following Mama's admission to the hospital back in November were learned.

"Your sister was attempting to locate discharge papers. She insisted her mother be released. Security had to be called to remove her. It would have been fatal for your mother to leave at that time," Dr. Nelson stated.

Upon our arrival back in Mama's hospital room she asked, "What did Dr. Nelson have to say?"

"The echocardiogram was not good." I made up something about the will to live. I certainly was not going to tell her she could die tomorrow for all the doctor knew.

"Dr. Nelson said you could be released to go home if you agreed to have hospice come in to monitor and help you. However, Jane also has to stay with you at night," I explained.

"Jane is against getting on hospice," she replied.

"They are there to help you, and Dr. Nelson will not release you to go home unless you are willing to accept hospice care. Jane will have to cooperate," I declared.

"I want to go home. I'll think about using hospice," she replied.

With that prospect Don and I left the hospital and went to dinner.

Lois called early Saturday morning. "We need to get Mama to agree to use hospice, she has been eligible for some time," I stated with high hopes.

Lois agreed to talk to her about it. They were very helpful with Hans before he died.

"Jane may be an obstacle though," I told Lois. "She will be calling soon. I'm not looking forward to talking to her about it."

It was a few minutes after 8:30 A.M. when the phone rang. I knew it would be Jane. I braced myself as I picked up the phone and began speaking. "Dr. Nelson has agreed to release Mama under the care of hospice. You will need to spend nights with her for a while."

Jane went ballistic, "I don't want Mama on hospice! They kill people! Everybody in hospice dies! This one hospice nurse was laughing, 'Ha, Ha, Ha' while she was bathing someone who was dying." Jane's high-pitched, mocking laugh was unsettling as she repeated herself again.

Jane continued going berserk, "Your husband's driving made me sick. He whipped the car around in the parking lot, and it made me dizzy. I'm glad he is your husband and not mine. You have to put up with him, but I don't!"

I broke in, "Jane let me interrupt for a minute."

"You always do!" she snapped back.

"If Mama is going to come home, she has to be on hospice, and you have to agree to stay with her at night for a while. Don't you want Mama to come home?"

Jane would not settle down. I hung up.

Don and I stopped by the hospital before leaving for home. Mama was finishing her breakfast as we entered. She had slept well and was feeling better. I mentioned Lois would be contacting her soon.

A nurse entered to clear the breakfast dishes. As she was leaving, Mama hollered at her, "Hey, bring back my applesauce!"

Don chuckled. That was the most energy we had observed in Mama since the event of her heart attack.

"We need to get going," I announced. "We will be back again. Goodbye for now." We gave her hugs and were on our way.

In the hours that passed, Lois finally persuaded our mother to accept assistance from hospice, and arrangements were initiated for her care. Mama wanted to die at home, and Lois promised her request would be honored.

Ironically, Mama went home on the day that had been set for her release from Horizons. Lois arranged to have Meals on Wheels bring by a noon meal Monday through Friday.

Jane was given a list of prescription drugs to have filled. The prescription for acid reflux particularly was not to her liking. The pharmacist gave her the name of a nonprescription drug that would work just as well, in her opinion. According to Jane, Dr. Nelson had prescribed a medication that would kill her.

Mama was getting along well with the current arrangements. Alternative plans needed to be found for when she needed around-the-clock care. Don and I offered to have Mama live with us. We had plenty of room and could arrange for home health care during the day when neither one of us could be around. Mama was not open to moving from Delta. We had to seek other options.

After a week of assisting our mother, Jane sent Lois an email saying she was tired and could use some help. Taking care of Mama was hard on Jane, but she was not alone. Lois had been spending many hours every week seeing to insurance matters, sorting and tossing junk mail, paying Mama's bills and talking to nurses and Dr. Nelson.

Jane wanted Mama's mail to be redirected to the condo in order to receive magazines and newspapers, in pretense for our mother.

Lois knew Mama was not up to reading. To satisfy Jane's request, Lois bundled up the magazines and personal mail and sent it to Jane. Jane was complaining about losing things "right and left." It would have been disastrous to depend on her to forward bills and important papers to Lois.

Jane was staying with Mama almost constantly. A lot of her time was spent on the computer and doing her own laundry as her washing machine had broken down. Jane said she had lots to do at home, but Mama needed someone to be with her.

"I need quiet," Mama told Lois. "Tell Jane to give me some space." It seemed strange that she did not tell Jane herself.

Lois complied with Mama's request. "Leave after breakfast to do your personal things. Stay only if you are asked."

"You can't tell me what to do," Jane said begrudgingly.

Jane needed a break, and Mama needed a break from her as well. Lois and I set up a preliminary schedule to relieve Jane. My daughter, Caroline, volunteered to take the first round, beginning January 30 and would leave Thursday February 3.

One evening, I called to talk to Mama, but she was tired. I ended up speaking to Jane. "It is much better having Mama here. The nursing home was not taking good care of my mother. They wouldn't do anything to stop her coughing. Dr. Nelson is not a good doctor. He doesn't know what he is doing. She would be much better off with someone else." Jane continued expounding how incompetent Dr. Nelson was. "Mama is vomiting. I need to go check on her."

❧

The preliminary planning for our mother's memorial service had begun. Jane had already informed Lois she wanted to sing at the memorial service. As much as we dreaded honoring Jane's request, trying to discourage her would only cause further discord. Jane would choose the songs to be sung and pick out the cover for the program. I had the perfect poem: *Miss Me, But Let Me Go*. Caroline agreed to read it at the service.

Lois and I compiled information on our mother's life for the obituary. I would keep the ashes until we got our bearings and could plan for spreading them at a future date. The flowers would be selected when a date was known. Everything else for the service was under control.

We had been going through the motions, seeing to the worldly issues, but had not expressed our feelings about Mama dying. Lois will always grieve for Hans and talked about surviving the grief. I knew all about grief also, from losing my newborn son. "I'm okay with her passing," Lois shared with me."

"I have always felt it is harder on the ones left behind. Even though we know things are well for the one passing, it does not keep us from missing them and dealing with the void. Mama told me she had a good life. I'm glad she said that," I replied.

Lois and I discussed the management of our mother's belongings. We needed a plan of action to put in place once she dies. At this point, Lois was mentally exhausted. To anticipate one more thing was too great. Lois suggested Caroline be invited to help come up with a plan.

Caroline willingly agreed to develop a detailed plan of what was needed to be done and assign who would accomplish each chore.

CHAPTER EIGHT

Caroline's Stay with Her Grandmother

Caroline spent the night with us before heading over the mountains the next morning to be with her grandmother. Upon arriving at Mama's home, her aunt Jane greeted her at the door. While Jane loitered aimlessly, Caroline sat and began to visit with her grandmother, who was in the living room, sitting in her favorite brown upholstered chair.

A large mobile oxygen machine stood against the wall next to the television. Mama was receiving oxygen through a long plastic tube.

"I'm here now," Caroline announced to Jane, "You can go home and get some rest."

Jane remained reluctant to leave. She finally left briefly but returned moments later, complaining about the snow and road grime that had fallen from Caroline's truck onto the driveway. Jane decided to sweep the drive, exclaiming, "They are particular how things look around here!"

Jane returned. "It is okay to go now," Mama said. "I'm in good hands."

Jane finally left and phoned Lois.

"You all are just waiting for her to die. IT'S JUST A DEATHWATCH!" she yelled into the phone.

Lois tried to answer her back, "No! No! It's NOT a deathwatch. We just want to assist you in taking care of Mama."

Jane kept interrupting as Lois talked and did not hear a word Lois said. Now that help had arrived, she was envious she had to share Mama's attention.

Caroline helped her grandmother get through lunch and straightened the kitchen. While Mama took an afternoon nap, Caroline took the opportunity to bring in her luggage. Boxes lined one side of the hall leading back to the bedrooms. The boxes obstructed the path and made it difficult for Mama to maneuver her walker.

The next morning, Caroline cleared the long hallway, moving the boxes to the guest room closet. It was exasperating that her grandmother did not want to get rid of anything.

There were still boxes full of junk mail, which Mama never seemed to get around to going through. Caroline eliminated most of it.

Caroline brought her own food to keep things simple. She catered to her grandmother, learning how to fix oatmeal and other things just the way she liked. Mama's appetite was poor. Jane had been eating more of the Meals on Wheels lunches than Mama.

The hospice staff arrived that afternoon. Bridget, a young hospice nursing assistant, was scheduled to come in twice a week to assist with bathing. Jessica, the head nurse, was a tall pleasant, redhead. Jessica wore her hair very short in back, but as Caroline described, the front was wild with long curls that fell on her forehead.

Jane appeared periodically unannounced, which Caroline and Mama did not appreciate. Caroline asked Jane to call before she came over and invited her to leave.

Caroline and Jane tangled several times. Caroline responded with logical answers, which got her nowhere. When Jane was on the attack, throwing out insults concerning us, Caroline did not say anything. She smiled and ignored her. Jane ended the degrading, saying she loved us anyway.

During one of Jane's stays she decided to sing. One song in particular that Jane said she wrote started out "Road kill, eating squirrels. . ." Jane hit some unnatural high, off-key notes. During the performance, Caroline observed her grandmother rolling her eyes then massaging her temples.

Caroline left the condo briefly several times. During one of her outings, she brought back a cordless phone. When her grandmother received calls, it was an ordeal wheeling her to the phone in the kitchen and keeping her oxygen cord from getting tangled in the cluster of boxes stacked near the phone. The cordless phone was conveniently placed on the end table next to her favorite chair in the living room.

In preparation for Caroline's visit, Lois had sent her a set of keys. Caroline decided an alternate way to enter was needed, especially if a garage door opener was not handy. The back door opened from the living room onto the large shared grassy atrium. A key was safely tucked inside a fake rock Caroline had brought. It was set outside the garden door inconspicuously with a group of real rocks. Even though the combination was known, earlier attempts to access the atrium had failed. It still was not known how the combination worked to get through the tall wrought iron gate.

The afternoon before Caroline left was spent pampering her grandmother with a "spa treatment." Caroline gently applied lotion to her hands and arms. Caroline was troubled to see how her arms and legs had withered away to skin and bone.

Mama began talking about Jane having meningitis when she was a teenager. Meningitis was one excuse, along with several others Jane blamed for her mental illness. "The doctor said not to do anything that would traumatize her and to treat Jane with kid gloves as she was vulnerable while she recovered. I should have spanked her like the other two, and maybe she would have turned out more like them," Mama remarked. The treatment ended in one of Caroline's wonderful massages.

The last day of Caroline's visit arrived. She packed and was getting ready for her departure. Nine o'clock came, then ten o'clock, and eleven o'clock. Mama was still sleeping. Caroline rubbed her grandmother's hands while tears rolled down her cheeks. The thought that she had died crossed her mind. Caroline kissed her on the forehead, but she still did not budge.

Within inches of her grandmother's face, Caroline said loudly, "Grandma it's getting kind of late." Caroline was relieved when she woke up with a start. She was surprised it was so late, but she was not quite ready to get up and stayed in bed a little longer.

Mama ate a small lunch. Jane arrived, staying a few minutes, but had to leave for a dental appointment. It was 12:30 and Caroline needed to go. Bridget would be there any moment. Caroline gave her grandmother one last long hug. As she drove away, she knew in her heart this was the last time she would see her grandmother.

Caroline arrived at our home in Farmington that evening and reported the events of her stay. She also shared Mama's comments regarding Jane's mental illness being caused by meningitis. I shared my thoughts on the meningitis excuse. "When Jane was in the ninth grade, she started being more weird than usual. She was letting mosquitoes bite her for some kind of *experiment*. She claimed she caught meningitis from a mosquito, and the mental illness resulted. That explanation is rather far-fetched to me. I was aware of Jane being really sick back then but didn't know what it was. She was so caustic to be around Lois and I stayed clear of her. She had mental issues long before the meningitis excuse."

Caroline left the next morning to rejoin her family. After Caroline had gone home, Jane told Lois she had seen Caroline trying to strangle Mama with the telephone cord.

CHAPTER NINE

A Challenging Visit

"I am changing my plans for staying with Mama," I explained to Lois over the phone. "Rather than going in March, I'm going this weekend. Jane will only have to stay two nights with Mama before I get there."

Don and I left Farmington early Saturday morning, arriving in Delta at 9:30. I entered the condo, expecting to see Jane, only to be greeted by the constant pumping sound of the oxygen machine instead. Mama was alone, asleep in bed. Jane was nowhere to be seen.

As Don brought in the luggage, I spoke softly to Mama, receiving no response. An hour later, she finally woke up. Upon dressing, she tucked a folded crisp $50 bill in her pocket, to my amusement. She proceeded slowly down the hall with the assistance of her walker.

"It sure is a lot easier getting down the hall since Caroline removed the boxes," she said. "I'm really thankful she cleared the way."

I was hoping for a quiet afternoon when Jane appeared with Ben. Jane talked about a drive they took, gossiped about a lady's family from her church, and talked about other things that had no relevance to anything in particular.

Jane and Ben joined us for a dinner of roasted chicken that Don picked up. When the food vanished, so did Jane and Ben. Their departure was Mama's cue to retire to the bedroom.

I assisted her as she struggled to get into her nightgown. "Jane does not help me," she expressed. "She says I need to do things for myself." That was silly. Mama needed help and I was not going to sit there doing nothing.

After a very long day, it was time to retreat to the guest room. The room was covered in a mass of boxes piled in stacks of two or more. The floor was hardly visible. A path led from the door to the bed. Care had to be taken when an object was laid down; otherwise it would disappear in the clutter.

A distant train whistle woke me. I had barely gotten up when the telephone rang. It was Jane. "I'll be over later."

"Okay," I answered, not looking forward to Jane's company.

I helped Mama dress and reach her wheelchair safely in the living room, while Don ate a quick bowl of cereal. As usual, he was anxious to get on the road. On Thursday, Don would return to bring me home.

I was rarely alone with Mama for any length of time; Jane made sure of that. The last time I could recall, before her heart attack, was shortly before Caroline was born thirty-three years ago. I remembered sitting in the wooden rocking chair at my parents' home, while going on three weeks overdue. As I sat there rocking, we talked about the new baby and watched my stomach go in and out of contortions as feet, elbows, or whatever else could be seen protruding under the maternity smock. It was getting considerably uncomfortable as Caroline finally settled down from turning somersaults and intervened with the hiccups.

I remembered the story Mama related about her pregnancy with Jane. Jane had kicked her so much she was black and blue under her ribs. I knew Jane was a kicker from getting kicked every night when I had to sleep with her.

Mama ate breakfast slowly. While trying to eat my own bowl of cereal, I stopped continually to meet Mama's requests. After breakfast, Mama was seated in her favorite chair in the living room, where she fell asleep.

Jane arrived after lunch. We sat in the living room, talking over the music coming from a little teddy bear Jane kept winding up that played "Home on the Range."

"Will you take me to Walmart to buy a Walkman for Mama?" I asked. I had brought a meditation tape that Mama was enjoying but had no means for playing when I left.

We left our mother resting in her brown chair as we walked out to Jane's dilapidated, old, rusty brown car. I handed her a $1 bill for gas that she grabbed and tucked in her purse, without saying, "Thank you." We rode down the street, listening to a rattle that sounded like a bucket of loose bolts rolling around.

"It is shorter to stay on this street," I pointed out as Jane turned toward Main Street.

"I like going my way. Your talking while I'm driving is distracting me."

I took a deep breath whispering, "Oh brother," to myself.

Even though there were many closer parking places, Jane parked an extraordinary distance from the store's entrance, which was isolated from other cars. "Why didn't you park closer to the entrance?" I questioned.

Laughing, Jane answered, "The way I drive, it is best to park way out here."

I picked up the pace. I wanted to buy the Walkman and get out of Jane's company as soon as possible.

"Slow down. You're making me sick. I can't walk that fast. It makes me dizzy," Jane complained. Jane looked frumpy as she limped along with a scarf on her head. Oblivious to people's stares, Jane trailed behind as we walked through the store, searching for the electronics department. This was not a fun little jaunt like it would have been with Lois.

Jane left shortly after returning to the condo. It was a good time to call my old high school friend Vonda, who had helped move Mama to the condo.

After dinner, Mama was helped into bed. I would have liked to turn on the television or radio, but for Mama's consideration, it was kept quiet.

I lay in bed wide-eyed for what seemed all night. The sound of the obnoxious oxygen machine seemed louder now. Not being sure how it worked, I imagined the sounds it made being related to Mama's breathing. Lois' email came to mind:

Remember if something happens and Mama passes when you are there, call hospice (Push the button that is on a string around her neck). Try not to freak out. Hospice will come and pronounce the death and help from that point on.

Monday morning found Mama sleeping soundly. At 9:30 she finally woke and dressed with assistance. As she reached for the walker to leave the bedroom, the doorbell rang.

I hurried to the door to find two men standing in the garage asking for Mama. She slowly made her way down the hall and sat in the wheelchair. Once she was situated, the men were let in. Mama greeted them warmly. Two kitchen chairs that were in the living room were cleared of their contents for the guests to have a place to sit.

The two men were Samuel Harrison and his son, who owned Equitable Insurance. They explained the benefits and insurance disbursements from Mama's policy for long-term care. There was a lot of small talk. They were old friends of Mama and Albert.

During their stay the doorbell rang. It was a flower arrangement delivery of carnations from Vonda. Soon after the Harrisons' departure, the Meals on Wheels lady made her delivery.

After lunch, Bridget and Jessica from hospice arrived. I knew who they were immediately from Caroline's descriptions. Bridget took Mama's blood pressure and asked if she wanted a bath, but she declined.

Soon after they left, the doorbell rang again. It was a handsome older couple from Mama's church. They visited for a while, said a prayer and then left.

Moments later, Jane called. "We are bringing over pizza for dinner. We will be there in about five minutes."

"Okay," I responded, wondering if the steady stream of people would ever end. Soon after calling, Jane and Ben entered carrying two pizzas. Mama ate a small piece, while I helped myself, biting into the card-board tasting crust. Ben and Jane gobbled it down as if it was a gourmet meal. Ben watched television most of the time, while Jane and Mama talked about subjects foreign to me as usual. Finally, Jane retrieved what was left of the pizza, and they left.

I began on Tuesday suggesting the yellow dresser from behind Mama's bedroom door be removed to make her bedroom wheelchair accessible. I explained again that it was more practical to be wheeled down the hall when she needed to use the bathroom.

Reluctantly, Mama agreed to the dresser being moved to the living room. "If we empty the dresser, it will be easy to move," I suggested as I was praying Mama would choose to get rid of most of the dresser's contents.

Mama was seated in her brown chair in the living room while each drawer was emptied. Mostly old slips occupied two drawers. They were all past their prime and should have been tossed ages ago. Mama decided to give a number of them away and then decided to keep several saying "I might need them."

Old *Writers' Digest* magazines filled another drawer, which Mama said could be given away. A red-and-white crocheted afghan, which she had forgotten she had, occupied the bottom drawer. It was kept out for when she got cold. The dresser was moved to the living room in front of a closet containing the vacuum. The dresser could be scooted easily out of the way.

Mama's need to use the bathroom provided the opportunity to test how well the wheelchair would get through the door. The footrests were in the way as I attempted to wheel her around the corner. They were removed. Upon returning to the living room, I began placing the drawers back in the dresser. I jumped when Jane appeared out of nowhere, shouting and attempting to belittle me. "HOW WOULD YOU FEEL IF SOMEONE WAS GOING THROUGH YOUR PERSONAL THINGS?"

"Mama agreed we needed to make room for the wheelchair to access her bedroom. We had to empty the dresser to move it out of the way," I responded defensively while my heart was still pounding from the abrupt scare.

"Humph!" she grumbled. I was invading her domain.

"I forgot to put the footrests back," I said while walking over to pick them up.

"I'll do it," Jane said.

"That's okay, I will." I protested

"I'll do it, I'm the oldest," Jane declared.

"What does being the oldest have to do with anything? You are here all of the time to do things for Mama. Let me help for the limited time I am here," I said as I proceeded to attach the footrests.

Mama was amused at the bickering over who would help her. Jane's "I'm the oldest" attitude, which in her mind afforded her privilege over all others, was most annoying. Jane left announcing she would be back later.

When washing dishes and gazing out the window onto the atrium over the last several days, I observed a neighbor taking her cat for a walk on a leash. "There is a lady out there with a cat," I said.

"Her name is Lotty," Mama informed. "They don't like to have pets running loose."

While Mama rested, I went out to meet Lotty and pet her cat. Lotty was short, on the chubby side with blond hair cut short in a boyish haircut. I enjoyed talking to Lotty about her cat and her daughter. "Do you know how to get the wrought iron gate to release?" I asked. "I know my mother's code, but we haven't been able to get it to open."

"Yes, I use it all the time," replied Lotty, and then gave a demonstration.

Jane and Ben appeared at dinnertime, which was becoming a habit. Mama was hungry for corn soufflé, which I whipped up with her instructions.

That evening as Mama was settling in her bed before going to sleep, she started to talk. "I have two normal daughters, and I have one who isn't normal, but she is getting there."

I was tired of Mama continually saying Jane was getting better. I blatantly spoke up. "Jane is not getting *normal*. She will never be *normal.*" It surprised me when this came gushing out of my mouth. I hardly ever challenged anything Mama said.

Wednesday was going to be spent cleaning. I planned to clean the house as quickly as possible. Waiting on Mama was wearing me out, and I needed quiet time to rest.

"I'll be over later this morning," Jane announced over the phone.

"Don't come," I told Jane, the self-appointed watchdog whose presence was not appreciated. "I am going to be busy changing the bedding, washing and cleaning."

"Aren't you overdoing it?" Jane said in a snotty tone. "I don't want to leave the house dirty," I responded.

"What about your so-called heart condition?" Jane chided.

It was time for some of her own medicine. "I lied," sprang out of my mouth.

"Well, this is the end of this conversation," Jane remarked.

I chuckled to myself.

On Wednesday morning, while the washer and dryer were running, Jessica and Bridget appeared. Mama still did not want to have a bath or have her hair washed. While Bridget was caring for Mama, I joined Jessica at the dining room table where she was refilling the pill dispenser with Mama's prescriptions.

"Jane told me she had a pharmacist recommend a different medication for acid reflux because she thought the prescription was too strong," I disclosed.

"I noticed she had substituted the prescription," stated Jessica. "I changed the pills back to the prescription medication that was prescribed, and she has left them alone. She has been interfering with a lot of your mother's care. I was at the hospital the first evening your mother was brought in," Jessica revealed. "Jane was physically trying to remove your mother from her hospital bed. She was pulling on her arm and leg trying to get her up."

I knew from the discussion with Dr. Nelson Jane had tried to get Mama discharged, but trying to drag her out of bed was news.

"Lois and I have talked. We are concerned about Mama being alone for any length of time," I stated.

"There is a grant that has become available recently for people in your mother's situation. She is a perfect candidate," Jessica explained.

The grant sounded like a godsend, but Mama had previously expressed she did not want people she did not know in her house. I could not see passing up the assistance. "You need help during the day when Jane can't be here. Would it be okay with you if we have home health people come stay with you?"

"Whatever you girls agree on will be fine with me," Mama responded as she sat back with her eyes closed.

"Lois and I know you need more help than hospice and Jane can provide," I insisted, purposely not mentioning Jane, knowing she would challenge the decision. "We are concerned you cannot be left by yourself."

"Okay then, if you think that is best," she replied.

From the list of home health agencies Jessica had provided, only *Loving Assistance* could provide around-the-clock care. Jessica made arrangements for Rosemary, the owner of Loving Assistance to meet with Mama after lunch. She tried to reach Sarah, the hospice social worker, who also coordinated grants; but Jessica was unable to contact her.

After lunch, Jessica explained how the grant worked, and Rosemary described Loving Assistance's payment policy. The necessary papers were signed to begin care the following morning. Jessica would contact Lois and straighten out the finances. The ladies left after the arrangements had been made.

I confronted Mama with Jessica's rendition of her first night in the ICU. "Jessica told me Jane tried to physically remove you from your hospital bed the night of your heart attack."

"Oh, really?" Mama's voice sounded in genuine.

"Don't you remember?" I said, wondering if Mama was playing dumb.

"I don't remember that. I was very tired and goofy from the drugs."

Maybe she had been too drugged to be aware of the situation, but she shrugged off hearing of Jane's effort to remove her from lifesaving care.

Mama snoozed in her brown chair while the beds were made, and the cleaning was completed. She was cold even though she was wearing a sweater and covered with two afghans. I was sweltering. I stuck my head out the garden door for a moment to get a breath of fresh air.

⁂

Jane was a certified nurse assistant and had been working part time as a home health aide before Mama's heart attack. The agency of Jane's employment provided service only between eight and five on weekdays. Having a different agency care for Mama would create another matter of contention. The dreaded call to Jane could not be postponed indefinitely.

"Hello Jane," I said as optimistically sounding as possible. "Since I'm leaving tomorrow, we have arranged for a home health aide to stay with Mama to make things easier for you. Mama needs someone with her all of the time. A home health person from Loving Assistance will be staying with Mama tomorrow beginning at nine."

I paused, expecting Jane to jump in yelling, but she was silent. "Don will be here around nine in the morning to take me home. I would like for you to come over and meet the home health aide and say goodbye."

Mount Vesuvius still had not erupted. "Jessica told me about a grant that is available to help defray some of the home health assistance fees. She said Mama meets all of the criteria, and all we have to do is apply for it.

"I'm checking into a grant, also," Jane stated in a subdued tone. "Hold off on your grant. My grant pays more than yours and it is a better grant. I have an appointment next Wednesday to learn more." Shortly after the conversation with Jane, the phone rang. It was Jessica. "Sarah's schedule is full today. She has time next Wednesday, I can represent your mother."

"My sister, Jane, said she is checking into another grant," I expressed. "I'm aware of only one such grant," Jessica responded.

A short time later, Jessica phoned again, "In talking with Sarah I learned Jane has made an appointment with her. Routinely, Sarah goes to the client's home, but Jane insisted on meeting in another place, which is unusual."

Jane was conspiring to get home health care for our mother without conferring with Lois or me, besides not wanting Mama to know what she was up to.

"I just spoke with Jessica," I conveyed to Jane over the phone. "The grants are one in the same."

"Mama doesn't want just anybody in her house. I want to use my agency. I know the aides, and I want to hand pick the ones to take care of Mama. I'm so angry we better end this conversation before I say something I shouldn't." Jane slammed down the receiver.

Meanwhile, Lois had spoken with Rosemary from Loving Assistance, and set up a schedule for a home health aide to be with Mama.

Angrily, Jane called Lois shouting. "You are so STUPID! I want people I know taking care of Mama during the day! Loving Assistance can come at night."

"I already asked if that was an option. They said it would be too confusing to have two different agencies involved. Besides, there will be a smaller group of people taking care of Mama, which would be more to her liking," stated Lois.

Jane continued yelling, "You are a self-appointed boss! You think everything has to be your way! Well, you don't know everything! You don't make good decisions. You—" Lois hung up.

Mama was finishing her dinner when her brother, Jack, called asking how things were going. "Is Jane giving you a hard time?"

Mama was sitting at the dining room table within several feet. I did not dare express my frustrations. Mama would have gotten very angry if she knew Jack was aware of Jane's actions.

"Yes," I responded. "Would you like to talk to Mama? She is right here."

After their conversation, Mama was given a fresh cup of hot spice tea, while I took out the trash.

My mind was on going home in the morning. Being with Mama for days with a steady diet of Jane, no radio or TV, having little time to myself, exhausted from the constant flow of people and telephone calls, not to mention missing Don, I was more than ready to get back to my life. It was good breathing in the fresh evening air. Relishing the idea of going home, I had forgotten after Jessica and Rosemary left, the door to the garage had been set to lock.

Upon returning and finding the entrance locked; I was highly distressed. Mama was too weak to wheel herself to the door. Thanks to the conversation with Lotty, I entered the atrium. Through the kitchen window, I could see Mama sipping her tea. Caroline's hidden key in the artificial rock was located. I slipped in quietly through the garden door without Mama noticing.

Finally, it was Thursday. I was elated to know Don would be here soon. Curtis and Claudia were coming with him. Joyce, the home health aide from Loving Assistance, arrived promptly at nine followed by Don, Curtis and Claudia. They stood around talking while waiting for Jane. I decided to familiarize Joyce with a quick tour of the condo, pointing out Mama's bedroom and bathroom. Joyce commented on the boxes stacked all over. "Your mother must like having her things around her. That is fine with me. It doesn't bother me," she stated.

After being out of Mama's eyesight a matter of seconds and returning to the living room, I heard Mama say, "What are they going back there for?"

I had forgotten how private Mama was and how she did not like people in her bedroom. I pointed out to Joyce where Mama's spice tea was, along with her strawberries, leftover corn soufflé, and the leftover Meals-On-Wheels lunch.

"CLOSE THAT REFRIGERATOR DOOR!" Mama hollered.

My heart jumped. Being startled in such a manner was not good for my condition. Between Mama's attitude and Jane's taunting, I was more than ready to go home.

It was ten o'clock and Jane still had not arrived. I phoned Jane receiving only a response from the answering machine. Surely she was there, choosing not to answer. A message was left. "Jane, we've been waiting for you to come by Mama's, but we have to go now." We said our goodbye's to Mama and left her in Joyce's care.

CHAPTER TEN

Management by Crisis

I had no sooner walked in the house with my suitcase and reached the bedroom when the phone rang. It was Lois calling from work in a panic. "Sarah called. Jane is not cooperating. She is refusing to stay with Mama."

Jane was not concerned our mother be left by herself. "After all, it isn't unusual for old people to be by themselves when they croak," she told Sarah, the grant coordinator and hospice social worker.

Lois was beside herself. "Mama should not be left unattended. They are talking about moving her back to Horizons. I told Sarah it would be very hard on her to go back. They are trying to find someone to stay with her tonight. Sarah wants to know how soon I can get there. I need to change my plane reservations."

Lois had already purchased an emergency ticket to arrive Monday. Fortunately, the reservation could be exchanged for the next available flight, which Lois hastily arranged.

Lois was back on the phone, advising Sarah she would be arriving Friday afternoon on a two-thirty flight. To her relief, Loving Assistance had found someone to stay with Mama that night. Lois phoned to inform Mama of the new plan.

"Hi, Mama, I will arrive tomorrow afternoon instead of Monday," stated Lois.

Rather than tell Mama Jane had refused to stay with her, Lois made up an excuse. "Jane isn't feeling well. Arrangements have been made for a home health aide to stay the night."

"Jane just called and said she will be over at six o'clock," Mama replied.

Lois was horribly upset. Whatever deplorable game Jane was playing, Lois was not amused. In between the flurry of calls, periodically, Lois tried to reach Jane, but she was not answering. Lois persisted, and finally, Ben reluctantly answered. "Jane is not here." Lois could hear Jane in the background barking out orders.

"You are lying. I can hear her telling you what to say."

Jane refused to come to the phone until Ben relayed the message that she did not have to relieve the home health aide.

Jane picked up the receiver as Lois was saying, "Arrangements have been made for an aide to stay the night since Jane has refused."

"Tell the home health people to go home! I don't want them over there!" Jane yelled belligerently.

"Arrangements have already been made. Don't interfere," Lois shot back.

Lois called Rosemary at Loving Assistance, not knowing if Jane would go by Mama's and demand the home health aide leave.

"The health care aide will not get involved in a confrontation. In the event Jane tells her to leave, she will leave," Rosemary replied.

Lois had to assure Rosemary her aide would get paid for the hours they had arranged even if Jane ordered her to go. They were to notify Lois if Jane appeared. The evening passed with no calls.

The next morning, Bill took Lois to the Memphis airport.

Once on the plane, Lois' thoughts turned to the possibility of our mother dying anytime. Along with the dread of dealing with Jane, she was overwhelmed.

Upon landing in Montrose, Lois rented a car and drove twenty-five miles to Delta. As she approached the condo, Jane's car was spotted parked along the street. *Oh great,* she thought as she pulled into the driveway and entered.

Jane greeted her with a hug and looked calm. "I didn't expect you to be here," Lois said with restraint. "You weren't going to take care of her."

"I was only joking," Jane said, laughing. Lois was livid. That was some joke. Jane was not confronted in Mama's presence. It was not the time or place to quarrel.

Jane took leave, and Mama started chatting. "I can't believe you kids are doing all this for me."

Isn't it natural to care for your mother and do everything earthly possible when she is very sick and dying? Our family had a huge void when it came to family togetherness and support. Mama did not generally go out of her way and did not expect anything in return.

Lois prepared dinner and helped Mama get ready for bed. I had informed Lois of the evening routine. Unfortunately, I left out one detail. After cleaning up the kitchen and settling in, Lois finally went to bed herself. Even though she was exhausted, the annoying sound of the oxygen machine delayed her ability to doze off to sleep. During the night, she was awakened by Mama calling out. She sounded mad. Lois leaped out of bed and ran into her bedroom.

"WHERE'S MY WALKER?" Mama demanded in a harsh reprimanding tone.

Bewildered and half asleep, Lois made her way to the dark living room and retrieved the walker, placing it next to Mama's bed. She was satisfied and went off to sleep.

The previous week when Lois was making travel arrangements, she had the foresight to call James King, Mama's attorney, to set up an appointment for Tuesday afternoon. Lois made the mistake of mentioning the appointment to Jane. Jane attended the same church as the attorney and cornered him at the Sunday morning services. She told James to cancel his appointment with Lois. That afternoon when Jane informed Lois she had canceled her appointment, Lois became incensed. She called James at home and told him she did not want the appointment cancelled. Lois was assured Jane was not taken seriously, and her appointment was still on.

Suspicious of everyone, Jane had assumed Lois was planning to conspire with him about her share of the inheritance. In reality, Lois wanted to talk about our mother's estate in general and her duties as the personal representative after our mother was gone.

In Jane's absence, Mama asked Lois to go through coffee cans that were filled with change. Lois was directed to check for valuable silver coins and old pennies. After the second night of sorting through thousands of coins, only a few collector coins were found. There were way too many coins to look at each one individually. Lois resorted to taking some of the cans to the bank and deposited them into our mother's checking account.

Lois wanted to get out of the house for a brief period each day. Rather than give Jane the power to decide if she would show up to relieve her, Lois arranged for home health aides to come in two hours every afternoon.

On Monday afternoon, Lois met with Sarah and Jessica in a conference room at the hospice complex. Lois was looking for help regarding how to deal with Jane. "Taking care of our mother's needs is comparably not as difficult as working around Jane to get things accomplished," Lois expressed.

Sarah could not believe Jane's disrespectful behavior and language. "Your family is one of the most dysfunctional families I have ever seen," Sarah declared. "It is a miracle you and Louise function so well."

Later when Lois relayed that conversation to me, I was very surprised. I had never considered our family dysfunctional. Does one mentally ill person make the entire family dysfunctional? Or maybe she was including Mama's personality into the mix. Perhaps but Lois and I did not operate on that premise.

"I am exceedingly tired of Jane's manipulation and interference. She is not a team player, and her reasoning is questionable. She goes off on her own, making decisions behind our backs. When I try to talk to her, she gets all hung up on who the *boss* is." Lois confided to Sarah and

Jessica. "The issue is not who the boss is but rather what the best things are that we can do for our mother right now."

"I would suggest you ask your mother if she wishes to have twenty-four hour care, in Jane's presence," Sarah offered. "Since Jane respects your mother as an authority figure, it would be easier for her to hear it from your mother."

Lois returned to the condo after the meeting. As she had expected, Jane was there. Following Sarah's advice, Lois approached Mama. "Mama, would you like to have twenty-four hour care now?"

"Yes, I think I need someone here," Mama replied to Lois' relief. Fortunately, this scheme did not backfire. Lois had already decided twenty-four hour care was necessary and would be arranged in any case.

After Jane's exit, Mama started to talk. "If I could just get some energy back, I could do some things. Then she went into her "I have three daughters" speech. In Lois' version, Mama told her she had different relationships and ties to each of her daughters for different reasons. Later Jane told me Mama had a similar conversation with her, only in Jane's version she was our mother's favorite.

Upon occasion, our mother displayed strange behavior, which embarrassed Lois and me. She did not care what anyone thought. Such an occasion presented itself the following day.

On Tuesday morning, Jessica made her routine visit, appearing with an abundance of red curly hair intruding over her forehead. "I don't like your hairstyle. It's in your face. I'll cut it for you," Mama offered.

Jessica was a good sport. She reached in her pocket and handed Mama a pair of bandage scissors.

"Lean your head down so I can reach your hair," Mama directed.

Jessica bent down to accommodate the request. Mama took a piece of the red curly locks in her fingers and snipped some of Jessica's hair. She was not very strong, and did not get a very large piece. The process was repeated. Jessica had a worried look on her face until she saw the small amount of hair held in her hand.

"Are you finished?" Jessica questioned.

"Yes. It looks better now," Mama answered.

Lois was horrified but relieved the missing hair was hardly noticeable.

Jane stayed with Mama, while Lois went to lunch with her high school friend, Gail, who lived in Delta. After lunch she kept her appointment with James King, her mother's attorney. Besides getting to have lunch with an old friend, the lunch provided an alibi for Lois' whereabouts. Lois gained the needed information from the brief meeting and returned; Jane none the wiser.

Upon returning from her appointment, Lois decided to wash the bedding. One of the pillowcases on our mother's bed was very old and worn. It had a small tear when it was put in the washer. After being removed from the dryer, the tear was quite large and the pillowcase was not usable.

Jane saw it and chided, "You better get the sewing machine out and fix the pillowcase that you tore, or Mama will be really mad!"

The fabric was so thin and worn there was no way it could be repaired properly. Lois replaced it with another pillowcase from the linen closet. At first Lois was worried about Mama getting upset. Then she realized it was not a big deal. Lois tucked the pitiful pillowcase into a zippered pouch in her luggage to make sure Jane did not see it in the trash. She would take it home to throw away. Lois had learned from an early age that sometimes it was best not to bring attention to irrelevant issues, to protect herself from unrealistic demands. It was best to let sleeping dogs lie.

Jane had been accusing Lois of wanting Mama's money when in actuality, Jane was already making plans for her inheritance. She wanted to go on a trip to Oregon to visit Uncle Jack and Aunt Lorie and perhaps to California to see Aunt Rebecca. Jane totally disregarded the stipulation of our mother's will for her share to go to Lois or me to be under our control to pay for Jane's major expenses, repairs and emergencies.

Jane said she probably wouldn't help us clean up the condo as it would be too hard for her. We knew Jane would be there, but she did not want to do any of the physical work because it would make her *sick*.

Our parents had purchased a number of silver bars and valuable coins. Mama told Lois the silver bars were hidden in two old green metal ammunition boxes way back in the corner of her bedroom closet.

Lois asked if she could locate the boxes for future reference. After getting past the barricade of waist-high boxes, the mirrored closet door was slid open. In a corner of the dark closet, countless old shoes were found piled high, camouflaging the ammunition boxes.

Without disclosing the hiding place, Lois suggested to Jane the silver should be inventoried. It was anticipated Jane would be helping herself to our mother's belongings at the first opportunity. Lois proceeded to document the contents of the boxes, carefully recording everything that was in each box. Afterward, out of Jane's presence, the boxes were returned to their hiding place. Photographs of the house and closets were taken. There was not a formal inventory, but Jane was lead to believe there was.

Later, after Lois had returned home, Jane phoned her, saying it was illegal for her to have gone through Mama's things and list them. Jane was full of hooey, and Lois told her so.

On Wednesday morning, Mama had just awakened and was getting dressed when the doorbell rang. Jane rushed to get the door to find Sarah from hospice, representing the grant assistance program. It was 10 A.M., the appointed time to make arrangements for getting the grant funds in place.

Upon Sarah being seated, Jane began grilling her with a series of peculiar questions. When Jane scurried off to the bedroom to check on Mama, who was having a bad coughing episode, Lois took advantage of her absence to apologize for Jane's bizarre conduct. Sarah assured Lois an explanation was not necessary. "Jane's behavior is well-known in this community," she responded.

Within minutes, Jane reappeared pushing Mama in the wheelchair. She transitioned to her favorite chair and was ready to begin. The terms of the grant were straightforward. It should have been a simple meeting to explain what the grant entailed and how the vouchers would be distributed. Mama treated it suspiciously and examined the wording with methodical thoroughness before signing the form. At last, Sarah was on her way.

Jane must have told Mama something to make her suspicious of the way Lois was handling her affairs. Later that morning, with no warning or explanation, Mama came at Lois in a harsh voice, "I WANT TO KNOW EVERYTHING AND I WANT TO MEET EVERYBODY. I'm going to get to the bottom of this," she exclaimed. Lois was taken aback. Get to the bottom of what?

Lois was told not to pay Loving Assistance one cent before she met them. Mama had already met Rosemary, the owner or Loving Assistance, the previous Wednesday when Jessica had initiated the preliminary arrangements for home health care. During that visit, I signed papers acknowledging the expectations of home health aides and agreed to pay the costs. At that time, our mother had been agreeable to the arrangements.

Mama was being unreasonable, and Lois was not happy. Mama's finances had been discussed with her every step of the way. She knew Lois was paying her bills. Lois was a good advocate. Upon noticing the bank had erroneously deducted fees from her account for several months, Lois requested the fees be reimbursed. She was told by bank officials their policy did not allow fees to be returned. Lois challenged, "It is not the bank's policy to charge the fees in the first place." The fees were reimbursed after that conversation.

As per Mama's demands, Lois arranged for Rosemary, Sarah, and the Harrison's, from Equitable Insurance, to meet with her, each at a designated time. Mama interrogated them one after another all afternoon. She was finally satisfied all was well after a grueling day.

It was becoming increasingly difficult for the home health workers to get Mama out of her chair. Loving Assistance asked for a lift chair to be brought in. Lois complied, and hospice delivered one promptly. Having the chair would keep Mama from being confined to a bed.

Jane went into orbit upon learning Mama had the chair lift. "She doesn't need it and it's too expensive!"

"Medicare is covering the $25 fee for the loaner chair," Lois explained to Jane, not that she heard one word, while lost in her tantrum. Even if it had cost something, Lois would have gladly paid.

Lois observed scenes of Mama eating breakfast or lunch, while Jane sat next to her at the table, staring at her. Perhaps she was trying to send her mental telepathy messages.

Lois took advantage of the final afternoon of her visit to hear our mother talk about her childhood and when she met Daddy. Mama also talked about when we were babies and young children. Lois took notes as Jane glared the entire time.

When it was time for Lois' departure, she was exhausted from Jane's interference and manipulative games.

CHAPTER ELEVEN

Entering Another Room

"I am going on a trip to Denver. It is very hard on me seeing Mama declining. I need to get away," Jane informed Lois. She was perturbed by Jane's announcement. One does not go far when their mother's death is imminent.

Jane had been talking to someone who told her Social Security could take claim of the condo to pay our mother's medical expenses. "Mama can't get thrown out because I own the condo," Lois replied.

"You are taking advantage of Mama! I know you are just out for yourself! Jane exclaimed. Even though the condo belonged to Lois, our mother did not pay rent or any compensation for staying there.

"If I were out for myself, I would never have helped Mama to begin with," Lois told her.

The old diesel truck that Ben drove was evidence of Lois' generosity as she had given them $5,000 outright several years previously to buy a vehicle.

Mama was losing ground daily. Lois and I had to make plans regarding how much time we could stay in Delta when we came for her services. Our accumulated leave time from our jobs was diminishing. After careful consideration of time limitations and the horrendous cleaning task, it was decided to have an estate sale before leaving Delta. With the joint forces of Bill and my family, the job could be accomplished. It had to be. There was concern about appearances, having the memorial service one day and an estate sale the next. It could not be helped.

⋙

A hospice nurse answered my phone call to Mama. The receiver was handed to Mama. It took a lot of effort for her to speak. "There are a lot of people here," she said in a weak, hoarse voice.

"Who is there?" I asked, receiving no answer.

"When are you coming?" Mama forced out.

"Chris and his family are coming Saturday. I am riding with them. Are you up for us all to come then?"

She did not respond. The nurse came back on the phone, "Her breathing is irregular. She is not eating or drinking anything and is refusing medications. She probably will not be with us by the weekend."

I was in denial, not believing she would be gone that soon. Mama had a strong constitution. Surely she would hang on a few more days.

Jane was still on her excursion, when she called Lois the morning of March 2, from Denver. "I will be back in Delta on the bus tonight around 8:30. I will go over to see Mama in the morning."

"Okay," Lois replied. "Yesterday, hospice brought in a hospital bed and set it up in the living room."

"Well, humph. You didn't do what I told you, did you? I have to go. Goodbye," Jane responded rudely.

Earlier, Jane had agreed the hospital bed was a good idea, but she wanted it in the bedroom; however, there was too much stuff in the bedroom.

Lois tried to ask what her plans were for moving our mother's car. It had already been established Jane would get the dark blue Plymouth Belvedere that our parents had bought new in 1965. Her name was already on the title jointly with Mama's.

When Lois called, the caregiver could not rouse Mama. She had gone into a coma and would be gone soon. Our mother had always said dying was like going from one room to another. She took the journey into the next room late that night at 11:30.

The caregiver who was present, notified hospice. Carmen, the nurse on call, arrived and confirmed our mother's death. The official cause was advanced congestive heart failure and coronary artery disease. She was six weeks short of reaching her eighty-second birthday.

Lois phoned us early the morning of March 3. Don answered the phone. "Mama died just before midnight," stated Lois.

Jane had already called Lois. "Where are the keys to the Plymouth?" Jane demanded.

"I have no idea," Lois told her.

"I need to move the car in order for Mama's body to be carried out through the garage!" Jane bellowed.

Lois started to suggest she open the sliding glass doors in the master bedroom, but Jane would not listen and hung up.

After locating a set of car keys, Jane called Lois back. "I can't get the car to start!" Jane declared angrily. She was nasty to Lois and acted like it was Lois' fault. The car had not been driven since November when Mama had her heart attack. It was no surprise it did not start.

The next morning, hospice came by the condo to pick up the lift chair, hospital bed, oxygen machine, and other items. Lois was notified the items were being removed. "Jane was at your mother's this morning while we were there. She was frantically going through things in the house and made a mess," relayed Sarah.

With the knowledge Jane was rummaging through our mother's things, Lois tried to reach James King but he was out of town. Foreseeing this situation could happen, Lois had previously discussed her thoughts with James. He promised he would *take care of everything* if Jane got out of control.

"Should I call the police?" Lois asked me. "She is trespassing, and I'm sure she is taking things."

"If we call the police, it could get pretty wild. Maybe we are over reacting," I suggested. It was decided not to call the police; it would cause more trouble for Jane, and she had been in enough trouble.

Nine months after our mother passed, I contacted Carmen, the nurse, who pronounced our mother's death. Some of the events of that night were learned.

"Jane was not present when your mother died but arrived shortly after I notified her," explained Carmen.

"Was Jane upset?"

"She wasn't crying. She was okay. She acted a little different. She didn't seem to be terribly upset. I called the funeral home, but Jane did not want them to pick up the body until later. She said it would bother the neighbors." Since when, was Jane ever concerned anyone was being bothered?

"Jane did not want to leave," Carmen continued. "I called the coroner to see if they minded waiting until morning to pick up her body. They agreed that would be okay."

When Daddy died, Mama anointed his chakras with frankincense. Jane had told me we should do the same for our mother. With that in mind I asked if Jane had anointed our mother's body with oil.

"She put oil on her forehead and feet. There was a sheet covering the body. I couldn't see where all she was putting the oil," Janet said. "She helped wash and groom the body and put in the dentures."

"Was she going through our mother's things?" I asked.

"I was busy and did not notice. I was gathering up all of the medications and flushing them down the toilet. She objected to wasting the medications."

Upon completing the established protocol, Carmen left Jane alone with our mother's body. Lois and I wondered what Jane was doing all night. One thing we were sure of was that Jane had taken our mother's wedding ring that Daddy had given her. Lois knew Mama was wearing it when she was there the previous week.

Jane wasted no time emailing Uncle Jack and the others about our mother's death. Her email stated she was there mopping up after Mama's passing.

Last-minute arrangements were being made. The memorial service was set for Thursday morning.

Through a phone number Lois provided, I contacted Marcus, who lived in Missouri. He was one of three of Mama's stepsons who was a minister. Marcus would get in touch with Pastor Bedford and assist with organizing the service.

CHAPTER TWELVE

Our Mother's Belongings

O ur mother had a tremendous amount of possessions that she had hoarded over her lifetime. A large part of her belongings was only of value to her. Knowing there would be an abundance of things to toss, Lois arranged to have four small dipsy dumpsters placed on the street in front of the condo.

The details for the estate sale were finalized. Caroline contacted the *Delta County Independent* in time to meet the deadline to have an ad placed in Wednesday's edition, the only day the weekly paper was published.

Meanwhile, Jane had an agenda of her own. She visited the Comrade National Bank and closed the POD account, retrieving the full balance. She also proceeded to claim her third of a CD.

Jane informed Lois she was going to take funds from our mother's checking account which was kept at a different bank. Lois was not going to wait around for another one of Jane's *jokes*. Lois contacted the bank, requesting the account be frozen.

Since Jane had limited space in her apartment, she was asked to reserve a storage unit to hold items she was getting. It was her responsibility to move her things to the storage area. Lois needed to have everything out of the condo by the time she left Delta in order for it to be put on the market.

Jane reported she had our mother's car but had not removed the items from the trunk because she was a little "addled" right now. The trunk was full of tools that were part of the estate. "You both can fight over Mama's beautiful set of china. We need to be concentrating on God and the funeral more than who gets what." In her next statement, she elaborated on items she wanted.

It had already been determined who would get the big items before our mother died. With all due respect to Mama, Lois and I made it known we wanted to have some of the countless smaller items. We did not consider the dividing process as being a fight. "I feel like saying grabby, grabby, grabby," Jane expressed. She did not like the idea of Lois selling the condo.

"Give Lois credit for handling a horrendous responsibility," I told Jane. "Lois is not greedy. She is one of the fairest and big-hearted people you will ever know. Keep in mind you are getting most of our mother's possessions."

Jane did not want Mama's obituary to appear in the Delta newspaper. She did not want the mental health agency staff to know her mother had died as they *might come get her*. Lois was in a quandary. It would be inappropriate not to acknowledge our mother's life. Lois decided not to let Jane's distorted motives dictate actions. Mr. Logan, the funeral director, was instructed to have the obituary printed in the Delta paper, but to satisfy Jane's fears, her name would be omitted.

Upon Lois and Bill's arrival in Delta, they checked into a motel. Early Wednesday morning, they arrived at the condo and began sorting items in Mama's bedroom, where the biggest challenge lay.

Don and I arrived with Caroline and her family shortly before noon. The first of the four small dipsy dumpsters was almost full from Lois and Bill's morning work.

In accordance with Caroline's carefully planned cleanup agenda, Don began working in the kitchen, emptying the cupboards tossing and packing items in an orderly fashion. Joe began removing Mama's collection of books from the shelves that covered an entire wall in the living room. Five-year-old Mathew was assigned the job of sorting the remaining coffee cans of change. He was doing a good job and having fun separating the pennies, nickels, dimes, quarters, and occasional fifty-cent pieces into piles.

Caroline began going through the multitude of boxes that were stacked up in the guest bedroom. Clara and Kayla were busily taking clothes off the hangers from the guest room closet, checking the pockets and neatly folding and placing the clothes in garbage bags for Jane. Jane had requested to have Mama's clothes to give to charity. I doubted she would give them to charity, after all, I knew her, but it really did not matter.

I joined Lois in sorting through dressers in the master bedroom, while Bill was buried in items from the master bedroom closet. Among the items Bill found was a front-page newspaper clipping declaring World War II over. There were ration books for sugar, flour and gasoline. All of these items would be kept, of course.

I kept getting distracted from the interesting things Bill was finding, such as my baby book. I did not even know I had one. Stopping to take a quick glance, I noted my, first words: "daddy," "don't," and "stop it."

Why would "*don't*" and "*stop it*" be among a baby's first words? Sadly, I knew why.

It was back to the dresser. Our mother's collection of old jewelry and odds and ends were discovered. Lois had been told there was money intermingled with the contents of envelopes in the dresser I was going through. The money was well hidden. At first glance, one would not realize there were all denominations of bills inconspicuously stashed inside envelopes with old bank statements, insurance coverage notices, and the like.

The blue Plymouth had been moved from the garage, but the tools that were not intended to go with the car were not in sight. According to Jane, they had been stolen from the trunk. That story was not believed, but she was not confronted.

Jane appeared after lunch to nose around. She had spent the previous week gathering a collection of things from the house that were boxed up and placed in the garage. We had no idea of the boxes contents.

Jane wanted some of the items Lois had claimed. Besides the old chiming clock that had belonged to our paternal grandfather, Jane wanted an antique end table. Apparently, Jane had taken the key that wound up the clock as it was nowhere to be found. She may have thought without the key, Lois would have considered the clock useless and let her have it. If that was her plan, it was spoiled by the discovery of several other clock keys that were found among the jewelry.

Jane arranged to have special services for the family to be held at 5 that evening at the church *to save Lois' soul* and socialize with Albert's family, the Archer's. Lois and I had an overwhelming amount of work to do. There was no time for socializing.

"Ben will be over later to load my things. He is taking a nap on the couch. He has negative energy." Jane announced then walked back over to her apartment to wait for Ben to get off his *couch.*

The condo was humming like a beehive with everyone fastidiously attending to our assigned chore. A nearby neighbor was enjoying the entertainment as he sat leisurely outside the front of his condo on a portable lawn chair. It surely must have been a spectacle to witness the parade of trips to the dumpsters.

Jane returned with Ben. She had not gotten a storage unit yet. She was not sure how to go about it. I reluctantly volunteered to go with her and Ben. Don joined us.

Ben and Jane were already in their old, white diesel truck, as I approached with Don. Don motioned them to go ahead, while we followed in our vehicle to the location of a storage company's office. I arranged for a unit and paid cash for three months from money we had found in the house. Having that accomplished, we went back to the condo. While Don put garbage bags of clothes in our liberty blue Jeep Cherokee, I carried Jane's collection of boxes to Ben as he organized them in the back of the truck. "Give me a hand," I called out to Jane.

"I can't. I have to save my energy for tonight," Jane declared as she looked on.

I was highly discussed with Jane's lack of assistance. This was her stuff!

Once loaded, we were on our way to the storage area. Don and I carried items from the SUV to the storage unit but did not stay to remove Jane's boxes from the truck, as we needed to get back to excavating the condo. Jane was furious when she and Ben were left to unload the truck themselves.

Upon returning to the condo, Lois asked me to accompany her. We needed to go by the mortuary to pick up our mother's ashes and also to go by the bank to claim our shares of the CD.

We waited in the reception area of the funeral home while our mother's ashes were being retrieved. Lois asked if they had Mama's wedding ring. We were assured she was not wearing a ring when her body was picked up.

A young woman with long brown hair, appeared with a gift bag-type container. "I put the snaps from the coin purse your sister insisted being held in her hand, at the bottom of the container beneath the ashes." Jane wanted the coin purse to be incinerated with our mother's remains to prove they did not replace her ashes with someone else's.

"All metal is removed before cremation takes place," said the lady.

"However, in this case, we made an exception."

Lois and I looked at each other with blank expressions. Then we thanked her and were on our way to the bank. It was almost 5 P.M. as our business was completed, and we left the bank. There was no way we could make Jane's family prayer service, which we never agreed to attend in the first place.

Don picked up a bucket of chicken for the working crew to share. After dinner, Lois and Bill took reprieve to their motel, and everyone else settled into their beds at the condo. As exhausted as we were, Don and I were restless and got up to sort through more items in yet another dresser. It was after midnight when we finally gave in and went back to bed.

CHAPTER THIRTEEN

Memorial Services and Aftermath

The Lord provided a gorgeous spring day for our mother's memorial service. Several of us set off to pick up the flowers that Caroline had arranged through a phone number she located on the Internet.

A short time later, we arrived at the church. The flowers were placed on each side of the altar, along with an enlarged picture of our mother in her pink dress. Already sitting on the altar was Jane's contribution, a poster drawing of flowers. Sloppily printed at the bottom were the words "Flowers for Mother."

Mr. Logan directed us to join family members in the basement as others attending the services began to take their seats in the auditorium.

While I had been in the auditorium attending to the flowers, Pastor Bedford aggressively confronted Lois in the basement, "Why was Jane's name omitted from the obituary?"

Jane walked up at that moment. Lois suspected Jane had brought the omission of her name to his attention. Looking Jane straight in the eye, she replied, "Jane ordered me NOT to put her name in the paper, but I was not going to let our mother's death go unnoticed." Without saying a word, Jane walked off, realizing she had been caught in her own web. As we were entering the basement, Jane, with Ben alongside, was escaping up the stairs.

"Aren't you going to stay down here with the family members?" I asked.

"No, I'm a free spirit," she said as she exited the basement area.

I met Marcus and the other Archer family members for the first time. They were all average looking. Everyone visited congenially until Mr. Logan announced it was time to join the congregation for the service to begin.

Pastor Bedford opened the services followed by short sermons from Jasper, the oldest of Mama's stepchildren, and Marcus. Lois and I breathed a sigh of relief to see the vocalists on the program were listed as Bernard and The Archer Family Singers. Jane and Ben joined The Archer Family Singers for their pieces.

Caroline delivered the poem "Miss Me, But Let Me Go" without a flaw. She began by saying her grandmother was a very spunky lady, to everyone's amusement.

After the eulogy, Pastor Bedford spoke again, acknowledging Caroline's observation that Mama was a very spunky lady. On those lines, he told a story of a previously portly gentleman in the congregation.

> "After services one Sunday Marie went up to a portly gentleman in the congregation and tapped on his stomach telling him he needed to lose that. Stating she had some books that could help him and if he would like to call her she would tell him what he needed to do. At first he was offended, but thought about it for a while, then decided to take her up on her offer. A little over a year later the gentleman had lost a significant amount of weight and was grateful to Marie. He was now off of his prescription medications and felt wonderful."

Mama did the same thing to Claudia's father. Claudia and Curtis had arranged a pre-wedding activity for their friends and families to enjoy the festivities at the Bar-D Chuck Wagon, north of Durango. Claudia had just introduced me to her father moments before Mama was introduced. We were standing outside the ticket building. After the formalities of the introduction, I just about died of embarrassment when Mama tapped on the stomach of Claudia's father's and said, "You need to lose that."

Fortunately, he took it in stride. Later, Claudia told me her father knew he needed to lose weight, and he should learn from the wisdom of someone who had been around as long as she had.

After the services, our family and the Archers, visited while indulging in a buffet of chicken, baked beans, rolls, salad, and desserts provided by ladies of the church.

"Jane is planning to take the flowers to a nursing home," Pastor Bedford informed me.

"She can take the flower arrangement our cousin furnished. I was planning for the church to have the flowers we brought for the Sunday Services. But I would like to keep the vases, in memory of our mother," I stated.

"I'll remove the flowers and bring them by later," Pastor Bedford volunteered.

Back at the condo, everyone changed into their jeans and went back to work. Chris' wife, Phyllis, was sorting through old files.

"Do you want to keep these files on Jane?" Phyllis asked.

"What does it say?" I asked.

Phyllis began reading an excerpt. "Jane was kept in a drug-induced coma for three days . . ."

I assumed it was referring to a time when Jane was taken to the state hospital in Pueblo after she had been picked up by the Delta sheriff. She had been walking out to our mother's farm down the middle of the county road with her dog, Ginger, while yelling obscenities at cars that were dodging and barely missing her.

"Shred them," I said without hesitation. This was sensitive information and I did not want to be reminded of it or hear anymore.

Phyllis found another piece of paper among Mama's personal files. It was an old evaluation of job performance. Phyllis read the evaluation. "Secretarial skills are excellent. Needs to work on interpersonal skills."

"Shred that, too," I announced.

The garage was filling up quickly with things for tomorrow's sale. Caroline and Joe had brought several folding tables. Items were piling up on top of the tables as well as underneath. A grouping of other miscellaneous things was starting to line the opposite wall of the small garage.

Great headway was being made when members of the Archer family appeared. They asked if they could look at the garage sale items. I had just set out some knitting needles and fabric, which one of the ladies asked if she could buy. There were other items they wanted also. Lois and I let them have what they wanted. It would not have felt right to charge them.

The sliding glass door in the master bedroom had been left open for a shortcut to the garage. The guests were gathering in the bedroom. The quilt Thelma, Jasper's wife, had made was still on the bed under copious boxes. The quilt was made especially for Mama in payment for a piano Thelma wanted. The old upright piano had been a gift from Albert. Not that she could play, but Mama had been trying to learn at one time. In exchange for the piano, Thelma agreed to make Mama a quilt.

Thelma had died the year before. Her grown daughter recognized the quilt and asked if she could have it. Lois agreed to let her have it. Thelma's daughter sobbed with sentimental tears as the quilt was removed from the bed for her to take.

Sometime during their visit, Joe and Bernard moved the two freezers over to Jane's apartment. The Archer's finally left. Our family resumed sorting and discarding.

While taking another load of sale items to the garage, I glanced up. In the distance, a frumpy-looking person wearing a coat and big hat was seen walking with a limp coming down the sidewalk. At second glance, I realized it was Jane. I went back into the bedroom and continued working.

Lois was in the living room taking a moment to look around, pondering what to do next, when Jane entered through the garage. Smiling, Jane approached Lois. "Well, I'd say we made a pretty good team taking care of Mama."

Through the entire ordeal, Jane was yelling at her, telling her how stupid she was. They were in constant conflict. Lois stood there assimilating Jane's words. *Team* she thought. It was a BAD team, if it could be called a *team* at all.

Jane then caught Lois off guard, grabbing her and giving her a big hug, and kissed her on the mouth. Lois was repulsed and pushed her away. Laughing, Jane ambled off, calling Lois a lesbian. Lois was speechless and so furious her face turned red.

There were probably thousands of dollars' worth of church cassette tapes in the boxes remaining in the guest room, which Jane claimed.

"I want the cedar chest also," Jane stated. "It contains books and tapes, and writings by prophets."

I objected, "You can have the chest's contents, but I am claiming the chest. It is the only other big item I am getting besides Mama's old Bernina sewing machine."

I proceeded to empty the contents of the chest into several boxes, while Jane watched from our mother's brown chair. "Would you help me with these?" I asked.

"I can't. It will make me sick," Jane excused. This behavior was typical, but as much as it did not set well, I said nothing. "I would like the answering machine," Jane stated

The answering machine had not been disconnected yet. Since I was engaged in emptying the trunk. I hollered, "Don, Don." But he did not answer. He was working in the guest room where the answering machine was. I thought he could get it for her.

Jane got up slowly and started to walk out, while I was bent over the chest with my arms full. There was a sudden thud against the back of my head. Jane had taken the palm of her hand and shoved me. It hurt, but I let it go, even though Jane deserved to be smacked back. Getting into a brawl would accomplish nothing.

I had foreseen the possibility of clashing with Jane and had discussed it with Lois. We decided neither one of us should be alone with her in case she claimed we hurt her but, with everyone working in different areas, this plan slipped away. It had already been decided we would not touch her under any circumstances for fear Jane would interpret any aggression shown toward her as an attack on a *defenseless* person. The occurrence passed without notice. Jane lumbered off without saying a word.

"You can't put Mama's nice dishes in the garage sale for strangers to use!" Jane shouted at Lois. That was how she felt about everything headed for the sale, for that matter.

"Then you can take them!" Lois exclaimed to console her.

Jane was checking out the garage sale items and gave Curtis $20 for things she had collected. Ben had driven the truck over and was selecting things he wanted. Jane came back in the house and was milling around. It was getting late, and the children were hungry. Giving up on waiting for Jane to sense it was time to leave, Don spoke. "You need to leave now so we can go eat."

Jane was highly insulted and became furious. Meanwhile, Curtis had given me the $20 bill. Curtis wanted me to return her money, saying. "Jane gave this to me for things in the garage sale. Would you give it back to her?"

Unaware moments earlier Don had asked Jane to leave, I followed her as she tromped angrily out to the truck.

"Wait, Jane. Here is your $20. You can keep it."

Jane turned, looking back, and shouted, "How would you like to get thrown out of your own place?"

She got in the passenger side of the truck, locked the door, and turned her back on me. I knocked on the window and repeated, "Here take your $20 back."

Jane halfway turned around and stuck her tongue out. With that childish gesture, I returned to the garage, where Ben had been checking out our mother's old tape player stereo system and gave me some money for it. After carrying it off to the truck, they left. I went back inside. "Don, what is going on? Why is Jane saying she is being thrown out of *her own place?*"

"She perceives the condo as hers. I asked her to leave so we can go eat." It did not occur to Don or any of us that we should have invited Jane and Ben to join us. We pretty much had all of her company we could stomach. After calling Lois a lesbian, bopping me in the head, and being an all-around nuisance, we did not care to have her glaring at us through dinner.

It had been an extraordinarily emotional day. Things were somewhat under control, and it was time to call it quits. We would be getting up early for the estate sale.

At 6:30 A.M., I dragged myself out of bed. I had just started to put hot rollers in my hair and was attempting to look presentable when the first of the bargain hunters appeared. Don jumped in his clothes. As I stood at the master bathroom mirror, brushing out my hair, Don let the first person in.

The whole plan was shot from the beginning. People were not going to be allowed in the condo. The items for sale were going to be carried outside. Considering the first person was Trudy Gray, who had been an old neighbor in Farmington, Don made an exception. We had not known Trudy had gotten married and moved to a nearby town. As Don led her into the living room, Claudia and Curtis were scrambling to get dressed. Trudy was into antiques and got the pick from what was being sold. She probably got a steal. We were not concerned about haggling.

In spite of how early it was, the place was already swarming with people. Breakfast was hit or miss with whoever could steal a minute to consume a bowl of cereal.

Bill's calving season was beginning, and he had to return back to his cattle. Lois drove him to Montrose to catch a plane and would join the estate sale circus as soon as she returned.

Chris appeared at 7 o'clock to help. I caught a glimpse of Chris and Curtis carrying a mattress out to the lawn that was probably still warm. Pillows were sold still in their cases. As the estate sale progressed, Don removed the bookshelves that were bolted to the long wall in the living room and took the shelving out to the front lawn to be sold. People were carrying things off right and left. Many items that were thought doubtful to sell went like hotcakes.

I was checking on some items that remained in the small storage area at the front of the garage when Pastor Bedford appeared with the glass vases from the memorial service. Stepping over some buckets that were blocking the door into the condo, I invited Pastor Bedford in to get away from the madhouse in the garage.

"Thank you for making a special trip to bring the vases by. I really appreciate it," I expressed. "We've been through a lot lately. It might seem premature to be having a garage sale so soon after our mother's services, but under the circumstances we have to take care of things when we have the chance."

We stood in the kitchen talking. "This has sure been taxing, especially dealing with Jane. She bopped me in the head when I asked her to help." Pastor Bedford said a prayer for Jane and our situation before going on his way.

Word was out the condo would be sold. A lady, who said her name was Edith, appeared, looking for a place for her mother. Lois showed her through the rooms, while I showed the condo to one of the neighbors, who was looking for a place for her aunt.

As the estate sale rambled on, Lois stole me away for a late lunch to regroup and slowdown from the whirlwind of the past few days. "This would be a good time to close the safe deposit box," I mentioned.

"Oh, that's right. I forgot about that," said Lois.

The estate sale was winding down when we returned. The entire town must have stopped by. It was the first estate sale of the season, and the weather could not have been more perfect. Joe and Caroline took the rest of Jane's items to her storage unit, while Lois and I dropped off the receipts to James King as he had directed her to do. He would deposit the funds into the bank account when the frozen status was released.

Our exhausted group was ecstatic that it would not be necessary to stick around to continue the sale into Saturday. Don loaded Lois' share of items into our vehicle along with my share. Lois' things would be held until she could come get them or have the items shipped.

That evening, Lois, Don, Caroline, Joe and I took Jane a large box of detergent and the second key to her storage unit. We entered her apartment from the alley in through the dark kitchen. A freezer took up the majority of the kitchen floor, forcing everyone to turn sideways as we passed, groping in the dark. Jane led us to the opposite end of her small apartment, passing through a narrow room, which housed the bed in which she slept.

We stopped in the last dimly lit room, where we stood the entire time. I recognized the couch that at one time had belonged to our mother and now was where Ben slept.

Jane was very cordial and acted normal. She talked for quite a while, speaking about our mother being gone and saying she wanted to be friends. She spoke of how happy she was when my children were born. Lois was shocked at how normal she presented herself and her friendly mood. This was the face she presented to my children, who had trouble believing Jane had been as abusive as I described. As we left the crowded apartment on amiable terms, I thought Jane should be nominated for an Oscar.

Since Bill had gone back home, Lois invited Don and me to stay with her in her motel room using the spare queen-size bed. Everyone else had also gotten a motel room.

The next morning was a mass exodus with everyone on their way back home.

CHAPTER FOURTEEN

Perplexity

In the week that followed, Jane contacted the Delta newspaper, demanding a correction be printed with her name listed in our mother's obituary. She would remain on *bereavement leave* indefinitely. Lois and I went back to work the following Monday with confused feelings of being relieved the inevitable was over but wishing it had all never happened.

As executor of our mother's estate, Lois was now busy probating the will and getting our mother's affairs finalized. It was depressing for us to think we would never see our mother again. There was a big void in our lives.

Lois received an offer from Edith for the asking price to purchase the condo. James King took care of the legal technicalities of the sale and drew up a contract. Lois agreed to have the garage wall repaired, where a previous owner had cramped their wheel and left a big dent on the right side, and the vinyl floor would be replaced in the washer/dryer area where it had been torn by a previous owner. The condo would also be painted and the carpet professionally cleaned. Don and I would take care of those matters.

The worst of the ordeal was over. For Don and me, it was time to visit Don's mother who lived in a tiny northeastern town, near the Nebraska state line. Don's mother, Mabel, had been widowed twice more after Don's father died; losing William after being married over fifteen years, and again, after being married to Wayne, after a number of years. Since Curtis and Claudia were planning to move to Kentucky and didn't know if they would see Curtis' grandmother, again, they went along and were present to celebrate Mabel's eighty-sixth birthday. An evening was spent with Don's brother, Adam, a divorcee of five years. During our stay, we took a trip to Mount Rushmore in South Dakota. It was good to get away. The upcoming weekend would be spent fixing up the condo.

Don and I arrived in Delta early Friday morning of the last week in March and started working immediately. At lunchtime, Jane appeared inviting us to go out to lunch. Don was wearing his old, torn, paint-spattered jeans and was engrossed in painting. We did not want to take time to get cleaned up. Besides, there was food in the cooler we brought.

Jane was unhappy and started to leave when I remembered I had a picture for her of our mother. "Wait Jane, I have something for you." Mabel had taken a picture of her the night of Curtis and Claudia's wedding. It was not a very good picture, her blue eyes looked brown. She had a stern look on her face and was not smiling.

I held the picture out for Jane to take, but after one glance Jane did not reach for it in return. "That's not my mother!" Jane said in an angry tone.

"Take it, Don's mom had copies made especially for each of us."

"No. I don't want your rejects. You may have to put up with Don's mother but I don't." With those words she marched out in a huff.

On Saturday, the professional carpet cleaner completed that chore, while Don continued to paint, and I cleaned.

Bright and early Sunday morning, the remnants of painting and cleaning supplies were gathered. On the way out of town, Ben was observed sweeping the sidewalk around a big white church. It was an odds and ends job he had.

Our mother had been gone a little over a month. Her ashes would be disbursed in the same place as our father. Lois wanted to take care of the ashes the end of July when Bill could get away from his cattle and she had accrued more vacation time. Jane was contacted to see if she could join us at that time and afterwards have a picnic in the park. Jane responded that July was not a good time for her as it might interfere with her travel plans. When asked when would be a good time, Jane did not reply.

⚬∞⚬

"I wish we did not have to go through Mama's things so quickly. Things were tossed that we might have wanted to keep." I suggested to Lois now that it was all over and done.

"That is true," Lois responded with a fresh memory of the enormous amount of our mother's things to go through and with a bit of resentment for our mother putting us through the ordeal. "It was her own fault. She should have never let that much stuff accumulate. Mama saved the strangest things. As Lois explained it, "She kept all the seeds from every apple she ever ate."

Looking back later, Lois expressed, "I was sorry we had to do the cleanout in such a rush. I know it was hard on Jane, but it was hard on us too."

The end of April was approaching. Lois and I were reminiscing over Jane's behavior in dealing with our mother's heart attack. "I think Jane was against so many things because of the cost. We were raised to do without things and cut corners to the extreme. Jane still lives that way. She never buys new clothes. She gets them from used clothing stores," I said.

Lois and I discussed visions of what could have happened to our parents' farm had Jane taken it over. She did not have the resources to pay the taxes, insurance, or up-keep. It also would have been too much work for her.

"I shudder to think of what might have happened if Mama had not sold the farm," Lois expressed.

"Yes, that is exactly what I have been thinking." I agreed. "Jane would have moved in lock, stock and barrel and assumed ownership of everything. And then she would expect us to pay the taxes or end up losing it. I don't even want to think about it. Thank God things did not work out that way!"

⚬∞⚬

Lois wanted to finalize her plans for flying out the end of July. Since Jane did not give Lois an answer, I sent Jane an email informing her Lois could get away the end of July to take care of Mama's ashes and asked Jane if that would work for her.

Jane had no obligations that would interfere with the proposed plans. The drive to Gunnison would only take an hour and a half; however, she was reluctant to agree. Lois and I were left dangling.

Plans were being made for the event, even though Jane had not agreed to the date. The ashes would be divided into three bud vases. Each of us would take part in disbursing our third. A verse from the Bible would be selected and read.

The end of May was approaching when Jane finally responded to Lois' earlier email. "Louise and I are supposed to spread Mama's ashes. If you had made different decisions, maybe Mama would still be around." She accused Lois of keeping her share of the estate below a certain level. "You are quite a rascal, but you always were." She also accused Lois of not telling the truth.

Fireworks were set off when Jane accused Lois of lying. She was not going to let the last set of insults roll off. Jane's cynical attitude toward Lois' judgment regarding our mother's care was unwarranted. Lois responded back. "Just because you lie, doesn't mean I do. No matter how nice I am to you, you always say bad things and yell."

Jane was not going to be allowed to call the shots. She was informed plans were made to spread our mother's ashes. "Are you going to be there or not? Yes or no?"

Lois placed another call to Jane regarding our mother's ashes.

"Well, we might be able to make it," Jane replied. "I'd have to make sure Don doesn't throw me into the river. In fact, I don't want him there."

"Bill is coming with me and Don will be there," Lois stated firmly. Lois could not resist jokingly adding, "I know Don won't throw you into the river, but Bill might."

Jane went into a slow rant yelling," IT'S SUPPOSED TO BE JUST US KIDS! I was eating before you interfered with my dinner!"

"You didn't have to answer the phone! Bye," Lois said as she hung up.

Lois called me to discuss the situation. "I told Jane where we will be that day. If she refuses to show up, we could send her third of the ashes to her. We both want our men there. If she doesn't want Ben there, it's her choice," Lois expounded.

"She has not given any reason why she can't be there. If we wait another year or ten years, we will still have to deal with Jane sabotaging the plans," I replied.

CHAPTER FIFTEEN

Oregon or Bust

Per Jane's request, Lois released $1,000 from the estate for her to visit our uncle and aunts on the West Coast.

June 7, Uncle Jack called regarding a card he received from Jane. "She says she is leaving for Oregon, June 13, to come for a visit, and something about having seven days. Does that include the two days she will take to get here by bus and return?" Jack inquired.

"I don't know." I answered. "She didn't even tell me she was going."

"Ben is coming with her. How stable is Ben?"

I was afraid to answer that question as I did not know Ben's history. "I don't know him that well. I think most of his problem is that he is lazy," I responded.

"Jane says she wants to see the ocean and her cousin Karen. Karen lives in Southern California, which is 1,500 miles from us. I'm wondering how she is going to get to all these places. Is she going to take the bus, or expect us to take her?" Jack asked calmly but confused. Here again, I had no idea.

"Jane has a bus ticket to Eugene and has asked Lorie to pick her up. Who does she know in Eugene?" Jack asked. He was confused as to why Jane did not purchase a ticket to Corvallis, where Lorie lived, in the first place.

"She is bringing her dog. We don't want the dog in our house. She has Lorie worried about whether she should go out and buy groceries and how she is going to entertain them and how long she is going to be there. Lorie has been having problems with her health and is on oxygen at night. She is not used to driving very far."

Aunt Lorie was a widow in her early seventies. She had contracted polio at the age of twenty-three, which had left her with weak lungs, limited movement in a crippled left arm, and other problems associated with the disease. Aunt Lorie was a pale, white-haired, stooped, gentle lady. "Does Jane expect me to pick her up at Lorie's and drive her and Ben the 150 miles to stay with us?" Jack wondered. "And when she is ready to go home, am I expected to take her back?"

Jane's plans were so vague that Uncle Jack and Aunt Lorie were in a quandary as to what to expect.

"I am worried about Jane traveling so far on the bus. Traveling is exhausting and when Jane gets overly tired she gets *sick*," I told Uncle Jack.

"Will she do something that might cause her to get put in jail?" Jack questioned.

"It is a possibility. She has been in jail before. With Jane you never know. As long as she stays on her medications, she should be okay." I promised to see what I would find out and get back with him.

Aunt Rebecca called moments after Uncle Jack. "We are trying to figure Jane out," Rebecca started.

"Well, when you succeed, let me know," I answered lightheartedly.

She was trying to determine whether Jane was going to visit her daughter, Karen. It did not seem logical that Jane would go that far by bus, but I could not answer that question either. Jane's thinking was so far out it was impossible to second-guess her.

I called Jane to simply ask about her plans.

"Hello Jane. How are your trip plans going?" I asked.

"We are getting our things gathered up and plan to leave Monday morning. We are going to camp out and we are taking Ginger, our dog, with us."

"Oh," I responded. "So you decided to drive rather than take the bus?"

"No, we are taking the bus."

"How can you take the bus with Ginger?"

"Ginger is a special care dog, and we can take her anywhere like a Seeing Eye Dog," Jane explained.

I did not understand why she needed a special care dog but did not dwell on the point. Later, it was learned the *special care* status of their dog was given because of Ben's condition, not that it made any sense either.

"Did you know it is against the law to make fun of people with disabilities?" Jane offered.

"No, I didn't know that," I answered. "Well, it is so people can't make fun of me."

"You aren't disabled," I said in turn.

"Yes, I am because of my illness. I'm thinking about letting my hair grow and going incognito."

"How can you take all your camping things on the bus? Isn't there a limit to how much you can take with you?" I asked.

"We checked, and we can take what we need," Jane replied.

"How long are you going to be gone?"

"That's none of your business," Jane answered brashly.

"Why is it a big deal to tell me?" I asked after feeling like I had been slapped in the face.

"You heard that click on the line a few minutes ago?"

"Yes," I admitted. I had heard an unexplained break during the call.

"That was the Elks Club. They monitor my line, and I have to be careful what I say."

"Why would they be interested in anything you are doing?"

"Because I know things," Jane responded in her know-it-all frame of mind.

As soon as the call ended, I phoned Lois with major concerns about Jane's plans. "Jane is planning to take their dog, with them, and they are going to take all their camping gear on the bus. Can you image trying to haul their tent, sleeping bags, and I don't know what all besides the dog? She wouldn't answer my questions about her trip because she said the Elks were listening. What if she does something outlandish and ends up in jail in another state. I'm afraid she is going to get in major trouble. Can we do anything to stop her from making this trip? I'm worried about what might happen," I declared.

"I'll call our mental health contacts in Delta and see if they can stop her," Lois said, agreeing this trip sounded like a major fiasco. During the conversation, Lois was told as inappropriate as Jane was, she could not be stopped unless she was a danger to herself or others.

I called Uncle Jack to inform him Jane would not answer my questions about her trip, and suggested he call her. He called Jane to learn details. She was not nice to him, stating she was not going to visit any of them except Aunt Lorie because she was mad at them all.

She told Jack they all helped hasten Mama's death.

Besides having no realistic plan, Jane had a big deficit of common sense. She must have thought Aunt Lori lived in Eugene. She had no clue how far Uncle Jack was from Aunt Lori, and especially how far it was to visit our cousin Karen, in California. Jane was overly presumption, assuming her dog was welcome. Jane must have realized she was in over her head, and was angry with Uncle Jack for his legitimate questions, for which she had no answers.

Jane left for Oregon as planned, arriving in Eugene Tuesday evening. She called Aunt Lorie, announcing their arrival. They were spending the night in Eugene and would catch a bus to Corvallis the following day. Jane did not know when the bus was scheduled to arrive but would call when they got there. She learned a bus from Eugene would arrive at 1:30 that afternoon and another that evening around 6. Jane and Ben were on the 1:30 bus but could not locate Lorie's phone number and did not call until late that evening. Jane explained that someone finally helped them find the number.

When Lorie drove to the depot, she did not see anyone and drove around the block. Not knowing what to look for, as she came around the block, she caught sight of them across the street from the bus station on the court house lawn, sitting on some of their things. At first, she did not recognize them as they resembled homeless people. They were both wearing big hats. Jane was also wearing an old stained, tan-colored raincoat.

Lorie's station wagon was packed with their things. They would have to come back in the morning to pick up the remaining camping gear that was locked inside the closed bus station. Lorie got the impression they were prepared to set up camp anywhere along the way if they saw a desirable spot. She was mystified as to how they would ever have gotten back on a bus to continue their trip. Jane had also mentioned to me they were going to camp along the way if they found a nice place. I shared the same thoughts with Aunt Lori. Was she going to try to flag down any bus she saw going in the right direction? Or had she even thought about it?

Before reaching Lorie's home, a stop was made to pick up hamburgers and some items for a salad for their dinner. As Jane entered Aunt Lorie's home, she caught sight of an old radio. "That is my dad's radio. He left it here years ago," Jane announced.

Lorie was not sure what Jane was implying but was now on guard for whatever other strange things Jane might be thinking. Jane and Ben spent the night in the guest room, while the dog slept in the garage. Ginger was not allowed in the house. She smelled putrid because of a very bad infection on her side. Lorie felt for the unfortunate people on the bus who had to tolerate the horrific stench.

On Thursday morning, the remaining camping gear was retrieved from the locker at the bus station, and a side trip was made for Jane to buy dog food. That evening Mark, Lorie's only son, stopped by with his wife, Sharon, and their two grown daughters. Mark was around five feet ten with brown hair and Sharon had medium length, brown curly hair. Sharon brought food for dinner and everyone enjoyed a delicious meal. After the group finished eating the satisfying dinner, Mark expressed his pleasure, saying, "I'm full."

"You are full of satin," Jane blurted. Mark ignored Jane, letting what she said go by unacknowledged.

Jane and Ben insisted they wanted to go camping. After dinner, they decided to set up camp near the creek at the end of Lorie's property. Ginger was left in the yard while they set up their tent for the night.

Lorie was concerned for Ginger, who was whining and barking while they were gone. Ginger was part poodle and badly matted from neglect of proper grooming. Jane placed a cardboard contraption around Ginger's head to keep her from chewing her infected side. The lesion was awful, and the poor dog was attracting flies.

After the campsite was ready, Ginger joined Jane and Ben inside their tent. Jane was happy and insisted on singing and talking, keeping Ben awake. Ben went to the house to get away from her. Lorie refused to let him in, telling him, "NO! Either you both sleep inside or both outside." Ben did not like it, but Lorie did not really care what either thought. They both remained outside.

During their visit, Jane chatted incessantly, telling Lorie all kinds of things, some of which she doubted was truthful. According to Jane, Lorie should have her lungs collapsed and reinflated to solve her breathing problems. Jane could not understand why it had not been done. Lorie did not share Jane's enthusiasm for having that procedure.

Jane talked about a correspondence course she was taking in law. She thought with the course and her writing, she should be able to make enough money to live on. She was planning to go off the antipsychotic medication.

Lorie wanted to take a picture of Jane, but she refused. Once her hair had been washed, she changed her mind. She started acting silly and donned three hats at the same time. She then told Lorie she could take her picture. Lorie wanted a more sensible picture so did not take any.

There were times when Lorie said something disagreeable to Jane. Jane would react by placing her hands on her chest, saying Lorie was causing her to have a heart attack. When Lorie asked her if she had seen a doctor, Jane responded by saying she was taking care of it herself. Lorie could see through Jane's childish behavior and pitied Lois and me, since we were constantly being bombarded by Jane's bizarre behavior.

Lorie skipped church to take Jane and Ben to the bus station. They would spend the night in Eugene and begin the long trip home Monday morning. Lorie sent a short email to Jane, asking if they got home okay. The following day, there was still no word. Jane finally called Lorie. She had not responded sooner because the public library from where Jane sent her emails was closed for renovations.

Jane reported the dog got home safely; however, twice someone tried to take the dog from them. Jane was going to complain to the bus company.

Jane left one of her pillows at Lorie's and wanted it sent back. Lorie suggested she get a new one and offered to send money to cover the cost, but Jane insisted she wanted the pillow she left as it was theirs. She had no regard for imposing or the inconvenience she was causing our fragile aunt.

During the time Jane was in Oregon, Lois and I discussed the matter of Jane's diagnosis. The mental health worker who Lois had spoken to regarding Jane's trip to Oregon, had revealed Jane had multiple personality disorders. She gave a brief description of different mental illnesses and disorders. Specifically where Jane stood in the mix was not said.

We did research on the Mayo Clinic website for more clarity.

Jane displayed dysfunctional thinking from all of the personality disorder categories. Noted behaviors included distrust and suspicion of others, hostility, constantly seeking attention, unstable mood, disregard for others, desire to be in control, lying or stealing, recurring difficulties with the law, and aggressive behavior.

I knew Jane was schizophrenic. It was a term our mother had used. Schizophrenics are out of touch with reality. They have bizarre delusions and can have difficulty organizing their thoughts or connecting them logically. The disorder needs constant management. It cannot be cured but can be controlled with medication.

Jane had told me she was bipolar (manic-depressive), which causes shifts in a person's mood, energy and ability to function. The mood changes from severe highs to lows of depression.

Both schizophrenia and bipolar disorder are genetic but are not likely a result of genetics alone. There are environmental influences. Even though there were lots of references to genetic vulnerability, Jane was the only one from both sides of our family known to be mentally ill.

Lois and I were satisfied we at least had a better understanding of classifications and behaviors Jane displayed. But it would not make getting along with her any easier.

CHAPTER SIXTEEN

Ashes, Ashes, We all Fall Down

Jane was back from her trip, and so were her problems.

Lois eagerly listened to a voicemail at work from Jane, expecting to receive an answer regarding whether or not she had decided to participate in disbursing our mother's ashes. The message started out, "I really need to talk to you. I keep losing your phone numbers. Ben has been playing a game of push and shove. I don't know what my plans are for August. But I think during July, we are going camping on Grand Mesa. By August, we have a special needs camping trip, WHICH YOU ARE NOT INVITED TO. It is going to take one weekend. When you pick this up my little dearest sister, maybe you'll realize that I've been your big sister for a long time. So get back to work and call me when you have a chance."

Lois called Jane after work. She shared the content of the conversation with me.

"Jane said a couple of days ago Ben said he was going to kill her. She is going to the Veteran's Administration to get him straightened out. Ben is out of the house now, but she has planned a couple of camping trips with him this summer. She said she and Ben are staying together no matter what."

"She said she loves her little sister, but I could have learned from her when I was little instead of being so 'smarty.' She should have been the first one to marry because the Bible says so. She said Mama and Daddy didn't give you and Don permission to marry until she said it was okay, and that you and Don sat down with her to decide who Don should marry."

Lois continued. "She said when Mama cut my bangs too short when I was a kid and I cried, that was just what needed to be done, that I should have been learning from her, blah, blah, blah…"

"I laughed at her and told her all this was just stories. She said 'NO THEY AREN'T.' I told her she was making up lies, and she started yelling. I yelled at her to stop yelling. She quieted down but kept moving from one pile of hooey to the next. I listened for about fifteen minutes and didn't say a word. Some of what she said was how bad I treated Mama after she had the heart attack and I better not ever do that to her!

"Finally, she was silent. I said, 'Oh, do I get to talk now?' I had some comments earlier, but she didn't let me speak, and I forgot what they were."

We discussed managing Jane's estate. Lois was tired of dealing with Jane's nonsense. I reluctantly agreed to take it on.

Aunt Lorie informed me of a conversation she had when Jane called her. Jane was preparing to go camping. Lorie asked how her dog was doing. Jane told her Ginger was biting herself all of the time and not getting any better. The veterinary could intervene, but Jane did not want to spend $300. Jane reported she had decided not to go back to work at the same home care agency where she was employed as they were crooked.

During Jane's conversation with Aunt Lorie, Jane sang "I'm Forever Blowing Bubbles," which she also sang continuously during her visit. Several years previously, Jane assisted our aunt in finding the words. Since then, every time they talked, Jane sang it to her. Once the library's renovation was completed, Lorie was hoping Jane would go back to writing her emails rather than calling so often.

Toward the end of July, James King, who had been our mother's attorney, phoned me regarding Jane. She is dressing quite shabbily. I suggested she get some new clothes," stated James. "She said new clothes are too expensive, and she has plenty of her own clothes."

He revealed an incident that happened at church. "Jane was acting inappropriately in the choir, being loud and obnoxious, and was asked to leave. She sat in a pew temporarily and then wandered down to the children's church in the basement and sat down with the children, where she talked baby talk."

"In another incident, the police were called to the Delta Super where she was causing a disturbance and almost got arrested. They let her go when she agreed to leave peacefully," reported James. It was learned later she had been banned from going there.

"I contribute her behavior to her medications. They need to be readjusted," James stated. I doubted she was on medications.

⌦

The time had come to take care of our mother's ashes. Lois and Bill arrived in Gunnison on Friday. Don and I arrived the following morning. It was decided to enjoy the afternoon by retracing Daddy's old mail route. The mail route was a contracted route to deliver mail to the rural residents who lived on Ohio Creek. Daddy or Mama delivered mail Monday through Saturday every week for twenty-five years.

It had been decades since we had been that way. The road had been rerouted and bypassed the deadly curve where Don's high school friend had been killed in a car accident when he was nineteen.

Memories returned of the pleasant summer days when my sisters and I would take turns going on the mail route with Mama and assisted putting mail in the boxes. Mama delivered the mail to free Daddy to take tourists down the Gunnison River in a rubber life raft on morning fishing trips. He was generally booked both mornings and afternoons beginning from May into the fall.

When Mama had finished sorting the mail, she would stop by the corner supermarket before beginning the mail route. The sister whose turn it was to go with her would be given a nickel to spend on a candy bar.

The two of us who stayed home took turns washing and drying and putting away the dishes. There was always quite a stack! Mama routinely cooked full-fledged dinner, which generally included the pressure cooker and other heavy, greasy pans.

Jane did not like doing dishes, not that Lois or I relished the chore either. Her approach was to tackle the task head-on and get out of the kitchen. There was no diddle-dallying on her part. She wanted to go read.

Lois was another story. It would take her forever to decide to begin, and then she would play with the bubbles and spend hours pouring the water back and forth between the cups and other containers. The water was stone cold by the time she finished, which was minutes before Mama returned.

The mail route ended at Baldwin, an old mining town where there was a water trough. Sometimes we would stop to get a drink from a pipe that fed the trough with fresh mountain spring water. It was the best-tasting water anyone could ever find and well worth sidestepping mud that had formed from the excess water tumbling over the edge of the trough.

Upon returning, Lois and I wanted to locate the residence that was listed on our birth certificates. Lois was only three weeks old when we moved from the Cricket House to the log house our father had built in 1950.

A For Rent sign listing a phone number was posted in a window of the Cricket House. Our group circled the empty old house, looking in the windows, yearning to experience the inside.

"Let's call the number and see if it is possible to go through the house," Lois suggested. From her cell phone, Lois reached the realtor, Mrs. Atwood, who agreed to meet us at the house after church the next day.

The day was getting away. Four boxes of our mother's papers that I had brought were waiting to be sorted. Many love letters Daddy had written to Mama while he was a marine in World War II, were found. Lois wanted to keep them and stowed them away in the corner of an empty suitcase she had brought for this purpose.

Picture albums full of people we did not recognize were given to Lois for the keeping. Countless miscellaneous items and souvenirs were found that had been kept in remembrance of a time long past.

Dinnertime was approaching when we decided to take a break. We walked along Main Street, which now had an entirely different demeanor than when we were growing up. The clothing store where I had worked while attending high school was gone. The old, yellow brick school building, reminiscent of most of our schooling, was now a government services building. There were numerous other changes that had gradually taken place. It hardly resembled our hometown. Whoever said you can never go home was so right.

After enjoying a relaxing dinner, it was time to return to the motel to finish sorting the remainder of the contents from the boxes.

A beautiful Sunday morning was emerging for the long-planned event. Our mother's ashes were divided among three bud vases, which included one for Jane in case she decided to appear. The snaps from the incinerated coin purse were found at the bottom of the ashes, where the lady from the mortuary had said they would be. The snaps were removed to give Jane as proof we had received our mother's ashes.

Our group arrived at the designated spot early, maneuvering the steep drop-off from the highway to an open area by the river. The rented SUV was parked in the shade offered by a grouping of willows. Close by, a blue pickup truck was parked on the small sandy area. Ripples of the clear blue water lapped against the bank.

It was 10:45 A.M. with no sign of Jane and Ben. Lois and I shared mixed emotions about Jane's absence. Even though it made things simpler and pleasanter, she should have been there to participate.

Standing by the SUV, Bill took the Bible out from under his arm and read a carefully selected verse, followed by the release of the ashes from our respective bud vases. I handed Lois the vase that was intended for Jane and the remaining third followed. There was an unsaid mutual feeling of sanctity in releasing all of the ashes at once.

Our goal had been accomplished. Our solemn group did not linger. An early lunch was to follow with browsing through shops before meeting Mrs. Atwood at the Cricket House.

Mrs. Atwood graciously unlocked the front door and waited patiently as we inspected each room with delight. The house had been well kept. There was a unique cupboard

The Cricket House – August 2005

that opened both from the kitchen side and the dining room side. The dining room harbored a cute built-in bookcase.

A bay window was the highlight of the living room. A small isolated room inconspicuously came off the living room. I could picture the space with a baby crib and envisioned it being where I had slept.

An addition had been built to the back of the house, which included a large master bedroom and a bathroom. "Where was the original bathroom?" I asked.

"It didn't have one," replied Mrs. Atwood. "They used an outhouse. The house was built around 1880 when most people did not have indoor plumbing."

I never had quite understood why Mama said when she went to the bathroom, the whole neighborhood knew. I followed her and stood outside the door, crying, "Mama, Mama." She failed to mention the important detail that she was referring to an outdoor privy.

Lois and I were mesmerized by the old stone house and were curious as to who owned it. With Mrs. Atwood's assistance, Lois later contacted the owners. The house was built in 1879 when Colorado was still a territory. It had been inherited by a man who had inherited it from his mother, who had inherited it from her mother, who was a midwife. The ranchers would come in to town to have their babies there. After Mary passed away, it was estimated she delivered over 1,000 babies there. Lois and I were fascinated to learn we had lived in a house which had served an important role in the history of our hometown.

After the tour of the Cricket House, the events of the gathering came to a close. Lois and Bill spent the afternoon fishing, while Don and I embarked on our five-hour drive home.

CHAPTER SEVENTEEN

Going Haywire

Upon returning home, Lois found a birthday letter from Jane. Jane drew a picture that depicted Lois and me releasing our mother's ashes. One figure in the drawing said, "We are finally rid of the old Hag." The other figure said, "Too bad the old biddy didn't kick the bucket sooner!"

The letter accused Lois of being a social climber and stated all Lois was interested in was money. Jane had drawn a picture of a head with teeth eating money. "Chop, chop, yum, yum." The letter ended saying, "Our dog, Ginger, died of maggots, same as Ben's mother. Lovely way to go! Sorry for the sarcasm, learn from it."

There was a message on Lois' answering machine from Jane. She tried unsuccessfully to return the call. Lois resorted to sending an email:

I have tried to call you several times and your phone just rings and rings. In your voicemail you said Louise and I are after your money and that I was mean to Mama.

First off, I followed Mama's wishes to the letter. I don't want your money. I know you are mentally ill, but do you have to be so mean? If you want to call and talk, leave out the lies and insults. Either be civil or stay away.

Two months later, in Mid-August Jane responded to Lois' email.

One reason I can tell you these things, is because, in my opinion, you follow the money. The answering machine is not plugged in.

I hope you received your birthday card. Sorry it was late. You do not understand me, and am not certain I ever will you, either.

I am taking some people camping soon and am working toward that goal—have been for the past few weeks.

There is a lot to do. The goal is to get people well, did you hear that? I am a nurse's aide with that milieu. I always was here or in heaven and I am happy that I never had to figure some things out, even though there are a lot of things I really need to learn more about.

It is a zany world, and I don't believe much I see and certainly not a lot of what I hear.

"We buried Ginger," Jane announced in a call to me.

"What did she die from?" I asked.

"The kids in the apartment next door go by the porch and tease her, which makes her bark and jump around. Ben left the saw blade uncovered," said Jane, leaving the rest to my imagination.

Ginger was very excitable, and that hint of an explanation sounded logical with the information Aunt Lorie had supplied regarding Ginger's open lesion.

Aunt Lori had expressed to Jane she had not been able to accomplish much lately. Lori was dumbfounded with Jane's reply that made no sense whatsoever. She forwarded it to me to see if I could understand it:

> *Not getting anything done is part of the grief we feel right now. Ride it through because it is a dear and tender time to reflect on how much she meant to us all. Remember the Old Oaken Bucket? And Silver Cords among the Golden Ribbons? I like Clementine and Old Dan Tucker. The Ship of Fools seems like the good ship Lollipop compared to today on the Spaceship Beagle (which by the way is the name of a book first written in the 1960's).*

> *Anyway, I hope you know that my time is come, like the old time song, Our Time Will Come. We pursue happiness all our lives. Mama and I had a very difficult time. We now live in the age of the Water Barer. We were in the Age of the Fish. What exactly does that mean? I do not know, but I do know that the change has been very gradual and we are simply in the decennium of Jesus, or maybe it is time for a new leader such as He.*

> *These are some thoughts in profoundness that came to me when I could not see when I lost my glasses.*

Jane sounded like she was headed for the state hospital in Pueblo to me.

Upon returning from an extended weekend out of town, I was greeted by emails from Jane.

> *It has been a long time since I have heard from you. Does Don still have the hiccups? I love you both, but I will not let you take me out of circulation by your proving what is not true. Did you catch that? I understand you are trying*

still. Gemini? Love you Louise. Are you there? Calling from outer space . . . this is Jane . . . No reply . . . Trying again.

I responded to Jane's email:

We have been gone for a reunion with Don's family. I have not been ignoring you. We just got home late yesterday afternoon.

Jane emailed the following response:

I am pretty worried about Lois right now. Did the storm fly by? And there's more to come so they say.

What are you all doing these days besides being swift and coy?

Do you want the next hurricane (Katrina) to be named after you?

So more of what you handed me. Toss it up in the air, catch it, and smile for the camera. Love you much.

Jane emailed me again:

I plan to have the business "The Columbine Plan" as the basis for a future LLC.

In going forward today I am hoping to work on another project: Assisting the American Red Cross over the internet in routing relief efforts to the disaster areas. (Hurricane Katrina) Lois could have died. Are you guys in some kind of selfishness fog or something?

Have you ever read James Bond pocket novels or followed the line of such authors as Katherine Anne Porter or Willa

Cather? The Maltese Falcon, I read shortly before leaving Colorado Springs. So, think about life, not just you. And please tell Mabel, Jane is very glad Mama and she had some quality time together in spite of the rest of you; (referring to when they spent time together when coming for Curtis and Claudia's wedding). Lois sent me the remains (snaps from our mother's coin purse) due me and it made me ill.

May the force be with you is out of Star Trek?

I answered Jane's email, telling her Lois was okay; I had talked to her last night.

It was already September. Jane was requesting funds from Lois.

Lois, I am working with the Red Cross relief effort for the Delta area as chief communicator something, so can you send me $300. Fast, no strings attached and I will use the paid qualifiable bills as fast as I can. When I can I will send receipts by US Postal Service mail. The less electrical stuff, the better . . . don't you think . . . sorry for the delay.

With much love for a really sweet slick little sister.

On September 2 at 6:30 in the morning, Lois received a phone call from the Montrose Mental Health facility. Jane had been *caught* by the Delta police and taken to the hospital in Grand Junction, where she would be held for seventy-two hours until she *leveled out*. The lady who called Lois said Jane had not been taking her medications. Jane was quoting English literature and had been singing to them for the past half hour. They were trying to locate Ben.

The following day after playing telephone tag, Dr. Clayburg from the psychiatric unit reached Lois. "Jane is not cooperating. I need her history. She won't tell me which medications she had been on or anything else."

"The Montrose Mental Health facility has a file on Jane. There are records at the state hospital in Pueblo also." Lois proceeded to give him

Jane's maiden name and her two married names. He was surprised Jane was married.

"Jane has been in and out of mental health facilities most of her life. She is bipolar and has other issues," Lois offered.

"That goes along with my observations. She is displaying manic tendencies," the doctor stated.

"Why has Jane been picked up?" Lois asked.

"She was out in the middle of the highway, yelling at people as they drove by. The speed limit is sixty-five, and she was in danger of being hit," replied Dr. Clayburg.

"What will happen to her at the end of the seventy-two hours?" Lois questioned.

"Depending on how things go, she may end up in Pueblo," he replied.

Lois called me to see if I knew how to locate Ben since he was not staying at the apartment. I knew Ben had a sister named Carrie and where she might work. She would know where Ben was. The following day, Lois spoke with Carrie and learned Ben had received the message left with her husband, Herman, and that Ben had gone to Grand Junction to check on Jane.

Carrie began speaking, freely divulging information that was new to Lois, "Jane started going off the deep end when her mother died. She almost got in trouble recently at Delta Super. She was threatening the customers because she thinks everyone is out to get her. She will pound on people's doors at night. A couple of months ago in July, Jane had set up camp at a Denney's in Montrose. I went down and got her. She had been out in traffic, yelling at cars."

Carrie acknowledged she had helped Ben "rescue" Jane on numerous occasions. Carrie kept spewing more information, "When Jane kicks Ben out, he sneaks back in and sleeps on the porch to watch that she does not go out. When she cannot sleep she takes walks and sings songs. Once she was arrested for being out in the middle of the night disturbing people.

"Ben will do everything he can to keep her out of Pueblo. The last time, he did research and found that she had spinal meningitis when she was a teenager. He got this information from her records. Ben found they had her on the wrong medications, which caused her to be really violent. When she gets this way, she especially hates men. Ben had to really fight to get her out"

Ben's family was aware of Jane's history before he married her. "I sat down with Ben and asked him if he really wanted to take it on. He really does love her. Ben is exactly like his father, very kind and loving." Carrie continued, "Jane is very intelligent, and Ben has the IQ of a genius in science and math, and that is why he understands Jane. Ben had a heart problem and epilepsy. They said he would not live to be two years old. When he was a teenager he was healed at a Billy Graham Crusade. Ben went back to his doctor, and the healing was confirmed. He went into the navy after that."

"Every so often, Jane stops taking her medications because she feels she is fine and doesn't need them any longer. Her mother didn't help as she believed in healing through vitamins and nutrition."

Carrie talked about the problems they had getting Jane to take her medications. Sometimes Jane would hide them. One time when Carrie was trying to get Jane to take her pills, she bit Carrie's finger. "She bit down very hard and would not let go, the tip of my finger was hanging on by a piece of skin. I had to go to the emergency room to have it sewn back on. It took a long time to get the feeling back," Carrie reported.

Another time when Jane did not want to take her meds, she scratched Carrie's granddaughter on the back with deep scratches. There was such a commotion the neighbors called the police. Carrie talked the police into dismissing the call.

Carrie made reference to Jane removing Mama and Daddy's clothing from the storage unit. She had not yet given the clothes to charities as she had claimed were her intentions; instead she was wearing them, coming up with some very strange outfits.

During the conversation Carrie confided that Jane resented us coming to help care for our mother. We knew Jane could not take care of Mama by herself, but having to share our mother's attention was too much for her.

CHAPTER EIGHTEEN

Trust Who?

I called Carrie to inquire if Jane had been released yet. "She is still in Grand Junction," reported Carrie. "They were going to transfer her to Pueblo, but yesterday Ben talked her into cooperating. They are going to keep her there for now. She is on a new medication. The medication isn't bringing her back as soon as Ben thought it should."

"It has been five or six years since she was in Pueblo. Since Ben and Jane have been married, she has had three major events, which led to her being institutionalized, and numerous minor times," Carrie volunteered.

"It has been a hotter summer than usual, which contributes to Jane having an episode. Heat and crisis could cause Jane's medications not to work as well," Carrie told me.

Whenever Jane went outside, she wore a hat. According to Mama, too much exposure to the sun contributed to Jane getting *sick*. Whether the sun was a legitimate excuse, or not, it was already known Jane had not been taking her medications.

"Between your mother and me, we were pretty much able to keep her somewhat under control," Carrie stated.

"Ben and Jane haven't been getting along very well," I related.

"Ben would not hear of divorcing Jane. He loves her so much. He took her camping throughout the summer to help her get over her mother's death."

Carrie's version was sugarcoated and inconsistent to what I already knew. According to Jane, she was going camping, and Ben would probably go along as he liked her cooking. And why was he punching Jane if he loves her so much?

I relayed the news to Lois. Lois reacted. "Just an interesting thought—if Ben can talk her into cooperating, doesn't that mean she DOES have control over her actions?"

"That is EXACTLY what I was thinking," I replied. "That means she does have some control and chooses to be a pain in the butt. It is rare that I've seen her when she doesn't get mad. We must be a catalyst for her anger to surface."

Lois was in the process of transferring Jane's share of the estate for me to manage. Lois informed me about the call she received from Jane at 6:30 A.M. at her home "Jane said she didn't know what I'm doing with her money, but whatever it is, she said, 'I don't like it ONE BIT!' I told her I didn't care whether she liked it or not; I am following the law.

"Jane said she had been in the hospital. I told her I knew. They called me. She was surprised. I said if they hadn't gotten in touch with me and I wouldn't have found Ben, they would have taken her to Pueblo. She started yelling something about when we were kids. Then she told me I needed to get married because people in the South didn't like women of ill repute. I told her I had to go to work and hung up. Sometimes I feel guilty for hanging up on her, but what am I really supposed to do. Just keep taking her abuse?" Lois stated in disgust.

"I'm in a quandary about dealing with Jane also," I replied. "Since we have always been out there being batted around in the wind with no direction, it is difficult to know how we should respond to her.

Just as I'm beginning to think things aren't that bad and wonder if we are being too sensitive, we get freshly raked over the coals again." Lois received an email from Jane.

> *Thanks Lois, for your take charge attitude. It does me wonders of nothingness... My glasses are not ready and I don't know how much the settlement was for.*

*It really hurts that Mama did not trust you two to make
sure I received my share and that is why she and I kinda
decided this would be the best way to go.*

Our mother trusted both Lois and I, completely. Jane had nothing
to do with her decision to assign Lois or me to oversee Jane's inheritance.
Lois responded to Jane.

*Your portion has been set up according to Mama's will. It
would make me very happy if you could take control of your
share, then you wouldn't call me names. I'm sorry you were
in the hospital. They said you were in danger of getting run
over. That is why they picked you up.*

Lois was Jane's favorite scapegoat for now.

Don and I were sleeping in as usually on a Sunday morning, when
the phone rang at 7 on the dot. Don answered, it was Jane. "You're
driving in circles made me dizzy. It's against the law." Jane was referring
to the time we took her to see Mama when she was in the Delta Hospital
and he turned around in the supermarket parking lot.

The phone was turned over to me. "Mama would still be here if we
had lived in a bigger city, where she would have gotten better care. My
optometrist told me not to go there again." Jane went on talking about
losing her bills, her glasses, and her keys.

"Clear off a spot and always put those things in that place," I
suggested.

"I do, but Ben plays tricks on me and hides them. He is staying at
the shed now. I am working on a newsletter."

Jane was referring to the *Columbine Plan,* which she named the
newsletter publication she prepared and sent out to a few subscribers
every other month or so. Her publication consisted of several pages
created on a computer. She wrote derogative statements about the
mental health care system, making reference to being forced to take
medications against one's will and being kidnapped by the system and
how the system exploits unfortunate people. She made little drawings,

quotes and jokes and even included a "Questions to the Editor" section, where she answered the questions she made up. For the most part, it was a bunch of malarkey but it gave her purpose.

Jane brought up her recent hospital stay. "I got put in the hospital because Mama wasn't there to tell me not to go out and stop cars."

"You are mature enough you should not need Mama to tell you that sort of thing," I stated.

"Yeah, in years but not mentally. I need Mama to talk to me about those things. The medication they have me on is making me lose my sight. The doctor is going to cut back on the medication. I want you to invest in a stable stock in copper. It has been around for years."

I was now in charge of managing Jane's share of her inheritance and she was insisting how she wanted the funds handled.

"I am not going to invest in that stock. It is too volatile," I told her.

"Put it in bonds like Daddy and Mama had during World War II. You can get a lot of interest from bonds. Why don't you just take the money and put it in bonds and send them to me?"

She went on and on, not pausing to give me a chance to speak. I began talking at the same time. "There is no way I am going to buy bonds and send them to you." I had to get my point across then; otherwise, by the time she came up for air, I would have been led through Wonderland and back and lost track of what I wanted to say.

Jane was on the attack again. "Mama didn't trust Lois or you to handle her money. Blah, blah, blah."

I jumped right in again, knowing Jane would not stop talking. "Mama trusted Lois and me, or she would not have specifically stated in her will for us to be in charge of her estate."

Jane responded with a deflated, "Oh."

Jane started talking about the truck needing repaired and other things that needed fixed. I tried to reel her in, but she was way down the road and started talking about a lady who came over and helped her wash dishes. Jane failed to mention she paid the lady.

CHAPTER NINETEEN

Never-Ending Conflict

It was the first few days into November when Jane called my home. "Call back this evening when Louise will be here," Don told her, but she insisted on talking to him.

"I found a new will, and I'm contesting the one used. Have investments been made with any of my money?" Jane asked.

"I don't have anything to do with it." Don answered.

"If Louise has, she is breaking the law." Jane knew the funds had been invested. She had been sent a bank statement copy, which included a note listing the investments.

"Stop your breathing thing," Jane spouted. Jane claimed Don used hyperventilation and repetition techniques over the phone that could set up an irregular heart rate, which made her quite ill. "Have Louise call me back this evening."

"You can call her," Don said in return.

Don notified me at work that Jane was claiming to have found a new will. I emailed James King, Mama's attorney who setup her new will only days prior to her heart attack.

James emailed back immediately.

> *There is no other will; Jane sometimes does not have the same reality you and I have. You __should be__ investing the funds. I have seen Jane twice recently. She is not tracking very well.*

That evening, Jane phoned, throwing out insults calling me stupid, and a weasel, and then went on with a multitude of topics. "I've read books on family dynamics. The middle child causes trouble. You played me and Lois against each other, just like the book said. "While Lois and you were playing, I read books and watched Mama cook. I'm better off for you shutting me out."

"You would not play with me," I responded back.

"We played paper dolls. Mama didn't like the names you gave your children. She wanted you to name them after family members rather than popular names." Jane quickly changed topics. "The preacher should not have called the ambulance because Mama told them not to, and they should have done as she said."

I broke in, "They had already called for an ambulance before Mama said not to."

"They shouldn't have taken her without asking her," Jane claimed.

"If they had not taken her to the hospital, she would have died," I chimed back.

"That is okay. That is what Mama wanted. They were overstepping their bounds. They should have taken her home like she asked!"

There were times Jane totally defied common sense. Lois would comment saying, "You have to remember she is nuts. Not that I had forgotten, by any means, but I was making a mistake in thinking Jane could be reasoned with.

The conversation continued. "I have a tooth that fell out," Jane reported.

"The estate will pay for your dental work," I stated.

Jane suddenly got very angry. "I don't want you handling my money! I don't want you to know my business. The bill for my hospital stay was $40,000. They are billing me for $900. I am paying a small portion of it."

"The estate can pay the $900," I mentioned.

Jane flew into a rage, yelling, "ONLY DENTAL CARE CAN BE PAID FROM THE ESTATE!"

While my ears were still recovering, the topic took an abrupt change. "You should have moved closer to Mama so she could see your kids and the grandkids."

As far as I was concerned, we lived close enough. If Mama wanted to see her grandchildren and great-grandchildren more, she could have made an effort to come see them.

I received a Christmas card from Jane with a scribbled letter saying, "We have a communication gap." She claimed I kept interrupting her every time she had something important to say. She made accusations of Lois and me playing dirty tricks on her. She claimed I would not release information regarding her money, even though she had been sent bank statements every month and been told over the phone besides written documentation of the particulars of the investments.

I answered Jane's letter, saying "You are right, we have a major communication gap. Since you dominate the conversations, you cannot blame me for not having a chance to say what you want. Lois and I are not playing tricks on you. We have never done anything to make things difficult for you." I ended by saying, "Here is wishing you a much happier New Year in 2006 than 2005 was."

Lois' responsibilities for settling our mother's estate had finally been completed. Issues between Jane and Lois had simmered down tremendously.

Lois spoke to me over the phone. "Jane told me she is going to take you to the Sixth District Court if she has to. She said she is going to get her birthright back as being the oldest."

As I was sitting down to eat dinner, Jane phoned. "The will says the money is for my personal enjoyment."

"My copy does not say that," I stated.

"There are three different wills. Each of ours is different," replied Jane.

Jane went on about needing dental work and would have to go to Denver for an evaluation. She talked about "potholes" in her kitchen floor and needing new linoleum, besides the truck needing repairs.

"We need to discuss one thing at a time," I told her in an effort to get Jane focused."

"Do you remember when we were kids, and you were playing with blocks, and I knocked them all down, and you didn't know what to do?" Jane touted, trying to get her point across that she was in charge, and I could not do anything about it.

"No," I replied. Later, I recalled when I was little, it was rare when I could play with the wooden blocks, or anything else for that manner, when Jane did not take great pleasure in messing up whatever I was doing.

"You are knocking me off my throne!" bellowed Jane.

"You were never on a throne!" I retorted back. "You are not better than Lois or me!"

"I don't mean to imply I'm better," said Jane. "Being the oldest has more clout. The pecking order is all messed up now. I stayed around to take care of Mama. If you and Lois had stayed around, you would have turned out differently. I don't even know you or Lois.

"You are a crook," Jane announced out of nowhere.

Angrily I quickly replied, "I am not a crook, and you have no business calling me that!"

Evading the situation entirely, Jane said, "We need to make a trip to Gunnison to spread Mama's ashes." Jane still had not realized Lois had not sent ashes. She had possession of the snaps from the incinerated coin purse.

"I can't talk anymore. My head is going to fall off," Jane stated, not literally meaning her head was going to fall off; it was a term Mama used to say when she was tired and had a headache. With that remark, she hung up as I resumed eating my now-cold dinner.

When Don and I returned home from work one day in February, there was a series of seventeen voice messages from Jane on our answering machine. When the machine clicked off, she pushed redial and kept going, not skipping a beat. Her stammering message began:

"What a pain in the neck am I? I paid $39 of the ambulance bill. I kind of think what I want to do instead of having you take care of my finances, I'm going to pay it on credit."

"I've studied a lot of English literature and stuff, and I love you, guys. We are getting ready to go to the VA today. I've been working on the computer quite a bit, and I've been under quite a bit of stress, but that doesn't mean I'm going to fold. It just means that's the way life is outside of things, and to tell the truth, I held out just about as long as I thought I was going to."

"It's the bills from the incarceration that makes my life miserable. I love you, folks, but as long as I'm staying away from you, folks that makes me happy too. I've been on the wrong end of the stick, and I don't want to stay there! So if you think I'm proud, if you think I'm haughty, if you think I am wrong, that's okay. That's your attitude, but I've got my pride, and I'm also taking a criminal justice course, and so far, my grades have shot up to an A."

"I think I know what I'm talking about. It's a government of the people, by the people, for the people, and I'm one of the people, too."

She talked about a spaghetti dinner she put on every year to raise funds to take people camping who had been in the mental health system. The funds were also used for taking clothing and books to the state hospital in Pueblo. Jane complained about how things from our mother's estate were divided up.

"I'm sorry, Louise, but that's not the way life is. YOU'RE NOT MY BIG SISTER! As far as you are concerned, I don't even exist. You showed that when you helped with the obituary."

"You guys live the wannabe, gonna be lives, while we live the rank and poverty mess. I will tell you one thing. I bet we are a whole lot happier."

"In the process of you guys having your fun, you are hurting my feelings. Also I might mention the monies from your trip to Disneyland were supposed to be deducted from the amount that everybody got from the will."

"I don't have very much time. I'm busy paying bills, and when I'm not paying bills, I'm busy working on the newsletter, and when I'm not doing that, I'm doing something else."

"I'm signing off. Too bad I just love to talk so much. Do you want to pay my phone bill? Thank you. Goodbye."

Two days later, Jane called again. She was chatting about when she was little and said she started walking when she was eight months old.

She talked about when we lived at the Cricket House before Lois was born. But mostly, she talked about Ben's relatives, his nieces, nephews, and how cute they were and Ben's aunts and uncles and who had divorced. She mentioned she wanted to buy the apartment next door.

In the days that followed, calls routinely came from Jane. One morning at 6:15, while I was rushing around getting ready for work, Jane phoned. I was later than usual, getting up with a headache and discovering a crop of cold sores on my lips. Jane was complaining about letters she was receiving for the ambulance bill, threatening to take her to court. "Every time I get one of those letters it makes me sick, same as when I get a bank statement from you."

Jane wanted to buy the apartment next door using estate funds. "The estate money is for emergencies and supplemental expenses," I replied.

Jane got mad "I never have emergencies! Can you remember all this?"

"I need to leave soon. Write it down," I told her as a diversion to pacify her for the moment.

"I don't have a pencil, and it is dark. If I write it down, it could become a contract, and I might change my mind," she said reinforcing her irrational thinking.

I repeated, "I have to go. Goodbye." I then hung up."

I received a copy of our mother's will covered in Jane's handwriting. It was the same as my copy. A note was written in the top margin saying "If I am not happy, I reserve the right to go back to a lawyer and get this corrected."

Speaking to Jane on the phone had proven to be an inefficient mode of communication. I sent a letter. The highlights of the letter stated:

> *To save telephone time and getting off on unrelated topics,*
> *I am writing you my thoughts on taking care of your needs.*

I suggest we pay the ambulance for starters. Then get organized to get the truck fixed, and then get your floor fixed, then check on getting your teeth fixed. Or at least set up a plan.

You mentioned you wanted to go to Ben's uncle in Denver for dental work. You could save a lot of time, hassle and money by finding a dentist that is closer, who could do a good job for you.

Let's stop spinning our wheels and get organized so you can benefit from the estate.

The first anniversary of our mother's death was upon us. Her death was most devastating to Jane. Our mother was the only one Jane could always rely on to be there for her. She was a part of Jane's everyday existence, and she had been Jane's stabilizing force. The chaos caused by Jane's actions had not allowed Lois and me the peace and serenity that we were entitled to in coming to terms with the loss of our mother.

Jane phoned one evening. "I want you to invest some of the funds in a stock I like. YOU BETTER DO WHAT I'M TELLING YOU!" I had no intentions of changing the investments.

"You are giving me a heart attack, and that is okay if I die. I'll go to heaven, and I won't need the money. And you will be in the *other* place," Jane said angrily.

I refrained from saying, "If I died and you were there, I would know I was in hell."

CHAPTER TWENTY

Potentially Toothless

J ane had not been heard from in several weeks. Suddenly, she popped up like a hydrogen bomb blast, flaring with fires from hell, demanding I give her money to go to the dentist.

Jane was hysterical, yelling, making accusations, and saying I was taking away her citizenship. She would not stop yelling. I hung up. I was concerned Jane may end up back in a psychiatric unit.

When I got home from work the following day, there was a message on the answering machine to call Megan Spice, explaining she was Jane's sister-in-law and needed to talk to me about getting Jane's teeth fixed. I returned her call.

Megan began, "Jane has talked to me about needing to get a tooth fixed because she is in pain, and she wanted to know if you could help. Can you see that a dentist gets paid?"

"Yes, of course," I responded. "Jane was yelling so much she didn't make sense. I couldn't talk to her. Jane never mentioned being in pain."

"I am a dental hygienist for Neil Mitchell. Since Jane is family, he has done dental work for her at little or no charge. I am no longer working for him. Eldon and I are preparing to move soon. I don't feel Dr. Mitchell should be asked to cover Jane's dental needs. Could you possibly bring Jane to Farmington to take her to a dentist there?" NO, NO, NO! I was screaming in my head. That was totally out of the question. I would rather be shot at dawn than have to deal with Jane going into one of her inevitable stark raving mad episodes at a dentist's office. Besides it would be a major thankless imposition to transport Jane back and forth. I replied calmly, "I would have to miss work, and it would not be practical for us to go that far to get her to appointments and back home."

"There are two low-income clinics in Grand Junction, but I do not know if they would be willing to work with Jane because she is so difficult. Jane gets mad easily and goes into temper tantrums," stated Megan. "She has a high pain threshold. She doesn't want to put Novocain in her system. She also does not want any x-rays or partials."

"Jane is very bad about keeping appointments. Because of that, it may not work to have a treatment plan. I will see if Dr. Mitchell will work on one tooth at a time."

Megan made several references to Jane getting out of the hospital. I assumed she was referring to when Jane was at in the in Grand Junction in September until I realized Megan was making reference to Jane getting out several days ago. Megan began talking about strange things Jane had been doing.

"Last summer, just before she went off the deep end, she disappeared for three days in the Dodge truck. By chance, I recognized their truck parked alongside the road. The police were there talking to Jane. I stopped to see what was going on.

"Jane was wearing a pair of your dad's long johns and was in the back of the truck making a tent. She got in the truck and drove off saying, 'You can't catch me.' She stuck her tongue out at the police and drove off. She had not done anything wrong, so they could not take her in.

"Another time she was out in front of a dinner in the back of the truck, wearing your father's long johns, and waving at people. The police were there. While trying to contain her, she somehow slipped away and got in the truck. She locked the doors and rolled up the windows. She yelled at them, 'You will have to catch me first.' She stuck her tongue out at them and drove off with a smirk on her face." I was mortified to listen as Megan, kept on going.

"Around Easter, she was making some spooky comments, threatening Ben. She said 'I don't know what I will do to you. You better go stay with your sister.' Ben sleeps with one eye open. She got worse when your mother died. She said to me, 'Some day they will take me away, and I won't be coming back. Then who will take care of Ben?' It is probably a matter of time before she gets committed. Her episodes are getting more frequent than usual."

"What did she do this last time?" I asked.

"I don't know specifically. She had been threatening the neighbors. They are really afraid of her. Jane is welcome at our family events like birthday parties. She gets tired, and we take her home. When she says off the-wall-things, we just smile. She licks the sugar spoon and puts it back in. We tell her 'No you can't do that here.' She does bazaar things to get attention.

"From the clothes she has of your mom and dad, she dresses up in these weird outfits, and she always wears a hat. She looks like a character out of *Hee Haw*. She was wearing a bicycle safety helmet and carrying around a lunch box. She is very entertaining."

Ben's family was used to Jane's strange behavior and did not seem to get upset with her outlandish actions.

"Jane is planning to build a wall by the alley and wants me to go with her to get blocks. I talked my way out of it." Megan talked about several other situations before the hour-long conversation culminated.

The following day, Jane called me, going into her bashing routine. "By the way, my phone might be tapped. They think I am a danger." In her next breath, Jane lit into me, "You are a weasel. Have you heard that before? Thank you for working with the dentist to get my teeth fixed. A couple of children said I threatened to kill them, but I DID NOT! Now we have that hanging over our heads." Changing the subject, Jane abruptly said, "Megan finally got through to you."

"I was able to talk to Megan in a civilized matter. She did not yell. You should have told me you were in pain and I would have arranged to pay the dentist," I stated. The attorney had told me not to give her cash.

"I was trying to, but I was too upset. You are a shithead," Jane blurted. "You are trying to get me committed."

"I am not—"

Jane broke in. "You are in trouble with God."

"I'm not in trouble with God."

"Yes, you are," Jane retorted back. "You said you were going to take care of me. I don't want you controlling me."

"I have no intentions of controlling you," I replied, doubting if it was possible for anyone to *control* her.

"I have to hang up. I am waiting for a call regarding my blood test."

"Wait a minute I need to tell you something—"

"I already know what you are going to say. Goodbye," Jane said as she hung up.

I called Lois to let her know Jane had been in the Grand Junction psychiatric unit again. Lois had missed a call from the Montrose Mental Health, where no message was left. Lois phoned to find out why they had called. She spoke with a member of the emergency team for Delta Mental Health. Jane had actually called to receive treatment.

They were working hard to coordinate Jane's medication, and she wanted to let Lois know. "Jane is very paranoid and very, very sick," the lady revealed. "She has severe bipolar. I have been doing mental health for a long time, and Jane is THE MOST severely mentally ill person I have ever seen. She suffers with mania a lot and mostly cycles in the manic side. Jane is difficult to examine. She will get up and walk out in the middle of her appointment. When she receives a bill for as much as $5, she goes into a manic mode, and it ends up finally being written off."

The dental office called me to remind Jane of her teeth cleaning appointment. In turn, I left a phone message for Jane.

Indignantly, Jane returned the call. "I already knew about the appointment, and I don't need you to remind me. Stop talking down to me."

"I'm not talking down to you," I said. "The dental office asked me to remind you of your appointment, so I did."

Then from nowhere Jane spewed, "Your teachers passed you because you were cute."

What is she talking about? I thought as I digested the remark. I was not cute; in fact, I felt ugly until I got contact lenses and refused to let

Mama give me any more home permanents. Besides, I WAS a good student.

"All you wanted was to get boys, while I got straight A's," Jane said with her superior attitude.

"I did not chase boys. They chased me." I threw back in her face. "People don't care what grades you made in school. You don't go through life with your transcript tattooed on your forehead."

"If you won't buy the apartment next door, Frank, Ben's brother, is going to help me buy it," Jane informed.

"I will not pay money out of the estate for the apartment." I said adamantly. There were not enough funds.

"So you won't give me the money to buy it?"

"No," I said firmly. We need funds available to care for your teeth like now to resolve your pain!" I replied.

"I'm not in pain," Jane claimed.

"Megan told me you were," I said back.

"Well, I'm not, I'm putting Numbs-It on it, and I'm NOT IN PAIN! The dentist is NOT GENTLE. He is rough, and I don't like that guy. It is his fault that I lost one of my caps!" Jane exclaimed.

"How could it be his fault?" I asked.

"I paid him $100 to get it fixed. When Ben hit me in the jaw, it came apart. The dentist charges too much. Dentures would cost less."

"Dental work is expensive," I explained.

"Well, I'm not going to have the dental work done," Jane ranted.

"That is not a good decision. Your teeth will start bothering you and you will lose them," I expressed.

"I don't care. I'll just pull them out myself," Jane raved.

After pausing for a second Jane said, "I will go to the dentist if you will let me buy the apartment."

If Jane thought she was manipulating me into letting her buy the apartment, she could not have been more wrong.

❧

I received a lengthy call from Jane one evening in June. "I sent a letter to the attorney general. You will get a copy. The neighbors next door are smoking marijuana. I can smell it in my apartment, along with the fumes from the traffic. The neighbors have a grandmother and two kids living with them, all in a tiny apartment the size of mine.

"The dentist is a crook. I've known that for a long time. I've heard people in his office screaming bloody murder. I got two root canals before, but I can't take any more dental work. I prefer to have my teeth rot in my head before I will go to the dentist. I don't care to look cosmetically pure," Jane expressed.

"I gave Mama a chance to be a person at the end. I am still suffering from losing Mama. When Mama died, I helped prepare her body with oils. I closed her eyes, adjusted her jaw, and put her arms across her chest. I was there when they came in with the body bag. Hospice was doing all kinds of things to speed up Mama's death as was Caroline. I was the only one with professional experience, so I could see these things," Jane explained from her point of view.

"I made good grades to please Mama and Daddy. I don't know why the oldest always picks on the next child, but it is natural." Jane went on. "I'm known as Jane the Clown. I love life sometimes. I'm happy sometimes, and I'm sad sometimes. I'm going to live until I die. If I have a heart attack, I don't want to be hooked up to all this stuff like Mama. I would rather die. We are scrimping a lot. We don't have enough money for food."

"Doesn't Ben contribute anything?" I asked.

"He gets paid $50 a month for sweeping around the church and feeding the minister's goldfish. He spends his money on cigarettes. He does not contribute anything. I am planting radishes and they are coming up."

The copy of the letter Jane sent to the attorney general arrived the following day. It was a big misrepresentation of circumstances. She kept referring to herself as being handicapped and stated she was having legal difficulties in freeing her share of her mother's estate.

After wading through the mixed-up rhetoric, my interpretation of the letter boiled down to Jane requesting to have the money from the estate so she could buy the mortgage to the "condominium type home" occupied by her "burdensome neighbors." Along with a number of irrelevant statements and criticizing me, the letter also stated Jane was fighting a rights issue that she hoped would be taken to the Federal Supreme Court if necessary.

If whoever screened the attorney general's mail had not figured out right away the letter was written by a mentally unstable person, it was clear to see toward the end when she stated she was becoming vexed.

CHAPTER TWENTY-ONE

Hodgepodge

J ane phoned talking about the place our parents had lived in Gunnison. "Our old log house is in receivership. You should buy it. I can run a guide service out of it, and it could be used as a place where the family can go to get away. My brown car needs repairs. It keeps stalling. It is having the same problem that we paid to have fixed before, and I took it back."

"Why don't you get rid of it?" I suggested. "Now that you have Mama's car, you don't need the expense of three cars to keep up."

"NO! The car has sentimental value, and it is one that Ben can work on. Besides, it is made of metal, and people avoid hitting me because it is so sturdy it would damage their cars a lot if they run into me. It is an excellent antique.

"I need it to take homeless people to a shelter. Sometimes I meet people hanging out in the alley by the supermarket, and they need help. That is what I do—I help people." Jane felt it was her duty to assist misfortunate rejects of society with whom she related.

"Why don't you use the blue Plymouth?" I advised.

"Sometimes they have accidents in the back seat, and it gets dirty."

The people at State Mental Health did not like Jane picking up indigents and were unhappy with her for presenting herself as their advocate. She was treading into territory for which she had no business.

The following day, Jane left a series of messages on my answering machine. "I am schizophrenic because I refuse to divulge information about my clients. I wouldn't give their Medicare numbers."

The answering machine continued with Jane's messages. "The maximum dosage by law takes three or four weeks to get out of your system. It makes your muscles jerk. It is making me go blind, and my senses are going down. I got a dog three days ago. He is a big hound dog, I call Topper."

Later, by phone, she talked about other puzzling issues, which I discussed with Lois. "They are going over her medical files and will make changes under authorized circumstances, whatever that means. She is on the docket for a hearing. According to her, State Mental Health wants to incarcerate her. She said something about them filing for the police to do surveillance on her. Jane would be committed to Pueblo now, except they don't have enough beds. She wanted me to talk to Judge Green."

Lois spoke to Ben's sister, Carrie. "Other than what we had already figured out, it was learned Jane had been taken to the psychiatric unit in May because she had attacked the grandchildren of her neighbor." Attacked?

In short, the DA was petitioning to review Jane's case. She was in trouble for not staying on her medications and as a result was facing being committed. Marvin Olsen, Jane's attorney, contacted me. He was representing Jane pro bono in a civil case. "Jane has missed her appointment for medication with State Mental Health and refused to come in. She said her husband gives her the medication. She feels harassed. Does the family feel she should be committed?" asked Mr. Olsen.

I was caught totally off guard. I was not prepared to answer that question. The state hospital had turned into a revolving door for Jane. If she was committed, when she got out, Jane would revert back to her old behaviors. I should have said, "Yes and keep her there or it won't accomplish anything." I was afraid to answer in that manner; it would come back to bite me. Jane would never trust me again.

"We want what would be best for her," I responded, assuming the powers that be would obviously send her back to Pueblo to get her back on medications.

⳥⳥

I had been dealing with atrial fibrillation by staying on heart medications. I was told it was unusual for someone so young to develop atrial fibrillation, without having any factors known to instigate the condition. Perhaps being overly sensitive, in combination with being kept in a subdued emotional flux by Jane, for the past fifty-six years, had taken its toll. Occasionally, I found myself slipping into fibrillation. During an appointment with the cardiologist, my pulse was found to be at 160. He said it was like I was jogging all the time. That explained why I was so tired. The frequent blood tests to monitor blood coagulation were annoying. The blood coagulation levels had gotten out of whack. My life centered on frequent trips to the cardiologist. I decided to have the ablation procedure on my heart to hopefully remedy the condition. Lois was informed of my plans to have the procedure and I relayed the most recent conversation with Jane.

"Jane said the attorney was very promising. She thought they will stop bothering her. She sounds relatively normal and then pops up telling me when she was in Pueblo they were doing experiments on her ovaries. They put her in an MRI machine and were banging on it to torture her."

⳥⳥

A lady from Montrose Mental Health phoned Lois. She did not know what was going on with Jane because Jane had been very quiet lately. Jane had not been going there for her medications. The lady thought Jane was getting them from a private doctor or possibly through Grand Junction. Lois was satisfied with the lady's assumption that Jane was taking lithium, and Ben was seeing she kept on it. They were fooled into thinking she was on her medications.

173

I took off a week from work to recuperate from the ablation procedure in mid-August. I was not feeling too great when Jane called.

"I've been cleared," Jane stated.

"Cleared of what?" I asked.

"Of what you talked to the attorney about."

Why couldn't Jane ever come out and give a straight answer? I was not in the mood to play guessing games.

"So you don't have to worry about being sent to Pueblo. So you are taking your medications?" I asked.

"Yes, but it is none of your business. I can't talk to you about it because you and King are plaintiffs."

"Why are we plaintiffs?" I asked.

"Because you won't give me any money," Jane answered.

Wouldn't Jane be the plaintiff?

Jane continued, "You are as crazy as me. Don and Chris keep you out of trouble."

"Don doesn't follow me around keeping me out of trouble!" I exclaimed angrily.

"I didn't mean he follows you around. . ." Jane said, trying to redeem herself. I was so angry it was a wonder smoke was not rolling from my ears.

"Can you hear the guitar in the background? Ben is playing," said Jane.

I did not answer.

"Maybe we should end this conversation."

"That is a good idea. Goodbye," I said.

Jane was still talking as I hung up the receiver.

It was mid-October. I was in a bout of coughing from the bronchitis contracted from when I had a tube down my throat during the ablation procedure, taking in cold air. I was not feeling well when Jane called one evening. "We want to put in a dishwasher. Could we just set up a charge account so we can get the supplies we need to do the plumbing?"

I was leery of setting up a charge account that would give them Cart Blanche to charging things. Besides, I was wondering how a dishwasher would fit in their tiny kitchen. When reacting without enthusiasm, Jane got mad. "I will talk to you about it later because I don't want to get mad at you when you are sick."

⁂

Aunt Doris, Uncle Jack's wife, notified us of the death of our cousin Teddy Winters. Teddy was the oldest son of Abigail, our mother's deceased sister. He was my age, being overweight with diabetes and had a heart attack.

⁂

It had been an unusually long period of time since Lois or I had heard anything from Jane. I decided to call. No one answered; however, Jane had left the strangest greeting on the answering machine, which included in the greeting, "If you are not a friend, don't call back." I wondered if Jane was in trouble again and contacted Carrie, Ben's sister, who informed me Jane was not taking her medications.

"She is not ready to be hauled off yet, but she is about to go off the deep end," Carrie reported. "We've been keeping her inside and away from people to keep her out of trouble."

"Should we contact the mental health people about her not taking her meds?" I asked.

"No," replied Carrie. "It only makes it worse as they send her to Pueblo, where they keep her about six months. If she gets in trouble on her own, they take her to Grand Junction, and she gets out in about three weeks. Sometimes she snaps out of it and decides to start taking her pills on her own."

Carrie went on, "Jane calls me every other day and accuses me of something, such as stealing her writings that she creates for her newsletter or accuses my son of stealing her grocery money. Recently, she would not let Ben out of the house."

"How could she keep Ben from leaving if he wants?" I asked.

"When she is in her manic state, she is very strong, and she picks up knives and things," Carrie explained. "He had been at my house. He was going over to the apartment for something and said he would be right back. When he did not appear after a while, I went over to check on him. Jane would not let him leave. I held up my cell phone and threatened to push the button to call 911. Jane is afraid of the police, so she let him out. She can be really scary."

⚬✖⚬

The second anniversary of Mama's death was here already. The date was noted with reverence while Lois was recuperating from a horrible virus, and I was back at the cardiologist for another followup on the ablation procedure.

"I have not heard a word from Jane," I told Lois. "Carrie is supposed to notify us if Jane gets 'hauled off,' her words. The last time I left a message for Jane to call, she did not get back with me."

"I called Jane on my way home from work. She sounded pretty nutty," Lois explained. "Michael, Bill's son who is a doctor, told me there are monthly shots that can be given to alleviate people like Jane from having to take their meds every day."

⚬✖⚬

Ben called me to report Jane was being sued by a collection agency on behalf of the Grand Junction hospital. There never seemed to be a break from Jane's issues.

I sent an email to James King, explaining a credit agency was after Jane. He phoned saying "When Jane gets released from Grand Junction, I will try to talk to her."

"I wasn't aware she was in Grand Junction again!" I exclaimed. I was getting dizzy keeping up with Jane's frequent admissions.

"The police need to be reeducated about Jane," stated James. "Apparently, there are a lot of new policemen who don't know the routine in dealing with her. When Jane is downtown doing weird things, people call the police. The police usually talk to her and take her home."

That evening, I called Ben. "I just learned from James King Jane had been taken to Grand Junction again. What happened?" I inquired.

"She was involved in confrontations at the library and with the neighbors," Ben replied.

I could picture in my mind's eye Jane flying off the handle with people for some perceived injustice. "Jane needs to stay on her medications. Lois told me there is an injection Jane could have instead of taking pills."

"We are aware of an injection that is available. She would have to go to the mental health clinic or the hospital for it, and she is not good at keeping appointments. The idea is to find a solution that will work for her," explained Ben.

"If there is a solution that would work, they should have found it by now. Getting committed is no one's fault but her own!" I exclaimed.

"Jane thought if she did not pay the hospital, they would not admit her as long as she owed them money," Ben shared.

"That sounds like Jane's reasoning," I said. "But it backfired!"

⚬⚭⚬

Lois called the mental health facility to learn details about Jane's incarceration. She only learned that Grand Junction no longer had a psychiatric unit but rather what they called a stabilization center.

Jane had been released five days before calling me at 7 A.M. The medications made Jane's speech slurred. "I'm going to take a bus trip to Denver to see Aunt Hazel. I am taking my hound dog, Topper, with me. I have rights. You are trying to take away my rights," Jane slurred. I got calls saying I was surrounded by the police. Carrie and Ben were playing tricks on me. I was in a trauma center for about a month."

Aunt Hazel was married to our father's brother, Uncle Curly. She was in her nineties. I could not believe Jane was bothering her.

Then she started quoting her version of scriptures from Isaiah about taking care of other people. "Look it up," she commanded.

Jane was speaking rapidly, jumping from topic to topic and stopped abruptly. "I don't trust you. You are helping yourself to my money. I'm supposed to be number 1, and you are number 2. It isn't fair that you made yourself number 1. You are trying to take away my rights, and you can't do that!" Jane went back to talking about her trip to Denver. "I'm going to see a dentist."

I knew she was referring to Ben's uncle. "Ben's uncle is not a dentist. He is an orthodontist," I said.

"I'M GOING TO SEE HIM ANYWAY," Jane bellowed. "My gums are hurting, and it is hard for me to eat. I have arranged for Topper to ride on the bus with me and stay in the motel with me. While I'm there, I'm going to the library."

I got the impression she was going to research her rights for being the oldest.

Jane quickly calmed down. "The windshield on the truck needs replaced. I need dental work done. The glasses I got two years ago have scratches on them."

I wanted to talk about getting dental work scheduled and new glasses, but that went to the wayside. "We need eggs and cereal. While I was gone, Ben ate all my food. I have a broken foot that causes me to limp. I haven't gotten it fixed because the doctor would not do it the way I wanted." Jane was getting hoarse and ended the call.

I informed Lois of recent events concerning Jane. "She wants to take a trip back East, something about visiting a company that will publish some of her poems. She said we could go to Disneyland, so she thought she should be able to travel, also. The trip we took to Disneyland was thirteen years ago. Her entire point has nothing to do with anything."

I continued, "Jane has been complaining her mouth hurts, and she has a boil. She has a semiretired dentist, Dr. Rice. He agreed to take Jane back. She said the receptionist in his office keeps throwing her out because she says things that offend people. I told her when she goes to wait for her appointments to not say anything to anyone and get a magazine.

CHAPTER TWENTY-TWO

Moving On

The day after my birthday in June, Don and I decided to put our house on the market to alleviate caring for such a large yard. We contacted our friend Gary, who was a real estate agent, and a sign was posted in the front yard on a Monday evening. We were shocked when a serious offer was received with no negotiations on Wednesday.

"You better start packing," Gary announced. "The buyers have cash and want to move in as soon as possible."

I began preparing for a garage sale and packing while dealing with more of Jane's concerns.

Jane left a series of phone messages on the answering machine.

"I've been accepted into a poet's society!" Jane exclaimed. "I have written some poems they like." She proceeded to sing one of them.

She went on to say, "A year before Mama died, she told me she did not want me to lack for anything. Aunt Hazel is going to come out sometime around the middle of July. I need to get motel reservations for her. I've joined the Christian Science Church now. I want to forget all the bad things I've done."

Jane called me again the following day. She wanted me to pay the utility company to move a telephone utility box. She explained the utility box was in the way of the wall she was building. "I need the wall to keep the neighbors from treading on my garden," she explained.

I arranged for funds from her account to pay the expense.

Jane wrote a letter to thank me for "helping with some things that are going to make our life more pleasant." In the same letter she wrote: "What would have happened if I had trusted that I would receive the parents' property? You two would have come in and demanded your share, just as you did." She was still angry about not taking over Mama's condo. The four-page letter included a lot of other thoughts from Jane's disturbed mind, including reminding me that I was born second in line.

Lois and Bill were discussing a wedding date. Lois was very busy preparing for the sale of her home, along with a lot of furniture and house hold items.

She had been working for some time cleaning things from the upstairs/attic area of Bill's substantial brick home that had been built by his grandfather in 1934. The collection of things that should have been discarded ages ago had not been touched in decades. It was comparable to cleaning out our mother's things.

Lois was given free rein to remodel Bill's family home as she liked. She had plans for completely changing the kitchen and renovating the master bedroom to include a roomy walk-in closet.

Things were happening very quickly for us as we had to be out of our home soon with no idea of where we were going to go. Along with packing, evenings and weekends were spent house hunting. We were considering finding a temporary place until we made an offer on an existing new home.

During the spring, Lois and I had planned a vacation to Oregon to visit our aging aunts and uncles. The time of our departure was approaching quickly.

Lois called, "Well, we leave on Friday for Oregon! I got a contract on my house this past weekend. I will close August 30. Bill has been moving some of my stuff to his home."

"Isn't it funny that we have both sold our houses about the same time and are moving? The trip to Oregon isn't happening at the best time. We hadn't planned on the house selling so quickly." I replied.

Don and I just moved in the day before. With boxes remaining to be unpacked, we were preparing to leave that evening to drive to the Albuquerque airport, over two hundred miles away. We would spend the night to catch an early morning flight. Don was giving his last final for an evening class. As soon as he got home, we were leaving.

Jane called at the worst time ever. "I'm looking at buying a travel trailer. I want to live in it when I work in Denver," she announced.

"We are getting ready to leave any minute. We can talk about it next week when I get back from vacation," I told her.

After our flight, Don and I met Lois at the Portland airport and rented a car. The first evening was spent with our cousin Anita and her husband, Evan, who lived in Beaverton. Anita, who was a few years younger than Lois, resembled our mother, and looked more like her than any of us kids did, being five foot two with short, white hair and blue eyes. Evan was a big, tall man of my age, with a full head of graying hair. Anita's younger sister, Jenny, was there also. Jenny was taller than her sister, but favored her mother, Doris. Her dark hair was cut in a short, boyish style. It was great getting reacquainted with our cousins whom we had not seen in ages.

I was in college, and Jane was living at home when our parents decided it was time to take us to see our grandparents and other relatives who lived in Oregon. Lois was a junior in high school at the time. That was the last time she had seen any of them.

The next morning, our group left to visit Uncle Jack and Aunt Doris who lived in Warrenton. Aunt Rebecca and Uncle Ralph, who had taken the train all the way from Southern, California, were already there, along with Aunt Lorie, who had ridden with them from Corvallis.

Lois had been concerned that she would not know who anyone was. I described them from when I had seen them several years earlier at a family reunion in Delta. Uncle Jack, who was three years younger than our mother, was tall, good looking, and slender with dark hair that was balding on top. His wife, Aunt Doris was a charming, warm, tall lady with white hair that was cut short in the same boyish hair style as her daughter, Jenny. Aunt Rebecca had grown to be a big, tall woman. She had short curly hair and a big warm heart. Her husband Ralph, was older, maybe in his seventies. He was of average height, wore glasses and was too skinny.

Mark, Aunt Lorie's son and his wife came later, as did Victor, Aunt Abigail's youngest son, and his wife. Victor was scrawny with long hair that curled on his neck. He talked in a loud voice. His wife was chubby, with long straight dish-water-blond hair. We were delighted to see everyone.

Everyone reminisced around the dining room table. I asked what our mother, the oldest of her siblings, was like as a kid. There was silence. Uncle Jack was not around that much as he was always off working with their father. Aunt Abigail, the next sibling, had died in an automobile accident. Aunt Lorie came after Aunt Abigail and was nine years younger than Mama, followed by Aunt Rebecca, the baby of the family, who was eleven years younger.

Aunt Lorie and Aunt Rebecca were so much younger they did not remember much about Mama when they were children. After completing her elementary education at the one-room country schoolhouse in Iola, Mama had spent her high school years away from the younger children, living in Gunnison and working for her room and board. After graduating from high school, Mama went to Denver to attend a business college and work.

"Marie would always bring candy when she came back from Denver every three or four months," Rebecca recalled. "I got to know Marie more after we had children when we had more in common."

"Marie was very independent," Jack stated. "She always felt she was right, overall. I do remember something else," he added. "We were poor, you know. This neighbor kid used to tease Marie. Once he told her he didn't like her ugly dress. She told him when he started buying her clothes, he could have a say in what she wore."

Yes, that sounded like the feisty mother we knew. It was getting late. Lois, Don and I retreated to our motel and returned the following morning.

Sunday was spent with more visiting, along with venturing out to the beach. It was a cold windy, dreary day. Jenny, Lois and I removed our sandals and walked out into the Pacific waters, just enough to get our toes wet. We took a group picture of our feet. Aunt Lorie, Aunt Rebecca and Uncle Ralph did not go down to the water. Don climbed all over the rusted out hull of the Peter Iredale shipwreck, while Uncle Jack and Aunt Doris strolled in the sand.

Our group got back into our respective cars and drove to a solemn cemetery to see the graves of our grandparents. As Lois and I gazed upon their shared headstone, we felt regrets of not being around them while growing up.

Our clan stopped at a cozy restaurant for lunch, and then it was time for parting. Lois and I left with fond memories of our aunts and uncles, who were above all, warmhearted, loving people. We vowed we would return, and it would not take so long the next time.

Upon returning home and getting back into her routine, Lois phoned me. "I talked to Jane on my cell phone while driving to work this morning. She got funds by writing a check on her Advanta credit card to buy a camper trailer that she could live in when she works in Clifton. She said you wouldn't give her the money."

"She called the evening we left for our vacation, saying something about wanting to buy a camper. I told her we were getting ready to go on vacation, and I had to finish packing before Don got home. I told her we would discuss it when I got back," I explained

"Doesn't Jane realize how much interest she will be paying?" Lois said in disgust. "She is really being taken.

"I will talk to Jane about it," I told Lois. "I will have her send me her Advanta statement and will pay off the camper before she is charged any more interest. I guess Jane is serious about getting a job in Denver or Clifton, or somewhere," I added. "Whether that materializes is yet to be seen."

Jane called during my lunch hour to report the phone company had moved the utility box, and she was continuing to work on the wall. She was happy about both.

I informed Lois of Jane's call. "They are taking the trailer camping this weekend. I thought she bought it to stay in when she went to Denver to work."

"Personally, I don't care what she uses it for, just as long as she doesn't come see us!" Lois exclaimed.

"It is parked on the street. I told her there were ordinances against keeping a trailer on the street for very long. They are going to take some people camping. When I asked her about it, she said they take handicapped people around. That is what the *Columbine Plan* does. She is planning to have a bake sale to raise money.

"She mentioned she will have Dr. Rice, her dentist, contact me when they are ready to start working on her teeth. She is working or, rather, volunteering, doing something with the library board. She works an hour a day and keeps her mouth shut, and it is working out. Jane had to go to work at 1:00 o'clock. She told me I am not the only one who is busy and important."

Jane called a week later, informing me of her latest plans. "Now that the trailer is paid off, I am thinking about publishing my poetry book and building an inner stairway to the roof!" Jane exclaimed. "I am going to take a trip back East for publishing research," Jane declared. "I will buy bus tickets and charge motel, food and incidentals. Ben and my dog, Topper, will go along."

Jane had already sent the manuscript of her book, *Swinging: Poignant Poetry with Purpose*, to Redco Publishing and got it copyrighted. "I need help with your *enthusiasm*," she informed me. In other word, she wanted the publishing costs to be paid through her estate funds.

"I need a check written to Redco Publishing Company to take with me."

"I'm not going to write a check to a publishing company," I said emphatically.

"Well then, I will mortgage my house if I have to, to get the money."

Jane sent Don a birthday card with a shark on it that when opened played the music from the movie *Jaws*. He called her to thank her for the card.

"I'm having problems mortgaging the apartment because it doesn't have a thermostat, which means I can't get it insured." Jane told Don.

Later, Jane called me. "I had a bake sale yesterday to raise money for the Columbine Plan. It netted $23. I had the bake sale and didn't keep the dental appointment."

"You should have kept the dental appointment and scheduled your bake sale for another day!" I exclaimed.

"I asked the dental office what would happen if I decided not to keep my appointment. The receptionist said 'I don't want to go there.' I told her 'Well, I don't want to go there either.' I am dressing nicer."

I was glad to hear she was making an effort to dress more sensibly and hoping Jane was donating the excess clothing to make more room in her tiny apartment.

Lois and I talked about the estate paying the publication costs for Jane's book of poems. "I don't think it is a reasonable expenditure," I expressed.

"I think it will be okay. Writing poetry is Jane's passion," shared Lois.

Jane had turned into a loose cannonball with jet fuel. It would be easier to harness a snake. I told her, Lois thought the publishing fee could be paid from the estate, and so I would pay it, even though it was against my better judgment, and it was a lot of money. Then she went into how this was a lifelong goal of hers. She talked about how everyone thought her poetry was so great, and she gets these awards. She thanked me "from the bottom of her heart." I told her not to thank me, to thank Lois.

The payments were to be made in three installments. Jane was getting ready to travel to Pittsburg to meet with the people at Redco Publishing before she signed a contract. I asked her if she was taking her dog with her on the bus. She decided to leave him with a friend. I agreed that was a good idea. She said when traveling with Ginger, it took a lot of time seeing after the dog, but it was good though too as people would talk to them.

While we were on the subject of Ginger, once again, I asked her what happened to her. I thought Jane would tell me Ginger died from an infection. Before, when we talked about it she did not really give an answer. Jane said, "She died." When I asked her how, she gave me the story that she had glass cuts on her stomach. Earlier, she had told me Ben had left a saw blade out with the blade exposed. People told her she should put the dog to sleep, but she did not want to do it that way. She said watching the dog go through the dying process actually helped her deal with Mama dying. It took two and a half months for Ginger to die. She admitted that sounded strange. That sounded sick to me. I'm sure the poor dog suffered a lot.

Our fortieth wedding anniversary was coming up. We had made plans to have a quiet anniversary by going hiking in the Durango area and spending the night at a motel when we received a call from Caroline. "How would you like to have some company this weekend?" It was agreed Caroline would bring Clara and Mathew and we would all go hiking together. Joe was scheduled for a National Guard drill weekend; however, his schedule had been changed at the last minute when he learned days earlier, he was being deployed to Afghanistan, which meant he would be coming also.

I was very surprised when Curtis and Claudia appeared at my office. I was so happy to see them; tears streamed from my eyes. Chris and his family joined in, which rounded off the celebration. It was a joyous occasion to remember with all our children and their spouses and grandchildren.

Sunday morning was too quiet. The excitement had faded, and everyone was going home. I was now in the middle of Jane's publishing escapade. Jane had given me the name of a person to contact and a schedule of payments with the amounts due. I wrote a detailed email to Redco Publishing with Jane's information, asking for confirmation. After jumping through some hoops with the publishing company, the accurate figures were provided, which were different from Jane's. The cost of the publishing was taking a big chunk out of what was left for Jane.

Jane made the trip by bus accompanied by Ben. Upon arriving, she called. "We got here and are fine. We just checked in a motel."

Upon returning home, Jane called. It was a thirty-hour bus ride and they slept on the bus. Jane was very happy and kept thanking me. Jane talked about promoting her book and traveling to do book signings. She had all kinds of grandiose ideas. At the end of the conversation, she sang a song she wrote titled "Sing a Happy Song."

Jane talked about the cover of her book. She decided to draw some pictures of children swinging.

I expressed to Lois, "As long as things are going her way she is very amiable. However, she has taken us to hell and back and I can't seem to get past it."

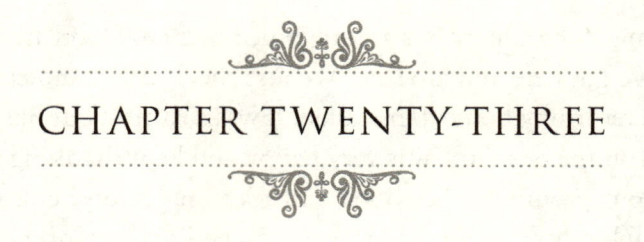

CHAPTER TWENTY-THREE

This and That

"I received a notice from the city to move the trailer, or it will be hauled off for being abandoned," Jane told me. "We got permission to keep it at the Methodist Church parking lot for now. I'm thinking about selling it. I put an ad in the newspaper. Three men came to look at it to use when they go hunting. When they came, I had been working outside, and my clothes were all raggedy. One look at me, and they scrambled for their car without even looking at the trailer. I might have you pay for a crane to put it on the roof of our apartment."

I almost broke out laughing. Where did she ever get such a cockamamie idea as that? The roof of the white-washed apartment was flat, so it made perfect sense to Jane. Her apartment faced US Highway 50. Anyone going through town could not miss seeing it. What are her plans for getting up there? I wondered. I could imagine what a scene it would be to watch Jane try to climb up a ladder and perhaps fall.

"I don't think putting the trailer on the roof is a good idea," I expressed.

"Oh, it will be okay. I'm not going to hook it up to the water or use the toilet. I am going to use it for an office. A city inspector is going to come out and talk to me about it in a few days."

She could not possibly be serious about such an absurd scheme. Surely the city had regulations prohibiting such things. With that in mind, I refrained from getting into an argument.

"I talked to Jane last night," I told Lois. They don't have the brown car any longer. They took it to a salvage yard. It was beyond repair. The reason she called was because the truck needs some work. They are having problems starting it and it needs new tires.

"I asked her if she had talked to the inspector yet about the camper. She responded, saying he talked about an ordinance that said it has to be parked a number of feet from the street, but they do not have enough property. I asked her what he said about putting it on the roof. As I expected, there is an ordinance against putting an existing structure on a roof.

"Jane talked about taking the camper to Denver when she works. She was going to keep it in a national forest, but there wasn't one close enough. Another idea was to park the trailer where it was handy, so she could go out to it when she needed rest. She could move it around every so often, but Ben would not be there to help her and she could not hook it up herself." There would never be an end to Jane's impractical schemes.

Later, Jane called to thank me for paying to have the truck fixed. She also said the reason she wanted to build the wall by the alley was to have a protected place to grow vegetables. And now she was telling me it is to keep people from encroaching on their right of way. Then she talked about when Mama had her heart attack. "Lois panicked, and that caused Mama to go back to the hospital, where the treatment hastened her death." Actually, the opposite was true.

Jane began talking about the incident she had with her first grade teacher. "Mrs. Barns spanked me because I was writing on the board. I did not hear her tell me not to, because I am deaf in this one tone."

I had always wondered what had happened, when Jane clashed with her teacher. Jane's poppy cock excuse of being deaf in one tone, had never been heard before.

Jane went on to talk about when she was in nursing school. She stayed up until 2 A.M. studying for a test at 6 A.M. Everything went blank. They took her somewhere and gave her some medications which were hallucinogenic that messed her up. She said she also had trouble giving shots to people when they did not need them.

I called Lois to chat. "I wanted to wish you and Bill a very Happy Thanksgiving. We are having Thanksgiving with Chris' family. We are spending Christmas with Caroline. Joe will be in Afghanistan by then," I informed Lois.

❦

The new year of 2008 slipped in quietly for me, while Lois was busy finalizing wedding plans. The wedding had been moved up from March to January. Don and I could not get away because of Don's teaching responsibilities and the expectation of hazardous traveling weather.

Meanwhile, Don's brother, Adam, learned he had early stages of bladder cancer. He had an operation in early January and expected to be released to go home after a week's time.

Jane sent a letter, telling us they still had the camper trailer and they would like to travel with it to come see us for business purposes to distribute some of the not-for-profit items. It would take them a while to figure out how to do that, unless we were willing to help. Her next dental appointment was in February. Ben had sold one cord of wood and she was getting ready to work on the tax records for her business, The Delta Columbine Plan. She asked how soon she could start working on glasses. They are due every two years, she wrote and she was wondering if she should wait until her teeth were repaired.

The following week Jane called. "I popped the boil in my mouth and it has gone away. The tooth in front is growing back," Jane reported.

"Teeth don't grow back!" I exclaimed.

"Yes, they do," she said, fully believing that they do.

"No, they don't," I asserted.

"According to the Christian Science Church, they will if you believe they will, and I can't talk about it not happening. I can see where my tooth is growing," insisted Jane.

"There is no way your tooth is going to grow back, no matter what you think," I reinforced.

"Yes, it will," Jane insisted. "If not in this lifetime, it will in the next.

"I am doing very well in my criminal justice course, and when I finish that I want to take a class in business administration. Lois was trying to take away my rights."

"What rights did she try to take?" I asked, wondering what she was dreaming up.

"I won't go into that now," Jane answered, evading her lie.

"You asked me when you could get new glasses. Go ahead and get them now."

"I want to wait and get my teeth fixed first. I don't want too many things going on at the same time," Jane replied.

I did not want Jane appearing at my house with the camper as she had suggested in her letter. "You cannot bring the camper to our house. There is a covenant in our subdivision against parking a trailer on the street." This was true.

"Are you going to Lois' wedding in March?" asked Jane.

"The wedding has been moved up to January and will be in about a week. We cannot go then because Don has classes to teach."

"I would like to go if I had a way of getting there," Jane hinted.

Enabling her to go was not even a remote consideration. She was not welcome. Lois and Bill had a simple wedding with thirty guests. Curtis and Claudia were present with Curtis giving Lois away.

Don and I were worried about Don's brother. Because of complications from the first surgery, he remained in the hospital and had four more surgeries. Everything that could go wrong did go wrong. He died in early March.

The third anniversary of Mama's passing came shortly before Adam died. Memories of events and struggles prior to her death and afterward were still fresh in our minds.

Don was concerned how his mother would manage without Adam, who helped her buy groceries and with many things in general. Don and I discussed asking Mabel to live with us. "No, I'll be fine here,"

Mabel answered. "I've got lots of friends, along with Wayne's kids and the people from my church. I'll get along fine."

Don and I attended Adam's memorial service. Upon arriving at Mabel house, she started talking about boxing up her things. "I need to figure out what to do with my cat."

"Where are you going?" I inquired.

"To live with you," Mabel answered, dropping a bombshell.

The move would be in May to give Mabel time to get organized. The house Mabel lived in belonged to the family farm, which her decreased husband, Wayne's, son maintained. There was nothing tying her down.

"I was surprised to hear from Jane this morning," I told Lois over the phone. "She has cancelled all of her dental appointments. The dentist wanted to build a partial. She claimed it would interfere with her chewing. She did not get the email I sent regarding Uncle Ralph having a stroke. She was having trouble at the library with the girls only allowing her a limited time on the computer. She asked, 'Who is Uncle Ralph?' I was going to tell her about Don's brother but, she hung up on me.

"We are preparing for Don's mom to come live with us. Don is leaving here around noon on Friday to go get her. He will be coming back with her and her cat Sunday."

"I hope you get along with Mabel, okay. It will be nice for the kids to get to know their great-grandmother," stated Lois.

"I get along well with Mabel, whereas, I know I would have had issues with our mother," I professed.

"Oh, by the way!" I exclaimed as I changed topics. "I haven't told you Curtis' wife, Claudia, is expecting." I was looking forward to welcoming another grandbaby into our family.

CHAPTER TWENTY-FOUR

Happy Times/Challenging Times

For a summer vacation, Don and I had plans to meet Curtis and Claudia in Philadelphia and then go on to Claudia's parents' beach house in Delaware. Caroline and her children were joining us for a family vacation.

I was sewing away happily, making a set of placemats with matching napkins to give Monica, Claudia's mother, as a thank-you for her hospitality. Jane called and kept talking using up my valuable sewing time.

Jane claimed Vonda, my high school friend, had hit her and pushed her around. She went on with more outrageous accusations.

"Vonda tries to get me in trouble," expounded Jane.

"What does Vonda do to get you in trouble?" I asked.

"I won't tell you, because you will try to do the same," Jane stated.

Jane talked about things that needed fixed on the blue Plymouth. "The plastic cover to the clutch is gone. Someone stole it. I don't really need to drive anyway. That is why I live where I do so I can walk everywhere. If Ben messes up the truck again, it can just sit. I don't want to spend any more on the truck. Don't tell your kids not to talk to me," Jane spouted next.

"My Kids can talk to whomever they want. I certainly don't tell them not to talk to you," I replied back.

I kept telling Jane I had things to do, but she kept on talking and talking. Finally the conversation ended.

The time came for our family to go on vacation to the East Coast. Every morning our group walked just under two miles from the beech house to Bethany Beach. Curtis spent time in the ocean with Claudia, who looked cute as she sported her maternity swim wear bearing her obviously pregnant tummy.

Clara and Kerry, Claudia's fourteen-year-old sister, enjoyed floundering around in the ocean on their floating devices. Don made sand castles with Mathew, while Monica looked out on the horizon watching for a school of porpoises to come by.

Caroline and I spent most of the time enjoying the beach from underneath a large umbrella. I ventured out in the ocean several times, reveling in the idea that the previous summer, my feet were in the Pacific Ocean, and this summer I was in the Atlantic.

Mathew was complaining about his leg hurting. Caroline thought perhaps it was from growing pains. She would have it checked when they got home.

❧

Upon arriving home, X-rays revealed a mass above Mathew's knee, which was diagnosed as osteosarcoma; bone cancer. The news was devastating. Caroline was trying to reach Joe by email in Afghanistan. Finally, Joe was contacted.

It was decided to take Mathew to St. Jude Children's Hospital in Memphis, which was near Lois. Hastily, Caroline made arrangements for Clara to stay with a friend. By noon the next day, she arrived in Memphis where she was met by the welcome face of her Aunt Lois.

Caroline contacted Joe's commander, requesting an early release. Lois met Joe at the airport and took him directly to the hospital. Joe was at Mathew's side when he woke up from being sedated for his first MRI.

"Jane called this morning and was going on and on. She asked if you had told me about Mathew," shared Lois. "I said yes, but I didn't offer any information. She said Mathew should be taken out of the medical system."

"We talked to Caroline last night. It is hard to explain because we knew in our hearts Mathew had cancer, but Caroline had a lump in her throat when she told us the biopsy was positive," I relayed to Lois. "Then we were blessed with Jane's call. She started rambling. I interrupted her to tell her about Mathew, which was a mistake. I think she said an insincere 'I'm sorry.' She said, 'Some children aren't meant to live. All the medical system wants is your money, and he should not be in the system.' That made me very angry! 'Sure, we're supposed to just sit back and let him die.' She said she has been in contact with Aunt Hazel, and our beliefs are very different. I said, 'They sure are!'

"I asked why she called. It was about her property tax listing. On the website, her apartment was listed under the name of some people who live in Hotchkiss. She asked if I got her package with Giuseppe. She had sent a Cracker Jack box type figure of an organ grinder with a monkey. She said there were two that we were fighting over as kids and Daddy took them away. She found them in some rags. I told her she did not need to send it to me as I was not into Giuseppe anymore.

"We had a disjointed conversation. She needs to make more money and is going to rent out the trailer. She is eating weeds. She cooks them, not to get high, but for vegetables. The neighbors keep pulling up her lilac bush and cutting back the rosebush that has been there for twenty years. They also spray her with the garden hose. She got their dog, Topper, back yesterday. He doesn't have rabies. He was in quarantine for rabies since the neighbors said he bit them. The neighbor kids make her mad by calling her by her first name. She said, 'We were taught to respect people older than us. It is disrespectful to call me by my first name.'"

"Ben has stopped slugging her so much since he is on the medication. She said something about the Old Testament saying it was okay to beat your wife. I think she was talking about where the Bible says the woman should be submissive to her husband. We got into a big argument about that. They are looking for a place for Ben to live."

"Jane wants to travel to pick up her poetry books in May. She wants me to help her sell them. When I wasn't very receptive, she said in her high mocking voice, 'I don't like poetry.' When I told her I never said that, she started singing a poem in the book. 'God, God, God, you are my friend, friend, friend.'"

"I got about the same conversation but not as long," replied Lois. Her poetry book came. I haven't had a chance to read it."

Caroline's family was assigned accommodations at the Target House that housed St Jude patients in Memphis. Mathew was inundated by more scans and doctors. Mathew was declared a candidate for a limb sparing procedure. Caroline was becoming proficient giving Mathew shots and was learning how to flush his central lines. Joe had ninety days readjustment time after his deployment, before he was required to return to his teaching position. He would be spending those ninety days caring for Mathew, while Caroline returned home to keep the home fires burning.

Lois had been through a crisis of her own. She was on her way home after shopping for a dress to wear at an upcoming wedding, when out of nowhere she felt a piercing pain on her left side. The pain gradually became more intense. After arriving home and fixing a quick dinner, Lois continued to feel strange. She took a steaming hot shower to relieve a cold chill, to no avail. She stepped out of the shower, quickly drying off, and then slipped into her warm pink nightgown to join Bill in the living room. She lay down on the couch, covering herself with two warm throws. She was still freezing cold.

Bill gently touched her forehead to find her burning up. Bill called his son, Michael. His daughter-in-law, answered. With Bill's description of fever and chills, she suspected Lois had a staph infection. Michael would come over as soon as he got home. It was comforting to have Michael, who was a doctor, nearby. His family occupied the brick house, where Bill had grown up.

Lois went to bed with a temperature of 103. When Michael arrived next door, he took one look at her and announced, "You have a staph infection. You need to go to the hospital now! Don't let it get worse, or you could be delirious by morning."

With that being said, Michael placed a phone call, arranging for Lois' arrival at the nearest hospital, which was a half hour away. Lois was placed in a curtained room and given an IV of antibiotics. Bill sat next to her bed in an easy chair while Lois slept. Her fever came down, and she was released to go home at 3 A.M. after receiving a vaccination of another antibiotic.

Lois described her experience to me. "I could have died from the staph infection. They believe the infection manifested itself in that painful spot on my side. I wonder where I could have come in contact with it."

I was grateful Lois was okay. Losing Lois would have been earth shattering.

❦

Jane phoned talking about the usual topics, telling me how she wanted the estate funds managed and demanding I get higher interest rates for the CD's; as if there were higher interest rates. She spoke at a slow rate, leaving an unnatural amount of time between each word, dragging on in a demeaning tone.

"Don't talk to me like that," I protested.

"I've been under a lot of pressure," Jane excused. "I'm mad at the guy who was supposed to fix the car. I'm going to stop driving. I've almost gotten run over twice. There are hunters out there, and farmers' crops are coming in, and they are all in a hurry. We had to go to court over the dog and pay a $250 fine. The neighbor kids were harassing him. He was tied to a sharp spike and a kid got cut on it and blamed it on the dog. The police came and got Topper and kept him in quarantine for two weeks because his rabies tags had expired. The judge told Ben he could be sentenced to a year in jail. We are looking for someone to give Topper to."

Jane sent me a copy of her poetry book; *Swinging, Poignant Poetry with Purpose.* The paperback cover was yellow, with a drawing of three happy children swinging. At first glance one would get the impression it was a children's book.

I did not care for most of the poems. Two of them looked familiar. I could not swear to it but I thought they were poems Mama had let me see many years ago. They had Mama's spirit, not Jane's. It could have been possible for Jane to include some of our mother's poems; she had been given Mama's writings.

❧

September 26, Curtis called me at work. Claudia was in labor and they were taking her to a hospital in Louisville. That afternoon Curtis and Claudia welcomed sweet baby Cole into the world. It was quite a coincidence that Chris was there. His job had required him to conduct a training session in the area.

Don and I put our heads together with Lois to plan a trip to see Mathew and Cole. Joe picked us up at the airport and we went to the Target House. They were having an early Halloween party which we attended. Joe had gotten an Elvis Presley costume for Mathew. After all, we were in Memphis. For a party with children, it sure was quiet. It was sad to see all the children who were fighting for their lives.

The next day, Lois picked up Don and me from the Target House and drove us to the farm. We admired the changes Lois had made to the home. We were introduced to one of Bill's prize young breeding bulls, which resided in a protected pasture area behind the house. The bull was used to Lois hand-feeding him tall grasses that she pulled off from her side of the fence. When Lois appeared, the two-thousand-pound bull bounded toward her for his fresh handpicked grass and to have the hide scratched behind his huge ears. Lois treated the bull like a big dog.

The next morning Lois drove Don and me to Louisville to see Curtis and Claudia and to meet the newest member of the family. We were delighted to see the new little bundle of joy. He definitely would have Claudia's blond hair and blue eyes.

❧

I received a call at work from Mabel. Jane wanted to speak with me right away. Jane was filling out some kind of form, which I later concluded was a questionnaire typically sent to perspective jurors. The form asked if she had been involved in a civil suit.

"Should I refer them to you?" asked Jane.

"What is this form?" I asked. After a jumbled-up explanation, I told her that was not necessary.

"I have to be careful how I fill this out so they won't drag me through the judicial system. The system will kidnap me if they get a chance," Jane claimed.

"That will not happen," I replied to Jane's objections.

"I would like to serve on a jury. It would be very interesting, and I could learn from it."

I could only imagine what kind of a free-for-all it would be if Jane ever got selected to be on a jury. Surely she would never squeak through the screening.

"The court could channel me through the judicial system!" Jane exclaimed.

"What do you mean by channeling you through the judicial system?" I asked.

"If you are that stupid . . ." Jane said in a condescending tone.

I was getting very peeved at Jane for assuming I should know what she was thinking in her cement-mixer mind.

Jane changed the subject. "The kids next door think it is time for the yearly ritual to send me to the nut-house. I'm trying to give away Topper, the big dog. People who are interested in taking him expect him to have all his shots and the amenities."

"I HAVE TO GET OFF THE PHONE! I HAVE TO GET OFF THE PHONE!" repeated Jane suddenly, yelling loudly.

"What is happening?" I asked.

"I HAVE TO GET OFF THE PHONE."

"Okay. Goodbye."

Mathew had successful surgery on December 1 to remove a large portion of the bone in his left leg. Caroline's family brought in the 2009

New Year together at the hospital. Caroline traded places with Joe in caring for Mathew, while Joe went back home with Clara.

❧

"I didn't go in to work today," Lois informed me. "I was attacked by a cow. I was helping Bill with a normally very docile cow that had recently given birth. Cows are very protective of their young. Bill's three-year-old grandson, Justin was next to me in the pasture. We were standing to the rear of the cow chute near her calf. The cow came out of the chute with her head down, ready to charge. I threw, Justin aside and tried to fend off the cow by kicking her nose with my foot. I missed. She threw me about ten feet. I landed on my back, partially on the side of a cattle scale. The good news is there was no fresh manure close by. Bill shooed her off. His grandson did not have a scratch on him, but I could hardly move. I rolled over on my stomach somehow and got up. Both, Justin and I were crying as I hobbled off with Bill to the truck. When we got to the house, Michael gave me some painkillers. When I called in sick, my boss said she had never had someone call in because they had been attacked by a cow."

❧

It was early April. "Jane called me yesterday and left a message on my work phone," Lois reported. "She wanted me to talk you into letting her have money to get T-shirts for her book signing. I called her back saying the cost would not be covered by book sales. This morning there was a phone message at work. She went on and on about how money isn't everything and how I threw cold water on everything when we were taking care of Mama's affairs. She never did get back to the T-shirts. The thing is that *swinging* is a reference to couples switching partners. I would not want to be wearing a T-shirt that says *swinging* on the front."

I burst out in laughter, "She apparently does not know the other connotation. Actually, back when Jane announced the name of her book, I was wondering about her title, *Swinging, Poignant Poetry with Purpose.*"

"I called Jane and reached the strangest message on her answering machine," I expressed to Lois. "She sang *Happy Days Are Here Again*, in a high-pitched voice. If you ever want to be entertained, call her number to see what she has recorded. She changes the message just about every day. When I started to leave a message, she answered, and before I could say anything, she started talking saying 'What is happening here, etc.'"

"She talked about leaving her apartment to the Forrest Service. She said Ben can live there until he dies, after that he can't. I said to her, 'You mean he can't live there after he dies?' We both laughed.

"I told her I was going to retire. All she said was GOOD, like she didn't approve of me working in the first place. Then she went on talking about her things. Did you know they had another dog?"

"No." Lois replied. "She should not have gotten a dog. She can hardly take care of herself."

"She has a hound dog named Topper and now she has another," I said. "The second dog's name is Strike, but I never heard her talk about the second dog again until she mentioned both of them died from something they ate. She said at least now she didn't have to worry about taking care of them."

I formally retired May 15, 2009, but continued to go into work just about every day for several hours and sometimes almost the entire day. My replacement would not be starting until July.

I had not heard from Jane in a while and decided to call her. The answering machine took the call as usual, which was Jane's screening device. The first part of the message was in a low mumble followed by Jane abruptly shouting ONE, TWO, THREE! I was startled and jumped. I left a message requesting my call be returned.

I called again to see if I could understand the first part of the greeting. It was undistinguishable. Perhaps she was saying, "Leave a message on the count of three."

Mathew progress was significant. The long haul for Mathew was drawing to an end. He had a two-hour session answering questions for a psychiatric study regarding the effects of stress. Mathew was asked what the saddest thing that had happened in his life was.

"The death of my great-grandma (Marie)," Mathew responded.

Caroline was amazed with his positive attitude toward his personal tribulations. We were all ecstatic and grateful, more than words could ever express, for Mathew to be going home. It was not long ago, when we did not know how his struggle with cancer would end.

CHAPTER TWENTY-FIVE

Do Not Pass Go

It was July of 2009. I received an email from Redco Publishing, reporting there were no earnings from Jane's poetry book. Rather than printing out the email and sending it to Jane, I decided to call. Ben answered the phone.

"May I speak to Jane?" I asked.

"She is not here," responded Ben. "She's in jail. They are waiting to do a psychiatric evaluation."

I was taken aback and was not sure what to say. "I was calling to let her know Redco Publishing sent an email stating there were no earnings from her book sales for the last period. I haven't heard from Jane for a while. I thought you had gone camping."

"We haven't been able to go. The truck needs new rings. It would cost between $5,000 and $7,000 to have it fixed," Ben explained.

"The truck isn't worth that much," I stated.

Ben talked about possibly selling the engine and other parts to get more money for it than trying to sell it in one piece. The truck had over two-hundred-thousand miles.

The conversation went back to Jane. "How long has Jane been in jail?"

"Since June," Ben replied.

"What was she doing?" I asked.

"She was trespassing in one of the vacant apartments in our row. She was in there fixing it up."

"For herself?" I questioned.

"I don't know. She never tells me what she is up to," Ben said.

"Do you know how long she will be there?" I questioned.

"She has a hearing the middle of August," Ben answered. "They have had some delays getting the psychiatric evaluation scheduled."

"Doesn't she know what she is doing?" I asked.

"She doesn't know what is real and what isn't. She is out of touch with reality and is not in control of her actions," Ben explained.

"Isn't she taking her medications?" I asked.

"No, she hasn't been taking her meds for two to four years. She is going to the Christian Science Church and is relying on that."

I kept grilling Ben, "Wasn't there a hearing that required Jane to stay on her medications?"

"Yes, there was a court order, but they don't know how to enforce it if she doesn't come in to get her medications. The last time when she was in the stabilization center, we learned of a new shot she could get instead of taking pills. I went to get it filled and it cost $1,000."

"Well, when you see Jane, tell her 'Hi' for me, and I hope everything works out okay." I hesitated. "Once when I was talking to your sister, Carrie, I asked her to let us know when Jane gets in trouble. She told me Jane gets in trouble with trivial things all the time, and it wasn't practical to let us know every time. So Lois and I never know what all she is up to. I guess she is always doing something strange."

"Did you hear about her getting arrested on Moth's Day?" Ben asked.

"Mother's Day?" I asked wondering if I heard Ben correctly.

"It was Mother's Day back several years before your mother moved to the condo. Jane was having delusions of moth people and computers taking over the world. She dressed up funny and took the dog with her into the church." The police were called, and they chased her all over town. Now we call Mother's Day Moth's Day."

I was very surprised to learn Jane had gone off in such a manner and wondered what other strange things Jane had done that Ben's family took in stride. For now, I was distracted from Jane's escapades as I prepared for a second trip to Oregon with Lois.

∽∞∾

Don and I flew into Portland as planned and met Lois at the baggage terminal. We picked up a rental car and were on our way to Uncle Jack and Aunt Doris's house. Uncle Jack wasn't as peppy as when we visited two years ago, but that was to be expected with his heart problems.

We had a wonderful visit, which included a stop with them at the historical Fort Clatsop the following morning. Upon bidding Uncle Jack and Aunt Doris goodbye we were on our way, stopping to see the Devil's Punch Bowl and charming Meer's Lighthouse. After spending the night at a motel, visiting Aunt Lorie was on the agenda. An aquarium visit was on the way, along with an unplanned tour of the Tillamook Cheese Factory.

Aunt Lorie welcomed us to her home. She was relying on a walker now. The affects from contracting polio when she was a young adult were causing her increased difficulty now as she was getting older. She moved slowly as we made our way to the entrance of a popular sea food restaurant for a late lunch. After lunch, we were on the road, traveling to Cousin Anita's, where we stayed the night before continuing on to spending another day visiting other sites.

The next day was dedicated to getting back home for Don and me, while Lois and Anita spent the day at the Zoo. Another memorable Oregon vacation concluded with disturbing thoughts of Jane spending her summer locked up in Jail.

A letter to Don from Jane was among the collection of mail awaiting our return. "**UNCENSORED** Inmate Mail, Delta County Jail" was stamped in bright red on the front side of the legal-sized envelope.

On the backside of the envelope, "Sign of Disapproval" was written in the center of a wavy circle, encircled by another wavy circle. Among other markings was a heart surrounded by loops. "John 3:16" was written inside the heart.

With a scrap piece of notepad paper and a pencil, Jane created her own birthday card. The front had a good drawing of a cake with candles. A note stated, "Hearing is August 14, be there please."

"Call sheriff and get me out of here!" was written at the bottom.

The date of Jane's psychiatric exam passed. In an attempt to call Jane, I was amazed to find Ben's voice was still on the answering machine. That was unusual since Jane dominated the answering machine messages. This meant Jane had not been released.

A social worker from the Human Services contacted me, asking if I knew Jane was in jail. The lady stated Jane was being sent to the State Hospital in Pueblo for stabilization. "Jane asked me to contact you to pay her utilities and taxes while she is at the hospital."

"She has plenty of money in her checking account. She should arrange to have her husband, Ben, pay them," I informed.

The social worker mentioned Jane was not on medications right now. I told her I had talked to Ben about Jane taking her medications, but he said they could not enforce it.

"It is up to a guardian to see that a court order is in place to mandate she takes her medications. A court order is only good for two years at a time," stated the social worker. The social worker seemed to think having a guardian to keep a court order in place was the solution. But Jane did not comply with court orders. "We need a long-term solution. Jane needs a guardian. We prefer to have a family member involved," stated the social worker.

"Neither I nor Lois, our other sister, can control her. We don't feel we could be responsible for her," I explained. "Ben is the logical person to be her guardian, or perhaps his sister, Carrie. She needs someone who lives in Delta who knows what she is doing. Neither Lois nor I could be her guardian because we do not live near her, and if we did, she would be too disruptive to our lives. It is a matter of self-preservation."

"I understand," replied the social worker."

I called, Ben's sister, Carrie, to ask if she knew details regarding Jane's arrest.

"Jane took an axe and broke into an apartment," reported Carrie. "We had all the papers ready to get Jane bailed out, but she refused to sign them. We wanted to get her out and back on medications before the trial. Jane insisted the apartment was hers, and she didn't do anything wrong. She was personally going to file habeas corpus. She had Ben bring her information on what to do. At the hearing on August 14, Jane was declared incompetent to stand trial and was ordered to be sent to Pueblo. Once Jane gets stabilized, she will have to face the charges."

Carrie considered Jane to be dangerous. She talked about the time Jane scratched her granddaughter on the back and the time Jane bit off the tip of her finger. They routinely got Jane off and protected her from getting into trouble. Carrie said it may have been a disservice to her; Jane had gotten away with an abundance of weird stuff.

Carrie told me some strange things. Ben had been really sick.

They suspected Jane was trying to poison him. He ate with them and got better. Once Jane baked cookies with glass in them and brought them over. They won't eat anything Jane brings them.

Carrie explained, "When Ben doesn't stay at the apartment, he goes over to the shop. It has a bathroom, but there is no bed, so he sleeps in a sleeping bag on the floor. It is hard for him as his health isn't the greatest. He has high blood pressure and heart problems contributed to by Jane. When Jane is at our house and starts getting weird, we tell her to go home and take a nap. Sometimes we tell her, 'Get out of here or we'll have to call the cops.' That is how we deal with her when she is out of control in a manic state."

Carrie talked in length about encouraging Jane to take her medications. "She takes them as long as she is being monitored. Then as soon as the monitoring stops, she stops taking them. When Jane was doing okay, your mother said she was well and didn't need to take her meds anymore. Of course, when Jane got off the drugs, she would go back into not being sane. I argued with your mother about keeping Jane on her medications, but she would not listen and hung up on me."

I had a conversation with Ben. "Jane wants me to pay the utilities, but I have a problem with that because it is not like Jane doesn't have the money. I don't want to leave Jane in a bind, but I expect her to cooperate.

"That is just it," said Ben. "She won't cooperate."

"We might want to talk to an attorney to see if you can get access to her checking account to pay her bills," I suggested.

"Jane called me about looking up her property tax back when she was using the library computers," Lois informed me "She was listed as owning another apartment. I accessed the records and found, indeed, there had been an error. It was obviously a mistake, but that may have been the reason Jane thought she was entitled to be there."

"When I have time, I will review the tax rolls to see if the records have been corrected," I replied. In the meantime I wanted to see if Marvin Olsen, Jane's legal advocate, knows of a way to pay Jane's utilities from her checking account.

While waiting for Mr. Olsen, to return my call, I began a quest to explore the Internet in search of the county tax rolls. The records showed Jane owned the apartment that she was occupying and none of the others. The site led to an image of the quit claim deed that was initiated to give ownership of the apartment to Jane. It was dated September 11, 1992 and showed transfer of the property from Jeff Ramsey to Jane, for the consideration of LOVE AND AFFECTION.

I had been curious about who Jeff was when Jane occasionally brought up his name. Jane had told me they wanted to get married but, Mama would not let them. Jane would have been in her forties. It was not as if she was underage. I found records saying he died in January of 2000.

While I was researching, Marvin Olsen returned my call. "Are you still Jane Jenson's advocate?" I asked.

"I'm not sure. I have not received anything from the courts lately. I received a call from Human Services about trying to get a family member to be her guardian to see that her bills got paid. I am aware Jane has been apprehended," he informed.

"Jane is a difficult case," he began. "She is always getting into confrontations with people, who should just ignore her, but she gets into spats with strangers who overreact to her antisocial behavior and they call the cops."

I had heard that dialog before. He continued talking about Jane doing annoying things and explaining her behavior was not a crime.

"I acted as her advocate in court some time back. I was able to persuade the judge that Jane was harmless, and her intentions were not criminal. Jane said she was alright and she didn't want to take the medication. Jane told both the judge and me just how the cow ate the cabbage. The judge let it go and did not force her into a compulsory treatment program. Jane does just about anything she wants, and sometimes her actions are treated as a crime. She is always going to get herself diagnosed as being someone who needs to be on stabilizing medication."

It was clear to me he had no idea why she had been arrested. "With this last incident, I could see why they have her in jail," I remarked.

"What was she accused of?" asked Mr. Olsen.

"Jane has the idea she is the manager or owns another one of those apartments in that row of apartments. She broke into it with an axe."

"That is a serious offense. Maybe she is not capable of knowing right from wrong, or she was hallucinating," Mr. Olsen suggested. "Jane is very self-righteous about things. She thinks she can tell anybody how things should be and then blames the judge, me, and the whole world. She thinks everybody is wrong in their judgment, and she is perfectly right, but she is very wrong."

"The reason I contacted you was to see if the court could allow for Jane's bills to be paid from her checking account," I stated.

"It isn't that simple. It has to happen through due process, and a guardian or conservator has to be assigned for that purpose, but no one seems to want to do that because it would create tense relations. Since Jane won't stay on her medications, she needs to be committed. A guardian or conservator could have her committed," he explained.

At least the court had her committed this time, but Lois and I had our doubts she would ever stay on her medications and stay out of trouble.

I was quite surprised to receive a collect call from Jane, who was still at the Delta County Jail. She had just talked to Ben, who had given her my phone number.

"I was fixing up the apartment. I am the apartment manager under Sunny Side something, something. I told Uncle Jack I was fixing up apartments. Have you talked to him lately?" Jane expounded.

"Yes," I answered. "I don't think he said anything about you fixing up apartments."

"Uncle Jack is more out for himself. Did you know Aunt Rebecca has an infection in her knee from the replacement?" Jane asked.

"Yes, I knew that," I answered. Jack had mentioned it during our visit.

Our Uncle Ralph had had a serious stroke before Christmas. He was in a wheelchair. Jane began to talk about him.

"Uncle Ralph could get better and manage a Baskin Robins like this guy I used to know who had a stroke. I helped him get his job," Jane bragged.

"Uncle Ralph could never manage a Baskin Robins, not that he would want to," I replied. Jane obviously did not realize he could not speak and had to have people lift him.

Jane got angry. "You shouldn't say he couldn't do anything because that sends out negative thoughts."

"Are you on medications yet?" I asked.

"Yes, I'm on speed and marijuana. I'm swifter than you are. I am the hare. You are the tortoise," Jane announced.

Bringing our conversation back in line, I remarked, "A lady from Human Services called and said you are being transferred to Pueblo to get stabilized."

"I can get stabilized faster at home. They won't take me because I don't have enough money. The social worker had me sign for Ben to get $300. They put me in manacles when I am let out of my cell to go to the sunroom. I need to get out of here. Call the sheriff and put bail up for me to be released so I can go to church," Jane commanded.

"Carrie and Ben have already made arrangements for your bail, but—"

The instant I mentioned Carrie's name, Jane burst out shouting, "CARRIE IS A LIAR, AND SO IS BEN! She has been trying to get me confined! YOU BETTER STAND UP FOR YOUR SISTER FOR A CHANGE!" Jane yelled hatefully.

I hung up. My heart was pounding as if I was being chased by an eight-hundred-pound gorilla. Jane tried calling back. I let it go to the answering machine. After several minutes my heart was still pounding. Jane's startling roar had caused my heart and blood pressure to go wild. I wrote a letter to let Jane know her actions were not acceptable:

As you can see I have enclosed some paper and envelopes. I will not accept any more collect calls from you, so stop calling. If you want to tell me something, send a letter.

Whenever I do talk to you, you are not allowed to yell. If you do yell, that is the end of the conversation; period.

I wanted to tell you when we talked previously that I spoke to the lady from Human Services. She said you wanted me to pay your utility bills and taxes. There is no need for me to pay those expenses. You have enough of your own money. Make the same arrangements you have in the past for paying your bills for when you have been incarcerated.

Several days later I received Jane's response, which was written on the back side of my letter:

I can hardly believe you, Louise. If I had acted, and by chance did, toward you in the manner you have in this letter, let alone every conversation we have, when Mama was around, I would have been severely verbally reprimanded.

Please allow me, via you to reach Lois. Does she know? How did you learn? I have been here doing hard labor.

Send care package, including street clothes so I may stand trial. By law it is required. Do you believe me or misinformed liars?

Tell Don and all your progeny I'd like to hear from them despite wedges placed by Mama. Are we going to lose the unsold Redco books for Redco while you "play games?"

Jane's response was typical. She could do no wrong, and I was the bad guy. It was unheard of for me to set boundaries.

"Jane wants us to send a 'care package.' Do you have any clothes in good condition you aren't wearing that might fit her?" I asked Lois.

"I don't know what size she wears," replied Lois" Neither of us knew.

I contacted Ben. "Jane needs some clothes to wear at her trial. Could you take her some?"

"I'm working on gathering up some clothes," said Ben. "There are piles of clothes stacked everywhere. It is a matter of figuring out what will go together. As far as the trial goes, people do stand trial in their orange overalls."

I had not envisioned Jane wearing orange prison uniforms and manacles. The image was disturbing.

"Doesn't she have to get stabilized at Pueblo before she faces trial?" I asked Ben.

"Jane is mixed up. She is preparing her case for a jury trial," he replied. Jane could not possibly be serious about representing herself. It would be a disaster.

"What is going on with the truck?" I asked."

"It is just sitting at the repair shop, and they are waiting for me to tell them what to do."

"Are you receiving VA benefits?" I asked. I knew he had little money of his own.

"I have not applied for them yet," he responded.

I was treading in an area that was none of my business, but I told Ben he needed to apply as he was entitled to them.

"Is Jane still in the Delta jail?" I asked.

"I haven't heard," he replied.

Lois spoke to the jailer, asking why Jane had not yet been transferred to Pueblo, where she could start getting help. They were waiting for a space to open up. The charges were trespassing and criminal mischief.

I called Ben to inform him Jane was still in the Delta jail. I mentioned Jane wanted me to bail her out. Of course, I had no intentions of doing so.

"It is a consideration of what kind of trouble she would be in if she was out wandering around on the streets," replied Ben. "She is always getting into confrontations with people. Sometimes they keep her in a separate area of the jail in a protective area, away from the general population. It depends on how she is behaving."

Many months later in a conversation with Jane, I was told about her jail experience.

"The jailers have some commodities they sell, and so I bought some colored pencils and paper, and I was doing a lot of drawing to stay occupied. I was waking up about three o'clock in the morning, yelling and screaming and usually singing. It made a lot of sense to me, but other people didn't like that because they could hear me, and they kept complaining. Then I stopped doing that. I was considered getting better.

"They started me out in an isolation cell. Then they put me in a cell that had room for more people, only they didn't have anyone in with me for a while. I had a television set and a shower. I was on good behavior. They had me in with two hardened criminals at the last, and we played Monopoly together.

"You had to clean your cell completely in the morning before they would let you do anything else. They come in with mops and we scrubbed the floors, and then we scrubbed the walls and we made sure the bed was clean and all sorts of things like that. They would come in with changes of clothes. I was wetting my pants.

"I found out my bail was only $100, but Ben wouldn't bring up the bail. Ben won't stand behind me. He lets me get in trouble and just watches. He can't give me good advice because he is stupid. He got D's in school."

Lois contacted an official at the Montrose Mental Health Emergency Services. Lois told her she was concerned about Jane being in jail so long, and she was contemplating seeing an attorney.

Jane's file was located. "We are aware of recent events. You are right. She has been in jail a long time. I am going to contact the jailer and try to get some medications to her."

In mid-September, I received a letter from Jane. It was mailed from Pueblo. I talked to Lois regarding what had been written. "In her letter she wrote 'I am to be evaluated for things that have already been proven. Please stop thinking I am crazy. I am not and have not been for a long time, and I think you all know that.' Well, I don't know that."

Lois replied, "I finally talked to Bea at the Delta jail. She took Jane to Pueblo September 16. The mental health people went by to see Jane. She refused to take her medications when she was in jail."

CHAPTER TWENTY-SIX

Certified Nuts

It was the third week of October. Lois was concerned that it had been especially rainy. Bill had not been able to get the last cutting of hay out of the fields and frost was expected soon, which would ruin the grass for hay.

"Ben called last night," I informed Lois. "He said the police turned over the ax to him. He thought the DA was dropping charges since they were not keeping the evidence. Jane had been going in the apartment before when it had been left unlocked. This last time it was locked, and that is why she used the axe. The neighbors called the police."

All my children and grandchildren spent Thanksgiving with us. Christmas was quickly approaching. I spoke to Lois regarding the latest encounters with Jane. "Jane has called me about three times recently. She sounded drunk. She is sensitive to the medications and the doctor has her on a new one. She is still planning to be her own counselor and is going to claim habeas corpus, which means she is claiming to be innocent."

"I'm getting together some clothes for Jane," Lois replied. "The sweater is roomy, and the pants are stretchy. I'm pretty sure the shoes will fit."

❧

Christmas was only three days away when I phoned Lois. "Jane called this afternoon. She is still pretty mixed up. She has a hearing in February to discuss her medications. She said she is incompetent to stand trial because she gets upset when they say bad things about her. They could keep her five to eighteen years. She knows that because she has been arrested for trespassing before. She has to eat with these big spoons because she is on a unit for the criminally insane."

"I had no idea Jane was in these circumstances," Lois expressed.

With the arrival of the 2010 New Year, Jane ceased to be heard from. I felt a need to contact Jane to make sure she was okay. After some detective work, it was learned Jane had been moved to a geriatric ward in a different building. Jane sounded drugged and her speech was difficult to understand.

"How are you doing?" I asked.

"I'm doing okay. I've got new glasses now. They are thinking about operating on my foot. They are taking a portion of my money out for my medicine each time. I'm going to have to take it."

"That will help you stay more stable. I was wondering how the clothes are fitting that Lois sent," I stated.

"They are fitting okay. They are just a little bit big, but I like to wear my clothes loose, so that is no big deal. I tried them on once. I want to wear them February 10 to a meeting. I do not want to get them dirty before that."

"What is the meeting for?" I asked.

"February 10, for drug reclaiming. That is what they are keeping me here on is the fact that I'm not making sense when they talk to me."

Drug reclaiming, I pondered. Is that Jane's terminology? "The last time I talked to you, you said something about the Five Times Rule. What is that?" I asked.

"Oh, they have a rule here that's part of old State law. If you've been in here over five times, you're considered incorrigible. People in my category can be on the streets, or their places would be too full. It is called certification. Have you heard of certified nuts? That's what I call it, certified nuts. That is what I am. So when they have the trial, I'll try to behave as best I can," declared Jane. "When I get out, will you come help me box up extra clothes?" I indicated I would try to help.

"If they say I'm up for trial, I will be sent back to Delta. The trial lawyer said it is not going to be nearly as bad as I think."

It was a big relief to hear Jane mention an attorney. Her mental health advocates insisted she have legal representation by a lawyer.

Jane started talking about the apartments in Delta. "There are two units at the end of that row that are under social services. I would like to find a way to start placing people from mental health there and me receive their rent. They are not owned by anybody. I can use the rent money to fix up their places.

"I'm trying to figure out a way to make a living. I could have one of those houses to rent and watch over. That house needs to be fixed up. Would you and Don help me, if I can get enough money gathered up to do it?"

"I don't know. I couldn't say right now. We are really busy taking care of Don's mother," I said, evading Jane's request. The entire idea sounded farfetched.

Jane was declared competent to stand trial. She wanted me to contact Dr. Rice, the last dentist who had agreed to work on her teeth and see if he would take her back.

⚬✲⚬

Ben phoned on February 19. "Jane arrived in Delta last evening. She is being detained at the county Jail for now until she sees the judge next week. I'll let you know what happens," Ben affirmed.

The evening of Thursday, February 25, I received a call from Jane. "I have the pants on that Lois sent. It is the only decent thing I have to wear right now. I'm planning on going to church Sunday."

"Tell me what happened yesterday," I commanded.

"They put me home on my own recognizance. Today Ben and I went downtown, and I went to the bank and nothing bad happened. I didn't expect it to, and I will be taking pills for the rest of my life, probably. I am on Zyprexa. It is bad for people with heart disease, so I don't know how this is going to work out for me. It may shorten my life."

"You don't have heart problems though, do you?" I asked.

"Yes, I do, a little bit."

"I didn't know that. What kind of heart problems, do you have?"

"Angina," answered Jane.

"Oh," I responded.

"You don't believe me do you?"

"Sure I do. You hadn't said anything."

"I didn't want you to know. Well, I had an, ah, ever since, ah, I was at . . . I don't want to go over it now, it is nobody's business but mine. I found out about it. I just wanted you to know. Okay?"

"I'm having to sign up for Medicare B and C, and so then they can have somebody come in my home and help me clean up the mess for free. I need to get off the phone. I'm expecting a call," Jane announced.

"First tell me, was it a jury trial?"

"No, it was just before a judge, and I was in a separate room completely. I was dressed in prison fatigues. I had to sign that I wouldn't drink, and I wouldn't use firearms for the next three months."

Later, I learned Jane's case was a hearing to set a date for the trial.

I called Lois to let her know Jane was home. "Apparently, Jane has resigned herself to staying on her medications," I stated.

"But she is going back to that church!" Lois exclaimed. "They may get her off her meds."

I called Jane to discuss loose ends. "Hi, Jane. I tried to call Dr. Rice's dental office, but it was a Friday, and he wasn't there. And then I decided to wait to see what was going on with you. I will—"

"I'm getting ready to go to the post office. Just get in touch with Dr. Rice. Tell him to call me if I don't call him."

"I won't tell him that. It is your responsibility to call him," I replied.

A pleasant-sounding lady's voice answered the phone at Dr. Rice's office. There was an instant coolness upon informing the lady I was calling on behalf of Jane Jenson.

"Jane wasn't happy with us and hasn't been here for a while. She is an inactive patient. I will ask if he will take her and call you back."

Moments later the receptionist phoned. "Dr. Rice is not accepting new patients," she said curtly. The rejection was not surprising.

I phoned Jane after allowing time for her to return from errands.

"Dr. Rice isn't accepting new patients," I stated.

⁂

Another year had passed since Mama's death. It was hard to believe it had been five years. We always knew it would be tough managing Jane when Mama was gone, but it was immensely worse than Lois and I had ever imagined. Soon after the anniversary of Mama's death we lost Don's mom. Mabel died at the life care center, the evening of March 8, ten days short of her ninety-first birthday. It was not until after her death that I had become aware of her role as a stenographer during the Nuremberg Trials in Germany, after World War II. If I had been aware of her experience sooner, I would have been compelled to ask her general questions; however, after more consideration, I am sure the horrors and atrocities she was exposed to were better left untold.

⁂

Jane decided to confer with Dr. Mitchell, another dentist to whom she had previously visited, and was able to schedule an appointment that week. I spoke with Trisha, the dentist's wife and receptionist. Options and costs were discussed. Jane would have one implant, a root canal, several fillings, and some extractions.

⁂

Jane phoned April 21, to inform us her trial had gone well. She had been acquitted of the trespassing charges. "They told me I had better never ever do anything like that again," Jane stated.

Jane's calls were coming every third day with nothing to talk about other than the progress on her teeth.

Our son, Chris was working in Denver. He came back to Farmington some weekends, which took him through Delta.

Knowing this, I asked him to drop off a red suit case for Jane the next time he went that way. The suitcase had belonged to Mabel and was packed full of her clothes that it was hoped would fit Jane.

When Chris stopped by Jane's apartment to leave the clothes, she was not home. The suitcase was left inside the screen door of the porch. He was aghast to see the condition in which Jane was living. "Jane's place is a dump," he expressed.

Don and I discussed going to Delta towards the end of May to help Jane box up her things, after we returned from Louisville to attend Curtis' graduation, where he was receiving his accounting degree. Don suggested he and Ben could explore car lots for a used truck, while Jane and I worked organizing the apartment. Ben had been hauling wood in the trunk of Mama's old blue Plymouth, which was currently in the shop. The suspension on the Plymouth had been compromised, and it drove like a boat. Jane explained it needed a tune up, and the radiator needed flushed, plus other things. They did not have any transportation.

I left a message on Jane's answering machine to tell her of our plans to visit. When she returned the call, she was panting like she had just run a marathon.

"Why are you out of breath?" I asked, as Jane gasped into the receiver, sounding like a creature from a horror movie.

"We just got back from buying groceries." Jane had walked to the adjacent supermarket. I informed her of our idea to help her clean up the apartment and find a truck if she wanted us to come.

"Ben is going to get a storage unit to move his things into from the shop. There should be room there to put some of my things."

"Are you going to keep it all?" I asked.

"Yes. I have a license to sell things. My apartment is like a warehouse, Jane explained. "I sell things now and then for a quarter and collect two cents tax that I send in."

Jane would never cease to amaze me with her wackiness.

"Sometimes I sleep in the camper, where there is more room. It is parked nearby on a vacant lot behind us. Tell Chris thanks for dropping off the clothes. I want him to know I really appreciate it," Jane expressed.

As usual, Jane was not staying on topic. The offer was made. I would wait for her response.

CHAPTER TWENTY-SEVEN

To Jane's House We Go

Upon returning from Curtis' graduation, Jane informed me she did not want me to come and take over turning her apartment upside down. "I don't want you going through my things!" Jane yelled.

"That is perfectly okay with me," I replied calmly. I was dreading the trip anyway and had decided to go only because I felt obligated. "I was only coming because you asked me."

"I did? I forgot," she said.

"If you don't want me to come, I guess that means you don't want to get a truck," I replied.

"You can get us a truck if you want to," said Jane.

"It doesn't matter one way or another to me. Do you want to get a truck or not?" I asked.

"Yes, Ben needs a truck to haul wood. While you are here, will you bring your sewing machine tools? My sewing machine is jammed up with threads."

❦

Several weeks prior to the expected excursion to Delta, Don had contacted a car dealership in hopes of finding something to suit the budget. Buck described a truck that sounded promising.

Upon arriving in Delta the afternoon of the specified day, Don's eye caught sight of the dealership. He stopped briefly to see if the truck in consideration was still available, which it was. We would return upon checking into a motel and collecting Jane and Ben. I called Jane from my cell phone to inform her, we would be there shortly.

Ben and Jane were waiting outside by their alley entrance when we arrived. Jane was wearing a purple flowered muumuu and had a straw hat on her head that resembled a flowerpot. A strap made from twine caressed her chin.

"How do you like my hat?" Jane questioned. "I made it."

"Oh," I responded while smiling my accepting weirdness as perfectly normal smile.

Jane's new glasses with lenses the thickness of pop bottle bottoms had slid down on her nose, causing her to look like Mother Goose.

The facial hair she had neglected to shave for a while was visible under her jaw and extended onto her double chin. She made chewing contortions with her mouth and clicked her teeth. Her dental work must have been bothering her.

Her head bobbed, and she had slight uncontrollable movements as one might have with Parkinson's disease. These were side effects caused by her psychiatric medication. Her eyes were exceedingly squinty and her face looked puffy. Perhaps this was caused by the medication also.

Ben looked as usual with his scrounge graying beard and tobacco stained teeth. His plaid shirt needed to be tucked in. His dirty jeans had a big tear on the upper right leg where the fabric was unraveling, and he smelled badly.

A truck was noticed across the highway from her apartment at a financial institution where repossessed vehicles were on display. We decided to inquire about it before returning to the Chevy dealership.

Jane took me by the hand as she wobbled along with her limp. We walked hand in hand across the grocery store parking lot to reach the street corner and crossed at the light. After getting information on the truck, we began walking back to Don's truck which was parked by Jane's apartment.

At the dealership, Buck pointed out several used trucks to consider. As Don and Ben drove off to test-drive a well-maintained white 2500,

4 X 4 long bed with a locked toolbox, Jane started to sing. "Way down upon the Suwanee River—"

"Don't sing here," I commanded.

"It is a Stephen Foster song," Jane expressed.

"I know. Let's go inside where we can sit down in the shade," I suggested.

A lady offered us drinks and popcorn while we waited at a table adjacent to the showroom.

Jane asked for water and popcorn. I asked for water but was also brought popcorn, which I later gave to Ben when he complained about Jane eating all of hers. We sat chatting as Jane crammed popcorn in her mouth. I pointed out the popcorn stuck to Jane's lip, not that removing it made her any less conspicuous.

The men returned from the test-drive. The truck was very much to Ben's liking. Don negotiated for two new front tires and a half tank of gas.

After gulping down the last of her popcorn, Jane belched several times. Fortunately, Buck's attention had been diverted by a couple purchasing a brand-new bright lime green Camaro. Buck returned, sitting directly across from Jane. Jane started coughing without covering her mouth. Buck gave her a quick glance, forgiving her uncouthness as he began collecting information for the truck title.

The necessary papers were signed and I wrote a check for the truck. Don and Ben would return at 11 A.M. the next day, to take possession. Meanwhile, we all went to dinner.

Ben selected a small café on Main Street. We all ordered hamburgers, except Jane who ordered a bacon, lettuce, and tomato sandwich. I glanced up occasionally to observe Jane taking large bites with food hanging on her lips. She took another mouthful before swallowing all of the previous bite. Food fell out of her mouth onto her plate as she chewed with her mouth gapping open.

After completing half of her sandwich, Jane complained to the waitress her sandwich hurt her mouth to chew. Jane asked if she could trade the uneaten half of the BLT for half of a hamburger. The waitress obliged her, taking away the uneaten half and bringing a whole hamburger, which had been cut in half, at no charge.

At the end of the meal, Jane yawned several times without showing us the courtesy of covering her widely opened mouth. Somewhere along the way, Jane had lost any manners she ever had.

After eating, Don and I escaped to our motel.

The next morning, Don and I joined Jane and Ben at the apartment. Jane was wearing a blouse from among the clothes Chris had dropped off. It fit very well and looked nice.

As I entered the apartment through the alley door into the kitchen, I was stunned to see the squalor in which Jane and Ben were living. Only one chair in the kitchen was free from being occupied with sundry items until Don placed some boxes on it containing more of his mother's clothing that we had brought.

The white steel sink unit was stained and dirty. Spills from dried food remained where they had run down the sides of the sink as well as the refrigerator. The ducted-taped linoleum kitchen floor desperately needed to be swept and mopped to be free from small wood chips and other debris. Absolutely no uncluttered counter space existed in the cramped kitchen.

First thing, Jane approached Don, asking him to help Ben install a portable air conditioner in the kitchen window. Ben was in no mood to start the morning with a chore. He cursed as he went out the door, saying he was going for coffee.

"Have you already eaten?" asked Jane.

"Yes." Don replied. There was no way we were going to eat anything at Jane's apartment.

"Good. I'm eating the other half of my hamburger for breakfast!" Jane exclaimed.

Don had the air conditioner set up in no time, completing the task long before Ben returned.

Jane kept bumping into me in the confined space, almost knocking me off balance several times. When I stood by the kitchen sink, Jane nudged me to get out of her way. "There is no place for me to go," I protested. "If you want me to move, you will have to back up and let me out!"

After making way for me to exit the trapped area and completed her task at the sink, Jane led me to the nearby vacant lot to see the camper. It was in ram-shackled condition, same as the apartment. Jane pointed out how she had rigged the broken ceiling vent to open and close with a bent wire hanger.

Back at the apartment, we passed through the kitchen to the center room, where a floor-to-ceiling mountain of miscellaneous stuff inundated one side of the room.

"This is normal for people in my condition," Jane stated. "Mama's place was like this too." She had taken on our mother's penchant for hoarding; however, she was much worse than our mother.

Jane wanted to get the rake to pull things down from the tall pile. "There is no need for a rake," I told her. "There is plenty to work with on our level."

I took the lead attacking the grueling chore by first assembling some boxes I had brought. Finding no space to set them, the vacuum cleaner and two of Ben's guitars that were encroaching onto the narrow path were placed in the back room. Now there was room for the boxes to sit on the floor in the limited pathway. I folded two large quilts and a blanket from the pile then placed them on the unmade mattress of the top bunk of the bed that was not being used in the back room.

Staring me in the face was an enormous pile consisting of clothes that had been tossed amid tangled sheets, towels, and boxes with heaven only knew what all.

A box was set aside for clothes Jane wore. Other boxes were designated for other categories. Jane was losing interest as I persisted diligently going through items one by one, asking Jane what she wanted to do with them. Jane disappeared once returning with a bag of potato chips, and another time eating an ice cream bar.

Jane was distracted by the newly delivered boxes of Mabel's clothes. She opened the box to find a pair of light-blue linen slacks. She decided to try them on. Clearing a kitchen chair of its contents and after removing her skirt, she sat down and attempted to put the slacks on.

"You should take your shoes off first," I suggested. Jane had not intended to go to the effort at first and would have gotten her foot stuck.

Jane could not get her leg high enough and asked for help.

I gathered the legs of the slacks and slid them on one at a time. Then I assisted Jane with her shoes. The slacks fit well.

Jane joined me briefly back at the pile before being sidetracked again to do a load of laundry, leaving me amid boxes waiting for her return. When the washer was finished, Jane took leave again to drape some of the larger items over the railing around the back door landing. She also had a line hooked up across the kitchen, where she placed socks and small items to dry. I turned around to see Jane standing under the line, gazing at me with a sock riding on her forehead.

Headway was being made slowly. Lots of papers that needed to be thrown out were put in a box by the woodstove in the back room to burn for heat when the weather got cold.

Jane wanted to keep part of a church announcement that had the words to a song she liked. "Glory to God . . . glory, glory, glory," Jane sang from the announcement in her high-pitched, off-key voice.

I was getting frustrated. Jane could not bring herself to throw hardly anything away. She was saving old calendar pictures because she liked them. An unused 1981 calendar had been kept because it would be accurate again if it was kept long enough. Begrudgingly, Jane tossed it in the trash.

Jane did not like being told she should discard a lot of the useless items. "How would you like your sister coming in your house and sorting through your . . ." Jane stopped in mid-sentence.

I was distracted, trying to decipher what the next item taken from the pile was.

"I fell," said Jane. "Help me get up."

I turned around to find Jane stuck in the box containing fabric remnants. At least she had a cushioned fall, I chuckled to myself.

"If you don't want my help, I will gladly stop and go home right now," I proclaimed as I pulled Jane out of the box.

"No, I need your help," said Jane.

Don and Ben returned from picking up the truck. Ben was thrilled and had already moved his tools to the tool chest. It was time for a lunch break. The four of us went out to another nondescript café on Main Street.

Upon returning to the apartment, Jane set up her sewing machine table in a space she cleared by the kitchen window. After presenting the sewing machine for me to fix, she retreated to the camper for a nap. Since it had gotten warmer, Jane was sleeping in the camper, which was under some shade trees. Ben slept in a chair next to the bunk bed in the back room.

The bobbin area of the sewing machine was impacted with a knot of threads, which was a simple matter to clear. Don helped unscrew the outside case, which was necessary in this model to access the places that needed oil. To have reference to locate the places requiring oil, the instruction booklet was needed. The pages of the manual were stuck together with dried jelly or some sticky substance. I peeled the pages apart carefully to reveal enough information to complete the task. Grunge was wiped from the outside of the machine, and then I sewed on a sample piece of fabric I had brought. The test piece was not sewn to my liking, but the machine was working when Jane lumbered in.

Don had already checked out of the motel and was ready to leave. We had not gotten as much accomplished as I had intended. I insisted we stay long enough to reach a section of the floor to have a level place to stack the boxes that blocked the pathway.

Jane wanted me to come back, but I had already told her this was a one-time deal. More could have been accomplished if Jane would have stayed on task. As it was, she had done little to help, and I was not going to take ownership of organizing the overwhelming mess.

Don and I left Delta with plans to spend the night in Ouray along the way. As we began the drive, I collected my thoughts, gazing at the peaceful countryside, taking note of horses and cattle grazing in the pastures. Contending with Jane had taken an emotional toll on me.

The motel room was a welcome sight. I retreated to a warm bath, putting another whacky experience behind me.

CHAPTER TWENTY-EIGHT

Ibee Weebee

Jane kept calling thanking me for getting the truck for them. She complained Ben would not let her drive it. She said the refrigerator was sounding funny and blamed it on the devil for giving her problems.

Lois and I received an email from Aunt Doris in Oregon with the news of Uncle Jack's declining condition. It was difficult news to accept.

❦

Lois and Bill had planned a Colorado fishing vacation to Gunnison, which involved a boating trip. Don and I joined them after the fishing trip that afternoon.

The following day, our group went on a road trip retracing Daddy's mail route again, only this time, we went further into the mountains. We hiked to an old beaver dam and then continued down the well-maintained graveled road until a place was found to share a picnic lunch of roasted chicken. Not a cloud was in view in the vast blue sky. The air had a familiar summer chill common to the high altitude. Nearby was an old abandoned graveyard located on a peaceful hillside which was covered in wildflowers. One grave of a teenage girl surrounded by a wrought iron fence stood out. Engraved on the large granite headstone was a message which demanded reverence. "As you are now, I once was. As I am now, you must be. Be prepared to follow me."

That evening ended at the rodeo, complete with bucking horses and a clown riding a motor cycle. The evening was followed by a gorgeous Saturday morning, perfect for viewing the parade of majestic horses and old pioneer wagons, which were occupied by ranch families wearing pioneer clothing and being pulled by teams of horses. The parade brought back memories of past parades that we had enjoyed as wide-eyed children.

Upon returning home to Farmington, three messages from Jane were waiting on the answering machine. Jane was worried she had not received anything from Redco Publishing regarding arranging to have her unsold books sent to her. She wanted me to check on it since she "did not have time." I spoke to a Redco Publishing representative and learned Jane's contract was still in effect, and they would keep her poetry books for now unless she told them otherwise.

I gave Lois a belated birthday call. During our conversation, I learned Jane had stopped taking her medications. The next call from Jane, confirmed Lois' information. "I can think more clearly when I'm not on medications," stated Jane.

"You need to stay on them, or you could end up back in Pueblo!" I exclaimed."

"I'll be okay because I go to church, and I'm doing okay," proclaimed Jane, pooh-poohing me.

"That is a big mistake. You are opening yourself up for getting into trouble again," I expressed, recalling the mayhem of the past five years.

"I'm not an animal, and I have the right to decide if I want to take them," Jane said arrogantly. "I'm just about finished with my dental work. They said I'm their best patient." *Sure, they like you for all the dental work is costing*, I thought.

Hardly a day passed that I did not receive a call from Jane.

"You are my full guardian," Jane announced, catching me totally off guard. "I met with a Social Security representative yesterday to notify them I had been receiving Social Security payments while I was in jail. Social Security checks are supposed to stop when you are incarcerated. I was unable to contact them to stop the checks because the jailer would not give me a telephone book to look up the number. They said the guardian usually calls."

"I gave the lady your address, and they will be sending my checks to you. So now you have control of my finances. They may want you to pay my bills."

"Wait a minute. They cannot make me your guardian without my consent!" I exclaimed.

"Well, anyway, you are going to be assigned that now. You are responsible for me."

"I cannot be responsible for you. Since I don't live there, I have no control over what you do," I declared.

"You are selfish and don't care about me!"

"You are not going to put me on a guilt trip!" I exclaimed. "We made the trip to Delta to help clean your apartment and find a truck for you. Plus, I've been giving you nice clothes that belonged to Mabel. How can you say I don't care?"

I didn't feel I could put myself in a position to deal with Jane any more than I already was.

"If you won't do it, then I will probably be in big trouble. There will probably be court proceedings, and I could very easily be declared incompetent," Jane proclaimed.

A lull of several weeks passed with no word from Jane. I was hoping things had been cleared with Social Security. My refusal to be Jane's guardian could not be as catastrophic as Jane portrayed. In any case, Jane was a worry. I placed a call to her.

Jane started talking immediately. "I went and saw a social worker, and they signed me up for food stamps, but they don't have all the paperwork done yet. I've been going out to the mental health empowerment thing in a building on Eighteenth Street and well, I had a good time today. We worked with each other, trying to improve ourselves, and can I be silent for a second and ask what you want."

"I was wondering how things are going with the Social Security Administration," I replied.

"I will be on Medicaid from now on."

Jane talked about the insurance company that covered her medications and her "shrink" who changed her medications and then began talking about unrelated topics. "So, were you going to say anything?"

"You told me you stopped taking your medications," I replied.

"Well, my insurance wouldn't cover it anymore. They said it was too expensive. So, I waited a month, and then I got back into their program. They have ordered me not to work ever again in my life."

"How come?" I asked.

"Because they have the power to do so. What they are going to do is make sure we don't have any money. I have been sleeping out in the trailer, and I finally got a good night's sleep. I've been getting along well with neighbors and everything else. I can even smile once in a while. My church says phooey on all that stuff, depend on God, and He will come through, and so that is basically what I am doing. Thank you for Mabel's radio."

"I'm glad you are able to use it," I acknowledged.

"I don't know how to put the CDs in it, but I've been listening to the PBS station quite a bit, and it is relaxing. It helps me when I go about my work in the house. Basically, Louise, I'm doing okay."

"I've been going to my church, and so I haven't been paying attention to the dogma of Mama and Daddy's old church"

"For a long time, I wasn't on medications, and I was doing just fine. One time when they brought me in for trial not too long ago, I claimed kidnapping and collusion. I had been working in the apartment complex, helping by sealing up the nail holes and stuff like that, but I didn't get permission from the sheriff or from these people. They had a SWAT team man take me away. That is what I was in jail for, Louise. As far as it was concerned in my mind, I thought I was helping them out. And it does look better in that apartment after I got through." Jane paused for a brief second.

"If I get in there one more time, they will keep me in Pueblo the rest of my life. We were planning a trip to New York when the bottom broke out of everything. I wanted to go to New York to see the people of the Academy of American Poets, which I am part of. It just ain't gonna happen."

After some more of Jane's long-winded conversation, I announced, "I need to go, and I'm sure you do too."

"Goodbye," Jane said abruptly.

&

I was focused on finishing Avery's quilt that was to be his high school graduation present. The days were starting to cool as the end of September approached. Things were generally calm. Jane called occasionally just to talk.

"Thanks for sending some more of Mabel clothes. Those clothes are distinctive. I love them. I really do!" Jane exclaimed.

"Don's mom really liked the bright colors and a lot of splashy prints, which looked great on her, and I think they will look good on you too, if—"

Jane interrupted me," The tops work fine. It's the bottoms that are a little big. Oh, do you know what Social Security did to me? They simply don't want me working any more at all." Jane kept on jabbering about her finances, not giving me an opportunity to speak. "As I send them a little bit each month, I think they are fairly well satisfied. I'm growing a beard. Did you know that?"

I laughed. "I could see where you had some hairs growing when we were there," I responded.

"I'm going out to the Vo-Tech school and let them use wax on my beard. I let it grow long, and I really look awful. Once I get rid of all the excess whiskers on my face, then I will look a lot more presentable. It hasn't been fun," Jane said laughing.

"Thank you so much for that box." Jane had just received more of Mabel's clothes that I thought would suit her. "Sometimes I get the feeling people don't love me. Most of the time people are wrapped up in themselves, and they don't worry about anybody else unless they come barging into their life, and I guess I have a habit of barging in. Do I? I don't know if I want you to answer that or not."

I laughed. "That is the last of her clothes. We gave a lot of them to Goodwill. I didn't think they would fit you, and I knew you did not have room for more."

Jane started talking about the Goodwill Store and the senior citizen's center and a lot of nothing in particular and then was back on the topic of Social Security. "I called up Social Security and found out I will always be on it because of the fact that I was sick in high school. And Social Security said that I am not to work."

"Why are they saying you are not allowed to work? How can they tell you that?" I asked.

"Well they did. They sent a mimeographed sheet out to me. So, the reason they don't want me working is because . . . I don't know why. I think I didn't do a satisfactory job, but that wasn't true. I think it has to do with the fact that I remind people of things they don't want to be reminded of and stuff like that. I haven't been sewing. I had a handbook with instructions for where settings were to be on. I really enjoy sewing when it doesn't have snags in it because of the tension. It needs some kind of adjustment."

"Take it to a professional sewing machine repair shop and get it adjusted," I suggested.

"I'm always afraid when I take something like that to get fixed, they will say it isn't worth beans, and they will want to sell me a new one and so . . . By the way, we really like the pickup. Ben has a new kiddy car. Oh, he loves it. We went down to the Veterans Administration last week, and they did some tests, and he is normal and everything. He has a good blood count and everything like that. They have him on some kind of stuff so that he doesn't bother me like he was there for a while. And I was there when we saw the psychiatrist. She was asking questions about craziness and most of them didn't fit the bill. It looks like Ben has got a lot of moral support since he was in the service. And I'm really glad I married him. He works in the evening from about eight to ten guarding a church, and he does the landscaping outside. Well, sometimes if you marry a sailor, what kind of a mouth do you expect it to have?"

"I was wondering if he is going to be able to salvage some of the parts from the old Dodge truck, or what is he going to do with that?" I asked.

"The neighbor next door said they want it for the chassis. They have a perfectly good engine on this one they have."

"Do you know that I am part of the Academy of Poets, and they send me materials, and I had one book signing of my book at the library? And you say Redco is willing to keep my books?"

"The man I talked to was supposed to send you a letter. Did he ever send you one?" I responded.

"Yeah, he sent me a letter and it asked if I want this person taken off my list?" and I certainly do not. They have around four hundred books of mine in their possession. I'm wondering if they like them enough that they want to keep them," Jane stated.

"He told me the contract doesn't abruptly end. If you want to end the contract, you need to send them a letter and tell them," I replied.

"I'm a different kettle of fish . . ." Jane continued talking about her experience in getting her poetry book copyrighted and lots of mumbo jumbo. "Redco is a vanity publisher. They sure know how to make a lot of money. Before I got sick, I was going to go over to the high school. They wanted me to pick out some poems and share them with the high school students. I'm waiting until I feel good enough to get in touch with them again," Jane stated.

"I need to go, Jane. I'm glad you liked the clothes."

When Jane phoned again two weeks later, she was very depressed. Her voice was shaky, and she stammered a lot. "Did you know I got my beard worked on, and they did it out at the Vo-Tech school a couple of times, and I don't know when my appointment is at the beautician, but I tried clipping off some of my hair, and it stands out in all directions at once. There is a woman who is a caregiver there at the mental health thing, and if we are not doing anything else, we can go there and work on psychiatric stuff. They also take us bowling and things like that.

"I'm going to a place downtown, and I don't know what time it is, so I think I'm supposed to be there at nine, I think it was, but I keep getting everything all mixed up right now."

"Oh, the man next door died about three or four days ago. His wife has claimed cancer ever since 1977. To tell the truth, most cancers have to do with self. Any that I have run across have to do with self-mutilation, and so once I found that out . . .," Jane did not finish. "Well, we are getting along better, and that little trailer is too cold now, but for quite a long time, I would go over there and just sleep and rest."

"What did your neighbor die from?" I asked.

"Congestive heart failure," replied Jane.

"He wasn't that old, was he?" I questioned.

"No, he wasn't, but he was really obese. What I do when I want to help the rest of the people who live here, is I buy a bag of oranges and put an orange on their doorknobs. That is what I have been doing for years. The only trouble is last year, I was gone most of the year. The judge apparently is running all the convicts through the mental health process, and lastly, what I am really grateful for is . . . Did I tell you how it happened that I got home?"

"How you got home from where?" I asked.

"From Pueblo. This lady, the one that determines the sanity of people who are put in the hospital, all I had to do was tell them I wanted to see her, and two days later, she came in and gave me a simple intelligence test. She sent back the report that I was okay to stand trial, and that is how come I am out of there now. The last ward they had me on, the geriatric ward, they were much kinder there than on the one where they deposited me at first. The geriatric ward is brand new. It has great, big, high-vaulted ceilings and they have them watch TV, so they know what the news is and stuff like that."

"The man who was going to do the surgery on my foot was told, "No." They didn't have enough money for it, and so really, it is doing pretty good right now. It is from some bones that were broken or misplaced over the years. So I left it alone. They put me over with the elderly on the geriatric floor, and I got along a lot better over there."

"And so some of the same feelings of depression that I would get there while I was in the hospital, my church seems to be the only thing that can pull me out of it at times."

Jane was in one of her talkative moods and kept on and on until I got a chance to get in a few words. "Jane, I need to go."

"Thank you for letting me talk. I have really been run through the mill. They expunged the charges against me and so my record doesn't show that I'm a convict or anything. I have an appointment with Dr. Fulton. He is a psychiatrist. He laughs at us a lot. He thinks we are funny. We run around crazily, I guess. I started to tell you about him."

"Okay, Jane, I need to go. We are getting ready to leave. I need to go."

"Did you hear what I said though? I really need to talk about it. Can you pray for me?"

"Yes, Jane, I do all the time," I expressed.

"Oh great. Thanks for telling me. I'm better after hearing your voice. Bye-bye."

❧

Lois and I got word our Uncle Ralph had passed away. "The news about Uncle Ralph is upsetting, but I know things will get easier for Aunt Rebecca once she gets through the funeral." I told Lois over the phone. "Jane called last night to wish us Merry Christmas. She was stammering all over the place, which makes it very difficult to listen to her. She said when she first got to Pueblo, she grabbed someone's arm and was put in seclusion because if they don't like you grabbing them, they can charge you with assault."

❧

Don and I had gone to visit our son, Curtis and grandson, Cole for Christmas. Curtis and Claudia had gone their separate ways. Several phone messages from Jane were left in our absence. "Thank you very much for the picture page. I showed it to the people that are my friends. MERRY CHRISTMAS. **HAPPEE NEW YEAR!**"

Jane lacked the ability to state anything in a straightforward manner. The gist of one of her messages was that she wanted me to locate a manual for her sewing machine on the Internet. "There are some really nice ladies who are working for me," Jane informed. "One of them worked with Mama at the last and the other one . . . They are helping a lot and YOU DON'T HAVE TO PAY FOR IT."

"I went in and had my face waxed at the college because I have a lot of facial hair where I tried to imitate papa. It is a side effect from a drug I HAD TO TAKE FOR A NUMBER OF YEARS. I'm sorry, I'm getting really angry, and I don't mean to do that."

"I hope you are listening to me when you come home. Please realize that what you did for Cousin Teddy was no favor. I tried to keep up with Teddy for years and every time I turned around, it looked like someone in our family was giving him a hard time. NO WONDER HE DIED. DON'T HATE PEOPLE WHEN THEY ARE TRYING TO DO THE BEST THEY CAN," she shouted harshly.

During the first week of January 2011, I phoned Jane. "I called to tell you some information I found on your sewing machine. I couldn't find the specific manual for your machine, but I found some that are close. That brand is basically the same," I informed.

"All I need to know is where the tension should be set at the stretch stitch. I have two girls coming in at three o'clock every weekday, unless I cancel them, and it would be ideal if you could call up then, and that would get me away from them a little bit because we are running one another ragged. I have a friend, and we were talking about atriums. Do you know what atriums are, Louise?"

"They are little areas where there are plants, like a small yard," I answered.

"You have caught up with me and then some. Okay to get back to what we were saying, we've been okayed for full disability by the U.S. Government. Is Uncle Jack still alive? Do you know?"

"Yes, he is," I stated.

Jane kept talking. "I talk to Aunt Lorie on the phone every so often. My heart is fine. We are probably in better shape physically than everybody else I see because I had a year of relaxation, you know."

"Oh," I said laughing. "I'm sure that was very relaxing."

Jane took over monopolizing the conversation, talking about Ben's family and other subjects.

"And so I worry about you guys an awful lot. I guess that worry is kind of a prayer from what I study. A moan is a prayer. A sigh is a prayer. A thought is a prayer. But that is what I believe. You don't have to believe a thing if you don't want to. I don't care it is my life, just like it is your life. Jane interrupted herself. "Let's get back to brass tacks. Over three minutes from here cars equipped with listening devices can pick us up, but I don't think that is happening all the time. Caroline sent an insignia a few years ago that was put on the same picture frame that I'm using for something else. I recognized the insignia of the Marine Corps, and I put it on a helmet. I wear those downtown every so often just for the fun of it, and everybody thinks I'm crazy. Well, I don't care."

After Mama died Caroline prepared shadow boxes for my sisters and me, that consisted of Daddy and Mama's wedding picture. To the right of the picture was a poem. Below the poem, Caroline had glued an insignia of the Marine Corps, as a tribute to her grandfather and a small wooden spool of thread that had belonged to Mama. Caroline went to a lot of work making the shadow boxes. I was appalled to hear Jane dismantled the tribute to our parents.

"What is it that you are wearing?" I asked.

"Oh brother, Louise, I shouldn't have told you, the Marine Corps hat. I've got three. I've got all of his safari hats. I'm getting off track again."

Jane started babbling about Ben. "He likes to dwink and so we had a whisky rebellion here a couple days ago, and I shared it with a neighbor, and I started talking in my sleep".

I kept listening as Jane chattered incessantly about our grandfather on our father's side and his second wife, whom he married after our grandmother died many years ago.

"So, we paid the bill off at my doctor's. We are in fine shape financially now, but we have got to get our marbles together because we have never been in a situation like this before. We are more prosperous now than I've ever been in my life since before Mama passed away."

I finally got another chance to speak. "Back at the beginning of our conversation, you were saying there are a couple of girls that come in to help you."

"Yeah, and I was trying to tell you their names. You don't need to monkey monk with that. We are cleaning in the kitchen right now, and it is up to me what they do. In the meantime, they are revving me up."

"I am in the process of trying to figure out a way to give a talk at Montrose High School, but I have a lead bird around my neck, kind of like the albatross, but it is not for real. Do you want to talk to Ben?"

"No, I don't. Did Redco Publishing contact you?" I asked.

"I called them like they said in the letter."

"So everything is straight with them?" I asked.

"Pretty much so. I invested in an advertisement just before I went to the hospital and it cost me 125 buckaroos of my savings. They are the biggest and the best in the whole world. Talking about that, Carrie across the way is mad at me because I have not dotted my i's and crossed my t's. I said it right that time." Do you think we should say good night?"

"Yes," I agreed, wondering how I could have let the conversation go on as long it had.

Jane started up again, "LEEP is going to help us with the heat we have in the front room, and they are going to pay us. It is a Colorado program that will help subsidize poor families. Arizona didn't become part of the union, I'm not sure it must have been forty-fourth, but anyway, it was one of the very last to join the confederacy."

"Confederacy? Don't you mean the United States?" I challenged.

"Yeah, I was wrong. You see, it comes out backward. I've got so much knowledge. I've probably forgotten more than you ever learned." Jane was laughing. "So, I must be the smartest thing on two wheels, but that doesn't mean a thing in God's eyes."

"Well, I think you are—," I was laughing and was going to say, "full of yourself," before being interrupted.

"Because you are normal. When somebody is smart and somebody doesn't understand them, they say they are crazy," Jane stated.

"And I'm sure that is your problem. You are just such a genius nobody can figure you out," I declared.

"Ibee weebee," Jane said in a shrill sound. "Well now did I prove it?"

"I need to get going," I said.

"I'm on medication," Jane kept going. "It doesn't make any difference whether I'm on or off. The only reason they have me over there is because I am socially undesirable because I'm so smart."

"Jane, you have delusions of grandeur," I expressed.

"Oh yeah, phooey on that," Jane blurted.

"I have got to go," I repeated. Our conversation finally ended.

January 28, 2011, Lois and I received an email from Aunt Doris, informing us of Uncle Jack's death the previous evening. Losing another relative was a sad blow.

Jane had not called for a while. I decided to notify her of the recent events with our Uncle Jack and Aunt Lorie, who had fallen just before Uncle Jack died. I also needed to speak to Jane about a call received from Dr. Mitchell's dental office.

"Hi Jane," I started.

Jane was in a grumpy mood. "Why don't we call it a day, and then we can write. That would be better," she muttered in a low tone.

"Jane, wait a second." She had already hung up. I placed another call. "This is Jane," she answered.

"You didn't let me finish telling you about Uncle Jack and Aunt Lorie, and also, I got a call from your dentist that I need to talk to you about."

Without responding, Jane slammed the receiver down. I was ticked off. I learned Dr. Mitchell had a serious heart attack when I was speaking with a lady from the dental office. She told me Jane needed to make another appointment. I told her Jane may have decided to stop her dental work, and she would not talk to me about it.

Surprisingly, Jane phoned the following evening, saying, "I called Aunt Lorie's house. She wasn't there, but I talked to Mark. He told me about her accident and Uncle Jack dying. Well, I'm glad I know now," Jane proclaimed.

"That is what I wanted to tell you," I expressed.

"I had a feeling you did, and that's why I didn't want to know it then. I worked really hard. I just sat down to rest now. We have our lives to live too. You and Don aren't the only ones who are important. Ben works around here an awfully lot. He cuts all the wood and stuff like that just like your husband, you know. There is no difference. We're not super people, and you guys aren't either. And so just because we have different ways of going about earning our livelihood doesn't mean we are any better or any worse off than you guys are. Did you know that?" Jane scoffed.

Where did that outburst come from? I did not react to Jane's derogatory statements. There was no need to have a battle over nothing.

"There are some bugging devices on the computer, and I am wondering if you all have tuned in to that," Jane expressed. "We get a lot of nonsense over the radio, and apparently, they are doing the Jane thing right now"

"What is the Jane thing?" I asked.

"Well, I wrote a lot of music, and Daddy did too. I think Mama did too. But anyway, a lot of the songs they sing —I was actually in the third grade, writing the poetry for some of the songs that they sing. Did you know that?"

I was marveling at how she could be emanating such blarney. Jane certainly did not write songs as a third-grader, and neither did Daddy or Mama. We were not a musical family. I answered saying, "No. I didn't know that. What songs were they?"

"Western songs, like *Back in the Saddle Again*. Well, the kids were beating on me at school. Mama was always trying to get my poetry.

I was so happy to be writing it I didn't think it was worth anything, and so what they did was they used it without my copyright, and it apparently went on some fund raisers and stuff."

She continued saying, "It has really been an interesting life now that I'm beginning to understand a little bit more, but the reason why you and Don are the way you are is because you have different lots in life.

Just like I said before, I mean, a professor is a lot different than someone who went into the navy. And Ben's family comes from an ordinary family. Have you ever seen what they look like when they go down the road? They are dirty, they smoke, and they drink and do all the things that common people do. And every time I turn around, I find myself doing something more and more common and yet I've been getting a lot of fulfillment in that respect.

"You guys came in like a whirl wind when Mama was sick, and I was sure glad you got a chance to see her. I wouldn't have called you guys in if I hadn't needed you. She didn't want you guys to know. One of the funny things about this whole mess is that Mama was feeding some of the neighbor kids, eggshells because they were not behaving, so I mentioned that over the public broadcasting that we have down here. If you stand too close to the radio, they will hear you on public TV. This stuff is confidential. So anyway, what happened, you see, I've been working all day long . . . I lost my train of thought there. Could you remind me?"

"You were talking about Mama feeding kids eggshells".

"Yeah. They were trying to get these kids to mind, and so what they did was—she did this at my suggestion—was she told them to crumble up the eggshells and put it on top of cereal. Everyone around here doesn't get enough calcium, and so what you do is mix it up with your food and chew it up. It is just like taking a vitamin capsule."

"Well, Louise, we all have our ups and our downs and I'm really sorry Uncle Jack passed away."

"I need to talk to you about something," I said hoping to stay on topic.

"No, you can't! So, thank you. You have a good night. God bless you."

"Don't cut me off," I squeezed in. There was silence. Jane had hung up on me again.

I poured out my frustrations to Lois. "Jane really sounds cuckoo, thinking she wrote lyrics to western songs she hears on the radio. I wanted to talk to her about going to the dentist, but she hung up on me."

"She called me last night also," Lois shared. "She went from one thing to another and also said something about a publishing company finally publishing all of her poems in a new book."

⚮

I phoned Lois in Mid-February. "I've been thinking about Jane a lot lately and am wondering if we might want to contact her psychiatrist, Dr. Fulton. I'm afraid she is about to get into major trouble again. I don't see how she can be on her medications. Can you?"

"No, I don't think she is on her medications," Lois agreed. "But she is a little different, not quite so combative."

"She is not behaving normally for sure. Not that she ever acts normally. She won't talk to me about her dental appointments. Right now, I'm feeling like she can just go do her own flipping thing," I expressed. "She keeps saying Don and I think we are more important than she is. Then she got mad about buying the truck. She said they didn't need it. She was screaming at me for getting the truck for them when she didn't want it. I told her Ben needed a truck to haul wood. Then she totally shut up on that point. The next burr she had up her butt was that she didn't want me to control what little there was left of her funds. That was most of the conversation. Talking to her is like being in a sparring match."

CHAPTER TWENTY-NINE

"I called to ask you if, well I can't remember, Dr. Daramandara, or whatever his name is, well he put a rivet in my mouth you know and attached it to my jaw," Jane began.

"Are you talking about the oral surgeon?" I asked.

"Uh huh. It is a direct line to the rest of my system and there is a little hole in the middle of it. I do of course need to get in and get it finished. In the meantime, I'm working on our income taxes. I've been having a lot of foot problems and that is basically why I've been having to be in a place where I get more rest than I do at home. It's not nutty nuts it's life. Okay?"

"Where are you going?" I asked.

"On a bus ride to Denver, just a day drive up, as soon as I can figure out how to budget in the ticket on my own. We've worked it so that every once in a while, when I'm about ready to blow my stack and my mind is rambling, when it does that, we find a way just to walk down the street, and there are motels close by."

"You go stay in a motel?" I questioned.

"For a night, anything to get it so that we are doing better. Ben is on a pension right now. We found a cheaper source for wood, and so he boogies down there on weekdays and gets some pine slats. I worked in a lumberyard once or twice. I think at least once when I lived in Grand Junction."

"Okay. My question is, has the dentist contacted you about my teeth?" Jane changed topics again.

"Only, to tell me they were ready to proceed," I answered.

"Probably next month, I will find the time to go into the dentist office," Jane announced. "I just thought I would fill you in on some of the things, so you know what kind of a spectacular life I have," Jane proclaimed.

"Yes. You are leading a really spectacular life," I said laughing.

"Okay." Jane said laughing. "Goodbye."

It was March 2, the sixth anniversary of Mama's death. Jane phoned that morning. "I talked to Aunt Lorie last evening," Jane announced. "We are working on this and that. Ben's relatives' names are Tate and Eve and their mother got remarried, and she has another little baby. It is really fun trying to get through to them. Wuacka, wuacka. I just lost my plate in the wood-stove. It is filthy dirty it has dog fur all over it. We lost our dogs, you know."

"What happened to them?" I asked.

"He froze to death basically out of lack of love and a worried wife. We lost Strike first he was a little border collie. We got him up in the forest. We lost Ginger, and then we got Topper. Topper lasted two years. He looked like a German Hound. He died about three days after Strike."

"What happened to him?" I asked.

"Froze to death."

"Outside?" I asked puzzled.

"He stiffened up and wouldn't get up," Jane explained.

"Did he have some kind of disease?" I questioned.

"A man threw a rock with hamburger on the outside of it and a rock on the inside of it," Jane answered. "All three of them had that happen over at the property of Ben's brother's."

"You lost me," I said trying to follow Jane's reasoning for the dogs dying since I knew Ginger had died from an infection.

"I said the grieving process is supposed to be something that some people never get over," Jane declared.

"Are you grieving for your dogs?" I asked. Jane was giggling wildly in a high-pitched, weird voice. "What's so funny?" I asked.

"We had someone who was dying next door to us. I told you that they died," Jane stated and then quickly changed her train of thought. You know what? I don't trust ya," Jane said laughing.

"You don't trust anybody."

"Yeah, I know. It says in the Bible not to. You know what?" Jane chimed in. "You are a very good sister because you trust everybody. And I like your bigoted attitude."

"Bigoted?" I said in anger.

"Uh huh. I think you're proud and haughty and have never learned humility."

"Well, you are totally—," I began, but Jane cut me off.

"Ben went out about three o'clock this morning to get a smoke. Your husband doesn't smoke. He couldn't be smoking because nobody smokes that's a teacher. We had a temperature of 71 degrees yesterday. Oh, it was beautiful. I was out working my fanny off and ran across some local yokels, if you want to call them that."

"What were you doing?" I asked.

"Cleaning things, moving wood around, trying not to hit myself with a ten-pound hammer," Jane exclaimed.

"Were you fixing something?" I asked.

"My life," she replied. "We buy used cars that are about twenty years old from individuals not from agencies because we get a better deal. It also means more upkeep. The fender on the right side of the Plymouth AND DON'T TRY TO FIX IT! It is still under warranty for miles, but it's not for years. We have an insurance agent who will repair it for a reasonable amount. Ben pays the insurance taxes."

Jane went on talking, "I'm tired of being put in the clink because I get upset about things I didn't understand. By the time I start making two and two out of things Ben does . . ." I could not follow what Jane was saying as I moved a load of laundry to the dryer. "I'm really pretty happy, aren't you?"

"Yes, things are going pretty well," I answered.

"Our place is so full of stuff. Is your place that way too?" Jane questioned.

I blatantly answered. "No way. I need to get going. I have things to do."

"Okay, goodbye," Jane said.

It was now well into March when I phoned Jane to see where she was with completing her dental work. I began the conversation, commenting about some typed pages Jane sent which was part of a story Mama had written. "I noticed it was some of Mama's writings."

"Yeah, it was something she had written when she took a journalism course through a writer's group at my suggestion, and she worked at it until she got it finished. She got all her assignments in on time and had good rapport with the instructor," Jane stated. "You sent only pages 2 and 3. If you are going to send me something, why do you just send part of it?" I questioned.

"All my stuff is in such a mess I thought you would enjoy what little I had together. I wrote one short manuscript. It turned out pretty good, just before I left high school. I wrote it under Mama's name. It took me a while to figure out that is what happened," Jane explained from her mixed-up thinking.

"How is your dental work progressing?" I questioned Jane.

"They want to charge way too much for what they are doing," she answered. "We've got the screw drive in or whatever you want to call it. I want to pay for it myself on a payment plan, since my inheritance is running out of money. I might end up with some baby teeth coming in, if I give them long enough," declared Jane. "The liquids that go through that rivet hole, actually is giving me a main line of nutrients into my body. And as far as I'm concerned, I probably would have to eat a lot less. I don't believe in the germ theory. We are going to have to slow this down. So, you tell me I'm not on a fast track due to some youngsters pushing me around. You tell me! Tell me!"

"I don't think—," I was trying to express my opinion, but Jane did not let me finish.

"COME ON TELL ME! TELL ME! And I'm not angry. I'm just telling you," Jane yelled.

"Jane, I talked to Dr. Mitchell—" I said in frustration.

"You can talk to him as much as you want," Jane broke in. "He has a lot of other clients besides me, and they take rich vacations every time they get through with me after they have drugged me up and make me as dizzy as they can possibly do because that is part of the professional ethic. Then Trisha comes over to me and gives me A GREAT BIG HUGE HUG and I walk out of there feeling like I've been smooched by a gorilla. Okay. DOES THAT HELP? DOES THAT HELP? Huh, Louise?"

"No, it doesn't help. It's your mouth, Jane," I said to no avail.

"I was listening to some of the stuff you and Lois were doing with the cassette recorder. I got batteries in that now. We have batteries coming out of our ears, and so why use electricity? I was absolutely astounded at how melodic and how original you two became while I was working on my scholarship. I do library work, and I might start working with them on a more regional level," Jane went on. "I have lots of fun in life while you pretend you are a worry wart with me. I need to hang up now. I'm really, really tired.

I phoned Dr. Mitchell's office to inform Trish that Jane was not cooperating. "I don't think Jane is on her medications," I told Trish. "I'm thinking about contacting Dr. Fulton when I find his number."

"I can give it to you," Trisha volunteered."

During our conversation, Trish brought up she was a good friend of Megan's, Ben's sister, who had worked in their office as a dental hygienist. Trish provided Megan's phone number, along with Dr. Fulton's.

Several days later, I spoke with Megan.

"Do you know what is going on with Jane?" I inquired.

"I haven't seen Jane since December," Megan replied. "She comes to our family activities. We don't dare leave her alone with any of the younger children because she has strange ideas on disciplining them. I make sure I am never alone with her either. There was one time when I was afraid of Jane. It was right after their dog, Ginger, died. Jane wanted me to go into the bathroom to point out the spot where Ginger died. I told her I could see it from the door. I was afraid she was going to corner me in there."

"I'm afraid Jane is headed for trouble again," I stated. "She is missing her dental appointments and keeps hanging up on me."

"She has used up all of my lithium crystals," Megan said jokingly. That was a good way to express the way I felt also. My energy had been drained to my core.

"Ben is being treated for depression through the VA. Not too long ago, I helped him fill out the forms for his disability. He has post-traumatic stress disorder," Megan explained.

I called the number Trish had given me for Dr. Fulton and reached his private practice. The receptionist provided the number to the State Mental Health office, which I called, leaving a message. A lady with a husky voice returned my call several days later, apologizing for not calling sooner.

"I don't know who to talk to about my sister Jane Jenson," I started. "She is acting very strange in her conversations, and I wanted to make sure she is taking her medications before she gets in trouble."

"You know I cannot tell you anything," stated the lady.

I asked her some general questions. Then phoned Lois who had taken off the day and was on the road, returning from a bull auction with Bill.

"Bill purchased a five-year-old prize bull named Starbucks," Lois informed. "We will name the bull's first offspring *Latte*."

"You could name others Brown Roasted, Hazel Nut, and other coffee-related names," I suggested. We laughed about potential names for Starbucks's calves.

"I just finished speaking to a lady from State Mental Health. They cannot force people to take their medications. If there is a court order and they feel there is a problem, they can notify the authorities, and the law decides what to do," I explained. "I'm guessing there is a court order for Jane to be on her meds. The most they can do is place her under police surveillance."

"Whatever happens, I'm washing my hands of it. I'm done. The purpose of my call was to alert Dr. Fulton to talk to her about taking her medications. Maybe he has. The ball is in Jane's court," I stated in frustration.

Several weeks later, I placed a phone call to Lois. "Jane has started calling again. Every peculiar call is followed by another one. She told me she is a 'technocite,' which is a title she made up since she works with technology. I asked her if she was on the internet now. She said, "Yes, no, yes, no, yes, no and started laughing."

"She is smart, but all of it has gone to waste," replied Lois. "Too bad she isn't normal."

"She isn't smart anymore," I replied. "She gets confused easily, and if she was smart, she would realize her condition requires her to be on medications. She has proven that enough times." I continued. "She called Monday morning. Mostly all she talked about was a bunch of hooey she has imagined. All of a sudden, she got mad and yelled, saying I killed our cousin Teddy Winters, which she has told me before. I asked her where she got that idea. She said I hated him, and that killed him. I didn't even know him. I had only seen him once, briefly, and had never even spoken to him. It is very irritating listening to the rubbish she dishes out. We have to chalk it up to her mental illness. Just the same I wish she would shut up," I expounded.

Jane generally called weekends when Don and I escaped to the mountains. She left insulting messages on the answering machine, telling me such things as Noah would not let me on the ark.

In other phone calls, Jane claimed she had written *The Mouse That Roared*, *The Revenge of the Nerds, Part I and II*, and also that she assisted in bringing *The Beatles* to America. Another trip to the state hospital was inevitable; it was just a matter of time.

CHAPTER THIRTY

Chaos Breaks Out

Just before Halloween, Jane started to pour paint in the woodburning stove of her apartment. Ben told her to get away from the stove. She started hitting him, pulling his hair, scratching his face, and biting him. She even hit him with a stick. Ben tried to call 911, but Jane yanked the phone cord from the wall before he could speak to anyone. The phone rang twice before the connection was broken, which was plenty of time for the emergency center to get a fix on where the call was originating.

Ben went outside after the incident. Shortly thereafter, the police appeared. As the police began to enter the apartment, Jane threatened them, saying she had a gun. Ben told them she did not. When the police got inside, Jane began throwing things at them. She was Tasered on her hip to get her under control and seated in the police car. She was charged with domestic violence and resisting arrest. Jane remained in jail several weeks until she was transported to the state hospital in Pueblo in mid-November.

I first learned of the situation when Jane called collect from the county Jail. I refused her calls but contacted Ben to see why she was in jail. Lois was notified that Jane was in trouble again.

Lois called the jail to learn more. Jane was arrested in her night gown. She was taken without her glasses. She was livid. She told Lois she was going to sue the police for $11 million.

In January of 2012, I finally decided to check on Jane. Rather than speaking with Jane directly, I phoned Ben, who revealed she was recently *jumped* by five staff members, who held her down to give her a shot. Obviously, she was still not cooperating.

I was extremely angry with Jane in general for yet another incarceration. I could not bring myself to call her until March. Upon reaching Jane, I was surprised she did not want to talk. Jane's exaggerated slurred speech was evidence of her heavily medicated state. She was not feeling well.

During the call that followed, Jane was more talkative. "There is a court order for me to take medications. I've decided I had better follow it. They should not have brought me here. I did not do anything wrong. The police beat me up," Jane complained. They should not have taken me away for a simple domestic spat."

"When do you think you will be released?" I asked.

"Never," Jane stated with flat affect.

Two weeks later during another call, I asked Jane once again, "When do you think you might be released?"

"I could be released anytime, but they do not know where to put me. I think I'm better off here in Pueblo. It is too hard to be on the outside. It is dangerous out there."

"I need some underwear, lipstick and talcum powder to put in my shoes," Jane requested in a conversation with Lois. "I have a review on September 26, and they will let me know if I can go home."

Lois sent Jane a *care package* with hand lotion and other personal items, while and I sent lipstick. I spoke to Lois over the phone. "By the time she has her review, it will be close to a year since she got arrested. She has burned me out. When they release her, she had better not be calling me like she was," I expressed to Lois. I did not feel I could stand any more of Jane's lengthy, chatty calls that were full of gibberish and insults.

Jane sent letters every now and then. In one scribbled handwritten letter Jane wrote, "I bumped my head, and finally, today it doesn't hurt as much. I have a new doctor. He has a ponytail and is in 'harmony.' I like him as a person. He lowered my medication. I felt better today than

I have in a long time. I walk like a zombie. I lose my balance often, so I am working on that." Partially colored pictures from a coloring book were enclosed.

"From the last letter, I would say she is not functional," I expressed to Lois. "Why is she sending half-colored pages? She has problems spelling, and she is still signing her letters, Aunt Jane."

⚭

September 26 came and went with no word from Jane. The second week into October, I decided to check on her.

"I'll be here in Pueblo a while longer," Jane replied when asked if she had any news on her status. "Would you like to talk to the nurse?"

A moment later, I found myself speaking with another person. "Do you know how much longer Jane will be there?" I asked. "No, but I can have Jane's social worker call you."

"Okay," I agreed.

I was surprised to receive a call the following week. "Hello. This is Cecilia, Jane's social worker. Jane is here with me now. She is a very sweet lady. She is one of our special patients."

I was surprised by Cecilia's enthusiasm towards Jane. *Could we be talking about the same person*? I wondered. "How is Jane progressing?" I inquired.

"Jane is evaluated every ninety days. The last one was September 26. It was to determine if she was ready to be returned to Delta to face the charges against her. Her psychiatrist felt she is not."

"Are they working with her to help her improve?" I questioned.

"Her psychiatrist is working with her, and she has a public defender, who is working with her also. Before she can be released, she has to complete the *competency restoration process* successfully. It is a complicated process. She understands what she must do," Cecilia explained.

"What I'm concerned about is when she is released from Pueblo, that she will fall back into her pattern of getting off her medications and getting back into trouble again like she has done more times than I know."

"When she is released, there will be something in place to keep her out of trouble. The system has failed her. If there was something in place, she probably would not have gotten into trouble this time," stated Cecilia.

A lot was learned from the conversation, however; I wished I had asked more questions regarding what the system could do. All *the system* had accomplished was to get her stabilized and then release her back into society to go amok again. Where was this allusive system Cecilia spoke of, which was supposed to keep Jane out of trouble?

The third week into January 2013, I phoned Jane. She was in a talkative mood and rambled, speaking in her familiar drug-induced, slow, slurred voice.

"I'm going to be here a while. I'm legally tendered here."

"What do you mean by that?" I questioned.

"That means I'm crazy. If you're in here over a year, you lose your rights. I'm schizoaffective, which is a mixture of disorders. I don't know when they will let me out."

"What have you been doing?" I asked, wondering how Jane spends her days.

"Nothing, I try to stay out of trouble by sleeping a lot."

"How can you get into trouble?" I questioned.

"There is this girl whom I try to help, but she tells me to leave her alone. There is a nurse I don't like. There is nothing worse than to be treated like a child when you are an adult. I've been trying to keep my head on straight. I'm not helpless, just hopeless," Jane said, laughing. "How is your family?"

"Everyone is fine," I answered. "Kayla will be graduating from high school in May and is applying to colleges. I told you Avery went into the Marines. He is engaged now and will be getting married in March. Mathew is the President of his seventh-grade class. Clara does well in school, is on the volleyball team and was the freshman attendant for the basketball home coming. Cole is growing like a little weed and is the terror of his preschool class," I stated jokingly.

"They bring in this little char-colored dog sometimes. I really like him. I pet him, and he wags his tail. They let me go outside in a protected area. The workers here are very cheerful and treat us well. I'm glad you called. I'm very lonely."

It was sad talking to Jane. There was nothing we could have done to prevent her from getting into this situation. Jane felt she had a right to do whatever she wanted, and she did, no matter how unorthodox it was. For the time being, Lois and I were saved from worrying about Jane getting into serious trouble.

CHAPTER THIRTY-ONE

Are We There Yet?

Late afternoon of February 28, 2013, a surprise call was received from Jane and Cecilia, Jane's social worker. Cecilia informed me of a meeting March 7 to see if the court felt Jane could be released from Pueblo.

"If it were not for the charges, Jane would have been released before this. I'm checking into getting Jane in assisted living," Cecilia informed. "They won't release Jane to go home to her apartment until it is cleaned up. The police saw what a mess it was and reported Jane was living in squalor. It was declared unsafe."

Jane broke into the conversation. "Ben's sister died. Louise is very upset over her death."

"Who is upset?" I asked.

"Louise is, I mean, Ben is very upset," stated Jane. She was obviously confused.

The news of Ben's sister's death was upsetting to me as well. Carrie was a stabilizing force in Ben's family, and she would be greatly missed. She had helped keep Jane out of trouble and tried to keep Jane on her medications.

Jane kept asking me, "Do you think I'm ready to go home?"

I had my doubts but certainly was not going to ruin it for Jane by answering, "No."

"How should I know?" I answered. "Things need to be in order."

Jane was hyperventilating. Cecilia directed her to take slow, deep breaths and relax. Cecilia asked about Jane's assets and Medicare, information needed to qualify for assisted living.

March 7 arrived with no word from Jane or Cecilia. The following day, I called Jane to learn the results of the meeting.

Jane spoke in her drugged, slow, shaky voice and sounded depressed. "I'm tired. I'm losing my citizenship."

I took that response to mean Jane was not going home yet. "When is your next evaluation?" I asked.

"Sixty to ninety days," responded Jane, talking more to herself than to me. "Talk to Cecilia, my lawyer."

"Cecilia is your social worker," I corrected.

Cecilia came on the phone. "I was going to call you next week." Cecilia assumed Jane had mentioned she was being released the following week. "The sheriff is going to drive her to Delta for the bond hearing."

"Jane didn't tell me that. I thought she was going to be there another ninety days," I said confused.

"I thought Jane understood. After the bond hearing, she will be released to go to her apartment," Cecilia revealed. "Ben is cleaning it up. Adult Protective Services will come in to check the apartment to make sure it is safe and sanitary."

I phoned Cecilia Monday morning. I wanted to learn more about Jane being monitored.

"The Delta sheriff picked Jane up at 3 A.M. and took her back already," Cecilia informed. "Jane was in bed asleep when the sheriff arrived. He was dropping off another person so took her back while he was here. She is in the Delta jail now, waiting for her bond hearing on Wednesday. Adult Protective Services has checked out the apartment. I assume it is livable. That does not necessarily mean it is neat. Between State Mental Health and other services, she will be monitored."

"Is the monitoring only for a limited time?" I questioned.

"It will be for as long as they think it is necessary," responded Cecilia.

"With Jane, it needs to go on forever, or most likely, she will decide to stop taking her medications like she has done before," I interjected.

"The hearing is scheduled at three," Cecilia stated. "The charges may be dropped, and then Jane will be released to go to her apartment. I checked into getting Jane in an assisted care facility. There are not many around. Jane had been in one before, and they did not want to take her. They said she didn't fit in. Her only option is to go to her apartment."

I took notice of Cecilia's comment that Jane did not fit in. Everywhere Jane went, she burned her bridges. She had been barred from the grocery store, the library, senior citizens' center, the church kitchen, and choir. She was always feuding with her neighbors and asked not to return by her optometrist and a dentist's office.

"At some point, you might want to move her closer to you," stated Cecilia.

"That would not work for us. She would cause too much turmoil for our family," I stated.

"A lot of families have told me it is too hard for them," Cecilia replied. "I can understand that after a lifetime of dealing with the situation."

"Is there anyone in Delta we can talk to when we are concerned Jane may be having issues?" I asked.

Cecilia gave me the name and number of a lady with State Mental Health. "Jane will have to sign a release with HIPPA for people to talk about her. I will make a note to encourage her to sign. Right now, Jane isn't very cognitive."

"Jane sounded confused the last time I talked to her. I was wondering if she is ready to be released," I confided.

"It will not accomplish anything to keep her here. Jane has met her maximum gain. Basically, all she was doing is serving time," Cecilia replied. *Maximum gain* was an interesting way of stating Jane was not capable of improving any further. She did not say Jane was functional. After being in Pueblo well over a year, Jane would be happy to finally be back home where she was not on such a strict regimen.

Four days after the bond hearing, I phoned Jane. Ben answered, saying Jane was lying down. A long moment later, Jane spoke. Both Jane and Ben sounded happy and upbeat during the lengthy conversation. Jane stammered while asking if I could come see her.

"I don't know," I responded not welcoming the thought. "But I will keep in contact with you."

"The judge said the next time she sees us, she wants to see us happy together," Jane stated. I surmised they must have been ordered to report back to court as a follow-through regarding the domestic violence episode. "Ben has been a lot of help. I told Cecilia I would keep the apartment clean without help from the aids from Loving Assistance. There are papers all over that I'm sorting through. Ben wants to talk to you."

Ben talked about his sister dying. "Carrie had bone cancer, then she got a tumor in her brain. She was in a nursing home and had seizures. When they decided there was nothing more they could do, her treatment was stopped, except for pain medication. She died two days later."

"I'm very sorry you lost Carrie," I conveyed with sincere sympathy. "I know she will be greatly missed, and what a major loss this is to your family. She was a very special person."

Jane came back on the phone, "Ben is still smoking, but that won't keep him out of heaven."

"No, it won't, but it could get him there sooner," I responded jokingly.

Ben and Jane laughed and sounded happy, to my delight. I had high hopes they would settle down into a compatible relationship.

Lois sent Jane cleaning supplies when Jane informed her, they were eating their meals out because the kitchen was too dirty. *How can they possibly afford to eat out,* Lois wondered.

Jane was always lying down whenever Lois or I phoned. She had lost her vigor and did not sound happy. The medications were suspected of making her groggy, causing her to sleep a lot. Lois and I had great compassion for what Jane was going through.

"What kind of life is that?" I remarked to Lois over the phone. "Maybe they can adjust the medications that zap her energy."

Lois always was concerned what it must be like to be Jane. "I understand more about her illness. However, I still think she can control it more than she lets on. I understand she really is in a horrible place." Lois conveyed.

"Understanding Jane is complicated," I told Lois. "Jane's distorted thinking is beyond my comprehension."

I had become acquainted with Russell Carpenter, who worked part time at the shop where I frequently spent time taking sewing classes. Russell was a pleasant, intelligent man who had retired from operating his very successful Mexican food restaurant.

In mentioning Jane to Russell, I was astounded when he revealed he had ADHD and severe bipolar, which were controlled by lots of drugs. He explained he had caused his family lots of grief. Russell expressed that he understood from both Jane's point of view and mine. I was in awe how such a successful, amiable guy could have serious mental health issues.

"You said you understand things from Jane's point of view," I mentioned to Russell. "When you were causing trouble, could you control what you were doing or did you even care?"

"I could control it, but I did not care." Russell expounded.

What a revelation! Our thoughts had been confirmed. Maybe Jane actually could control her actions to some degree, but chose to go off in her tantrums.

Russell spoke of his two sons who shared the same disorder. "One is in jail right now. He refuses to take his medications. The other is doing fine. He is taking the medications."

"Are you still taking medications?" I asked.

"Yes. I have to take them the rest of my life to stay in balance, or I will revert back. It is just like being an alcoholic. I'll never be cured."

I shared my interactions with Russell to Lois. "He even writes cookbooks!" I exclaimed. "I'm very impressed with Russell and how he has turned his life around. I know there are mentally ill people who maintain their careers and function in society. I've been thinking about it and wonder why with all Jane's promise, she was not able to amount to much."

After contemplating how Jane differed from Russell, besides refusing to take the medication, it came to mind that drugs are not the only answer. Medications cannot change one's personality or change the basic core of who a person is.

"I have been thinking about where we are now and I honestly don't think that if we *understood* Jane any better, we would react much differently," I expressed to Lois. "We act on instinct. She is always verbally attacking us. She constantly tries to put us down, calling us stupid and calling me a weasel. She said I am in trouble with God and that I'm going to hell, not to mention keeping on saying I killed our cousin. We cannot just sit back and say, 'It's okay, she can't help it.' We have learned to ignore some things she has said, as it would only put us in a no-win conflict. She does not respond to logic. When we challenge her, she gets mad. It is demeaning to us to let her get away with it all the time."

"When she is stabilized, she is still weird," replied Lois. "She needs our support, and we will be there for her as much as possible, not to our detriment."

It had been weeks since I had spoken to Jane, when I decided to phone her. Jane answered, sounding much more energetic than usual. "I've been going over to Herman's, my brother-in-law's, to take baths. He is very affectionate. He keeps kissing me." Jane was back in her pattern of rambling. "They want to operate on my eyes for cataracts. They could cause me to go blind. I could have holes in my eyes."

"The operation won't make you go blind. You will see much better afterward. Remember how much better Mama saw after the cataract operation," I reminded her.

It was strange that Jane was going to Herman's to take baths and what was stranger, was his advances toward her. I surmised it must have been his way of coping with the loss of Carrie.

I phoned Jane every few weeks as promised. Something was strange about the call placed the morning of June 24. Jane was talking quickly. "Ben expects me to wait on him. He calls me 'you fuck'n Jane bitch,' and he keeps telling me to shut up, Herman keeps kissing me. I told him he can kiss me when he first sees me, then at the end."

Without skipping a beat, she began singing, "I love you, I love Ben, Ben loves me and all is good. They have changed me over to private care. I have an appointment with a regular doctor. I have a cleaning lady that is paid for by Medicare. I have to go give him some loving, will you call me back?"

"I will call you back another time," I said, bewildered from the bizarre conversation. The call wasn't at all what I had expected. Jane was not focused, changing topics so quickly she hardly made sense like she had done previously. Jane appeared to be in a manic state.

It was time to phone the person Cecilia had said would be a possible contact in Delta regarding Jane's welfare. A message was left. A return call finally came several days later. The woman coldly stated at the beginning of the conversation she could not tell me anything.

"Cecilia, Jane's social worker when she was in Pueblo, gave me your name and number, she said you would be Jane's social worker or would know who is," I stated.

"I can't tell you anything," the woman repeated.

"Cecilia said she would try to get Jane to sign the HIPPA form so that you could talk to me," I said feeling very frustrated.

"I'll check on it and call you back if she signed." The lady never returned my call.

A few days later, I received a call from Herman. He was confirming he had reached the right person and then passed the phone to Jane.

I greeted Jane cheerfully. "Hi Jane."

"You said that like you love me." I did not reply. "Herman had your number. He has free long distance and said I could use his phone."

Jane talked about her upcoming cataract surgery and chattered about having floaters that bothered her. "Medicaid is paying for the surgery. People look down their noses at you when you are on Medicaid. I could go blind. You don't get as good of care when you are on Medicaid."

"You won't go blind," I stated. "Many people have that operation all the time. Lois said she sent you some cleaning supplies. Have you cleaned up your kitchen yet?"

"The cleaning lady is allowed only in the kitchen and bathroom," replied Jane. "I would thank Lois but I lost her address." Jane jabbered on and suddenly got mad about me not meeting her in Grand Junction a number of years ago when Ben's family was having a get-together."

"There was this girl whose family turned their backs on her. No one would go camping with her. The girl went camping in a tent by herself, and they found her dead. She committed suicide by letting the elements kill her."

Jane changed topics. "Ben keeps telling me to shut up. He says it so much that I made up a song." Jane started singing, "Shut up, shut up, shut up, shut up, shut up . . ."

"You've lost sight of God!" she screamed. "I'm not crazy!" she yelled as she verbally bashed me up one side and down the other. "You need to see a psychiatrist!" she shouted. "My eyes are going to be poked out!" she exclaimed. "Ben's sister died last week."

"No, she didn't." I challenged, "She died the end of February."

"You have social issues with me. We think very differently."

"You are right on that one," I agreed.

"It is because I am so much smarter than you. You only call me to find out my business," Jane taunted, shoveling out more demeaning remarks that she was so good at.

"My phone is dying. I have to go," I announced.

I was very upset as I hung up the phone. My heart was pounding out of my chest. "Why does she upset me so much?" I asked myself. I was used to Jane's unpredictable explosive temperament, but it was not healthy for me to tolerate.

I informed Lois of Jane's tirade. "I can't remember all the garbage she was throwing, but I cannot take it. Since Jane accused me of only calling to find out her business, I'm not going to call anymore."

My wishes of sustaining a compatible association with Jane were dashed. It was clear underneath it all, Jane harbored unjustified feelings of anger and hatefulness that would never diminish and would never go away.

The summer of 2013 passed with no contact with Jane until I received a call September 13. Jane stammered around.

"Today is Thursday, isn't it?" questioned Jane.

"No. It is Friday," I responded.

"Oh. Well, I lose track of things."

"How are your eyes since you had the cataract operation?" I asked.

"I didn't have the operation. I kept missing my appointments. After you miss the third one, they won't take you anymore. I don't see very well, I'm almost blind without my glasses," stated Jane.

"I want you to call me," Jane expressed next.

"Why, so you can yell at me, saying the only reason I call is to find out your business? The last time I spoke with you, you were very nasty to me."

"I don't remember that," Jane responded. I sure remembered how hateful she was. "It is because of my illness. You should know I didn't mean it. When I get some bills paid, I would like to get together and go on a picnic."

I did not give an answer. I truly did not want to deal with Jane in person; over the phone was bad enough. The call ended.

∽∞∾

It was November, and Jane's sixty-seventh birthday was tomorrow. I was compelled to wish Jane a happy birthday, even though I had promised myself I would never call again.

The conversation began as usual by me saying, "Hi Jane. I am calling to wish you happy birthday."

"Oh, I had forgotten about that. I'm busy right now. They are delivering a new refrigerator, and there is a woman in the other room. Would you call me back?"

An hour later, I phoned again. Jane answered in an annoyed tone, "Joe's Bar and Grill."

"Hi Jane." I responded, recognizing Jane's grumpiness.

"You are calling to check on me. The cleaning lady just left, and I'm getting ready to lie down. Call back when I'm in a good mood. Do you want me to hang up now or later?"

"NOW would be good." I heard a click, and the call was over.

I was consoled by my attempt to be a good sister but was disturbed by the rudeness that resulted. Any contact with Jane was subjecting myself to potential offensive treatment.

Over a span of time some things, are destined to remain the same. A consistent compatible relationship was not attainable.

CHAPTER THIRTY-TWO

The Last Time

On Friday evening, several days after New Year's Day of 2014, Jane phoned. Jane was congenial at first but then announced she was going into a diatribe.

Jane lit into me giving no mercy. "You don't care anything about me. You think you are so much better than me. I should have married first. The Bible says so. You didn't take good care of Mama. You should have moved closer to Mama so she could see your kids more often. You shouldn't have bought the truck. All the diesel needs is a new battery, and it will run perfectly fine. You hated Teddy Winters and you killed him with your thoughts. You never listen to me. You never do what I say . . ."

The phone was put on speaker and was sat on the kitchen bar. Jane ranted on and on without pausing for an extended period. I held my forehead from the headache that had developed. Jane was unleashing all of her built-up anger, plus spewing some X-rated information I had never heard before. Several times I almost hung up and should have. When Jane slowed down, Don picked up the phone. After talking to Don briefly, her anger vanished. She calmly said, "Goodbye."

A week after the call, while I was in a sewing class, Dr. John Bancroft brought in a vacuum for servicing.

Dr. Bandcroft came over to say "Hi." He was a psychologist, whom I had known many years. I asked him if I could talk to him sometime about an upsetting telephone call I had received from my mentally ill sister. "Call me, and we can set up a time for you to come to my office."

On Monday morning, January 27, I met with Dr. Bandcroft. In answering some of my questions, he stated Jane did not develop schizophrenia from spinal meningitis as she claimed. "It is in her genes. It was determined upon conception. The gene could not show up for six or more generations, which could explain why no one on either side of the family had known of its presence. Her condition cannot be controlled by diet. Eating fruits and vegetables does not make a difference. Her medication isn't working. Her counselor or whomever is determining her medication level should be able to pick up on that. She will only get worse with age."

I showed him a scribbled note from Jane that had been received a few days earlier.

"Her handwriting is like a child's, and she jumps all over the place," stated Dr. Bandcroft.

I relayed the story Jane had told me about a girl who went camping by herself because her family would not go with her. As a result, she died, committing suicide by way of the elements.

"Do you believe that?" he asked.

"No, of course not," I replied. "She was trying to make me feel guilty for not paying more attention to her."

"She is a great manipulator," responded Dr. Bancroft. I already knew that she tried to be, but we could see through her tactics.

Dr. Bandcroft was aware I had a cardiologist appointment the following week. He gave me the names of two psychologists who he thought could help deal with the stress Jane was causing. "Whether you are aware of it, she is causing you stress, and that can affect your heart. Make sure your cardiologist is aware of her," he emphasized.

"I really don't think I need to see a psychologist. I know the best solution is to avoid Jane, and I've been doing that as much as I can." I shared.

"You need to be at peace. Cut off all communication with her. Totally cut it off," Dr. Bancroft repeated, "You are not equipped to deal with her."

⚭

"I went to the cardiologist this morning," I mentioned to Lois." My blood pressure was the highest I've ever seen it. That may have been a result of Jane's 7 A.M. call. Don told her I was still asleep. I thought she would call back again, but she hasn't. I'm trying to take Dr. Bancroft's advice and not talk to her."

"Maybe I should step in," Lois suggested. Then you wouldn't have to talk to her at all." Lois was worried about my health. She had recently retired and felt that she might be able to relate to Jane.

Lois' offer to keep up with Jane, lifted the weight of the world from my shoulders. Being alienated from Jane relieved tremendous stress for me, but on the other hand threw overwhelming stress back onto Lois. After three months of dealing with Jane, Lois was totally fed up. "Jane is separated from Ben," Lois informed me. "He is living with Herman, his brother-in-law. There are restraining orders against both Jane and Ben. Jane wants to sell the truck. Ben was arrested for drunk driving after running into a fence and lost his driver's license." Lois wanted to be freed from talking to Jane.

"If you lose communication with her, we won't know what is happening with her," I expressed.

"I don't care," Lois replied. "Mama told us we were not responsible for her."

Jane continued calling Lois, leaving continuous marathon phone messages, the same as she had been leaving for me. She was told to leave only one message at a time. Any more would be deleted without listening to them. Lois was hanging in there, coping with Jane's harassing calls.

Instead of dreading anticipated calls, Lois chose to try something new. She would turn the table and call Jane once or twice a week. Jane's ranting stopped and Lois was more in control.

It was now October. "Jane's calls have slowed down," Lois told me. "She talks about when we were kids, we would go up to Aunt Mildred's and write songs with Gene Autry. Of course, I don't remember because I was too little. When Jane says things like that, it reinforces how nuts she is.

"Jane has a homeless woman living in her basement," Lois reported. "It is filthy down there."

◦◈◦

Don answered a call from Jane. "We have two satellites going around Mars. Martians live underground. They don't like us sending satellites around their planet, so they are shooting rays at us, which is causing me to lose my balance." He hung up. She did not call back.

In mid-October, Jane called, leaving several messages throughout the day on my answering machine. She wanted me to call her. During one message, she stated she was going to check on a poet's scholarship. "I still have enough years left to do that."

The final message was left that evening. "I haven't seen the lady living in my basement for a while. There is nobody here but me and the door knocker. I'm having a ball. I'm registered with the federal government as Jane the Clown."

Jane was supposedly being monitored and complying, but the question remained. How come is she acting like such a fruit cake? My suspicions were correct Jane had not been on her medications for months. She had gone to court to remove the mandate that required her to take them. It was a civil rights thing. As long as she was staying out of trouble, it was not enforceable. Jane got away with so much.

In mid-November, Jane was taken to the psychiatric unit in Grand Junction. Jane told Lois she got in trouble at the courthouse for heckling at a political event. But that was not a crime. Later, I heard Jane got in trouble for yelling at a judge when checking on getting a divorce. Could that lead to grounds for sending her to Grand Junction?

The Grand Junction psychiatric unit could only keep clients ninety days. She was released January 8, 2015, but that was too soon.

CHAPTER THIRTY-THREE

A Place for Jane

Walter, a social worker from Adult Protection Services, contacted me. Jane had provided them with my phone number previously when she was being sent to Pueblo. Since Lois was riding reins on Jane, he was referred to her.

"I have a good rapport with Walter," Lois told me. "Walter checked on Jane's apartment while she was in Grand Junction. When she got released, they wanted to put her in a halfway house, but no one would take her. She is back in her apartment."

Jane was still getting in trouble. She was going to the Catholic Church. She went in for a while then decided to lie down on the floor. They were going to call 911, but she talked them out of it. Ben's brother-in-law, Herman came and got her. She was in conflict with Fingerhut. She ordered a pair of earrings but lost one. She refused to pay for it. Lois told her she should pay the $20, but Jane didn't see it that way. A collection agency was after her for $400 for something else.

Jane had put something on the stove and then left to go to church without turning the burner off. She was not permitted to stay at the apartment for fear she would cause a fire. Herman called Lois, saying they had put her up in a motel for a week. She had stayed at his house the night before.

March 10, Walter spoke with Lois saying Jane had dementia and did not have the capacity to take care of herself. She was declared incompetent by the state, and would not be allowed to return to her apartment. That day, Jane was taken to Colorado Springs and placed in a behavioral facility. Walter was trying to convince Lois to be Jane's guardian.

Lois found herself talking with the Delta City building inspector. The city was planning to put a lien on Jane's property for leaving some mattresses and trash on the side of her apartment. A notification letter was being prepared telling her to clear it out. "She won't receive the letter, Lois informed him. "She is in Colorado Springs."

The last day of April, Walter informed Lois the behavioral facility was ready to release Jane. "If they are going to release her, at least they need to bring her back to Delta," Lois demanded.

Walter continued to pressure Lois to become Jane's guardian. Under duress, she agreed, but after an agonizing sleepless night, she recognized she could not put herself in that position. James King had advised against it; however, suggested Lois could be assigned conservator, which would give her authority over Jane's finances. Lois had already been receiving Jane's mail and paying the utilities from her own funds.

In early May, an emergency court order appointed Renee, with a local senior care company, to be Jane's temporary guardian. She worked with clients in the Montrose/Delta area and would represent Jane until a new guardian could be assigned.

Walter was overwhelmed with frustration in seeking a facility that would accept Jane. In an attempt to let Jane go back to her apartment, city inspectors checked out the condition of the apartment. It was declared uninhabitable. The wood-burning stove was a major fire hazard. Lois was informed the electricity was being shut off because of electrical violations. Renee, the temporary guardian, cleared the food from the refrigerator.

Jane would never be allowed to live on her own again. The time had come for Lois and me to step in to look after the apartment.

Mama's words echoed back to us; we were not responsible for Jane. But Lois and I agreed, it was our Christian duty to take care of our sister. We could not just walk away. Lois chose to pursue the conservatorship for overseeing Jane's finances. Lois and I began discussing the logistics for cleaning the apartment.

The allotted time for Jane to remain at the behavioral facility had long passed when she was finally sent to an assisted-living facility in Colorado Springs, where she would remain. The assisted living facility closely monitored its residents. If Jane was cleared to leave the building, she would be accompanied. She was mandated to stay on medications. If she got out of line, she would be sent back to the behavioral facility for a "tune up."

Tony, the director of the assisted living facility, spoke with Lois regarding providing clothes and personal items for Jane. They would not accept clothes, bedding or other belongs from her apartment that could harbor roaches, bedbugs or rodents. Lois bought clothes and other items which were mailed to Jane.

A hearing date was set for June 15 to assign a permanent guardian for Jane from El Paso County. Jane failed to call in. She had an "episode" declining to receive her injection and was taken to the behavior facility for a "tune up." To proceed, Jane needed to be included on the conference call. A new hearing date was set to June 30.

A hearing date to assign Lois as Jane's conservator was set for June 25. Meanwhile, Lois conferred with James King several times. Lois learned Ben had been living in a tent in Herman's back yard, where he had spent the winter. He had seen Ben around town using a walker. James expressed the neighbors hated the graffiti Jane had painted on the side of the building and asked if she could arrange to have it painted over when she came to clear out the apartment. The hearing date to assign Lois the conservatorship was postponed because of a court oversight.

Meanwhile, the guardianship hearing went well, with little comments from Jane, other than her citizenship was being taken away. Lois spoke several times with Rachel, the new guardian. Rachel thought Jane was sweet and they would get along fine. Lois warned her Jane's temperament may be short lived.

Finally in July 2015, the conservator hearing transpired smoothly. Lois was now Jane's legal conservator. There was one complication. Jane stipulated the apartment could not be sold without her approval. There were financial limitations that would prohibit Lois from correcting the code violations. Selling the apartment was the only logical solution. It was learned Jane's opposition to the sale would be overridden by the court since the court had declared her incompetent. That required another hearing.

CHAPTER THIRTY-FOUR

Farewell

"I hope we aren't getting in over our heads," I said to Don as we approached the Durango airport to pick up Lois, Tuesday, July 21. From there, the three of us drove to Delta to tackle the overwhelming task of cleaning out Jane's apartment.

Fortunately, Lois' plane was on time. We were on our way to an unforgettable experience.

Lois was on top of things. "I have done as much as I could to save time once we get there," Lois announced. "Herman, Ben's brother-in-law, gave me the name of some men who can haul the mattresses to the dump. James King has word out we are looking for help. He gave me the name of a car dealer who may be interested in buying Jane's vehicles. The city is going to deliver dumpsters which should be there now. I have talked to the lady at the utility department about temporarily turning on the electricity. Since we cannot send any of Jane's belongings to the assisted living facility, we have to dispose of everything!" Lois exclaimed.

Upon arriving in Delta, our group checked into a motel with joining rooms. Renee dropped off the keys to the apartment and talked about Jane's situation. "Jane has lost a lot of ground," Renee explained. "Every time a person stops taking their meds, they do not obtain the level they were at previously. She has only gotten worse."

After having dinner at a cafe on Main Street, we decided to survey the condition of Jane's place. We saw the mattresses that had been propped up against the side of the building among the tall overgrowth of weeds. Boxes and miscellaneous items pressed against the windows inside the small enclosed porch area. A notice stating the apartment was not safe and not inhabitable was posted on the door to the porch. Upon opening the screen door, which was not locked, a scene of junk greeted us. Sticks and weeds had been tossed on top of the debris. It was surmised they were to be used for fuel in the wood-burning stove. The door to the apartment was barricaded behind the squalor, forcing us to go around to the back door, passing the graffiti Jane had painted on the outside wall.

A notice was posted at the back door as well. The key did not work, but with a slight push, the door opened to reveal the largest mess imaginable. The apartment was filthy. Using some empty boxes that were handy, Lois and Don started filling them with trash from the kitchen that I emptied into one of the dumpsters, returning the boxes for more loads. Two hours later, insignificant progress had been made in the ubiquitous chore.

On Wednesday morning, our cleaning brigade returned at eight o'clock. I began carrying out more boxes to dump and decided to pick up large pieces of broken glass by the dumpsters. The last thing we needed was a flat tire. I was greeted by a tall well-groomed man who, introduced himself as Norman Johnson. He occupied the adjacent apartment. After a brief explanation of the situation, Norman asked, "Do you mind if I look inside?"

"Go ahead," I replied.

He entered and looked around, surveying the overwhelming disorder. "Where Is Jane?" he asked.

"She is in assisted living in Colorado Springs," Lois replied. "She is not coming back."

Continuing to look around, getting the full impact of the disarray and clutter, he asked, "What are you going to do with this place?"

"We haven't gotten that far," Lois answered. He left to go to his office.

Roger, one of the neighbors, stopped by and offered to help. His wife, Sandy, asked if she could have a set of unique bookends consisting of small globes that she admired. They were covered in decades of dust when Lois handed them to her.

I spoke with her briefly in the kitchen. "Jane was my friend," Sandy shared. "She would come over, and we had conversations. We watched TV and ate ice cream. Sometimes she would get upset and yell at me for no reason. I told her she was in my house, just calm down. I will miss her."

An electrician Lois had contacted arrived to check what needed to be done with the dangling wires in the cellar. He returned later and corrected the obvious problem; however, he could not declare the electrical problems corrected as he did not have access to a large portion of the area that was blocked by piles of Jane's and Ben's possessions.

I cleared out the medicine cabinet above the bathroom sink in conjunction with a standing cabinet. A rectangular tin container with a handle, labeled "POISEN" was found. I handed it to Roger along with a bottle of some kind of citrate, to discard. While cleaning out a closet off the kitchen, Don came across Jane's old chemistry set. "She could have blown up the entire place with this," Don remarked.

Many boxes of discarded items filled the dumpsters quickly. The waste management company was called to empty the dumpsters several times and were asked to bring two more containers. "Sometimes when we came by, she smiled at us. Other times she would cuss us out," shared the driver.

A Baptist minister stopped to inquire about Jane. He helped get word out that we were looking for help. That evening a call was received from Ethan, whom the minister had referred. Ethan was a short, but strong, energetic young man. He became a lifesaver and stuck it out through the last day.

Between five and six o'clock each evening, the cleaning was suspended. Covered in grime from head to toe, we headed straight to the motel to shower and change clothes before going to dinner.

On Thursday morning, Roger stopped by to see if there were any books he would like to take. "You have a very big job here!" he exclaimed as he left. He could not stay to help.

Three Hispanics appeared with a truck and trailer. They hauled off the mattresses and made several trips of large items to the dump. Monty, one of the Hispanic helpers, stayed to help.

Don had purchased a gallon of medium gray paint and painting supplies in preparation for Thursday morning's goal to paint the entire lower area of the outside wall to cover the graffiti. While Don painted the wall, Lois and I filled boxes with family photos and miscellaneous items, which were salvaged from the middle room.

After dumping a number of boxes that had been lined up, Ethan asked, "What should I do next?"

"The cellar needs cleaned out. I don't know what all is in there. "The city inspectors need to get in here," I expressed as we opened the door from the outside near the back steps. The dark space appeared impervious.

"This is more than a two-man job," Ethan declared.

"Just do what you can," I told him. "We will have to leave the rest."

The enormous quest to clear the cellar lasted through Saturday during which time Ethan and Monty brought out camping gear, tools, stray pieces of wood and boards, and more boxes of clothes among countless other items. A dresser belonging to Ben was retrieved that contained two handguns. "They are not loaded," announced Ethan as he removed one from its light-colored leather case. The guns were Ben's. Jane probably did not know they were there.

As more of the cellar was cleared, we were relieved to discover the cellar did not extend the length of the apartment but reverted to a two foot crawl space.

The garbage truck was not keeping up with the need to have the dumpsters emptied. Lois arranged for the dumpsters to be replaced with a twenty-two foot roll away container.

Don had widened the narrow path through the middle room the previous day. The outside wall was still piled high with a mountain of clothes and a variety of objects that were encroaching on the ten-foot ceiling, barely letting in light from the window. I cleared a portion of the floor that was covered with a variety of objects, such as wire clothes hangers, buttons, spools of thread, yarn, stray change, unused checks, part of a set of encyclopedias, vinyl records for lessons to speak German, outdated canned goods, bottles, purses, stray socks and shoes and copious other items that were all covered in a thick layer of dust.

Lois had been going through papers from the desk and two file cabinets in search of vehicle titles and was collecting stray keys and coins, until it was time to meet Ben at the police station, which was within walking distance. Because of the restraining order against him to stay away from Jane's apartment, he needed to be cleared to enter to claim his belongings.

After being gone over an hour, Lois returned with Ben. Lois was impeded by Ben, who relied on his walker and moved excruciatingly slow. He looked older than his actual years, being younger than Lois. His gums had receded badly displaying teeth with wide gaps, which were black at the roots and yellow from tobacco stains. Ben reeked with the smell of tobacco and urine. He smoked a hand-rolled cigarette as he sat on the seat part of the walker, which he had placed at the bottom of the back steps, making it difficult to get past him as the workers made trips to the dumpsters. He then migrated to various parts of the apartment and observed as others worked.

The paid workers took a lunch break, while Don and I returned to the motel to make peanut butter and jelly sandwiches. Lois and Ben remained at the apartment.

We had not brought enough bread to make sandwiches for everyone. From the motel's mini refrigerator, I removed the last bit of my submarine sandwich from yesterday's lunch and the piece of chicken leftover from my dinner of the first night, which served as my lunch, to allow for Ben to have my sandwich. For drinks, delicious Wendy's strawberry lemonade was purchased. The lunch set precedence for Ben to appear succeeding mornings before lunchtime.

After lunch, Don was dealing with loose ends in the middle room. He pulled on an extension cord that was duct taped to the floor, not realizing it was plugged in. An arc flashed from the cord as did hot sparks that landed on his socks. He yelped as he instinctively brushed off the sparks to prevent his socks from catching on fire.

After calming down, Don and I unearthed a twin bed and kitchen chair from beneath the mountain of miscellaneous articles that had overtaken the middle room. Two guitars and other items that were thought to be Ben's were stacked against the wall under the window in the kitchen. The helpers with the pickup loaded Ben's belongings to deliver them to his storage unit.

That afternoon, Norman, from next door, appeared saying he was interested in possibly buying the apartment, which he discussed briefly with Lois, explaining both he and his wife were realtors and there would be no realtor fees.

It had been decided to have a garage sale Friday and Saturday, even though there were still areas that needed cleared. In preparation for the garage sale, first thing Friday morning, Monty began working in the first room, sprucing up the wood-burning stove area which was surrounded by aluminum cans, paint cans, ashes and trash. With a barely working old vacuum cleaner, Ethen had found in the closet, he began vacuuming in the first room, with the nozzle pressed against the brown carpet, picking up dirt and small pieces of trash. I swept dirt and grit into piles from the small porch and removed as much as possible in anticipation of people coming through this area to inspect more garage sale items inside of the apartment.

Small garage sale items were placed on an orange tin folding table and a dilapidated card table with wobbly legs that were located in front of the porch. Lois brought two garage sale signs that were placed outside the apartment. Ethan had made two green neon posters the night before. At nine o'clock he placed them strategically on the busy street near the apartment for people to see. A stream of bargain hunters appeared in full force.

Some people were curious and asked where Jane was. A lot of them knew her and wished her well. Among the garage sale customers was a tall, older man who entered the apartment looking to see what else was being sold. He sported a long white beard that rested on his chest. His long neatly groomed braid nearly reached his waist. "I like your braid," Lois commented.

"I was a Hell's Angel in California," he shared.

"But you look like a good guy, now," Lois responded. He had sparkling blue eyes with a pleasant demeanor.

"Yes. It cost me a lot of money to get out. I'm sixty-nine and lucky to be alive."

"Did you know Jane?" Lois inquired.

"Yes. I spend a lot of time at the Elks Club. She came over frequently causing trouble."

He came back out to pay for the items I was holding for him. "You both are Jane's sisters?" he questioned in disbelief.

"Yes we are." I responded.

"But you two are so nice," he said in disbelief. "She was very nasty and rude. So rude," he repeated as he walked away."

Roy, a man who owned a used car lot and dealt in antique cars, came by asking about the vehicles. Lois took him out to the vacant lot near the apartment where the blue Plymouth Belvedere was parked along with the camper trailer and the two non-drivable trucks. Upon opening a rear door of the blue car to exam what was on the seat, Lois disturbed a wasp nest. She flew away at lightning speed.

"I bet you've never seen a sixty-five year old woman, move so fast!" Lois said jokingly to Roy, who was laughing. Don helped negotiate the sale of the vehicles. Another car dealer had previously agreed to buy the newer truck. The buyers would haul the vehicles away.

I manned the garage sale the majority of the two days. It was interesting talking to the neighbors who came by. Norman spoke to Don and me while waiting for his wife. "When we were moving in, Jane met us in 'full battle regalia.' She had an ice cream bucket on her head with the handle under her chin and was holding a broomstick."

Norman's wife, Rita, stepped out of their apartment and joined in relating more details. "You can't move in here. I'm the manager, and this apartment is mine, Jane told us. She tried to keep us out by duct taping the doors and windows in the front and back shut. She wrote 'Quarantined' on the door." They were both smiling and speaking about Jane in a jovial matter.

"I came home to find vomit in the mail slot. It smelled really bad. I wondered how she got it in there," Rita said laughing. "She almost threw a container of urine on me. I threatened to call the police."

"She appeared at our door, saying we could not have noisy children here. She insisted she could hear them," stated Norman. "We have two dogs that she may have heard but no children. She came to our door and slipped past me, looking for children under the bed and in the living room. We escorted her to the back door and told her to leave. She kept telling us to push her off the back steps."

"She said when we are gone, our teenage children come in and have sex, and they should not be doing that. We don't have teenage children. Our children are all grown. She got in loud arguments with the guys who live near the end of these apartments. She called them jerks and got right up in their faces."

"Did it get violent?" I asked.

"No," Norman stated. "I called the police before it got that far. I've called the police many, many times."

"Before she went away, we were woken up several times in the middle of the night. It sounded like a parent was beating their child. We could hear the voice of a parent telling the child to behave, and a child was screaming 'Don't beat me! Don't hurt me!' Jane was really good at mimicking voices. It sounded like two people over there!" Norman exclaimed. "We called the police. It sounded real."

"I used to talk to Ben a lot before he was banned from the apartment. I had conversations with Jane also about Charles Dickenson," stated Norman.

"We talked about flowers," Rita added. "I planted some for her, as well as strawberries that we told her she could eat. She is a character. She was very entertaining. We are going to miss her."

When people said they would miss her, we wondered how they could miss the turmoil she caused. In all fairness, though, most people probably were not aware of her endless antics or the countless times the police had chased her around town and were beckoned to remedy her disturbances. Whether, Jane realized she was a form of entertainment, we did not know, but she must have derived attention from some of her unconventional behavior, which she loved.

While I manned the garage sale, Lois and Don ran errands.

Lois entered the bank to close Jane's checking account. "I've known Jane for fifteen to twenty years. These last two years she has gone down significantly," stated the lady who was assisting them. "She came in and bothered the tellers. Sometimes I had to tell her to leave and she did. I felt sorry for her. It wasn't her fault, but at the same time it was, for not taking her meds."

Another stop to acquire duplicate vehicle titles provided the opportunity to speak with another lady who knew Jane. Lois explained she was Jane's sister, bringing her to attention. "You are Jane's sister? We wondered what happened to her."

"She is safe living in an assisted living facility in Colorado Springs," explained Lois. "She is supervised and required to be on her medications."

An appointment had been made to meet with James King, the attorney, at two o'clock that afternoon. Lois and I walked to his office two blocks away. We entered the law office together with Ben, who had just arrived. He looked scrounge as ever, and was still wearing the same clothes we had first seen him in, since our arrival. James ushered us into a conference room, where the topic of Ben and Jane ending their marriage was discussed. Since both were low income they qualified for free legal services.

Jane had begun the separation process but was confused about their marriage status. She told Lois they were divorced but Lois had a court document stating they were still legally married. Ben declared he had no claim to the vehicles or apartment and its contents, except personal items. Everything was in Jane's name.

Ben was invited to stay while conservator issues were discussed. He chose not to stay. James noticed the chair which Ben had occupied, was wet with urine. The secretary came in to clean the chair while James led us to another conference room where our meeting convened. He explained the financial reports Lois was required to submit as conservator and provided examples of items to include. The topic of selling the apartment was discussed. "It will be difficult to sell. A realtor will not make much profit," James declared.

After the business portion of the appointment, James shared some amusing incidents about Jane.

"We attended the same church. There had been a fire, and the congregation was meeting in a temporary building. When the church building was completed, we had a big service. Jane sung in the choir and was in the front row center, directly in front of the microphone.

When the choir sang, Jane was the only one that could be heard," he laughed. "She was off key and hit wrong notes. After the services, it was suggested to move the microphone."

"There was another time when Jane was misbehaving. The choir director told her she was out of the choir. She appeared the following Sunday and put on the bright-blue choral robe as usual. The director told her to take off the robe and leave. She left but did not remove the robe. She walked down the street in the blue robe to the Catholic Church. Of course, my church wanted their robe back, so they called the police. In the meantime, she joined the Catholic choir. They didn't know what to do with her, so they called the police. My church got back the blue robe. She kept things interesting.

"They had a strange marriage. Ben walked behind her following ten steps back. They did not sit together in church. She sat on one side, and he sat on the other. You would not know they were married."

After the appointment, I went back to the apartment while Lois made one more stop at the courthouse. It was raining lightly. Don and Ethan had brought the garage sale items into the porch area and Ethan had left. While waiting for Lois to return, Don and I walked to the vacant lot. We watched as Roy hooked up the camper to his pickup truck. After pulling it a short distance, he realized it was too heavy to pull over the curb and tried to back it out. He decided to return for the camper the next morning.

Meanwhile, Lois returned, spotting Don and me at the lot as she walked down the street. Renee, Jane's temporary guardian, had gone by the open apartment and joined our group on the street. "You all have done an amazing job clearing the apartment. It looks so much better from the outside, too," she stated with enthusiasm.

"We still have another day for the garage sale and there is more stuff in the cellar, but we have made a remarkable amount of progress with the help from some workers," Lois agreed.

The garage sale was back in business at eight Saturday morning.

People were not coming early, but traffic picked up as more items were carried outside to sell. Ethan and Monty continued to remove items from the cellar; however, they were running out of room in the dumpster to toss unwanted items.

Don plugged in a metal drill to see if it worked for a potential buyer. Sparks began to fly wildly. "This isn't safe to use. It needs to be tossed along with that other one. I'm not even going to try it." He had had enough unsafe encounters with electricity.

I was taking a break in the first room, sitting on the beat-up desk chair, when the building inspector, entered the first room. The woodburning stove was in full view. "I won't approve this for occupancy until that stove is removed," he stated sternly. "That bathroom sink is about to fall off the fall. It has to be fixed."

I nodded as he pressed on toward the kitchen. He checked the cellar where an old washer and dryer that did not work remained. He could see where the small stackable washer/dryer unit in the kitchen was vented directly into the cellar. "The venting is not in compliance," he told Lois.

Upon the inspector's exit, we stood in the kitchen in our collective exhaustive states, evaluating the horrendous disaster of affairs we had undertaken, when Norman and Rita stopped by. They were interested in making an offer for Jane's apartment and asked for the lowest acceptable price. After some discussion, a fair price was agreed upon.

They would purchase the apartment as is, complete with the items that were remaining. Norman and Rita were fully aware that the apartment was currently uninhabitable and would require lots of improvements before the inspector would approve it for occupancy.

Thank goodness the nightmare of putting the apartment on the market and finding a buyer was avoided! The prospect of finding a buyer would be nearly impossible and the apartment could remain on the market indefinitely. We were especially thankful Norman and Rita saw the apartment's potential and were willing to take on the extensive restoration.

Our group checked out of the motel Sunday morning and met Norman and Rita at their real estate office on Main Street. After the purchase agreement was discussed and completed, a copy was made for James King. It would be dropped off through the mail slot at the attorney's office, along with the set of keys. Lois included a note explaining the details. James would handle the legalities of the sale.

By the grace of God, things had fallen into place, down to the detail of Don finding the keys to the apartment on top of the refrigerator.

The week had been a taxing ordeal both physically and mentally. We had gotten through it, and things would be better for all. "I know it will be hard for Jane to let go of this place." Lois expressed.

The sale of the apartment had yet to go through. Lois had many details to contend with, including a potential blowup from Jane. Sure enough Jane objected formally to the sale.

"I talked to Jane yesterday," Lois told me over the phone. "She said she is happy where she is and would like to spend the rest of her life there. I asked why she objected to selling the apartment. She said 'That's just what I do.'"

It was a no-brainer when the court ruled to allow the sale.

CHAPTER THIRTY-FIVE

A New Era

A new chapter had begun for all of us. The assisted living facility would maintain stability and provide a safe place for Jane to stay. Lois and I would no longer have to wonder what kind of trouble she was getting into or worry about what would become of her.

"Do you think you will ever go see her?" Lois asked me.

"I am ambivalent on that. For now, she is okay. That is all I need to know. What about you, Lois?"

"I will go see her eventually. I will call her and make sure her needs are met and pay her monthly care bills and co-pays from her Social Security. She won't come into my personal life."

I had finally attained the calmness I had aspired all my life. Lois would inform me how Jane was doing now and then, which was good to know from a fly-on-the-wall perspective. Lois felt reassured in her role as Jane's conservator, knowing she would never be put in a compromising situation.

Upon returning home, Lois diligently took over her conservatorship responsibilities. Working in tandem with Jane's guardian, Jane's living quarters were spiffed up with new furniture, bedding and a desk. Since Jane had left Delta with only the clothes on her back, Lois spent considerable hours on the internet buying her clothes and other items, which Jane appreciated.

Jane settled in adjusting to her situation, in which she would never be released to live freely. Lois sent Jane's general studies diploma and her poetry books to make her feel more at home. From time to time, Lois sent books, cookies or something to cheer her up.

Jane's conversations with Lois were "disconnected," with unrelated responses. Sometimes Jane's words were slurred and other times she spoke somewhat normally with less rambling.

As 2016 arrived, Jane was not living much of a life and was not happy. She did not want to have a phone or computer, expressing they were too complicated. The medications impaired her thinking. Jane was losing weight, and she was depressed. She gradually snapped out of it as summer arrived.

Lois felt a need to check on Jane and informed me she was going to visit Jane in September. Time had paved the way for me to consider joining Lois, but I would have to wait and see how my shoulder was progressing as I had just undergone surgery in mid-August to reattach torn tendons. Lois put her trip on hold, waiting to see if I would be up to going later.

I decided to join Lois' road trip the end of September. Don dropped me off at the Durango airport to meet Lois where we rented a car. We spent the night at our cabin in Pagosa Springs, Colorado. The following day, Caroline's family joined us in their sunroof truck. Don drove us in the sunburst-orange jeep to sightsee the mountain views and admire the spectacular golden foliage of the Aspen trees that were presenting their incredible fall colors. Upon returning from the drive a short hike was on the agenda up the Piedra River Trail.

Lois and I spent Sunday, October 2, driving to Colorado Springs. We joined our friend Pat for dinner at a Mexican Food restaurant then went on to spend the night with Lois' friend, Lindy.

Monday morning at nine-thirty, Lois and I arrived at the assisted living facility that had become Jane's home. It was a red brick complex that was originally built in the 1950s as an Army barracks. It was not fancy, but it was well kept.

Jane was not there upon our arrival. She had gone to have her blood drawn and was expected back in two hours. This provided an opportune time to meet with Tony, the director of the facility, who happened to stop by the home. We followed him by car to his nearby office. Tony, a tall, slender man of six foot seven, was very pleasant. He commented on how sweet Jane was. Monthly or bimonthly, dental cleaning appointments were suggested for Jane as she was neglecting her teeth, and they needed attention. A senior citizens' center was across from his office. He thought Jane might be interested in signing up for activities. The assisting living facility could provide transportation. Knowing we were treating Jane to lunch, in parting, he recommended going to a small café not far from there, which served good food.

Upon returning to "Jane's house," as Tony called it, we went to her room. At first glance, I was not sure it was Jane. She was thin. Her hair had grown long and was in a ponytail. But most of all, her face looked like that of an eighty-year-old woman. She was smiling and happy to see us. She babbled something that was indistinguishable.

"Would you want to go to lunch?" Lois asked.

"Let me get my coat," Jane responded.

"Do you need a new coat?" Lois asked. We had planned to take her shopping for clothes since we knew she had lost weight.

"No, this one fits fine," Jane replied while looking for her cane. She had left it at the health clinic that morning.

As we walked to the car, Jane picked up a twig that had fallen from a tree onto the lawn and was looking for more. Tony had assigned her to keep the lawn picked up since she insisted she needed a job. "You can do that later," Lois told her as she took the twig from Jane and laid it on the ground.

Jane chose to sit in the back seat. Lois had to assist her with her seat belt. As we drove off, Jane said, "I don't care much for men anymore."

"They are a lot of trouble," Lois agreed with a big smile.

"I'm very religious," Jane said next.

"What church do you attend?" Lois asked.

"You can take me to any church. It doesn't matter."

"We aren't going to church. We are taking you to lunch," stated Lois.

Our group arrived at the small crowded café Tony recommended. Lois had to unbuckle Jane and pull her out of the back seat. Jane moved slowly through the parking lot towards the restaurant's entrance. Once inside, we were seated in a booth; Lois sat next to Jane. The waitress smiled sweetly as if she thought we were taking our elderly mother out for lunch. It was difficult to believe we were less than two years apart in age.

While our orders were being prepared, Lois presented Jane with some gifts. Jane liked the pocket book that contained $60. Lois then gave her a silver drawstring pouch, which contained two bracelets and a turquoise cross on a silver chain.

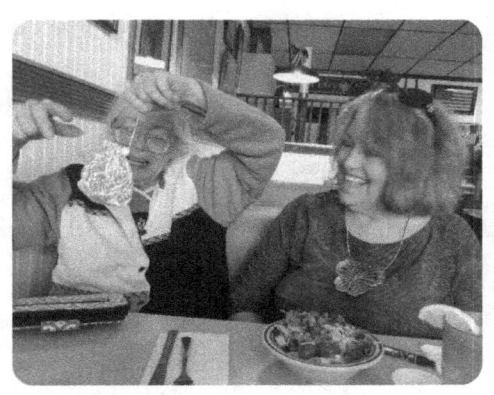

Jane and Lois at cafe

Before exploring the contents, Jane held up the pouch and dangled it before her eyes. She then attempted to loosen the string, while tilting her head. Her vision was very poor. She should have had her cataracts removed when she had the chance. She put on the bracelets and attempted to put the chain over her head, but it was too small. Lois helped her with the clasp.

After eating, Lois suggested we go shopping. Jane said she was tired and did not need anything.

"Would you like to stop by the senior citizens' center while we are out? Tony thought you might like to check out the activities," I suggested.

"That costs money," Jane expounded.

"I'm sure the fees are very reasonable if you are interested" Lois said encouragingly. Jane did not respond.

"Before we go back let's go to a park where we can talk," Lois suggested.

I pointed to a large park that just happened to be across the street. We had already taken our places in the car. This time Jane wanted to sit in the front seat. Upon arriving at the park, Jane began picking up pine needles from the grass. "You don't need to do that," I told her. "You are on vacation."

A cold breeze had come up, and Jane was tired. Back to Jane's house, we went. Jane was unsteady on her feet and wobbled when she walked. Lois stopped to speak with the staff about retrieving Jane's cane.

Jane scurried off to her room in a hurry, with me on her heals. Jane abruptly opened her door and entered quickly, slamming the door in my face. I knocked, with no response. I knocked again, only louder. Still with no response. Lois arrived just then and, without knocking, entered the room to find Jane wrapped up in a gray blanket on her bed taking a nap.

Jane was startled and rose from her bed.

"We want to get some pictures before we leave," said Lois.

Jane removed the rubber band from her hair and located her brush. Her gray to white hair was thick and pretty when it was brushed out. She sat in a chair and started singing. After taking pictures and departing chitchat, Jane was left to rest.

Rachel, Jane's guardian was awaiting our arrival. Along with Rachel, Irene, the owner of the agency, joined the meeting. Rachel was a brunette in her forties. Her supervisor was a lovely slightly older lady. Changing Jane's residency to El

Jane singing

Paso County, where she now lived was discussed, along with topics pertaining to Jane's well-being.

There was one more stop to make. Lois needed to meet with the mortuary director where she had begun to make arrangements for Jane's passing. After completing some forms, we were back on the road headed for Lindy's house.

Lois and I took leave the next morning headed for Durango to return the rental car and to meet Don. We mulled over our experience on the drive back. "We didn't know what to expect, but she was very amiable," Lois related.

"I am glad I went with you. I can't help but feel sorry for her," I expressed. "The Jane we just saw is not the Jane I dealt with for over sixty years. It is like she is not the same person. She appears to be cordial, sweet, old lady who wouldn't hurt a fly. If she would have displayed the same temperament to us earlier, dealing with her would not have been so daunting. Mind you, she is now monitored to be on psychiatric medication."

"Her life has been full of turmoil," Lois expressed. "All is well now."

That night we stayed at a motel in Durango for Lois to make a quick getaway to catch an early morning flight back to Tennessee.

CHAPTER THIRTY-SIX

Whatever Will Be, Will Be

Lois and I had returned to our busy lives. Lois had retired from her technical advisor position in the computer world. She enjoyed working part-time in an antique store, managing the accounting for her church, handling paperwork for the farm, and being the grandmother to five growing grandsons as well as keeping track of Jane's well-being. There was an endless list of tasks on her plate.

January of 2017 found me hurrying to complete a quilt project and other responsibilities prior to undertaking a total left shoulder replacement. The plan was to be mostly recovered before May to fly out to attend our granddaughter, Kayla's, college graduation.

All was well with Jane, or so we thought. On February 23, Lois received notice from Jane's guardian, Rachel, that Jane had gotten out on her own. She slipped out a back door of the assisted living facility unobserved. Our information was sketchy. Her *outings* as we understood had been in the daytime and at night. She came upon a lady walking her dog and was pulling the dog's fur. She was trying to get in people's cars. Jane was picked up one night in her night clothes by the police and taken to the behavior facility for a "tune up."

Jane phoned Lois from the behavioral facility. She had taken up where she had left off with her peculiar thinking. She claimed she had set Lois up with her first husband, Hans. Worst of all, though, Jane talked about getting her things back and returning to her apartment.

She wanted Lois to return her check book. Jane remained true to her life-long pattern of defying reality.

March 8, Jane leveled off and was moved to a different assisted living facility. It sounded like a lovely place to live on the outskirts of the city. But most importantly, it was a lock down facility and monitored constantly. She would still be able to go out with an escort

Lois and I were disturbed by this incident. We had assumed there would be no more concern for Jane's well-being, but she proved us wrong.

Again the following year, we visited Jane to see how she was adjusting to her new living facility. Lois flew into Durango where Don and I picked her up from the airport. The night was spent in Pagosa Springs at our cabin, leaving early Thursday morning. Don accompanied us as we drove to Colorado Springs, on the dreary fall day in early October. The night was spent again, with Lois' good friend, Lindy.

Friday morning, Lois drove as we ventured out into the country to the house which was Jane's new living quarters. Many of the rural homes accommodated horses, in the nearby pastures. Upon arriving, we were directed to the basement which housed several residents. From the basement, a sliding glass door opened onto a back yard which extended onto a golf course.

One of Jane's care givers had braided her hair, and it looked nice. She showed us her room where we met her roommate who spoke very little English, then we followed her out to the open sitting area. Lois brought her some new socks. I asked her if she liked the cloth picture of an appliqued cottage with flowers and clouds, and hearts coming out of the chimney that I had made for her. "I can't see it she responded." No wonder she could not see it. There was lotion or something, smudged thickly across her glasses lens. I took her glasses to clean them in the bathroom.

Jane and I walked together back to her room, to put the applique away. "I'm not doing badly for someone who is sixty-seven," Jane announced.

"You aren't sixty-seven," I responded, "You are seventy-one."

"Really?"

"Yes. I am sixty-nine and you are almost two years older than I am." Apparently Jane did not take notice of her birthdays or perhaps dementia was an issue.

"I am going to die soon." Jane kept repeating.

"How do you know that?" I questioned.

"I just know," she responded.

As we entered the sitting area, she said, "I want to go to heaven. Will you look for me when you get there? I'm not sure I'm going to heaven." Lois jumped in and told her she needed to accept Jesus Christ as her savior and explained more on the topic.

Racheal, Jane's guardian, appeared to see Jane and speak with us. While chatting with Racheal, I noticed Jane was wearing a pair of new white tennis shoes that were not tied. I tied them for her. It was ironic that she refused to tie my shoes when I begged her to, as a child of three.

"Would you like to go for ice cream?" Lois asked.

"I sure would," Jane answered. We followed Jane into her room to retrieve her coat, which she could not find, until it was located on the floor behind a chair. After getting her settled in the car, we began our quest for ice cream, not knowing where we could find some. Luckily, we came upon a small shopping area that had a Burger King. Jane was hungry and wanted a "Whooper."

Upon entering the Burger King, Lois purchased a burger for her with fries. She chewed in such a fashion that Lois, who was sitting next to her, caught the fall-out. Amazingly, she downed the entire burger and still wanted ice cream. I got a cone for her with lots of napkins that came in handy to catch the ice cream as it

Lois and Jane at Burger King

rolled down her chin. Getting back to the car, Lois led her around a big puddle of water that she was preparing to walk through.

We could see Jane did not have much of a life, but there was no way we could take care of her.

After dropping Jane off, back at her residence, we headed back to Lindy's for the night and stopped back to tell Jane "Goodbye," the following morning.

We did not visit Jane again, the following year while she remained at the country house. Lois spoke with her occasionally, but Jane did not have anything to talk about. A lot of Lois' time and energy was spent managing Jane's expenses and preparing an annual report for the State. Lois decided it was time to turn the conservatorship, over to the agency which handled Jane's guardianship. Kevin, a new person to be working with Jane, would take over as guardian in conjunction with Racheal. Racheal notified Lois of Jane's transferal to a different facility because the cost of keeping Jane in the country facility had increased, substantially.

Because of the Covid 19 pandemic, it was not a consideration to visit Jane in 2020. Kevin was in close contact with us regarding Jane's health. He called me to inform Jane had lost eighteen pounds while being hospitalized. She had gotten very sick with a bad cold or something non-Covid related. He was concerned about her extreme weight loss in such a short period of time. She was on hospice and palliative care. To encourage Jane to eat, a group of doctors and health care givers decided to take her off all the psychiatric medications, to determine a baseline. It was thought she would do better since the medications made her very drowsy. Upon hearing Jane would not be on medications, Lois and I knew that would be a big mistake. We were waiting for the mayhem to begin. And it did. Jane reverted back to her manic state and had to be sent to Mountain View Behavioral Health for stabilization. She was returned to her home, but had to be sent back to the behavioral facility a second time. Taking her off the medications proved to be a disaster, as we knew it would be. It was deemed necessary to keep her on medications to settle her down and prevent her disruptive behavior.

In July 2021, Kevin spoke with Lois concerning Jane's decline. She was not eating well and spent most of the day in bed. "Louise, we need to visit Jane before it is too late," Lois told me over the phone. We had been discussing a trip for this summer, but because, Bill needed hip replacement surgery, trip plans were put on hold. Bill was in no hurry to have the hip surgery since harvesting the hay crop had become his priority. Now was the time to go.

Our agenda mimicked previous visits, where Lois flew into Durango, rented a car then drove to our cabin for the night, before beginning the trip to Colorado Springs the following morning. Lois and I had a fun experience, non-stop chatting and following signs to check out the treasures of several yard sales along the way, and then on to Lois' friend, Lindy's house.

Upon arriving in Colorado Springs, a stop by Lindy's medical office was made to get instructions how to enter her home, which was in a gated community. After being greeted by Lindy's two huge, lovable Bernese Mountain Dogs, Austin and Hudson, the luggage was brought in. A visit to King Super's was in order, to stock up on snacks and items to make sandwiches. It had begun to rain as we headed for the store entrance. My cell phone was ringing as I struggled to retrieve the phone and close the umbrella. It was Don calling to report Colorado Springs made the national news with the deluge of rain. The rain was coming down in buckets by the time we were prepared to exit the grocery store. It let up as we made a dash for the car, wading through standing water. Shortly after arriving at Lindy's, a flood alert came across our phones saying not to go anywhere, except to evacuate flood areas.

Lindy's friends who had stayed the previous night had turned the thermostat to 60°. It was freezing cold. Lois located the thermostat and turned it up to sixty-seven degrees, which still was not high enough by my standards. It took a while to warm up our soaking wet freezing feet.

On Sunday morning, Lindy met a farrier at her ranch to shod her horses. With directions written out by Lindy, Lois and I made our way to the ranch later that morning. While Lindy tended to the horses, we rode around the main property on an ATV, checking out the remains of where the homestead had stood before the devastating Black Forest

Fire burned down the house and barns, eight years previously. The barn that housed the horses had been rebuilt, with plans to rebuild the house as soon as things settled down more from the pandemic.

Lindy prepared a special healthy dinner that evening. Mary, a charming old friend of hers and Lois', who had lost her husband to cancer recently, was also invited. Besides enjoying the wonderful dinner, we all had a very lovely evening.

Plans had been made to see Jane, Monday morning, on August 2. Lois was unsettled and stressed, continually forgetting where she had left her glasses and the keys to the rental car. The reality of Jane possibly dying relatively soon, was disheartening.

As it so happened, Jane's current residence was relatively close to Lindy's house, alleviating a long drive. Lois parked the rental car in the graveled parking area on the side of the house precisely at ten. We walked up the handicap ramp to the entrance, Lois looking as pretty as ever, with her thick blond hair and big blue eyes. Upon entering we were asked the routine questions regarding any exposure to the Covid virus and our foreheads were scanned for temperatures.

We noticed an elderly lady with long silver hair in a neat pony tail bob on top of her head, sitting with her back to us at the dining room table. Bree, one of the care givers addressed the lady, "Jane, your sisters are here to see you." She stirred from her napping state, turning around, to our surprise, it was Jane. She was wearing a heavy long sleeved sweater with a stain in the center of the maroon horizontal zig-zag repeat design, which concealed a turtle neck. Her maroon leggings revealed how thin she was.

No one had told her we were coming. She was very surprised, giving us a big smile revealing her missing upper front teeth. She relied on her walker and was very wobbly as she stood. She was very happy to see us, first hugging Lois then hugging me. It was obvious at first glance she was in no condition to be treated out to lunch. Jane quietly told me she was going back to Mountain View.

"Where are your glasses?" I asked.

"I don't need them. I got a procedure that was not surgical."

We were preparing to sit in the front area, which accommodated a sofa and some leather easy chairs, but Jane decided to go to her room instead, talking on the way, "I am happy here. I am happy anywhere they put me. I am waiting to go to heaven."

No sooner had we sat down on her bed, when Jane began singing "Ho, ho, ho, ho, ho—" continuously.

Lois asked where the fuzzy white teddy bear was, that she had sent Jane a few months ago. Jane did not know. The dresser, under the bed and the closet, which was full of adult diapers, were searched. No teddy bear was found.

"Let's take some pictures," Lois suggested. The sun was coming in the window behind Jane in such a manner only her silhouette would be seen.

"Come sit on the other side of your bed," I said to Jane. "We cannot get a good picture with the position of the sun. Jane and I went around her bed

Louise and Jane in Jane's room

where we both sat down. Lois was already sitting on the other bed under the window that was currently unoccupied by a roommate.

"Lois is fatter than you are," Jane spouted. Both Lois and I could afford to drop a few pounds, needless to say. Jane was in true form.

Out of the blue, Jane began a rendition of Beethoven's 5th symphony. "Dun-da-da-dun, dun-da-da-dun,—." Bree had said she really liked her music.

A few pictures were taken, when Jane decided she needed to lay down. Lois removed her black slip-on shoes. A small soft blanket

Lois next to Jane as she lay down

was laid across her body, followed with the bed quilt. With no chairs in the room, I remained sitting next to Jane. She started grabbing me, not particularly paying attention to where, and then hanging on to my hand and arm. She laid there briefly, then decided to get up, saying she was hungry. Exiting her room, she announced to the care takers she was hungry.

"Lunch will be served soon," responded one of the ladies.

"I'm hungry now." Jane demanded. Bree asked her to take her seat at the dining room table and asked her if she wanted green grapes, which was agreeable. I sat next to Jane as she ate several grapes. She sat there with her eyes closed, as Lois and I chatted. Jane's head bobbed around, then fell forward, face first, headed for an encounter with the plate of green grapes, until I caught her.

"Would you like to lay down?" I asked. She nodded her head, yes. She was shivering. We wrapped her in two small soft blankets and tucked her in bed again, under the quilt. As she laid there in silence I began talking about my grandkids as some time back she had asked about them. "Avery has two little boys so we have two great-grandsons now. He was in the Marines. He will be graduating in December from college. His wife, Rachelle, is a nurse. His sister, Kayla, is graduating from PA school in December. She has a serious boyfriend. Clara got married in November. She graduated with a BSN in May and is working in an oncology clinic. Mathew is doing well since struggling with osteosarcoma. He is a senior at West Texas A & M. He has a cute little girlfriend, with long blond hair, who is majoring in neurology. Curtis has two little boys. Cole will be thirteen soon and Knox is five. Curtis is not married to Claudia now. He has a new wife Jana, who is Knox's mother. Chris is in Dallas. He has a very demanding job and we don't see him very often. Caroline retired the end of June. She and Joe moved to Pagosa this summer, since they enjoy the mountains and cool weather." I could have gone on, as could any grandmother expounding on their kids and grandkids.

Despite appearances Jane was not asleep. "Lois, tell her about your family."

"My step-grandson, Justin is driving now. He grows water melons. I let him borrow my SUV to sell them on the side of the road. He and his mother have beehives, also. He and his brother, Jared are second degree black belts in karate. The other grandkids don't live close by. I have a booth where I sell things that I fix up. I also sing solos at church."

"You should hear her sing. She is very good!" I announced with enthusiasm. It is true, Lois is a singer with talent, as opposed to Jane who has illusions she can sing and write songs. Lois began singing a praise song she was practicing for a solo in church. Jane listened as Lois sang, accompanied by the music in her cell phone.

As Jane laid in bed, a clean-cut young man appeared, looking in and ducked back out after mentioning he and his father were the new owners of the facility.

"What do you do all day?" I asked Jane.

"I don't do anything."

"Do you read or watch T.V.?"

"No. But I watch baseball. The Cincinnati Reds," Jane announced to my surprise.

Lunch was being served. Jane stopped to talk to the new owner as she headed to join the other residents in the dining area. "You are a fine specimen of a good-looking man," Jane said to him as she proceeded on her way to the dining room.

Lois and I had a pleasant conversation with the young man, who previously had informed us he and his father were owners. He introduced himself as Coleton. "It is nice that you are spending time with your mother."

"She is not our mother. She is our sister," I explained.

With a puzzled look on his face, he proceeded to speak. "I am trying to get to know the families of our residents."

"We don't visit often," Lois shared. "We live in different states."

"We enjoy Jane. She is very funny. She had a cup of coffee— she drank the entire cup in one chug. I asked her if she wanted more. She said, 'No.'"

Bree agreed she was very funny. According to other people we had met in Delta, she was very entertaining. Jane did silly things to get attention.

While we were speaking to Colton, Racheal entered the home, sitting down in one of the leather chairs. We joined Racheal in the sitting area. She explained Kevin was unable to meet with us. He had an emergency appendectomy, which explained why he had not responded to our calls to confirm a meeting time with himself and Jane.

"Jane said she is going back to Mountain View," I expressed.

"No, she will remain here for the duration," said Racheal. "She had been going into people's rooms at night waking them up. Her medications have been adjusted to keep her out of the manic state, but to the level she can still function. It's a fine line to keep her calm and keep her relatively normal."

After lunch, Jane gave Racheal a big long-lasting hug, and they sat on the couch briefly, until Jane wanted to lie down again. We assisted Jane back to her bedroom. When she lied down, her leg was hanging over the edge of the bed. I lifted the dead weight of her leg onto the mattress. We tucked her snuggly back in bed, for yet another time.

We had been there more than three hours. Since Jane wanted to sleep, we hugged her as she laid in her bed and told her "Goodbye," for what was probably the last time we would see her.

Upon returning to Lindy's house, Austin, the female greeted us, while Hudson, who had hurt his back leg, pretty much did not move once he was settled. He was sprawled out on the floor in front of our bedroom door. He was too big to high jump over, so we had to maneuver around him. I started making Liverwurst sandwiches which we would eat on the road, while Lois packed up her things. Lois finished building the sandwiches and packing the lunch while I gathered my things for the trip back. Lifting the suitcase over Hudson without falling on him, was a real trick.

We decided to take a detour on our way back to the cabin, by way of Gunnison where we were born. We wanted to take our time looking over the town and checking out the house we lived in that Daddy had built. We were on the road, when Lois realized she did not have her glasses. It was imperative we find them. Since the cataract surgery she had difficulty focusing on close objects. After stopping to search for them to no avail, we returned to Lindy's for a thorough search. After looking every possible place we could think of, including getting over the dog barricade, they still could not be located. As frustrating as it was for Lois to accept her new bifocals were lost, it was time to leave without them.

Off we were again, headed by way of South Park. I did not remember ever going this way from Colorado Springs, through these breathtaking mountains. It was very familiar to Lois, from when she lived there. On the way we discussed our feelings about Jane. Jane had taken an underlying toll on both of us, which still remained. "If Jane had been a normal sister, I would not have left home soon after graduating from high school. My life might have been very different," Lois shared. As mean as she had been, she was still our sister who we could not turn our backs on.

We were exhausted by the time we reached Gunnison. Precooked chicken tenders that we brought back in Colorado Springs, were heated up in the hotel microwave for dinner. We watched television until it was time to call it a day.

Getting up later than planned, we had a hot breakfast of scrambled eggs and coffee provided by the hotel. After checking out, the first mission was to find readers for Lois and find something to relieve the headaches she had been having. Walmart was on the agenda. While waiting a long time in line at the pharmacy, we struck up a conversation with a lady who knew one of Lois' old boy friends. Bumping into someone we could talk with about familiarities was a happy coincidence.

Reminiscing while driving down Main Street, revealed some places that looked the same, while others were completely unrecognizable. As we entered the government services building that once had been the old Pine Street School, I recognized the area which had been a dirt playground where I played hopscotch every day during the lunch hour with my friend, Nancy. The entire previously dirt school yard, now, was a paved parking lot and neatly landscaped with grass and shrubs. The inside had been repurposed so much it hardly resembled the original building. Even yet, the building brought back nostalgia and warm memories of previous teachers and the children I grew up with. Lois did not remember much about the school except for the oak hand rails which remained on the stairways throughout the building.

Lunch consisted of sandwiches that had been made before checking out of the hotel. We stopped to eat at the park, where we once had played on the merry-go-round, swings, teeter-totter, slide and monkey bars, which all had been removed decades ago due to their dangerous reputations. The old high school where I attended freshman year through mid junior year which over-looked the park, had been demolished decades ago, leaving no evidence of ever existing.

We checked out a thrift shop Lois wanted to explore. Then drove down the boulevard for a quick glance of the Cricket house. It didn't appear to have current occupants. Onward to the "new" high school.

"This doesn't look like our high school," Lois exclaimed. It certainly was not how she remembered it. The single level school had been expanded to an unrecognizable size.

Time was getting away and we had yet to go by our old house, which was the main reason for the trip to Gunnison. We drove out west of town on the familiar highway past the airport and through the motel which wound back to

Memory of log home

our parents' previous property. The road ended at a locked gate. Tall grass and trees had grown up obstructing the view of where we thought the house was. Being frustrated we had not seen the house, I suggested we go across the river to see if we could see it from there.

Entering the road that lead behind another motel on the opposite side of the river, Lois drove slowly to grab a peek between the houses that lined the Gunnison River. The houses were too close together to get much of a view. Lois turned around for another look. "Why don't we stop and ask someone if we can have a look from their back yard?" I suggested.

Lois thought that was too presumptuous, but we had spotted a lady working in her yard and thought perhaps we could ask her. The pleasant lady was more than gracious as she invited us to walk around to the back yard, where we introduced ourselves to her and her husband. Her husband said he had been in the area about fifty years and thought maybe he recognized Daddy's name. After desperately looking up and down the river both ways, our old house still could not be seen. The man said he thought the house had been demolished. He suggested we go back in town and approach the property from the other direction through a trailer park.

The thought of our log house being demolished, took my breath away. How could that be? It was built sturdily with love from the sweat of our father. However; from all indications, the man was right. There was no evidence we could see that our old house was still standing. This was very sad.

It was raining and we needed to get to Caroline's for dinner, in Pagosa Springs before dark. Outside of Gunnison was a sign saying the road between Gunnison and Montrose was open. That was curious. Of course the road was open, not that it would affect us though, as we were heading South through Lake City. Later it was realized the sign was applicable to people needing to get from one side of the state to the other, because of the closure of Interstate Highway 70. The exorbitant amount of rain had caused a ginormous mudslide bringing tons of debris from the tall mountains down onto the highway. It was estimated to take weeks to clear the Interstate.

As we approached the cut off to Lake City the shortage of water filling up Blue Mesa Reservoir was very evident. The tall pylons supporting the bridge were mostly visible. In the past the water was just below the bridge. This was another blow to us.

The way through Lake City was new to Lois, as she had never had occasion to go this way before. Gorgeous mountain views were to be seen in every direction. We were getting weary as we finally got over Wolf Creek Pass and shortly thereafter, arrived at Caroline's new residence.

Caroline was excited to see her Aunt Lois and show her around her new home. Even though Caroline had only been retired since the end of June, she and Joe had purchased the property in December 2018. The house had been run down and the property was overran by prairie dogs. Caroline and Joe had made many improvements before moving in.

We ate dinner while admiring the view of the high majestic mountains from the dining room picture window. Caroline talked with Lois until it was time to retreat to our cabin a short distance away. We would return tomorrow for another day of catching up, and a short jaunt to Echo Lake to venture out in the pedal boat.

The following day was spent as planned. Lois got to see Mathew, now, twenty-one. He had been diagnosed with osteosarcoma at the age of eight. Lois was happy to see how well he had progressed with his leg since his battle with cancer and his time spent at St. Jude Children's hospital in Memphis.

Lois' trip was coming to an end. Thursday morning Lois spent repacking and organizing her suitcases. The lost glasses were not found among her things, however; later Lindy found them where they had slid between the bed and night stand in the bedroom we were staying. More time was spent with Caroline, until it was time to meet Don at the Durango Airport to return the rental car. The night would be spent in a hotel at Durango to allow for an early getaway to catch her flight.

Lois is planning to come out again next summer to spend time with me and Lindy, even if Jane passes away. As for now, I don't plan to see Jane again. I prefer to spend my time with family and friends and working on sewing projects, rather than making a trip to Colorado Springs to watch Jane sleep.

CHAPTER THIRTY-SEVEN

The Final Chapter

Lois and I were back in our routines keeping up with our families and active lives. Jane continued to exist in her mundane life, never leaving the home, except for medical appointments. Jane had no quality of life.

We sent birthday cards for her 75th birthday in November. We hoped she appreciated the thought and our efforts to brighten her day. Her medications kept her in a drowsy state, though. It had been years since she passed the point of being able to write a note or initiate a phone call on her own.

Saturday, the evening of February 5, as I was in my sewing room watching television and working on a sewing project, a call came from Laura, a joint owner of the facility housing Jane. "I am sorry to tell you, Jane passed away at 5:20."

I might as well have been slugged in the stomach. I could hardly breathe. It was impossible to say anything. An endless stream of tears started flowing uncontrollably, as Laura continued talking. "Jane was very sick with Covid, She did not suffer. She was not in pain." I knew Jane was on morphine. I was listening but in shock, not actually hearing what she was saying.

Finally, I blubbered, "Was she alone?"

"No. I was holding her hand when she passed peacefully." Laura was very companionate and said they would miss her, and offered condolences and assistance.

After the call, I sat in a daze as tears continued to roll down my cheeks. Why was her death affecting me this way? There had been times in the past, when Jane had made my life a living hell. I had wished she would just drop dead! We were never close, loving sisters, even though we could have been, if she had not resented me so much for existing.

My response was apparently a normal expression that burst from the sudden release of stress which I had been subjected to all my life. There were feelings of loss which I contributed to losing the sister I wished her to be; not the hateful abusive sister her mental illness had turned her into.

Lois, being used to dealing with death, shed no tears over Jane. However, Lois had deep empathy for her. "It seemed everything was sad about Jane," Lois expressed. "Especially her excessive failures to stay out of psychiatric facilities; specifically the state hospital in Pueblo. Sad she had a caustic personality. Sad we did not share good times or have the natural comradery sisters generally share. The disappointments and trials our parents endured was sad." Way too much sadness had been caused by the turmoil Jane created.

As did I, Lois felt a huge relieve that Jane would no longer suffer from the ravages of mental illness and ensnare us in her drama.

Now there was just Lois and me, which felt very strange. In a way it seemed lonely. My big sister had always been there in one form or another. What about her soul? Was she watching us from above as a sane entity?

Getting back to reality, there were the usual formalities that the world requires. Lois was able to locate Ben, still Jane's legal husband, who was now living in an apartment in Delta. "I wondered if I would ever see her again," he told Lois upon hearing the news. Jane's possessions would go to Ben, which besides her clothes consisted of a bed, dresser and a desk. "I have no way to pick them up," Ben explained. "Those items can be donated."

Lois provided a brief obituary for the Delta newspaper, for which we were sure many people would take notice. There was no purpose in having services as she had no friends or relatives in Colorado Springs and arranging something in Delta was not practical. We would conduct our own private service at the time her ashes would be released. As previously arranged, Jane's ashes were sent to me. We did not open the parcel. Jane was placed on a shelf in the garage for now.

∾

Since our efforts to see the log home daddy built had not materialized the previous summer when we were in Gunnison, Lois researched the current property owner and got his information. Victor Carter was contacted. She explained to him our wishes to revisit where we had lived as children. He agreed to let us access the property on our next visit, explaining the house was no longer there. It had been badly neglected. The stairs had collapsed. Raccoons and pack rats had destroyed the inside making it impractical to renovate.

∾

It only seemed appropriate to take Jane's ashes to Gunnison. Lois flew to Colorado Springs in August, to visit her friend, Lindy, for a couple of days prior to coming to Pagosa Springs, where we planned to meet.

It was great to see Lois when she arrived in Pagosa. Time was short for visiting. We would be leaving the following day to spread Jane's ashes. Early the next morning, we left for Gunnison, by way of Lake City, taking Lois' rental car. Don did not go but my daughter, Caroline, joined Lois and I.

The spreading of Jane's ashes in the area where Mama and Daddy's ashes had been was on the agenda after first checking out our previous home. Victor Carter agreed to meet us. The gate was already unlocked when we arrived. Lois parked on an area which had remnants

Unregonizable parent's previous property

308

of the original graveled circle driveway. Nothing was recognizable. We could not even determine where the house had been. We walked around, gazing in bewilderment. We were devastated to see the present condition of the property daddy had painstakingly maintained. Some skidoos were sitting on a trailer and other large items were sitting in the open. Tall grass and weeds loomed everywhere. Lois disturbed a small gray garter snake that quickly slivered back in the grass. I turned my ankle when walking on previously level ground which was now lumpy mounds overran by weeds. What happened here? I wondered.

Victor, a tall pleasant gray haired man of Lois' age, arrived as we continued to check out the property. He explained the previous owner had turned the property into a trash dump for his construction company. Victor had hauled off a lot of junk that had been left, defacing the land.

We inundated him with questions. "Where had the house been?" I asked. He led us to an area closer to the river than I remembered where the house had stood. There was no evidence of the foundation except a stray broken piece of cinderblock. Oh my gosh! There were clumps of Iris growing where our mother had planted them over sixty years ago. Victor found an old bucket and a shovel and dug a clump up for us to take, which Caroline later planted in her Iris bed in Pagosa Springs.

We checked out the view of the river from the steep rocky bank. It was nostalgic to watch the glistening water as it flowed calmly on its way down stream. I remember falling asleep to the soothing sound of the river in the summer time when my bedroom window was open.

When Victor learned the reason for our trip, he agreed to the releasing of Jane's ashes on his property. That would have made her happy. We had a simple

Gunnison River flowing serenely past previous home

ceremony for Jane. Lois read a passage from the Bible and I said a few words.

The day was waning as we hurriedly headed back. Caroline was dropped off in Pagosa. We were on our way to return the rental car to the Durango airport by 6:00, getting caught in a torrential downpour. Don met us at the airport, taking us back to Pagosa. It had been a long emotional day.

Lois stayed another day at the cabin before flying back to Tennessee. We accomplished the task at hand. Jane is back where she spent happier days.

On occasion we talk about Jane and the crazy times, with much relief that things are better for her now.

IN MEMORY OF JANE.

November 21, 1946 to February 5, 2022.

Succumbed to Covid.

ABOUT THE AUTHORS

LOUISE KILLIFER completed two years of college with a major in accounting, working as a bookkeeper and administrative assistant forty-one years. Her life has entailed raising three children whom have excelled professionally. She is an avid quilter, generally with several projects going simultaneously, while participating in a book club. She spends as much time as possible at their mountain getaway. She and her husband, Don, have three children, six grandchildren, and two great-grandsons.

LOIS MARTIN became a computer programmer/analyst after receiving her Bachelor's degree in Information Systems Development, from the University of Maryland. She retired after working forty years in the field of software development. Upon retiring, she keeps busy refurbishing old furniture and buying and selling collectibles. Lois lived in England and Germany while her husband, Hans, served in the Air Force. She became a widow when Hans died of cancer. Lois remarried Bill, acquiring three step-children. Lois is the proud step-grandmother of five grandsons.

Printed in the USA
CPSIA information can be obtained
at www.ICGtesting.com
LVHW040524220224
772413LV00051B/1202